MW00714800

Euterra Rising
THE LAST UTOPIA

Mark A. Burch

PUBLISHED BY Mark A. Burch

Copyright © 2016, Mark A. Burch

All rights reserved under International and
Pan-American Copyright Conventions. No part of this
book may be reproduced in any form or by any electronic or
mechanical means, including information storage and retrieval
systems, without permission in writing from Mark A. Burch,
except by a reviewer, who may quote brief passages in a review.
Published in 2016 by Mark A. Burch.

Library and Archives Canada Cataloging in Publication

Burch, Mark A., author
Euterra Rising: The Last Utopia / Mark A. Burch

Printed by CreateSpace
Design and Layout by Tracey O'Neil, simplelife designs

Issued in print and electronic formats.

ISBN 978-0-9784528-4-1
eBook ISBN 978-0-9784528-5-8

PRAISE FOR EUTERRA RISING: THE LAST UTOPIA

"At once thought-provoking, philosophically charged, and packed with action, *Euterra Rising* is an antidote to the dystopian storm clouds we thought we saw looming on the horizon."

— **James Frey,** *writer, consultant.*

"We live in a time where the stories and myths of our civilisation are failing both people and planet, and yet we have not found a new story or stories by which to live. In times like these what the world needs more than anything else are creative writers who are bold enough to tell new stories and break open new pathways into the future, using words to expand our imaginations and help us envision radically alternative ways to live and be. After all, before we can build a new world, first we must imagine it. In Euterra Rising, Mark Burch uses fiction to do precisely this, and he does so with that rare mixture of literary skill and immense intellectual, even spiritual, depth. Ultimately this book gave me renewed hope that another world is indeed possible - a world where human beings discover and create new forms of flourishing that avoid the needless violence, suffering and destruction of which we know far too much today. Burch explores an alternative future with such beauty and depth that its plausibility becomes unquestionable. Having liberated his readers old assumptions, Burch leaves us with the challenge of building the new world within the shell of the old, but he also leaves us with new energy to get moving."

— **Dr. Samuel Alexander,** *Ex. Director,*
The Simplicity Institute, Melbourne, Australia.

ACKNOWLEDGEMENTS

Many people deserve recognition for the roles they played in the development of this book. My friend and colleague Rod Kuene-man who pointed out that no utopias are being written anymore and that someone should try. My spouse Charlotte who continues to encourage me even through my physical and emotional absence when writing. My children, stepchildren and grandchildren to whom the future belongs—may they know that I tried to imagine something better.

Many others contributed through their review of early versions of the manuscript, their encouragement, their steady affirmation and sometimes through their sage advice. Sig Laser, Dr. Samuel Alexander, Dr. Rodney Kueneman, Maria Kruszewski, Eszti Nagy, Elaine Bishop, John Samson-Fellows, Coby Friesen, James Frey, and Tracey O'Neil. Thanks as well to Keith Barber for his kind permission to use the term "Lightminder," a word he coined that I found hugely evocative, and to Michael Dudley who introduced me to the inner world of librarians and archivists. Special thanks to Alex Merrill whose copy editing skills have added immense value to the manuscript.

AUTHOR'S FOREWORD

When all appeals to reason fail, tell a story.

Euterra Rising aspires to be a new work of utopian fiction. It began with a suggestion posed by a friend of mine over coffee. We were reminiscing about the many utopias we had both read over the years, especially in the 1960s and '70s, and the power of these works to inspire our imaginations. We also noted the almost complete absence of such literature in the popular culture of the twenty-first century. To our knowledge there had been no new works of utopian fiction for several decades—the field of what today is called "speculative fiction" instead being more or less dominated by dystopian visions. This suggested to me that the popular imagination might be unwilling, or perhaps even incapable, of envisioning a positive future for humanity in any form whatever. It was as if our vision of the future had turned entirely dark, holding out no attractive or plausible alternatives to the grinding, daily tragedy of the status quo. This might even suggest a loss of belief in ourselves, a loss of belief that we could hope to be better people, not just better makers of things. Moreover, the popular imagination seems to me to be truncated on the one hand by the claustrophobic limitations of 140 character "tweets" and on the other hand, fragmented by both multimedia and multi-author mash-ups presenting a cacophony of voices at the expense of coherence.

When this sand got into my oyster, it wouldn't let me rest. Though not his intention, my friend's casual remark opened my mind to a playful notion, which became a recurring preoccupation, then rather more of a challenge, and finally an obsession. Something "in the air" was daring me to make this attempt—daring me to imagine something positive and alternative to more of what already ails us. This turned out to be much more of a challenge than I at first appreciated.

For one thing, I spent several months blocked by the dystopian visions so prevalent in popular culture these days. Once I really began to pay attention to them, I felt nearly overwhelmed by the flood of negative imagery, fear and despair that, consciously or unconsciously, pervades post-modern society. And not without reason. Our efforts to leaven this psycho-social reality with super-heroic feats of daring-do tend mostly to ring hollow—never fully convincing us that heroes are super enough to overcome the darkness crawling toward the edges of their charmed circles of protection. So in a later conversation with the same friend, I announced that I would take a swing at writing a utopia, but I couldn't see my way clear to it without first transiting a dystopian near-future. I promised not to linger there feeding on the corpse of despair. But modern consumer culture is dying. And unless I wanted to write an escape fantasy (Long, long ago, in a land far, far away…) I had to begin from certain facts: Climate change is already impacting human communities and promises much worse ahead. There is profound dysfunction present in most human institutions. We face pervasive vulnerabilities created by globalization and global technologies like the Internet. And plainly, there are simply too many of us humans trying to make a living on this tiny blue marble if anything else is to have a chance to survive. These are all debts that will have to be paid. Any work of utopian fiction that aims even for the most modest claim to plausibility must face these facts and somehow accommodate them. I wanted to write a utopian fiction, but not one that required my readers to suspend disbelief entirely out of reach.

For another thing, if the barriers that now stand between humanity and a good life are to be crossed, given our past choices and behaviour, the world in which we build our utopia will be very different from the world we live in today. As I imagine it, two facts of life will have a pervasive and inescapable influence on any future good life we can imagine: The first is that a good life would have to be possible without cheap fossil fuels. It must also evolve in the context of ongoing climate change and its consequences. I cannot imagine any future for human beings, dystopian or utopian, that aspires to some measure of plausibility that is not also dramatically shaped by these two realities. There are many correlations and consequences that follow even from just these two considerations.

For yet another thing, I cannot imagine us shaping a new way of life without also reshaping the foundational assumptions of the culture that profoundly configures our present lives. The dysfunction which is everywhere visible today is clearly the result of a bankrupt and death-dealing worldview. Worldviews are long-term collective projects, not the work of a solitary author or thinker. So to escape the lethal cul-de-sac where capitalism and consumerism have brought us, we will need a different (not necessarily historically unique) understanding of human nature, the human place within nature, the meaning of a good life, and an etiquette of livelihood. It would have to be based on very different assumptions and *a priori* assertions about human beings from those that have guided the modern project since the Renaissance.

And for a final thing, I wanted to write a novel, to spin an engaging yarn, but not to provide a detailed master plan for some future society with all challenges addressed, all solutions in place, all critiques answered, and all risks anticipated. Such an undertaking is beyond me. So in risking this book, what I hope to offer is a vision, not a plan; a sensibility, not a list of answers; maybe a thematic line or two, but not a whole symphony; and certainly not a new list of commandments. These things we must do together over some period of time, hopefully *sans* the commandments.

Mark A. Burch
Spring 2016

CHAPTER 1

SPRING, THE 276TH YEAR OF THE EUTERRAN AGE (E.A.)
(2298 C.E.)

Every moment is Opening. On uncertain ground, wait
with patience, like an ambush hunter. The Central
Harmony manifests everything in its own time.

— THE BOOK OF PRACTICE

"THEY'RE ARRIVING," announced Zephyr Fey.

Lars Beckett set down the tiny forest he had been pruning, a two-hundred-sixty-year-old stand of bonsai Yeddo spruce, its roots entangling a slab of black slate the size of a serving platter. The trees were nearly as old as Euterra itself but hardly taller than a man's hand. Zephyr stood motionless in the late morning light streaming into the sunspace of their Dan. Her lithe frame stood poised in the robe that flared around her the colour of flame. If she was unsettled by the news she brought, she gave no sign. She watched Lars with a serene, unflinching gaze. Being a Euterran Helder—a healing elder—she was exactly the sort of person he would want beside him if things went wrong.

"Where?" asked Lars.

"Dawngate."

Lars laid down his pruning nippers and wiped his hands on his apron. "Very well," he said. "Is Otis bringing the foundling himself, or did others come from the Watch?"

"Others came too," Zephyr said. "The foundling is still unconscious. Otis stopped Tarshin to bring him back. Some from the Watch came back with him. It only seemed prudent."

"Aye, prudent," said Lars, half to himself. "How far did Otis get?"

"Far. Sixty kilometres at least. He was on the homeward circuit when he came on the foundling." Lars could scarcely imagine the labour involved in retrieving a foundling from so far away. The sunspace in which he stood was still dripping from the storm of the previous evening, a particularly violent one; not the sort of weather to be crashing about in the bush carrying someone on your back. But then again, Lars reminded himself, Otis was Tarshin-ru.

He nodded. "I'll go right down. Please come as soon as you can. Thank you."

Zephyr joined her palms in front of her chest and dropped her gaze ever so slightly, mindful of the Light in Lars, turned silently and left their commons room.

Lars pulled off his apron and placed it carefully on the work table. He returned the miniature stand of spruce to its place among the dozens of other bonsai crowding the sunspace. Fifty-something, he was not large for a man but strongly built, and his sturdy hands could still manipulate nippers with surgical precision when it came to his bonsai. He wasn't sure what awaited him at the Dawngate, but he cast his eyes around the sunspace as if surveying it before what might be a long absence.

He glanced over the balustrade of the sunspace and saw Loch Speare glistened three hundred metres below him and to a far distance east, south and west. For now the sky was clear with the fresh yellow light of spring, but clouds could build in from the west with remarkable speed and give them another drenching. At least the cisterns were sure to be full.

He turned to leave but paused. There on a table beside the door he kept a field stone of granite the size of a watermelon. It had been split in half and polished to a glassy finish on its flat side. An inscription read: "Tatum Barnes, b. 26 August 2004, d..." but there the inscription stopped. Lars had literally stumbled on it decades before when he was part of a survey team reconnoitring a pre-Ruination village far west of Euterra. It had puzzled him from the very start, lying out in the open the way it did, when by then so many pre-Ruination artifacts were being buried by floods and winds and the sheer passage of time. The stone was probably a grave marker, made for someone who had not yet died. Or maybe it was a lost artifact from someone's workshop, someone who had had no time to finish it before other events interrupted its fashioning. Certainly it was now cumber, an unnecessary possession that most Euterrans would avoid keeping on principle that it compromised their simplicity. But Lars felt a mysterious resonance with the stone. It spoke to him of a time almost three centuries past when people were so beset during the Ruination that they couldn't even bury their dead. And who was Tatum Barnes? How had she lived? How had she died? Who sang her wending song? Did they even have a wending song in those days? Always more questions than answers.

Lars glided his hand over the face of the stone as if consoling a friend, then went out the door of the sunspace, through his Dan's commons room, down a short passageway and through another door into Ariel Drift. Just outside the door he pulled down a spinner from its wall rack, mounted up, and started peddling toward the Dawngate Lift. It was over two kilometres away, but the ride through the drift, a broad passageway hewn through living rock, was pleasant and late enough in the morning that most people had already left their Dans for the workshops and food forests.

Even as he peddled Lars invoked Practice to keep his thoughts from running ahead of events. What was known was very little. What could be imagined was limitless. Prudent. What was prudent in the circumstances? It had been years since the last foundling, and never one from the east, and not during Lars's lifetime. But Euterran history showed that the discovery of foundlings was always—complicated. He had to have come from somewhere. And where there was one, there were probably more. But then it could be said that everyone in Euterra was a foundling, or a descendant of foundlings. Otis had done the right thing to stop Tarshin and fetch him back. He couldn't leave a foundling to die. But now Otis would be two weeks in quarantine and would have to start the Tarshin again, if his Practice Telder, a teaching-elder, would even allow it. And who could tell the consequences of the foundling himself?

Lars racked up the spinner at the Dawngate Lift and stepped on the elevator. He selected the lift control that would stop the elevator at the Dawngate station. It began its slow descent. He lived in one of the highest and oldest drifts in Euterra, hollowed only a couple of generations after Beamer Farris dug First Haven. It would take the lift over a minute to descend all the way to Forest Drift and the Dawngate. Lars mused: *What would Beamer Farris have done with a foundling?*

CHAPTER 2

SPRING, THE 276TH YEAR OF THE EUTERRAN AGE (E.A.)
(2298 C.E.)

When facing death, nothing is gained by drama.

— THE BOOK OF PRACTICE

JAEGER'S MEMORY of his last hours with the Brotherhood was painful. He dimly recalled days of being blindfolded and pushed roughly along a narrow bush track, then dragged when he could no longer stand, then dragged farther until what had passed for his clothes hung in rags and his limbs were a collage of bruises and abrasions. The exhaustion which had become a continuous drone note in his body was interrupted now only by the torrential downpours of cold spring rain that made the boar track slick and mucky. Mercifully, they had not had to endure hail, an ever-present risk in such storms, but usually not so early in the year. He was in the custody of three other men, which seemed more than sufficient given his physical condition even before this most recent ordeal—an instance of fear fuelling excess.

After days of crashing through bush, bramble and meadow, they'd come to this no-place. It was an opening barely wider than the muddy boar track they'd arrived on. Suffocating hazelnut and black alder thickets pressed in from all sides beneath a forest canopy of black spruce, white birch and poplar. Seeing any distance sideways was impossible, the sole views available being that forward or back along the trail they walked. Many of the trees looked like moss-bearded trolls leaning over them, drooling the last icy drops of the cold rain from the night before.

"Stop here," said one of the men who seemed to be in charge. He looked ten kilos heavier and half a head taller than either of his companions. His grizzly-bear gaze was sullen, dull and devoid of compassion. It was easy to imagine that his sole source of amusement might be found in sadism. Jaeger was dropped unceremoniously on the slimy mat of twigs and poplar leaves that smelled sweet in their decay. Then another of his captors pulled him into a sitting position against a tree trunk and tore off his blindfold. His head swam with the effort to stay upright.

"Take off his shoes," said the first man, who then picked up a sturdy fallen branch nearby.

"Listen to me. Do you know who I am?"

"Yes," said Jaeger weakly.

"Who am I?"

"You're the Expediter."

"That's right, skrala. I'm the Expediter. And do you know where we are?"

"No," Jaeger sighed.

"I can't hear you, skrala!"

"No," Jaeger replied, somewhat louder, not daring to look up.

"No," his captor mocked. "No skrala knows where this is. Not even most of the Brotherhood know where this is. There's fucking nothing that way," he said, pointing farther down the trail, "but howling forest, then howling desert, and then howling fucking mountains. And there's nothing that way," pointing back the way they had come, "except *us*. And whichever way you go, there are a fuck of a lot snakes, and cougars that like humans because they're less work to kill than boars. So I want you to remember *this*," he said, hitting the soles of Jaeger's feet with a vicious swing of the branch. Jaeger shuddered, too weak to utter anything but a moan.

"Remember this well!" The Expediter swung the branch again, sending another bolt of pain from the soles of Jaeger's feet that ricocheted from the top of his head and back to his feet again. "You were crazy to dream!" Another whack to impress the point.

"You were crazy to tell skrala they could be free," his captor persisted. "We're not giving you the chance to be a martyr too. If you ever," whack! "*ever*, come back to Mainbranch, we'll kill you—but not until you watch us kill everybody you ever knew. Is that clear?" Whack!

"Yes," Jaeger managed.

His tormenter paused as if weighing the sincerity of Jaeger's reply. He then swung the branch at him again, barely missing Jaeger's feet, but clearly by intent. Jaeger cringed reflexively. The Expediter roared with laughter. Then he hit Jaeger again, connecting this time.

"I can't fucking hear you, skrala!"

"It's clear," Jaeger hissed through gritted teeth.

"Good!" said the Expediter. "True communication is always so—satisfying—wouldn't you say? I think you're ready to move on to new opportunities now." Whack! "Good luck." Whack!

Turning to the other men, the Expediter said, "Leave him." The man who pulled off Jaeger's shoes tossed them on the ground near his now shivering body. "No," the Expediter barked, "he doesn't need those." Expressionless, the other man retrieved the shoes again. To Jaeger, the Expediter growled, "Don't even think of trying to follow us. Don't even think of watching us leave." With that, he gave the soles of Jaeger's feet one last bash with the branch, tossed it over the hazelnut break, then turned and headed back east down the boar track they had arrived on. One by one the other men trailed along behind him. Jaeger glanced after them through the one of his eyes that was still open as they disappeared into the bush. He watched long enough to see the last man in line drop his water bottle on the trail as he walked away. It was a casual gesture, arguably accidental should he be challenged by the Expediter, and yet calculated to be visible to Jaeger. The image circulated in Jaeger's mind only a few moments before he slumped to the ground, unconscious.

———◆———

Some way down the trail, the Expediter abruptly stopped his retinue. "You know," he snarled, "maybe we should just go back and kill him."

"Sir," said the man who dropped the water bottle, now perhaps worried that his gesture might be discovered, "he's never been in the bush before. He won't last the night. It's hundreds of kilometres back to Mainbranch and he wouldn't dare come back. Who's he going to tell his dreams to out here? The squirrels?"

"Ha!" the Expediter snorted, turning roughly. "The squirrels. Ha!" He looked back down the boar track, saw no movement, no sign, and shook his head as if he could physically dislodge his misgivings. "Ha!" he repeated. "Squirrels." Then he turned and they all trudged eastward again.

CHAPTER 3

SPRING, 2027 C.E.

When the world is passing away, attend to what is essential. Solitude and silence are helpful in this.

— THE BOOK OF PRACTICE

AMONG THE THINGS that can bring a person to hermitage are spiritual aspiration, guilt and grief. And the greatest of these is grief.

Beamer Farris had already been days on the road. Much of it he spent walking, interrupted occasionally by rides offered by strangers until, coming to a certain place which was an uncertain place for all that, he took his leave from the last ride he was offered. Then he struck off cross country into the boreal forest under burden of his gear. He headed south. It seemed the right way to go, springing from an intuition he had learned to trust, come what may. He passed several more days picking his way through dense walls of spruce and fir, around the edges of beaver ponds and lakes, their centres newly clearing of ice, and sometimes over the naked cheeks of rocks turning themselves to the leaden sky for perhaps the hundred billionth time. All this perfectly mirrored his mood.

Grief pursued him from back there in the wall of trees. It perched like an animal watching from the penumbra of his campfire. It felt cold and liquid, flooding him with tears just when he thought he might have come to the last of them. If he walked fast enough, maybe he could leave it behind, silently tangled in the roots of some fallen tree, until spring became summer, and summer autumn, and the thing would fade away quietly on its own.

But sometimes grief enticed him, drawing him onward, but onward to what? It felt like some inescapable ordeal he could not get around but must get through instead. His role was to find that hidden door and pass through it. And all this maelstrom turned around the memory of Tatum, a slide show in his mind featuring her, only her, sometimes this way and sometimes that, but always her. Their love, so new, so fresh, and yet doomed. And her death, so arbitrary, so impersonal, solitary, violent and unknown. How had she suffered? He didn't know. And, honestly, he didn't want to know. Details could not ease his pain. He simply wanted to get somewhere else, somewhere away, where he could watch the slide show of her in his head, alone, those flashbacks of love, and regret, and imperfectly expressed longing, and unmentioned admiration, all her slides, until, like Tatum herself, they were torn away from him.

Within the spectrum of unfairness that life has to offer, Tatum's fate was toward the profoundly unfair end, well into its deeper shades of violet. He and Tatum had both been young—in their mid-twenties. Never would they be younger, nor stronger, nor more beautiful, nor more astute, than when they met. It was especially unfair that Tatum should die this young, and Beamer should feel so much like a widow.

Through the days and nights, it was partly the memory of her, and partly their unrealized possibilities that Beamer dreamed, and that kept him moving—moving away from what had been even as he moved toward whatever was next.

But he was also looking for something. Tatum's death was a personal loss to be sure, but it was something more: A harbinger, a warning, a prophesy perhaps. He sensed this as clearly as he did the noisome cloud of grief that both pursued him and led him. So he pressed on within these nested bubbles of obscurity, not at all clear what he was leaving behind or what he was pursuing or what he was looking for between the two, consoled only by the prospect that he would recognize it when he saw it.

And then there was the eco-village at Badger Coulee and all those gathered there, the friends they had become to him, who grieved Tatum as much as he did. Perhaps Badger Coulee was the remnant of something passing away. Perhaps it was the seed of something that was yet to be. They were a community that didn't know which way to turn, a ghost town, believing itself to be an eco-village, but perhaps something more, something *much* more—surrounded by danger, all paths of escape seeming closed, except perhaps the possibility of jumping straight up. But how could a whole community jump straight up? And what could be Beamer's role in that?

The Starsis Massif appeared looming over the bush ahead. How anything so enormous could conceal itself in the forest canopy and then a few steps later burst into view was one of the eerier properties of wilderness. Beamer gazed up at the Massif as if it was an apparition. It reminded him of Ayer's Rock in Australia, but not as curvaceous or as friendly. The mesa thrust up from the Pre-Cambrian granite at least four hundred metres, sheer vertical walls, craggy enough to scale without climbing gear, but only just. A more gradual ascent might be possible along its north face, but most of what Beamer saw looked like sheer cliffs. Added to this was a sizeable river approaching from the north, slamming into the Massif's north wall, then boiling around to the east. From his angle on the ground, it looked like a fortress surrounded by a moat.

He spent most of the morning hiking around the eastern and northern sides of the rock looking for a way across the rapids that roiled against its north face then roared around its eastern edge to pass through a rugged gorge and empty into Loch Speare. Finding no easy way across, Beamer bundled his gear in a plastic bag he carried for the purpose, strapped it under his chin and started walking across the slippery cataract as far as he could until the current caught him and swept him down stream. An able swimmer, he stroked with the current, letting himself be taken toward the far bank. He estimated he had about ten minutes before he would lose consciousness from hypothermia. He came to shore again on the other side a hundred metres farther south than where he entered the stream, his arms and legs so numb he could barely move them.

He staggered up the river bank, then peeled off his pants and shirt and wrung them out. Having carried his socks and boots on his floating bundle of gear, he found them still dry. He put on his clothes again, and resumed his march to the mountain. Despite the pall that had settled on his heart, his body knew the wholesomeness of the land. The climate was changing, sure enough; but life in the bush was tenacious. And out here the terms of relationship were clear. Gravity would never mess with your head. You pay attention and respect it or it kills you. Simple. Honest. Clear.

He reached the bottom of the Massif, looked up, and searched for his first hand hold. Stretch by stretch, step by step, he made his way up. It was not high by rock climbing standards, but it was his destination, he felt sure. Today it tried his body and focused his mind. Today it threatened his life enough to keep his attention, to keep his mind off what life was becoming down below. Enough to keep him alive. After about two hours, he scrambled up to the broad, flat top of the mesa.

Before him floated an island in the sky. As far as Beamer could see, there was no evidence of human presence before his own. Surely the Anishinaabe would have known this place, and maybe the occasional climber like himself. But there were no other signs of the creeping cancer that humans had become in nature. It was, after all, the middle of nowhere, and not even the captains of commerce would set up in the middle of nowhere without a market. The mesa was heavily treed on top, as if the forest floor had been thrust up into the sky in one gigantic piece. But this would have happened millions of years ago. It was a little cooler than down below, the air redolent with the moist scent of sphagnum mosses and balsam fir. He noticed some plants that were not growing at ground level—probably descendants of plants that had thrived in cooler conditions before the climate started changing. In any case, the plateau would have been too high to clear-cut, which probably spared it from the worst of human predation. The rock was mostly granite, but with quartz intrusions here and there shot through with wire gold—probably not enough gold to be commercially valuable, thus escaping the claims of prospectors and miners as well. Best of all, Beamer thought, it was too inaccessible for the yahoos to reach on their ATVs. This might be a place where he could hear himself think.

He sat down on the crest of the cliff, his legs dangling casually over the abyss. Far below, the surf crashed upon rocky debris that had fallen from the cliff face under the steady pressure of centuries of frost and rain. The tiniest push, Beamer thought, would be enough. Then he could be with her. There was no sensible restraining hand. But one moment of delay led to the next until enough moments had accumulated that the forward bend in Beamer's spine became a subtle backward bend. He rolled back on his haunches, rocked a bit, then stood up. He guessed he would have time tomorrow to throw himself over. He turned around to inspect his new domain.

While he couldn't see all the way to the other side, he guessed the Massif was at least ten kilometres long and three or four wide. There were some rain water catchment pools, and rocky outcrops thrusting up from the bedrock of the mesa. But below him must be solid rock—an incredible mass of it. It was crowned with white spruce, aspen, paper birch, some lodgepole pine, and white pine as well. At first he thought that given its relative isolation, there should be nothing but climax forest on top. But both fire and birds could reach this place, more or less assuring forest succession and renewal, given enough time. He felt like he was laying eyes on a new world, or perhaps an ancient one.

A raven creaked from a treetop close by. "Hello to you too!" Beamer replied. *I'm barking mad*, he thought. *Now I'm talking to birds.*

He decided that he would stay in this place for a while. He'd stay until he felt good and damn ready to leave. Many people found wilderness threatening, he knew. But to Beamer there was something consoling in it, a welcoming quality. So he sat down on a rock some paces back from the brink, crossed his legs, his eyes filling with the sparks of light that danced over the lake below him. He felt the warm sun drying his clothes. He felt the breeze slide around his body. He heard the air sighing through the trees, endlessly inhaling and exhaling, even now. Was it the ancient breathing of all life in this place, or the last breaths of something passing away? Was it ending or beginning?

Part of Beamer thought it possible just to cast off his clothes and return to a life of hunting and gathering, back along the path humanity had come by, back to the womb in the forest which had gestated human intelligence long ago. But he realized that there was no *way* back. That passage was now closed, and the forest kept it closed. And when he tried to look back, he realized it was only images arising from some twilight space within him, not true memories, but impossible wishes. The forest was what lay behind and that which had brought him here, now. If there was any moving forward, it would not be possible by falling back into that emerald embrace, or into Tatum's either. He had to move forward, but toward what—and guided by what?

In the white spruce, the raven continued to eye him, creaking now and then, until they were both sitting motionless in the same place together. Beamer waited.

CHAPTER 4

SPRING, THE 276TH YEAR OF THE EUTERRAN AGE (E.A.)
(2298 C.E.)

*The First Happy Memory is that of relationship.
We feed on other life in order to live. There is no life
for us apart from the life of the Other. This truth
has many implications. Meditate on it daily.*

— THE BOOK OF PRACTICE

JAEGER LAY IN A HEAP where he had been left, feeling light-headed, his heart thumping loudly like a wood grouse drumming in his chest. His feet, for all the pounding they took, were a distant storm of sensation, occasional claps of pain subsiding to the dull rumble of a steady, throbbing ache. But the pain felt far away, as if it belonged to someone else. And that was how he felt, as though he was standing beside himself, watching himself lying there, not moving. *This must be shock*, he thought, then perceived the dark humour of naming the obvious. He smiled weakly.

Mostly his thoughts weren't thoughts at all. They were images that whirled into view for a moment, and then whirled away again, back into the darkness. Maybe memories. Maybe fantasies of things that never happened. Maybe wishes that could never be uttered. *Men who came in the night, his mother screaming, him being carried off—off into the night—without her—and the sky, red and smoking. Him small, cowering, powerless—crying and crying, his screams summoned from his heels, surging up his legs, his loins and belly, bursting from his throat until he gasped for air. Then a deep quiet, too terrible to cry about anymore, the core of terror and hurt inside him scabbing with a kind of numbness, a numbness that was comforting, but somehow—wrong.*

More images—*being hungry and seeing food, smelling food, but he couldn't have any—food being eaten by others but not skrala—not skrala food—and the faces of others who stood by, silent, unmoving, docile.* He was trying to remember something more, something important, still out of reach. Again, the flow tide of memory—*the boredom, dullness, like the endless ocean horizon, water pushing and pulling against the grey hem of the sky, everywhere the same, but pierced by moments of terror. Training for his job with the Brotherhood—(Brotherhood!)—and all those years, all the work, passing in a moment, ashes in his mouth, leaving nothing. But learning to read, in stolen moments full of fear, sampling the forbidden.* Something important, something that happened recently and had to do with the present situation... *Huddling in the shadows with some others (who?), in a ruin somewhere, whispering. What were we talking about? It seems brilliant, revolutionary, but what exactly? Too hard. Too far away after all this, this...*

Thirst. That's what it was. That was the *important thing* he was trying to grasp. He wasn't merely thirsty, he was thirst itself. This startled him back to consciousness. He opened one eye a tiny bit. There, on the trail, but seeming half a continent away, lay a water bottle. In his confusion, he debated with himself about whether such a thing might contain water even as he felt his body beginning to crawl in that direction. Maybe the hope of water was a final torture—a last insult left there for him by those who brought him to this no-place. Maybe he would reach it and open it only to find that it was dry as mummy skin. Ha! What a good joke that would be—a perfectly horrible end to a perfectly horrible life—but how apt, how fitting. Slithering those dozen paces to the water bottle felt like...*he is in the Human Resources Office—why did they call it that?—certain he would be moving on to new opportunities—his heart pounding thunderously—the Expediter sitting on the panel of review glaring at him—why were they all glaring at him?...* He was unscrewing the bottle cap with clumsy fingers working through their own body memory of how to do it, and then he was drinking, feeling each gulp of water passing down his throat, a cool bolus of moisture that he continued to feel even as it reached his stomach. He kept swallowing the water until there was no more left. He felt completely exhausted. He continued to grip the empty water bottle even as the world around him again wobbled and dissolved.

Some time later he awakened. The delirium was past, for the time being. He rolled over to assess his situation. The Brotherhood Retirement Party was gone. This was a great relief, but was alloyed with an overpowering desire to be away from this place, to be anywhere else but where he was. His hand still clung to the water bottle though it was empty. No boars had gored him, no snakes swallowed him and no cougars had jumped on his back to break his neck. But as his awareness cleared he noticed that any exposed part of his body, which was nearly all of it, was covered with painful welts that had tiny bleeding wounds at their centres—and a cloud of black flies and mosquitoes now swarmed around him. In a warming world, they had grown larger than their ancestors from previous centuries and were hungrier as well. Jaeger's first practical lesson in bush survival thus began with the realization that he probably wouldn't die in the jaws of a cougar or the coils of a python, but instead one drop of blood at a time from a hundred thousand insects. He was again very thirsty.

He lurched to his feet both of which throbbed painfully but the miracle of endorphins pushed the pain back, blurring it, subduing it, for the time being. He needed to find more water soon, and also do something about the black flies. He stood on his now insensate stumps, mere clubs of flesh that did what he asked them to, performing their habitual motions, but with neither feeling nor complaint.

He set off along the boar track the Retirement Party had been following, but not back in the direction the Party had taken, even though he had no idea where that might lead any more. In fact, he had no idea what direction he was taking except that it was *not back there*. Every step was painful and he was very weak. But he moved forward, staggering along the narrow track through hazelnut bushes, Labrador tea, clintonia, bear berry and poison ivy, unable to see more than one or two metres into the dense bush on either side. Moving about liberated new clouds of mosquitoes and black flies and even larger deer flies that buzzed around his head in a vexing swirl. He lost track of how long he stumbled through the forest, but noticed that the track was getting muddier as he went. A few more paces and he stepped into a rill, barely half a metre wide, so tiny that it made no sound as it passed, but it was water nonetheless. Jaeger's second practical lesson in bush survival was that in dense country, one step could make the difference between seeing something and not seeing it—water, food, a predator, the Brotherhood.

He fell to his knees, plunging his face as far into the stream as it would go, and drank to satiation. Some minutes later, he did so again, then filled his water bottle to brimming. Tormented to desperation by the vampirous insects, he smeared his skin thickly with the black muck of the stream bank. If they were going to bite him anyway, maybe a coat of mud would at least slow them down. A moment later he noticed a small trickle of blood seeping through a crack in the mud that caked his left leg. Digging into the spot with his finger he discovered a leach as big as his thumb, sluggish as it gorged on him. Jaeger grabbed the thing, removing it in a single twist, but he kept on bleeding until the anticoagulant from the leach had spent itself. Jaeger backed away from the stream and stepped off the boar track to discover a sheltered, somewhat drier nest in the tangled bowl of a half-fallen fir tree. Despite his pain, he noticed with gratitude the crisp aroma of the balsam sap, and that his mud pack treatment was reducing his insect bites. He slumped into his little shelter and let sleep take him.

———◆·◆———

Some hours later Jaeger awakened, still caked with dry mud, but considerably less bitten. Stiffly, he stood up to take stock of his situation. Clearly, it was impossible to stay where he was or to try to return to…what? Torture? Murder? Another Retirement Party? His head spun with the recognition that he had no idea where he was or how to navigate, anywhere, in such surroundings. He couldn't even be sure if, setting off in such confusion, he would not be heading back to Mainbranch. Staying where he was, despite the supply of water, he would die in a few days from starvation, for what prospect could there possibly be of rescue? And who might rescue him? He would not try to return to Mainbranch, even though he thought there might be some who would shelter him there. The one option remaining was to set off in hope of finding something, *anything*, that offered some new possibility. He hoped, dimly, that he might stumble upon some ruin and find shelter at least. He would need food eventually and water before the end of the day, but there was nothing for it.

Jaeger gathered up his water bottle—his sole worldly possession—and added to it a crutch he made from a fallen branch. He drank a last belly full of water from the stream, topped up his canteen, and set off unsteadily down the boar track heading roughly west, though he didn't know it.

He walked all morning but by mid-afternoon was beset by intense belly cramps. In another hour he was doubled over with diarrhoea along with nausea and alternating chills and fever. Despite his ebbing strength, he pressed on for another two days, not willing to die. The bush seemed to go on endlessly, every metre corrugated with ankle-twisting tree roots covered in moss or fallen leaves. Night offered little rest as damp fog rose up from the forest floor and he shivered under a dark sky of cold stars. But this test came on top of many days of exhausting marches and little food in the custody of the Retirement Party. He was young, to be sure, but had never been an exceptional physical specimen, and dehydration was a dogged adversary. Presently, he found himself walking upslope, away from the boar tracks and toward a large fallen tree with a puddle of sunlight warming its southern side. He lay down there—*for one moment*—he told himself. *Just a short rest.*

But he was being watched.

CHAPTER 5

SPRING, THE 276TH YEAR OF THE EUTERRAN AGE (E.A.)
(2298 C.E.)

It is helpful to bear in mind that whatever may at first
appear to be misshapen acquired its form through its
co-dependent arising. Had our own terroir been different
than it was, we too might resemble what we despise.

— THE BOOK OF PRACTICE

OF COURSE the Expediter had a name, though he seldom used it publicly, the better with which to intimidate everyone, such being his principal job. Axel Caine had been born in Mainbranch and raised as a member of the Brotherhood, as were his minions Dax Mason and Massey Ferguson. It was rumoured that Ferguson re-named himself after coming upon a pre-Ruination artifact bearing the moniker which he liked better than his birth name. It had been affixed to some complicated, technical-looking pile of machinery which he didn't understand and on that account alone found appealing. Whatever a Massey Ferguson was, it was from before the Great Recession, a time long ago when everything was possible, and above all, he wanted to be *that*.

After leaving Jaeger launched upon his new opportunity, Caine led the way back in an easterly direction toward Mainbranch, the principal Brotherhood settlement from where they had come. Not wanting to leave signs that might help Jaeger follow them, should he be foolish enough to do so, they had cut no blazes or other markers to guide their return. For the time being then, the whole group had to rely on Caine's dead reckoning through the bush, along the boar tracks, and over hill and dale. In truth, they could walk for a week bearing generally east and would not stray far from their mark. Eventually they would come upon some landmark or the remains of one of their earlier recycling expeditions, would recognize their place, and Caine could then navigate them back to Mainbranch.

The shadows of late afternoon were lengthening when Caine ceased his stolid trudge eastward, looked around, and announced, "Here for the night." As one they dropped their gear on the ground, exhausted. "Ferguson," said Caine, "find us some fire wood."

Mason had unstrapped his water bottle from his belt and was quaffing from it when Ferguson asked, "Can I have a pull on that?"

Mason stopped after one more swallow. "Where's yours?"

Ferguson shrugged, his face tensing up: "I lost it. I mean, I must have dropped it or something."

This captured Caine's attention. "You lost it?" he sneered. "What do you mean 'you lost it'?"

"Well," Ferguson said, feeling caught, "I had it last night. But I guess pounding on Jaeger and all, it must have got loose or fallen off my shoulder back when I took a leak there, you know?" Ferguson's heart started pounding so loudly that he was afraid Caine could hear it. Compassion was not prized among the Brotherhood, and any such gesture on his part toward a skrala like Jaeger would meet with swift rehabilitation.

Caine rolled his eyes. "Yeah," he mumbled, "I know. Do you think you can find some firewood without losing that too?"

"Yes."

Caine now to Mason: "Give him a drink."

Ferguson took two hasty gulps, handed the bottle back to Mason, and headed into the bush in search of wood. "*Dry* wood," Caine called after him.

Presently they kindled a fire and made a meagre meal from the scant provisions they had left after several weeks in the bush. After reviewing the menu Caine said, "Pretty soon we'll have to kill something." The Brotherhood were not highly skilled in bushcraft, yet even for those with deeper knowledge and more tested skills, spring offered lean fare compared to summer or fall. Nevertheless, there were boar markings everywhere, many sows would have farrowed by now and snares were easy to set. There would be mule does with fawns, and of course there was always the possibility of coming upon the kill of some other predator and sharing in the bounty, if it was still eatable.

For the night, however, they pitched a tarpaulin lean-to for shelter and sat close to a small fire.

Mason sighed, leaning back in the meagre firelight. "Damn," he moaned, "I'm bone tired. We sure are a helluva long way from anywhere. Was that damn skrala really worth it?"

"The Chief thought so," Caine said with finality.

"Humph," said Mason. "I don't know why we didn't just hang him."

Caine poked at the fire with a stick, glancing briefly at Mason and then back into the flames that licked lazily at the dead fall that fuelled them. "Well," said the Expediter, "guess that's why he's the Chief and you aren't."

"Be that as it may," Mason persisted, "if I'm going to walk for two weeks into the howling wilderness full of snakes, boars, cougars and black flies—fuck the fucking black flies!—I'd like to know why."

"You don't need to know why," Ferguson chimed in with what he thought the Expediter would say—ingratiating himself?

Caine glanced at him briefly, unimpressed, then returned to poking at the embers of the fire. He was in a more communicative mood than usual. "The skrala had a dream or something," he said, "which is nothing earth-shaking, except the other skrala started listening to him telling about this dream of his. What concerned the Chief was not that he had a dream, but that other skrala were listening to it. Killing him outright would have made a hero out of him, so the Chief thought it would be better if he moved on to other opportunities—you know—the way we usually handle such things. So here we are."

"But people have dreams all the time," Ferguson interjected.

The Expediter shrugged. "Not like this one," he objected. "The Chief is right. We have to handle shit like that carefully. There is only one dream for us—you know that. We have to get out of the hole we're in. We've been in a fucking hole ever since the Great Recession. We get a little boost now and then, and then we just fall back in again." His jaw became more set as he scanned the wall of the forest shrouded in night. "You have wives and kids—you know that too. I believe the Motherlode is out there, sure as hell. We just have to find it. And when we do, the Brotherhood is gonna be great again. We'll all be sitting pretty in our own HQs with hot water and all the bling you can imagine. The things they had back then would knock you out—you've heard the stories. You just wait and see. Somewhere out there that Motherlode is waiting for us. We just have to find it. And guys like this skrala scum we left in the bush back there, he's a distraction, see. It's guys like him that can set one of us against another and blow all our chances of finding the Motherlode, of keeping it together. We *have* to keep it together…" Caine's voice trailed off.

Mason looked up from the fire, then off west, the direction they were leaving behind. "I wonder if it's farther west there somewhere," he said.

Caine shook his head resignedly. "Doubt it," he said. "All the good recycling we've found has been farther east from Mainbranch or else south. It's been a long time since any of the Brotherhood went farther west than we did to dump the skrala. But when they did, they said the forest went on and on until it came to a desert, which went on and on, until it came to mountains, which is where they stopped. Nobody home. No Motherlode. So it's probably east somewhere, or maybe south, if we can find somebody else to recycle. We just *have* to keep it together until we find it. Then everything'll be better."

"Do you think things could ever get better if we don't find the Motherlode?" Ferguson tried.

Caine shrugged. "I dunno. Maybe. Maybe one of the Brains in the shop will tinker something up someday that'll take us back to the days before the Recession. I dunno."

"Time machine, maybe," Mason snorted derisively.

CHAPTER 6

SPRING, 2027 C.E.

All things speak in their own voices. One who listens
hears. None of this is to be taken literally.

— THE BOOK OF PRACTICE

BEAMER FARRIS stayed where he was for the rest of the day. Eventually, the lengthening rays of afternoon roused him from his meditation. He had struggled up the Massif carrying all his trail gear, though it had grown lighter with every day since he passed through a town where he could re-provision. Despite having a small tent, he surveyed the area for shelter.

He walked for half an hour until he came upon an outcrop with a shallow depression in its south face and its rocky backside turned north. This offered enough space for him to pull together a spruce bough bed with a margin in front for a small fire. This he assembled from some scraps of birchbark, and the dead-fallen twigs of tamarack. Happily, he thought, this spot gave him a spectacular view of Loch Speare to the east and south.

Having made himself at home, his next concerns were water and some supper. Rummaging through his packsack he retrieved two energy bars, some jerky, and a packet of granola left over from his last breakfast. And water. He still had some in his canteen but more would be needed eventually. This might be a problem. There would be no springs or creeks atop the Massif, but there could be a rainwater-filled pond, or at least some catchments in the rock that might hold water. Drinking it would be risky, but Beamer carried water treatment tablets as essential gear. There was also an abundance of mosses which could filter water and, given their antibiotic properties, add a measure of protection as well.

So as darkness descended, Beamer built a tiny fire, made a frugal supper from the victuals on hand and settled down for the night. He felt peaceful here. He would continue here—continue to be still as the distant lake surface was still.

———————◆·◆———————

He awakened to a raucous duet of ravens shouting at the blushing eastern sky. He felt remarkably well considering how basic was his hostel. He luxuriated in the sun that reflected warmly from the back wall of his grotto, feeling no need to hurry on to anything. One of the ravens took wing but the other remained behind, flapping from tree to tree over the space of many minutes, edging nearer with each move. Presently, it landed on the ground and waddled closer until it stopped a few metres away. It eyed Beamer and the remnant wisps of smoke rising from his fire circle with apparent curiosity.

"You woke me up," Beamer accused.

"Ache—uck!" the raven gargled.

"Yes," Beamer echoed. "Wake up!"

"Ache—uck!" it repeated.

"Are we having a conversation here or what?" Their exchange reminded Beamer of Fisher's advice back at Badger Coulee—that if he dreamed again of ravens, he should ask them what they might have for him. Fisher had been a dream worker after all, so such advice made perfect sense to him even if what he meant wasn't always clear to Beamer. Now he missed Fisher's counsel, but realized it made no more sense to him now than it did in their first conversation. What could he expect from a raven?

The raven walked back and forth in front of his campsite, inspecting him closely with one obsidian eye.

"I'm not dead yet. You can eat me when I'm dead. But not right now. Is that what you want? Or do you have something for me? I can't see anything for me."

"Ache—uck!"

"Yeah, yeah. Wake up! Wake up! I know. I'm awake now. Thanks. Why don't you go kill something? Earn a living for godssake. Or go wake up somebody else." Beamer rummaged in his knapsack for that stale granola which he'd saved against the need for breakfast. The raven hunched down, then sprang upward, launching itself into flight. "Easy for you to do!" Beamer shouted after the retreating bird as it flapped, then glided over the cliff toward the Loch below.

Beamer sat back and slowly munched his granola. During the night, fog had settled over the Loch and totally obscured it. Here and there the slowly heaving ocean of grey vapour shone pale yellow where it was lit by the rising sun. The mesa looked like an island of rock floating in a lake of clouds. In the distance other islands mingled with low mountains, most of them lower than the Starsis Massif. The scene was robed in the deep grey-green of spruce and pine trees, some being strangled in the ever-denser embrace of kudzu vines. Kudzu did well almost everywhere these days.

Up on the Massif, Beamer felt above that strangling vegetation, a green hand that was no longer friendly to human beings. The clutching green was a portent, impossible to see clearly and yet a presence that couldn't be denied. It loomed over humanity. Beamer felt it and everyone Beamer knew from the Coulee felt it. But no one was able to speak of it or name it exactly. Something was about to pass away, but it was so *large* it was invisible. This paradox had settled in Beamer's thoughts many times before: The paradox of something so big it was invisible, so close it couldn't be touched, so pervasive and implacable that it would go on its way, no matter what. Could this be a place to watch it roll by—a hulking beast hauling itself up from some belching hole in the skin of the world, crawling on its way somewhere else, like a modern-day eryopsid? Was this what his intuition had led him to—to discover this place? It was a difficult place for a refuge, this Massif in the sky.

The sun climbed slowly from the east, thinning the fog and gradually revealing the sparkling dark face of the Loch. Beamer felt no inclination to move. He sat utterly still, watching the Loch and the trees and the rocks and all the changing shades of colour and shadow that passed in the depths of the scenery. Not far off, the hushed rustles that fill the night forest fell silent and gave way to the dawn chorus. The birds, though they could hardly know how few they were these days, still offered the morning their boisterous greeting as if the day depended on their invocation. And down below, Beamer imagined, Great Grey Owls were noiselessly swooping into the trees. There, they were settling and preening their feathers before the day's sleepy vigil.

Beamer felt his imagination stretching back, back before the mess the world was in, before Europeans appeared with their belching, roaring machines, and everywhere, their guns. Big guns. Little guns. Every sort of gun. Lots and lots of guns. He started imagining a time before all that, when human beings would have grown up in places like this—where most sounds were those of the air and the trees and the water, and where the daily lives of people were unspoken, unvoiced, as they followed ancient, well-known customs. He pictured himself being born into such a world, where the first sounds to enter him were his mother's groaning in childbirth, the sound of tumbling water that was dipped and poured to wash his shivering skin, the soft brush of rabbit fur that received his naked body. And then the endless days stretching into a childhood filled with the sounds of squirrels rummaging in leaves, the swoosh of birds' wings visiting the camp, the hushed hiss and pop of the cooking fires, the sound of laughter as his mother sliced venison and fish, the perfume of balsam fir trees and, in spring, the musky aroma of aspen. He imagined himself growing up and living his entire life awash in such sensations—how different it would have been, how calm, how centred in the moment. He knew, of course, that this was the fantasy of someone raised in completely human-made surroundings and scarcely capable of grasping what his mind, his heart, was reaching for. And yet—and yet—it *was* a compelling fantasy.

This place was full of change. Even in its silence, Beamer sensed it changing beneath and around him. It was evolving to become whatever it was capable of becoming in the circumstances it found itself in. Human beings were merely part of this fullness, part of the great flood that moved into the way opening before it. At this thought Beamer felt a stab of guilt and of sadness. He knew what people were doing to the world. Unlike all the other extinction events of history, this time humanity was an asteroid smashing into itself. If a rock had come from space, Beamer thought, the passing of humanity would qualify as a tragic event. But when we ourselves were the asteroid, could anything so blindly suicidal also be tragic?

Beamer watched and listened, utterly still. An intuition seeped into him like a vapour. This was a stillness he never wanted to end, never wanted to leave, a stillness from which he would never again hurry away. This stillness that swaddled him was both hard and soft. The hardness of it he could feel in his numbing buttocks as he continued to sit on the brow of this enormous rock. The softness of it wrapped around him in the warming air that wafted up from the very same rocks. The dream that the forest was dreaming of itself went on and on as if he wasn't there, but then he realized, with a sudden ecstasy, that the dreaming went on and on, *including him*. What was he in this dream, he wondered? A hero? An ogre? A witness?

Emotions washed through him in spate. He had no words for such feelings, no thoughts to ponder them. He only knew there was nowhere else he needed to go, nothing else he needed to do except *be* here, in this place, in this impossible place, and pay attention. And being here, he no longer felt alone. He was no longer the stranger, the outsider, the alien. He belonged, but he was also emerging. He would not, could not, fall back. But he could watch for whatever was opening ahead. Maybe that's what the Quakers back at Badger Coulee meant when they talked about watching for way opening. They weren't meditating on some mantra or guided image. They were watching for cracks in the wall of darkness that always threatened to foreshorten what people were capable of becoming. They were watching for the light of emergence, that appearing which was always greater than the sum of its parts and always surprising when it appeared. To perceive it, you had to mind the Light.

He sat for a long time.

Then there came a rush of air and noisy wings. The raven landed a metre from his knee, carrying an enormous pancake in its beak, still dripping with maple syrup. *Someone's breakfast*, Beamer thought, *camping down the beach maybe*. Ravens could be thieves and brigands. The bird waddled over, then dropped the pancake in Beamer's hand. But before releasing it completely, the bird tore off a piece and, flipping her head back, gulped it down. "Ache—uck!" it croaked.

"So be it," said Beamer as he brought a morsel of the pancake to his lips, dripping sweetness. This might be the way…

CHAPTER 7

SPRING, THE 276TH YEAR OF THE EUTERRAN AGE (E.A.)
(2298 C.E.)

All are under concern to relieve suffering
if possible. For all are flesh.

— THE BOOK OF MEMORY

OTIS BEDE HAD BEEN running through the bush since dawn and it was
now well past zenith. He was moments away from stopping for Mindfulness
of Zenith but pressed on for a little longer. In appearance, his body didn't seem
well suited to Tarshin running, being short, strong, and blocky with muscle.
But he had set upon the Practice of the Tarshin-ru like a mortal adversary
and to his Telder's surprise, had mastered running as deftly as any. Now in
his late thirties he was also defying the odds as to his age. He pressed forward against both limitations with undramatic determination. This run was
his sixty-seventh in as many days over a course that was eighty-two kilometres
long. Once having completed this loop, he would run sixty-three more circuits
until he completed all one hundred, in one hundred days, more or less. Injury
or illness might slow him, but nothing else—except perhaps the Memory of
Compassion—if it came to that.

Tarshin running was neither a jog, nor a sprint, nor a race. It consisted in
traversing wilderness territory that included a variety of terrains and obsta-
cles that required continually changing one's gait and stride. The object was
not to win something or to set a record. Tarshin running was about sustaining attention over uneven ground and persisting in this practice to the end
of the circuit. The Tarshin-ru—a Tarshin practitioner—then engaged in the
practice of Stillness, which was immeasurably deepened by the running. The
entire Tarshin Practice consisted of seven consecutive years of the practice of
Stillness, study of *The Book of Practice* and *The Book of Memory*, together with

one hundred consecutive circuits of eighty kilometres each, in each of the first three years, followed by one hundred consecutive circuits of one hundred kilometres each, in each of the last four years. For those who were physically capable and spiritually drawn to Tarshin, it represented the summit and synthesis of the practices of Stillness and Action.

Today, however, Otis was stopped in mid-stride by the appearance of a human foot. It was about fifteen metres away, but the rest of the body, if there was one, lay behind a fallen log. It was not unheard of, though now very rare, to come upon human body parts, the orts left by feasting cougars, or the remains of recently dead people scattered about by rooting wild pigs.

Otis stood still, then slowly settled toward the ground in meditation seat. All his concentration had been focused on his running, but now he must refocus on opening in this moment. Gradually his breathing slowed and his whole attention was given to the foot. Breaking Tarshin was not right Practice except at greatest need. If the person to whom the foot belonged was dead, it would not be a situation of great need, but if alive… How could one tell without stopping?

Otis kept his vigil for a long time, watching the foot for any sign of movement, and letting his aural awareness expand in every direction, waiting for any sound of approaching people, of animals, of any change in the elements. The foot didn't move. But neither did it have the pallor of death, though it was hard to tell because much of the skin was caked with mud. The sole of the foot looked painfully lacerated. *Tarshin-ru make decisions in the space of seven breaths*, Otis reminded himself. He had been sitting for far more than seven breaths.

Resolved, he stood up and approached the fallen tree, looking over it to see what lay on the other side. Jaeger's body was still except for the slightest movement of breathing. Otis took in his appearance at a glance but then was immediately assaulted by the stench of what remained of Jaeger's diarrhoea-stained clothing and emaciated body. Certainly, whoever he was, he had been wandering in the bush for days and drinking tainted water. And just as certainly, Otis's Tarshin was over.

He rounded the fallen tree and started attending to Jaeger by trying to give him some water, which he sipped weakly. Otis quickly surveyed the area and decided that their location was a relatively favourable one for shelter and warmth, at least for the moment. But he would have to range farther afield to get what he needed to treat Jaeger's most pressing afflictions.

Leaving Jaeger where he lay, Otis made his way upslope toward an opening in the forest which turned out to be a meadow covering an old forest fire burn at the top of the hill. Here he found both some patches of desiccated blueberries from the previous year, and a stand of stinging nettle fresh in its spring growth. He harvested some of both and brought them back to Jaeger where he crushed them together into a dense, moist paste. He then assembled some fuel for a fire, retrieved his cooking pot from his Tarshin bundle and proceeded to make a tea using the paste and more water. He hoped the blueberries would be sufficient to suppress Jaeger's diarrhoea, and hence the risk of dehydration, and that the nettle would start to replace lost minerals and offer some nourishment. Jaeger accepted the tea, but took a long time to ingest a significant amount of it. Otis knew he would have to fetch this foundling to the attention of more skilled help and it was clear the man wouldn't be making it on his own feet.

Jaeger emitted a groan.

"Can you hear me?" Otis asked, shaking him gently.

Jaeger's eyes rolled part-way open. He barely managed another groan.

Otis tried to make eye contact. "Who are you?"

There was a pause, then a dry rasp, "Jaeger."

"Jaeger who?"

"Just Jaeger," he struggled, giving up a sigh of exhaustion.

Otis repositioned Jaeger's body to afford him more comfort, and said: "I'm Otis Bede. I'll take care of you." Jaeger made no reply, but Otis could feel him relax slightly with this assurance.

Having offered rescue, Otis wondered if he could actually deliver it. He was still at least forty kilometres from the end of his run, and another twenty-five or thirty kilometres to secure aide. The gear he carried was minimal as the eighty kilometre Tarshin run was in right Practice completed in a single day, or at most, two days. So he didn't have what he needed for a prolonged stay in the bush treating an invalid. He inspected Jaeger more closely. He estimated him to weigh at most sixty-five kilos. He was apparently uninjured except for severely battered feet, a multitude of insect bites, and many bruises and minor cuts as if he had been thrashing around in the bush for a long time. Judging from the lacerations on his face, he had also tried to travel at night. But all things considered, dehydration was the worst enemy. Otis took the additional step of administering a drop of phero-seven to Jaeger's lips, a systemic insect repellent. He then busied himself making more blueberry nettle tea which he gave to Jaeger over the next several hours until they were enveloped in darkness, a darkness relieved only by the waving pennants of a tiny cooking fire.

At sunrise Otis awakened to find Jaeger more or less where he left him the night before, his breathing stronger and no signs of any new diarrhoeal episodes, though they would probably stop of their own accord as Jaeger approached the extreme of dehydration. Otis meditated for some time, preparing himself for what he was about to do. The embers of his cooking fire had died out long ago. A thin, cold fog pooled on the forest floor below them. He looked again at Jaeger, imagining him becoming a bundle of eider-down, then of thistledown, and then of the thinnest of vapours. He repeated these visualizations over and over again until Jaeger appeared to be entirely weightless. He then arose, lifting Jaeger by one of his arms and hoisting his motionless body and draping it over his shoulders like a shawl. He shook a lit-tle as if to get Jaeger's body to conform more to the contour of his own shoul-ders, took a deep breath and released it slowly. Then he started loping along, as he had learned to do, as he had vowed to do, as he would do once again, when he had delivered this charge. And the old stories he'd heard about foundlings bearing plagues, he forced from his mind. His sole task now was to run.

CHAPTER 8

SPRING, THE 276TH YEAR OF THE EUTERRAN AGE (E.A.)
(2298 C.E.)

Not everything that appears fortunate is fortunate. Not everything that appears ill-begotten is a cause for regret. Many things are resolved most simply by non-action.

— THE BOOK OF PRACTICE

LARS BECKETT STOPPED the lift at ground level, stepped off, and made his way through another short drift. This one opened into a larger gallery cluttered with cargos, a few spinners, larger wains, and people on foot passing in and out of the Dawngate, many on their way to the orchards, gardens and permasites. Dawngate opened onto a small plaza and a bridge that spanned the Snake River cataract. The river was only about fifty metres wide, but wild and noisy in the rocks below. Its source was far to the north but its stream turned abruptly eastward when it met the Starsis Massif, boiling around its base, then turned south again, to empty into Loch Speare, an inland body of fresh water, now grown almost to the size of a sea. A century before, near Clippersgate at the west end of the Massif, Euterrans had built Molly's Gate and Molly's Quay to provide moorage and access to the Loch.

The view through Dawngate was that of a forest lane paved with flat stones removed during the construction of Euterra, as was the Dawngate Bridge. Being granite, they were many times harder and more durable even than the concrete made before the Ruination, but took more patience to work and skill to lay. In the near distance, Beckett could see Otis Bede leading a cargo with a human form on it and flanked by half a dozen of the Watch.

Lars waited until he caught a glimpse of Zephyr stepping off the lift. She had changed before descending to the Dawngate gallery, trading her morning robe for the more utilitarian pants and tunic of a working Helder. She had little information about what shape the foundling was in, or even if she might have to share his quarantine with him, for he would certainly be quarantined. She also carried a large bundle of fresh clothing. She hurried forward to join Lars, and then the two of them walked out onto the Dawngate Plaza. "Here they come," he said, half to himself.

"Yes," Zephyr replied, uneasily.

Lars joined his palms in the customary Euterran greeting as Otis Bede approached, but kept a discreet distance. "Otis Bede, well met. And to you of the Watch."

"Well met, Lars Beckett," Otis replied wearily. He stepped aside, giving a clearer view of his charge who was still unconscious on the cargo. "A foundling from beyond the Watch."

"So this is him?" The hair on the back of Lars's neck bristled as he saw passers-by notice the cargo. "Let's take this one inside so he's less of an attraction." The little group moved back toward the Dawngate and stepped inside its sheltering archway, then off to the side to a more isolated corner of the entrance gallery.

"Please strip," said Zephyr, her voice firm, trucking no objections. All the men present including Otis began doffing their clothes and tossing them in a single large pile on the floor. When all were naked, Zephyr handed out simple kudzu fibre robes which everyone donned. "Watchers can go to the right," she directed, "shower there, dispose of these robes too. You'll find better clothing there after you shower. Please speak to no one, and touch no one for the prescribed time. Food and drink will be brought. Otis, please wait here." She then conducted the others down a short passageway and out of sight.

Lars turned to Otis. "Where'd you find him?"

"I was in the second day of Tarshin, on the Path of Return, when I saw him. First I thought he was dead but it turned out not. Might as well be. He was out when I found him. Tricky to wake up. Trickier even to keep awake. He's half starved and pretty beat up, even after I've been feeding him this long. But running the Tarshin, I had very little gear—so no supplies really to help him. I ran back toting him as far as the Watch. There I got him on a cargo and peddled the rest of the way. The Watch-keepers came as escort, but they haven't touched him or me. I think they should be well enough. I'd pretty much guarantee he won't know where he is or how he got here when he comes to. He hasn't even seen a paved road yet."

"Good," said Lars. "Very good. Has he said anything about who he is or where he's from?"

"Says his name is Jaeger; just Jaeger. He's pretty confused. Dehydrated. I would guess he'd been crashing about in the bush for at least ten days by the look of him. Dumb luck that he's alive. If he knew the bush, he wouldn't be in the shape he's in. So my guess is he's an exile, or he was set loose in the bush to make it or break it on his own. Or maybe he's merely loopy and wandered out there and got lost. His feet are really beat up, like he walked a long way without shoes, or maybe the wounds were inflicted. When I asked him where he was from and how he wound up where he was, I'm pretty sure it was dehydration talking. He sounded really mixed up. He speaks well enough, like he's educated. But he doesn't know squat about how to find a meal in the bush."

"Did he ask you anything?"

"Asked who I was. I told him my name. But he didn't ask much else. He's hardly been awake the whole way. We've no record yet of any people from east of here, at least not groups of them. Too many blow-ups, too much fighting in the Ruination, too much contamination. Now it's mostly kudzu, boars and snakes. Hard country—but good for Tarshin." Otis gave a tired smile.

"About that," said Lars. "I'm sorry this happened, after all your preparation."

"It's not your doing. I know the Way. I may be able to spend my quarantine and still finish this cycle before winter. Be at peace. But maybe we should send a surveyor east."

The two men regarded each other closely, both thinking the same thing. Then Lars said, "Let's see if he lives first, and if so, what he can tell us about how he got in such a predicament. But I agree; it may call for a survey, and probably farther east than we've ever gone before."

"Humph," said Otis. "Nothing good comes from the east."

Zephyr joined them after asking a gallery worker to isolate and burn the pile of discarded clothing. "I think we should keep him here on the Forest Drift during quarantine, and not let him wander around by himself for the time being," she counselled.

"You speak my mind," Otis agreed. "We don't know anything about him. I think we should give it a few days until he can tell us more about where he's from and how he got out in the bush. And he has to decide where he wants to be. Maybe after quarantine, we can take him into Mizar Dan, provided we're in unity about it. I can keep an eye on him there and Lydia Ross might be willing to introduce him more to Euterra. I'll give him a day or two and then stop in to see him. So far I guess, I'm the one he knows most, little as that is."

"Yes, a bit of time," Lars agreed. "He'll need to be in someone's Dan to have a place here if he stays with us. If not, then we'll need to meet for clearness on what else to do. He needs clothes—and a bath." A chuckle rippled around the group. Lars turned to Zephyr: "Could you please care for him in recovery? Take all precautions. Please let me know what, if anything, you learn about him."

"I will," Zephyr replied. "Tell the Dan that I'm going into quarantine with the foundling but should be out in two weeks at most."

"Take no chances," said Lars with concern. "He would have died anyway if Otis hadn't found him."

Zephyr smiled. "I'm a Helder, not a martyr. You know that Lars. And we both know history." She gave the ceremonial bow to him, then turned. She and Otis disappeared in the direction of the quarantine gallery.

Zephyr and Otis pushed the cargo with Jaeger on it into Forest Drift toward the quarantine cells. While it was now a distant memory, the epidemic of 15-16 E.A. that swept the world very soon after the Ruination had touched Euterra as well. For the first few years following the Ruination, Euterra remained mostly hidden from the turmoil that engulfed the world. But from time to time people appeared who had somehow stumbled upon their community and begged for refuge. And in the same way that Otis Bede had acted in Memory of Compassion to retrieve Jaeger, the first Euterrans welcomed any who found them and wanted to stay. It was inevitable therefore that the plague ravaging the remnants of the human population beyond the Massif would also be borne to Euterra by one or another foundling. When it arrived in late 15 E.A., it persisted for nearly a year and carried off almost a third of the early Euterrans. It followed then that all the Drift Councils were in unity with the General Council that Forest Drift should be expanded to include quarantine cells for any future foundlings and that in such cases, volunteer Helders would join the foundlings for the duration of their confinement to render treatment as needed. While there had been no further incidents since the infections in 15-16 E.A., and following that period, the discovery of other foundlings was extremely rare, the experience of the epidemic was so imprinted in their collective memory and popular legend that the gates of Euterra were never again opened to foundlings without extreme caution and mixed emotions.

So it was with some care and caution that Zephyr and Otis attended to Jaeger, at first by stripping and washing him, then binding his still open wounds. Zephyr extracted blood samples and cultures for analysis and screening, and once Jaeger had been transferred to a proper bed, both Zephyr and Otis made their ways to their own quarters to begin the quarantine vigil.

CHAPTER 9

SPRING, 2027 C.E.

For decades before the Ruination it was feared that environmental collapse would ruin the economy. It was therefore ironic that it was an economic collapse that saved the environment. At the time, this was called a 'market failure.' Today we recognize it as an ethical failure. While the civilization of the day, which thought of itself as the ultimate human achievement, almost completely disappeared with much human suffering, a window was nevertheless opened for the Emergence.

— THE BOOK OF MEMORY

BEAMER HAD BEEN on the Starsis Massif for several days. His meagre provisions ran out long ago and the raven, while a diligent provider, sometimes brought items that Beamer couldn't agree were food—a scrap of raw meat of unknown origin, an empty beer can, some shiny shards of plastic, a metre of twine, foil candy wrappers… The bird had apparently decided that he was an abandoned chick for whom care was required. While male and female ravens looked identical, Beamer decided this one who seemed so attentive to his every need was probably a female for she attended, in her way, not only to his feeding, but also to the decoration of his nest. Beamer's own foraging efforts provided some additional supplies, but he was feeling weaker every day and began to ponder with some uneasiness the need to make his descent. He had also to ford the river again, and walk for at least a day in hopes of meeting a road closer to the Massif than the one he had departed from.

Thinking back over his trek to the Massif and his time upon it, he realized that somehow, the wilderness had done its alchemy. His grief at the loss of Tatum was still present, but instead of him being contained by it, it was now contained within him. He would always remember her, always love her, but the loss of her would not define his reality as it had for the past month. The bush was gaining colour and there seemed to be more light in the air. It was possible to breathe.

But as soon as he had decided to leave, he found himself again caught in stillness on the veranda of his little grotto. As if for the first time, he noticed jumbled about the scene many rocks that by ice and rain had been cleaved from the outcrop along lines so straight they looked like they had been cut by tools. He lifted a piece of this stone as big as a briefcase, and set it down again on the expanse of naked rock where he had set his fires. He looked at it there, so immovable, so solid. In a time when everything else seemed to be whirling around him, this stone stood still, an ancient fact—a two-billion-year-old fact. Beamer liked that.

He fetched another piece of rock, turning it until one of its sides matched almost seamlessly with the first rock. He found a third, this time one that fit with the other two. He placed this third stone carefully and sat down again, admiring his handiwork. *You could build things with this stuff*, he thought.

News of Beamer Farris's return to Badger Coulee spread through the community like pollen in the springtime. Some thought he had returned to his old life in the city, before the tragic death of Tatum Barnes, who had been his lover. Others thought he might have wandered off somewhere in his grief and done himself harm. A few understood that he might need time in solitude simply to find himself again after such a painful event. But soon after news of his return had made the rounds, the community gathered in the Barn—a large quonset building they had converted to a community meeting and party house—to welcome him back.

"This is totally messed up!" groused Jako Menpaa. He was hunched over a table in the Barn stabbing away at the face of a tablet computer. It glared back at him with its blue corpse-light, stating: "You Are Not Connected To The Internet." Beamer mingled in the group, enjoying the fire that had been laid in the fireplace that dominated one end of the room. The ambience was serene, but such appearances were misleading. Here and there people were pecking away at tablets and smart phones. This was a common occurrence as everyone had these devices, even at the Coulee where the group had installed WiFi at several locations throughout the village. On this occasion people were poking at their devices with noticeably more force and less patience, as if doing so would somehow rouse them again to working order. But all screens carried the same baleful message: "Service is temporarily unavailable." Which was, of course, a lie.

"Those things need electricity, you know," Beamer needled Jako.

"Of course they do," Jako snapped.

"Well?"

"Well what? I've got ninety-two percent battery left," he groused.

"Look out the window, friend," said Beamer.

Jako glanced out the windows that usually offered a view of the city in the far distance. It was an indistinct smudge of light in the sky, a wall of darkness peppered with surprisingly visible stars. A general blackout had descended on the city, the fifth time in a month.

"So?" Jako said, returning to his screen, "It happens all the time these days."

"Ninety-nine point nine, nine percent of what that thing needs to work isn't even in that thing," Beamer said. "It all depends on the grid. How much battery you have left doesn't matter. The grid is down. If the grid is down, servers are down. If servers are down, the Internet is down. If the Internet is down, so is the Cloud and so is WiFi. While the Cloud is down, we're toast. If the Cloud stays down, we're even toastier. Thank God it isn't winter." Turning to the larger group, Beamer walked to the front of the room and mounted the dais that was there. He had never stood on the dais, told a story, read a poem, or led a meeting. But on this night, he did, and the residents of Badger Coulee were listening. "Does anyone find this interesting?" he asked them. To Jako, he said, "You might as well save your battery until you see the power back on."

Slowly, throughout the room, the tiny blue screens winked off one by one, and with them the buzz of conversation became muted—as if someone had announced another death.

"Does anyone find this interesting?" Beamer repeated. The candlelight glowed around them, enfolding their silence in a warm golden sphere.

"I think it's scary," said Laurel Fey, a woman who looked like she wouldn't really be scared of anything. Her frame was slight and her hair so blonde as nearly to be white. But her body was a tightly coiled spring, as if everything about her was held in reserve, like a wave about to break, or a crocus ready to burst open in the snow.

"Yeah," Beamer nodded. "And the more you think about it, the scarier it gets." He sat down and the others in the group found spots to settle down, lean against a wall or sit cross-legged on the floor. "So why don't we take some time and be scared right here—together—for a while."

Moments passed. From somewhere in the room came a muffled sobbing sound. A woman put out her arm to comfort the person sitting next to her, but the silence continued.

"This is awful!" said a woman in the far corner.

Beamer looked up. "What is 'This'?" he asked, "and why is it awful?"

"I don't know," the woman said.

"Yes, you do," Beamer pressed. He surprised himself to hear an echo of Tatum's voice—that unrelenting, uncompromising demand for clarity, for awareness, for meaning.

She glanced at him, her face a gibbous moon passing through its phases—first puzzled, then angry, then sorrowful, then rising to the question. "It's like it's everything," she said, "and nothing at the same time. This stuff like the electricity being off, it's happening more and more and I'm afraid that some day it won't come back on again. And there's more and more people without jobs. Most of *us* can't even find jobs and we've got university degrees. We don't even know what to do or say or think if the bloody Internet is offline for more than ten minutes. The stores are full of fake food. The corporations run everything, even our governments. And people are getting sick and killing each other for stranger and stranger reasons…" Her voice trailed off, silenced by the weight of all she left unsaid.

"And…" Beamer pressed.

"And," she sighed, "it scares me."

"Me too," Beamer said. "This friend speaks my mind." He looked around the room, holding the gaze of everyone present. They looked back at him expectantly, as if he had The Answer, which he knew he didn't. What could he say? Finally he spoke. "I've been away for a few days since Tatum died. Went walkabout in the bush. Spent some time on a mountain. Sort of got a different perspective up there. Lots of fresh air. Made a new friend." He smiled.

"When things are this screwed up," he continued, "it seems to me that fear is an informative emotion. It tells us what's bad for us. The question is: When are we tired of being afraid?"

"Right fucking now!" Jako burst. The room erupted in laughter, a relief, as if oxygen had come rushing back in.

Beamer smiled. "Yes, right now. I think we all sense, we all somehow know, that we have to start moving toward something we want or we'll go crazy trying to dodge around what we fear. This way of life we have breeds more fear than anything else. It's pretty to look at, but it feeds on fear, multiplies fear, controls by fear. But it's so big, so complicated, seems so powerful, it's overwhelming to figure out what to do about it, or with it, if anything. So we stay stuck in fear. We keep our mouths shut. We tell ourselves we don't know when we damn well *do* know."

"So you've found the doorway out of this fun house?" challenged a red-haired man leaning on one of the tables. His tone was deeply cynical, almost bitter; but he'd bothered to ask the question.

"No," Beamer said. "At least I'm not sure. But I think we can make one together."

"You gotta give me more than a kumbaya moment," the red-haired man scoffed.

Beamer nodded gravely. "Yes. We certainly need more than that. This is what I've got, at least for today. Suppose for a minute that we don't try to figure it out. Maybe it can't be figured out. Maybe we don't need to figure it out. Suppose we just give up trying. Suppose we find somebody who believes all of this still has a future and we say, 'Here—You have a robe and a staff. You rule this heap of ruins!'" The group looked back at him, puzzled. "You see," he said cheekily, "we're all useless ten seconds after the Internet goes down. If it was on, you could all Google that and find out it's from *Isaiah*." They looked equally blank. "Never mind," he said, waving it away.

"When I was on the mountain," he continued, "I realized how much of our fear comes from trying to hang on to stuff we really don't have or control. Or we're trying so hard to maneuver in this crazy mess of a society, to find a way to live a good life, but it's so rapacious, so much like a minefield with hidden little traps everywhere. And I guess I got to a point where I didn't try to figure it out any more. I gave up hope of fixing it, or making it better, or contributing to its 'sustainability.' Sustainability! Ain't that a joke?" Beamer let go a laugh as if this was the funniest thing he'd ever heard.

"So what do we do?" asked Laurel.

"We make something different," said Beamer. "Maybe we start with that Periodic Table you've been working on. I don't know. But we have to start somewhere with something different."

"Just like that?" barked Jako.

"Well, more or less."

"What the fuck were you smoking on that mountain?"

Everyone laughed again.

"Well, maybe not 'just like that,'" Beamer conceded. "But what I'm trying to say is that every culture is made by people. If the one we live in is in a death spiral, and I think it is, we need to make something new, or we can go down in fear and misery with the rest of it. I think that's what scares us most is the idea of crashing because we can't think of anything else to do. But no person can do that on their own. We need to create the alternative, on a different path than the old one. It's fairly simple."

"And how do you propose that we do that?" pressed Jako.

"Well," said Beamer, "we've already made a start right here at Badger Coulee. And beyond that, we simply need to wake up."

"Of course! Why didn't I think of that?"

"I'm serious," Beamer insisted. "We live in a sort of dream. I know that's trite. Everybody says that—but it doesn't make it any less true. I think it has a lot to do with what we pay attention to, what we're on the lookout for. We're not on the Titanic here. We're mashed up like a flock of birds flying toward a wall. We could change course any time. We could turn on a dime if we wanted to. We might have to leave the flock to do it. But a tiny change now could cause a huge difference down the line. We need to stop focusing on the past, stop clinging to what was, stop trying to make a sane life in a delusional situation, and wake up. We need to stop trying to make 'This' work even as it terrifies us. We do this not by looking back, but by paying attention to what is opening for us. It's like the Quakers say—that guy, where are you Alex Brighton when I need you? —it's an *opening* we have to watch for, not what is closing. This is not a rational thing."

An old man stood up in the assembly, thin as a stick, with shoulder-length white hair and impossibly massive glasses precariously close to the end of his nose. He was one of the elder Quakers who had been part of the Badger Coulee community from the beginning. For months, whenever the opportunity arose, he would simply announce: "Wait. Way is not yet open. Wait." But on this night, when he stood, his eyes were wet and his whole frame shook like a rag in the wind. He turned slowly surveying the group until he had turned completely around and was facing Beamer once again. "Way is open," he said. Then, looking around once more at the others and pointing toward Beamer, he added, "Do what he says." He continued to shake like an aspen leaf but said no more and sat down.

There were some moments of silence until the red-haired man spoke again. He addressed Beamer, this time pleading, "Even if I knew what that 'opening' stuff meant, is that all you're giving us—all we've got to go on?"

"I've got some more," Beamer offered tentatively. "Not so much a 'what' as a 'where'—where I went walkabout. We might start there. You all have other bits too."

"You do hack riddles!" someone piped from the back of the room.

"Okay," Beamer said. "Try what I did on the mountain. Imagine we're all climbing that mountain. It's slow going, but we're pulling and pushing each other along because we know there's a different world at the top. We stick together. And we keep climbing. It's a long day, but in the afternoon we reach the top. We fan out in this new place. What do you see?" Again a silence settled on the group. The minutes passed. "Anyone? Anything?"

"Trees," said someone.

"It's quiet," said someone else.

"We're awake."

"There's food everywhere. Good food."

"It's simple. It's beautiful."

"Everyone is there, children, elders, everyone. All of us."

"No government. No corporations."

Someone giggled. "Grey is no longer recommended. Everything is in colour."

"There's Light! Light everywhere!"

More voices spoke out the vision-bits of some as-yet-to-be place, some as-yet-to-be way of living. Beamer listened as the bits came out and the room filled with a sense of something lightsome and life-giving. Then he said, "You see? We already know what it is. And we're already practicing parts of it here. It's practice that matters. Everything else will come from that."

"And when does all this happen?" Jako asked, sounding skeptical.

"Oh, five-thirty tomorrow morning," said Beamer. "Be here with enough gear and nosh for a week. We'll climb the mountain and see what happens. By then you should be able to decide where you want to place your bets—and how long you want to be afraid."

"What makes you think this'll work?" asked the red-haired man.

"A raven fed me. Maybe she'll feed you too."

CHAPTER 10

SPRING, THE 276TH YEAR OF THE EUTERRAN AGE (E.A.)
(2298 C.E.)

The Central Harmony is also present in its manifestations
whether they seem congenial to human interests or
not. This is a deep mystery that cannot be opened by
meditation alone. It requires insight born of Practice.

— THE BOOK OF PRACTICE

LATER, HE WOULD REMEMBER only murky visions—an image of himself lying on a bed, as if watching himself from a distance, surrounded by other people, silent, motionless. He saw them through closed eyes, unable to make out any of their faces. Dream people. A mist of light suffused the gathering. He sensed a presence, close by, moving about ever so softly, as if *inside* him, pausing to listen…then moving on…pausing again. The light dimmed, the figures turned away and disappeared one by one, no sound but the soft rustle of clothing as they moved away.

Some uncountable time later, a woman's face, comely and strong, hovered into Jaeger's view. "Hello. I'm Zephyr Fey," she said. Her hair dark, close-cut, framing grey eyes that were searching his carefully. There was no pretence to familiarity in her expression. It showed detached clinical interest, softened by a measure of compassion, observing, not communing.

He, about thirty-five, emaciated, disheveled, an unimpressive physique, lay naked and motionless on a cot, covered with a light blanket. His eyelids fluttered open and closed again as he struggled to stay conscious. His body testified to a life of hard work and undernourishment. One could imagine him eating voraciously only to lose it all in the next day's work.

"I'll be your Helder until you feel better," Zephyr said as she went to the end of the bed, pulled back the cover, and inspected the dressings that swaddled Jaeger's feet. "We'll need to change these dressings in a minute."

"Helder?" Jaeger asked, his voice raspy.

She looked back. "Yes. I'm a healing elder—a Helder. Do you have none such where you come from?"

"You don't look old."

She smiled: "Being an elder has nothing much to do with age."

Jaeger tried to look around but the effort made him dizzy. He lay still. "Where am I? What's happened to me?"

"You're in Euterra."

"You-what?"

"Euterra. You're in the Forest Drift of Euterra, near the Dawngate, in a sort of guest house, you might call it. Otis Bede brought you here after you got lost in the forest. Do you remember?"

"Otis? Where is Otis?" He searched for anything familiar, some memory, some emotional purchase in this strange place.

"Nearby. Both of you are in quarantine here, on Forest Drift, until you're well enough and we're sure it's safe for you to leave."

"Was he hurt too?"

"No," Zephyr assured. "Otis is fine. And you'll be fine. Otis will probably visit you. Tomorrow maybe. For now, just rest and drink." She then busied herself with removing Jaeger's dressings, washing his feet, and plastering them again with a poultice of herbs, honey and aloe. She bound them again in fresh dressings.

"How did Otis find me?" Jaeger pressed.

Zephyr was unsure of how much to say. "By accident. He was running Tarshin and came on you in the bush. You're very fortunate."

"Tarshin..?"

"It's part of Practice. He was running his sixty-seventh circuit, I think, when he found you. This quarantine will break his vow and he'll have to start over, unless the Siderium makes an exception. So getting you here came at a high price for Otis."

"Sider..?" His voice now sounded abstracted, like he was speaking with effort through fatigue or confusion.

"Siderium," Zephyr said. "It's a place. I'll explain some other time. Right now you need to rest." She gathered up Jaeger's soiled dressings and turned to leave. "Now that you're awake," she said, "you should start feeling better. You'll still be weak and should probably stay off your feet for at least another day. Food will be brought in another couple of hours. If you need help with anything, pull the cord by your bed. I'll stop in again this evening."

"But I have so many questions," Jaeger protested.

"So do we," said Zephyr. "We'll have lots to talk about. Rest now." She turned and left through a door that Jaeger noticed for the first time. It was made of skillfully carved wood set in a massive stone wall.

He raised himself up on one elbow and looked around. At first he felt nauseous but it soon subsided. Light poured in one entire wall of the room, a wall which was made of glass. It overlooked a terrace of closely laid flagstones and planters dense with flowers and ornamental shrubs. Along the terrace's far side ran a balustrade of carved stone and beyond that, a wall of forest.

His room had been hollowed from living rock. The walls were plumb and true, and their surfaces had been worked smooth, revealing feldspar and quartzite flakes in pink granite. A soft mat covered part of the floor. It was braided of many coloured strands of material that might be hemp or kudzu. Two niches were set into the stone wall, one sheltering a female statuette carved from wood, and the other a composition built up from dozens of shards of stained glass. At its centre was an orb of clear glass surrounded by three blue shards of glass above and nine amber shards below. This made a sort of sunburst composition surrounded by many smaller bits and fragments. Its facets caught and scattered the light around the walls in blazes of colour.

Jaeger spent some minutes looking out over the terrace, slowly realizing that despite the view, he really couldn't see much. The mist rising from beyond the balustrade he guessed might be coming from a cataract or rapids, but the forest beyond revealed nothing about where he was. He considered these things as he swallowed another glass of what appeared to be water, but tasted both brackish and sweet. With his conversation with Zephyr Fey spinning in his exhausted mind, Jaeger was again overcome by sleep.

———•◆•———

When he awakened, he felt much stronger, but still very thirsty. A meal had been laid for him on a narrow table close to his bed—a melange of vegetables and fish on a bed of some sort of cooked grain mixed with wild rice and cranberries. In Mainbranch, skrala never ate such food. It was reserved for the Brotherhood. But those who served the Brotherhood sometimes caught a glimpse of such delicacies as fish and berries. Moving slowly, Jaeger discovered he could sit up without feeling too dizzy, and fell to his supper.

The terrace beyond his glass wall was bathed in the coppery hues of a setting sun and the light seemed to billow up in clouds of luminous fog steps beyond the balustrade. That brightness reminded him of something, an image of a fish lying still in a sun-shot pool, and then, fanning its tail, dissolving in the watery depths.

When he finished eating, he rose gingerly and approached the glass wall. There were two glass doors set in the wall that didn't budge when he tried them. He went to the carved wooden door of his room, but that wouldn't open either. Before he could think of what to try next, a soft rap came to the door, which opened revealing Zephyr. She stood in the doorway holding a pile of folded clothing—Jaeger staring blankly back at her, still naked.

"I brought you some clothes," she said matter-of-factly. "You must feel a little better to be up and around?"

Jaeger looked at her steadily, suspicious: "Am I a prisoner here?"

"A what?"

"A prisoner. Am I having a time out?" His voice was edged with defiance and fear.

"What a strange expression," Zephyr said. "What is a prison?"

Jaeger's eyes darted about, anxious. "A place they lock up Citizens. The hole."

"Decidedly not, friend! There are no prisoners in Euterra, if I get your meaning. And no prisons, for that matter. You're in temporary quarantine, strictly for health reasons, and I do want to talk with you a bit before you go wandering about—for your good as well as ours."

"For my good?"

"Yes—and ours. Please be patient with us until we come to clearness on what's best for everybody." Her sincerity seemed genuine and Jaeger decided to take what she said at face value for the time being. "So, do you want to try these on?" she asked as she proffered the clothes.

Jaeger reached for the bundle. It had a pair of soft-looking shoes woven of kudzu, which he laid aside. There was also a pair of pants with a drawstring at the waist, made of a soft but substantial textile dyed pale blue with clouds of darker blue blushing through the fabric. There was a matching tunic with a hood. Jaeger realized that he had never worn clothing as fine as this, nor as simple. "I'll try the shoes when I'm rid of the bandages," he said.

"A wise choice." Zephyr smiled. "Come. Let's sit," she suggested, indicating a pair of chairs made of braided willow with cushions of gaily coloured hemp, and a small willow table between them near the window wall. The sun continued to lower in the west, and the view offered by the window now showed clouds above the forest line tinted by the first rays of sunset.

"So tell me," asked Zephyr, "where are you from?"

Jaeger's face tightened a little. "I lived in Mainbranch," he said, and after a pause, "but I don't know where that is exactly."

"Mainbranch," Zephyr repeated. "Otis found you in the bush, far travel from here to the east. You were unconscious, near death. He said you looked like you had been in the bush for many days."

Jaeger nodded. "Yes," he said. "Many days—ten at least, twelve maybe. I lost count."

"How'd you get there?"

Jaeger's face tightened and his body tensed, curling slightly forward, drawing himself in protectively. His feet pulled back under his chair. "The Expediter brought me. I was supposed to move on to new opportunities."

"The Expediter?"

He nodded with a shiver. "When the Chief no longer wants you in Mainbranch, the Expediter takes you. They bind you, blind you, bounce you away and leave you to move on to new opportunities. Far away." His eyes appeared hollow, distant.

"Was it the Expediter who hurt you?"

Jaeger nodded without speaking.

"You're from Mainbranch," she repeated, "but you don't know where that is?"

"Yes…I mean no," he said, confused. "I've never been out of Mainbranch. I lived in Mainbranch since I was a child. But I wasn't born there. I came from…somewhere else…I don't know where I'm from." Zephyr was mindful of Jaeger as he spoke. His body contracted noticeably when he talked about Mainbranch, as if expecting a blow. She weighed whether to pursue the topic any further. Adopting as neutral a tone as possible, she asked, "So, how many people live in Mainbranch?"

Jaeger's eyes darted around the room. "I don't know. Many. Maybe two thousand skrala, but many more of the Brotherhood. Millions of the Brotherhood. That's what they say. We never see them all at once. Only a few now and then. But there are millions of the Brotherhood. Millions."

"And you are skrala?"

"No!" Jaeger burst angrily. "I'm a *Citizen*!"

"You're a Citizen, then," Zephyr repeated, soothing.

"Yes," Jaeger confirmed. "Workers. We do the work. I was a Citizen in Mainbranch. I kept records, kept books, wrote things down. I can read." He showed a flicker of pride. "Skrala is what the Brotherhood calls us." Jaeger's lip curled in contempt.

"And not all Citizens can read?" Zephyr probed.

"No," he confirmed. "Not all."

A silence lengthened between them. Zephyr continued to watch him, her gaze steady but gentle. The foundling was an enigma to be sure, but she sensed no threat. "Jaeger," she said evenly, "you're safe here. No one will bounce you. No one will bind you or blind you. Understand?"

He looked up, nodded tentatively, but didn't look convinced.

"That's good." She paused, then said, "Listen. I don't know what sort of place Mainbranch is, but this is Euterra. Many people live here, but for the time being you'll stay on this drift until you feel more like going out. For a while, I will go with you outside, and this room will be your home, but only until you feel well, until you've rested and feel steady. You're in a place where we take care of people who are sick or hurt. We want to look you over and do some tests—to make sure there's nothing you need to help you feel better. Some time ago a foundling brought sickness here and it was very difficult for us. So now we take more care. Otis asked about you since he brought you in. He'll come and see you. How does that sound?"

Jaeger nodded again. "Thank you," he said.

"Of course," said Zephyr. "Now rest well this night and we'll see if we can get you into those shoes tomorrow."

CHAPTER 11

SPRING, THE 276TH YEAR OF THE EUTERRAN AGE (E.A.)
(2298 C.E.)

*Consider the python: Its movement is sinuous; its camouflage
perfect; its senses remarkably acute; its hunting skills
unmatched; and on cloudless days it can be found lying in the
sun. But seeing one in such repose, it would not do to think
that even for one moment does it cease to be a python.*

— THE BOOK OF MEMORY

BY THE TIME Caine, Mason and Ferguson reached Mainbranch, they were
ragged and half starving. They had managed to snare one small boar on their
journey but had definitely suffered for lack of grains and vegetables. The boar
had been perhaps fifteen kilos, but after gutting and skinning came in at less
than ten kilos; then one had to subtract the bones. Little enough for three men
making their way over difficult ground for thirteen more days.

At the best of times, Mainbranch did not appear welcoming, even to someone who had been away for nearly a month. But it did offer human company,
warm food, and an alternative to sleeping on beds of sphagnum moss and
spruce bows.

Mainbranch had once been a city, although its original name was now forgotten. Since the Great Recession, nearly three centuries before, most of it had
fallen into ruin. Any building made of wood was decayed beyond recognition
except for shards of plastic, ceramics and stainless steel. That there had ever
been a time when its streets were edged with single family houses with SUVs
parked in front had now become splintered memory and myth. Even concrete
buildings were crumbling before the relentless forces of frost, moisture, corro-
sion, and shelter-seeking creatures intent on colonizing any niche they could
find. Despite the general state of collapse hidden by an overgrowth of kudzu,

Virginia creeper, and wild grape vines, it was still possible to discern a grid pattern of streets and lanes that had formed the bones of the original city. The side streets had long since been riven by frost, potholes and vegetation, but some of the main streets were still passable.

Within this collapsing carcass of concrete and glass, however, there was an island of human presence and modest order. Not everything could be maintained. It was possible to see different standards being applied over time as to what to keep and what to let go. Whoever was making the decisions alternated between periods of more defensiveness and periods of less. Someone had made choices to conserve this building and sacrifice or renovate that one. Fragile buildings had been sacrificed for sturdier ones. High rises for low-rises. Airier, more open facades, for solidly bricked-in walls. Quirky architectural ego statements were traded off for reinforced parking structures converted to living quarters. All in all, the general impression was that of a city forced to contract defensively upon itself in the face of threats, perceived or real. It most closely resembled a medieval castle: grey, hulking, cold—its only redeeming feature was that it offered a credible defence against enemies that no longer existed.

The approximate centre of Mainbranch was dominated by a single building the Brotherhood called the "HQ." It was in relatively good repair as an example of late twentieth century brutalist inspiration. Much of it was still clad in plate glass, but broken or missing panes had been replaced with masonry in-fill, lending it an oddly 'mixed media' appearance. At twenty-two stories in height it utterly dominated its surroundings as did its sole occupants, the Brotherhood.

Over the centuries since the Great Recession, the building had been modified repeatedly, its street level floors having been walled in with the exception of some large doors that could receive shipments of goods for the Brotherhood. These floors housed the twenty-fourth century version of a twenty-first century shopping mall, though nearly all the goods on offer were retrieved from landfills or made of materials recycled from landfills. Nevertheless, considerable effort and ingenuity had been invested in repurposing what amounted to historical artifacts. What was old was new again among the Brotherhood, and it reinforced the sustaining myth of the Brotherhood that soon, any day now, the good times from before the Great Recession would return.

Another two floors above the mall levels were the Brotherhood's barracks, weapons stores (which were themselves museums of only partially functional curios) and restricted access passageways that together amounted to a protective layer standing between the Brotherhood and the hoi polloi of the skrala who served them. Higher still in the building were living quarters, government offices, and a variety of other areas within the building that served it as a school, a clinic, entertainment centres and shops. Reinforcing the impression of being a castle, most of the Brotherhood resembled maidens hidden by dragons in their high towers as far away as possible from any influence that might awaken them. The Brotherhood depended utterly on the labour of Citizens for their own survival, but this dependency rendered them vulnerable, insecure, and therefore prone to be vicious and oppressive.

Metastasizing around the HQ were the walled-in parking structures and warehouses that were the homes and businesses of the skrala—or Citizens— depending on their caste ranking in Mainbranch. Close at hand, but down-wind of the HQ, were various small enterprises that processed foods, plastics, metals, forest products and textiles for both the Brotherhood and Citizen markets. All of this, except for a spacious paved square that surrounded the HQ, was tangled into a mat of ever-growing vegetation that in an ever-warming climate threatened to bury all of Mainbranch like a Mayan metropolis.

It was shortly after midday when Axel Caine and his minions returned. The plaza surrounding the HQ and many of its side-streets were populated by several hundred figures who ambled about their various errands, some of the amblers seeming to have no direction at all.

Caine and his companions ignored all of this and headed straight for the HQ. As the gang forged through the throngs, Citizens looked askance or turned into the doorways of buildings so as not to come to the Expediter's notice. Whenever he was rumoured to be away, many harboured the fantasy that by some happy chance he might not return. And every time he *did* return, their fancies were dashed, leaving them only a residue of guilt they hoped he would never discover.

In his own way, Caine felt a similar oppression, although he would never call it that. He would call it duty, or the impress of responsibility, or perhaps even the weight of hope that someday, somehow, the Motherlode would be discovered and all things would be well. Despite being exhausted, starving and dirty, he felt his first duty was to report his mission accomplished to the office of the Chief. Only then would he release himself for a meal and a bath while waiting for a summons to the Chief's office to report in full on his journey. Feeling no such onus upon themselves, Mason and Ferguson returned to their own families in the HQ building, without delay.

No summons came from the Chief or any member of the Commission for two days after their return, during which Caine did little more than sleep and eat. He lived alone in Spartan quarters on the fifth floor of the HQ, his self-assumed charms as an eligible bachelor apparently never having been fully appreciated by others. Eventually, however, the summons did arrive and Caine boarded an elevator—the only one still operating in Mainbranch and utterly unknown to the skrala. It laboured upward with many dry squeaks and more than one doubtful shudder. Having attained the top floor, Caine stepped out to face a door with ancient lettering which read "Chief." "…of Police" was scratched out, but which nevertheless left a shadow like an old scar.

The Chief too had a name: Niles Edwards. But virtually no one used his personal name apart from his family and his closest associates, and always in private. He was 'the Chief' and felt obliged to reinforce his authority among the Brotherhood, and especially the skrala, at every opportunity—a role that amounted to autocracy accountable only to the Commission—the coterie of kleptocrats and oligarchs who were the top of the food chain in Mainbranch.

Caine hesitated outside the door, but not for long. It wouldn't do to keep the Chief waiting. He let himself into an anteroom office where he was met by the Clerk of the Commission, and conducted down a hallway to a large room with a massive table in the middle and twenty-odd figures sitting around it, all men. At their head sat the Chief. All were chuckling at some joke they must have shared before Caine entered, but when the clerk conducted him to a seat opposite the Chief, the room fell silent and all eyes were fixed on Caine. Their expressions ranged from boredom to mild interest to impatience that the proceedings get over so they could be somewhere else. Caine stood behind the seat he was shown, knowing that proper protocol in these situations was to wait until he was given leave to sit.

"Axel!" the Chief welcomed genially. With a sweep of his hand he indicated that Caine was to sit. "Welcome back," he said. "You look like shit." A ripple of laughter went around the circle.

Caine nodded with a tentative smile. "I've been missing meals," he replied.

The Chief made eye contact, still smiling, but with something hard in his gaze. "I bet you have," he allowed. "And what of your skrala there…what was his name?"

"Jaeger," Caine put in.

"Yes, Jaeger. So what of him?"

"As per your order, sir, we took Jaeger westward two weeks' march with a Retirement Party led by me and including Dax Mason and Massey Ferguson. We kept him on minimum rations the whole way and then left him in the bush. I would be surprised to hear that he had survived the day. But we didn't do any more than take him to new opportunities, sir—as per your order."

"Yes, yes, of course," the Chief said. "So you're saying we probably won't be seeing any more of Jaeger."

Caine nodded. "I'd be certain of that, sir."

"And what else of your vacation?" the Chief asked sardonically. "Any recycling prospects?"

Caine shrugged resignedly. It would have been well for him if he could have returned with news of recycling opportunities. As it was, "Nothing, sir.

We went farther west than any prospecting team in Mainbranch history, but there's nothing there that we haven't already found. The bush goes on and on. It seemed to me that we took him far enough."

"And you're quite sure this skrala, Jaeger, will not come back?" asked another of the Commissioners.

Caine glanced at him briefly, trying to parse if there was some other reason for repeating this question, but he couldn't detect any. "No sir," he repeated. "I can't imagine how he could survive with no food, no shelter, no gear, and no idea where he was. Not even I know exactly where we were. We just marched west. A long way west. Left him there, and then marched east again until we ran into something familiar and made our way back here. The skrala is snake bait by now."

His questioner raised an eyebrow. "Graphic," he said, half to himself.

"This Jaeger was gathering a following of a sort when he was here in Mainbranch," said another of the Commissioners. "What of that?"

Caine glanced around the table uneasily. This was a question he couldn't answer with as much confidence. The Chief eyed him closely from the far end of the table. "I would say, sir, that his following, if he had one, has probably already died down with his disappearance. We're keeping an eye on it."

"I expect you to do so," the Chief said, his tone dry and slightly threatening. "There are rumours that his disappearance has actually increased his following. Do you know anything about that?"

Perspiration appeared on Caine's forehead. "I've only been back for two days, sir," he said tightly. "But I'll check with my people and send you a full report."

"Report to me only if there's something to report," the Chief said, sounding weary. "But do mind the store, Caine. This Jaeger and his so-called dream could be a problem for us, you know. We have to keep it together until we find the Motherlode."

"I know, sir," Caine nodded.

The Chief sighed. "Well, maybe we can consider this Jaeger matter closed."

"I'll let you know if there is anything unusual."

The Chief glanced around the table one more time. "Anything else, brothers?" Most heads around the table turned from side to side, except for a few whose gazes were still fixed on the Expediter, but their silence resigned them to agreement with the others. The Chief nodded in Caine's direction. "Dismissed," he said.

CHAPTER 12

SPRING, 2027 C.E.

The seed of a thing may at first appear unpromising. But night and day, in the darkness of the Earth, it grows by itself; hidden but awake; serenely emerging to become what it may. Our life in this world is not different from this.

— THE BOOK OF MEMORY

SOME HUNDRED ADULTS and forty or so children had clambered up the sides of the Starsis Massif and pitched their tents among the spruce and aspens that adorned its top. Here and there thin wisps of smoke threaded up from tiny cooking fires as they finished their morning meals. While making his first ascent, Beamer had noticed a somewhat easier way to climb the rock, but it was still physically demanding. The sheer task of getting up that stony face ensured that everyone brought only the essentials and nothing more. But of course there was a diversity of understandings of what was essential. Beamer had brought along a wind chime salvaged from a garage sale. It rang with a wonderful mellow note that he struck now as a summons.

There had been no agreement among the group to respond to the chime, but everyone assembled nonetheless. Beamer sat at the entrance to his little grotto as people arrived, at first in ones and twos, then in small groups, until everyone was assembled. All sat down on the mossy expanses and outcrops that spread away from the grotto and a silence came over the group. As the minutes passed, the silence deepened, which everyone could feel drawing them together in some mysterious way—a delicious silence that was the warp holding a weft of chickadee calls, the sighing of spruce bows, the creaking of a snag deeper in the forest.

Presently, Beamer spoke. "Good morning friends," he called out. "Wake up!" Some responded with their own greetings while others kept still.

"This is where we start living differently. In this rock." Some of his listeners looked up with a start.

"You mean *on* this rock," said a bearded man in jeans and plaid shirt.

"No," said Beamer, "I mean *in* this rock." More faces looked up at him, incredulous. "Think about it," he continued. "For thousands of years we've always built our cities exactly on the land we should have left alone. We should have saved it for growing food, or as habitat for other beings. We especially liked building cities in flood plains with rivers in them. We had to bring materials from far away, so rivers were useful, but they could also flood. We built with stuff that burned, blew away, or melted in water. And when that happened, we'd rebuild them over and over again. We destroyed the richest places on Earth by pouring concrete on them, poisoning them with chemicals, or paving them over. What we've done in the past was a disaster for us and for other beings as well."

"But," he continued, "consider the ant. She builds by subtraction—by removing material or rearranging what's already at hand—not by dragging stuff from other neighbourhoods and piling it up where it doesn't belong at great cost in toil and energy. What we have in this mountain is a ready-made pile of material, already lifted and placed for us. All we need to do is remove bits here and there to suit ourselves. Nothing else grows inside this rock, so if we move inside it, we bring no death to other beings, no suffering. This rock won't flood. It won't burn. It won't blow away. It won't wear out. It heats and cools itself. It's been here for two billion years, so it should suffice for us."

"You mean you think we should mine our way into this stuff and live here?" someone called from the group.

"Pretty much," said Beamer.

"But I don't want to live in a cave!" an artist moaned.

"Then we'll cut lots of windows," Beamer grinned, "and make it not look like a cave. It needs to be an artwork. That's what you said the other night. Friends, look at the alternatives. When we can no longer use fossil fuels, and that day will soon be here, the drywall and strand board suburbs will fall apart in a decade. We won't be able to rebuild from the floods and storms that are already happening every year. In less than a generation, we'll be homeless. Think of the ancient city of Petra in Jordan. The whole thing was carved into a sandstone mountain twenty-four hundred years ago and people still live there, thank you very much. The Nabateans built Petra with hand tools."

"Yes!" Ai Changming jumped up suddenly, sweeping his gaze over the assembly, his eyes blazing. He was an architect who had joined Badger Coulee from its first days. "This will not be a cave!" he exclaimed. "I will build a palace here. All this place will be a palace. We can stay here ten thousand years. Longer than the emperors, longer than the trees. I can make a palace here for everyone." He bounced with enthusiasm like a kid on his way to recess.

"And who are you?" demanded the man in the plaid shirt.

"I am Ai Changming," he said, smiling brightly. "I'm an architect! I make buildings."

The man in plaid rolled his eyes. "I know what architects do," he said.

"Ah!" Ai Changming retorted, "You don't know what *I* do. But you'll see."

"Building in this will be a real chore," chimed in a muscular man from the middle of the group. "I've got a degree in geology. This stuff is granite, man. It would be glacial going, especially with hand tools."

"Well," Beamer chuckled, "In that case, it's lucky we have you. You can tell us how we should do it. We do have you, right?"

The geologist held Beamer's eyes for a moment and in that moment, seemed to grow slightly larger than he already was. He glanced briefly at the architect. "Yeah," he rumbled. "You've got me."

"And me too," declared Ai Changming.

"Outstanding," Beamer smiled. "Then let's build a new world beginning here, even as the old one is passing away. Let's build nothing here that's temporary. Let's think of everything here through our vision of the deep future—everything solar powered—everything built to last. We need to fit our lives to what the Earth and the sun can provide—for everyone—forever. Let there be no classes or distinctions among us, no special titles—just one people, one species, seeking our place, our symbiosis with everything else that lives. Here we have to build everything on foundations of humility and simplicity, learning always from the lessons of our ancestors who built with hubris and excess. Let's be ever mindful not to consume the home that sustains us but always to work on behalf of life and more life."

A murmur spread through the group like a ripple in a lake, like the voiceless call that turns a scoop of pelicans.

Suddenly, the raven swooped down and hopped to a landing close to where Beamer was sitting. "Ache-uck!" it creaked. "Ache-uck."

Beamer smiled. "Yeah," he said. "We're waking up."

The geologist leaned toward a woman standing beside him and whispered: "Well, fuck me! I finally got something to do with my geology degree besides mining tar sand."

CHAPTER 13

SPRING, 276TH YEAR OF THE EUTERRAN AGE (E.A.)

Opening sometimes appears in dreams. Dreams are truthful manifestations. It is right Practice to befriend your dreams. But not all dreams are helpful. Discernment is required.

— THE BOOK OF PRACTICE

ZEPHYR FEY APPROACHED Jaeger's door and tapped lightly. There was no response from inside. She tapped a bit more forcefully, but still no reply. She pushed the door part way open. "Jaeger?" she asked. Jaeger's bed was un-occupied and a quick glance around the room revealed no one. But Zephyr could hear snuffling sounds coming from behind the bed, near the window wall across the room. She pushed the door inward and discovered Jaeger sitting on the floor, his back against the wall, knees drawn up to his chin, arms encircling his legs and his forehead pressed against his knees. He rocked slightly from side to side, his whole body wound tightly into a coil of self-protection. His breathing was rapid and through clenched teeth, not exactly sobbing, Zephyr thought, but gasping nonetheless, holding himself in, holding himself together.

Zephyr approached him slowly and sat down on the floor facing Jaeger, her back against the bed frame. She slowly pulled her knees up and wrapped her arms around them, bowing her head slightly toward her knees, though not so far as to obscure the sight of him. She said nothing. Instead, she followed Jaeger's rocking movements although without noticeable imitation of him. She allowed her breaths to become shorter and more gasping, though only very subtly so. They remained thus, facing each other, rocking and breathing and clinging, for several minutes. Then Zephyr began to even out her breath-ing and slow down the rocking of her body. This change was so subtle that it would have been undetectable except over many minutes. Little by little, Jaeger's breathing also slowed as did the rocking motion of his body. And by degrees, he started to uncurl. In a few more minutes Jaeger sat up still with his back against the window wall, but now cross-legged, his hands in his lap and his head leaning back against the wall. Zephyr Fey sat in the same position, her rocking stilled, her head against the side of the bed. She let her eyes drift closed and let out a deep sigh. And there came from Jaeger a deep sigh of his own, like a worker at the end of his day.

"Ah," whispered Zephyr, "that's better." She opened her eyes a crack to see Jaeger still leaning against the wall, his own eyes closed. "Yes," he sighed. "Better."

They sat this way for several more minutes, breathing and waiting. Zephyr was the first to speak: "So," she said, her voice gentle, "what happened there?"

Jaeger kept his eyes squeezed shut and tears leaked down his cheeks. His breathing started to choke up again, but with less audible strain than before. "Don't know," he cried, gagging.

Zephyr sighed again. "No hurry," she soothed. Jaeger sat for another space, struggling to hold back his sobs. When he prevailed, he let out another sigh. "Better," he repeated.

"Better," she echoed, and continued waiting.

Presently, he spoke again. "I was back in the bush. I mean I *felt* like I was back in the bush…The day they beat me up the last time and left me there."

"And the memory of that came back to you?"

Jaeger opened his eyes, blinking in bewilderment. "Yes," he confirmed. "It was just like I was there again. Alone again. Dying…"

Zephyr sighed, deliberately this time. "But you didn't die, Jaeger. Otis found you and now you're here. And you're not going to die."

Jaeger nodded slowly, taking this in. "No," he said. "Not dying…today."

"Not today," Zephyr confirmed. "Not on my watch," she smiled.

Jaeger nodded again, sighed again, and looked directly at her. "Not on your watch," he repeated.

"So, are you feeling like some lunch?" she asked.

"I must wash my face," he replied gravely.

"Indeed you must." Zephyr looked amused.

Jaeger stood unsteadily and walked to the washroom attached to his room. Zephyr heard water running briefly, and Jaeger emerged again looking somewhat refreshed, but still red-eyed. She rose from the floor. "Ready to face the world?" she asked.

Jaeger nodded again. "Yes," he said. "Lunch, at least."

"Then please follow," Zephyr invited, walking toward the wooden door, stepping through the threshold of his room.

After three days of recovery, Jaeger was feeling more restless and curious about his surroundings. He followed Zephyr into a passageway that went both left and right. Its ceiling was arched in gothic style and its walls featured columns fashioned to resemble the trunks of trees with branches that arched over the passageway between them in a tracery of limbs. Care had even been taken to sculpt individual leaves among the branches and in the interstices between the leaves, amber stained glass had been inlaid and was somehow lit from behind to suffuse the entire hallway with a soft yellow light.

Zephyr turned right and started slowly down the drift as Jaeger took in these new sights. A number of doors opened into the drift behind them and a few more ahead, but there were few people to be seen. They walked down the passage until it became a much larger and higher gallery where scores of people were mingling, racking up spinners and parking wains as they headed off through another half dozen passageways. To their right, another much larger doorway opened onto a paved plaza awash in the light of late morning. The plaza, only about thirty metres wide, was bordered on the far side by a skillfully carved balustrade and curved off out of sight to the west. At one point a gap in the stone course marked the near end of a bridge that arched toward the wall of forest beyond. Below could be heard the roaring sound of rapids, which was sending up sprays of mist.

"This is Dawngate," Zephyr said. "If you come this way, we can enjoy the sun on Loch Speare with our lunch." She conducted him to the side, out of the flow of human and vehicle traffic moving into the gate. The plaza wrapped around the eastern edge of the Massif which reared upward in a wall of granite. The rock face appeared featureless, curving away toward the west while skillfully concealing any view of what lay beyond. Apart from the entry to the Massif offered by Dawngate Bridge, the plaza was furnished with tables, chairs, colourful shading umbrellas and planters with flowers making it all resemble the sort of street cafes common in pre-Ruination times. A few people who noticed Jaeger and Zephyr making their way to a table clasped their hands and bowed in greeting, smiling broadly.

Jaeger glanced around self-consciously, taking in the scene. "Why are people doing that?" he whispered.

"It's one of our customs," Zephyr replied. "We're all enspirited beings. Bowing reminds us of that. It reminds us of who we are. Did you do nothing similar in Mainbranch?"

"Nothing," he said. As Jaeger looked around, he could see that the terrace was a flat expanse of close laid flagstones that gave a view of Loch Speare to the east and a bit south. There were more islands far distant to the east, but only barely visible through the haze over the water.

"We're on the Starsis Massif," said Zephyr, guessing his question. "It looks like a mountain, but it's really a mesa—has a flat top. Beamer Farris had a good eye for real estate."

"Real estate?"

"An old expression," she shrugged. "'Real estate' used to mean any land or building, back when people still owned land and buildings—or owned anything for that matter."

"Who is Beamer Farris?"

"You mean who *was* Beamer Farris. He was the First. The first to climb the Massif and the first to settle here along with his friends, almost three hundred years ago."

Jaeger followed along, still gawking at the rolling forest landscape and, to the south, the shining expanse of Loch Speare. He was listening to what Zephyr was saying, but also distracted by what he was seeing. Sometimes he felt anxious as he struggled to take it all in. Mainbranch being totally landlocked, he had never seen a body of water so large. "How big is it?"

"Very big," she said. "Have a seat." She gestured to a table and the two of them sat down. A number of other people were being served food and drink. Still others, already seated, took note of their arrival, looked Jaeger over, but soon returned to their own conversations.

"Do you like fish?" Zephyr asked.

Jaeger nodded.

She turned to a server and asked for some pickerel, fried vegetables, wild rice and white wine. She handed the server a small metallic pendant from which he recorded a number, and handed it back to her. She turned back to Jaeger.

"It's good to see that you're feeling better," she smiled. "I'm still interested though about your family, where you grew up?"

Jaeger looked around, visibly uneasy. "I told you," he said, "I don't know."

"But surely you have a mother and father."

Jaeger's expression grew distant. "Of course. But I don't remember who they are or where I'm from." He shuddered. "I was very young. I still remember though. They came at night. They killed people—my family I think. Maybe they killed everyone. But they took me. They took others too. But no brothers or sisters. They didn't want us to have any people from before or even to talk about them. I was four—maybe five. They made us work. They taught us only things we needed for our jobs. I learned to read and write. I was called a 'scribbler.' Admin. Others of us just worked—until we died. Those who didn't die, but got old, went on to new opportunities."

Many expressions Jaeger used sounded strange or incomprehensible to her. She was particularly struck by the word "work" which was an ancient expression with exceedingly unpleasant overtones, as she recalled. She resolved to visit the Hall of Memory and look up as many expressions as she could remember from their conversations. Their food arrived, giving Jaeger time to compose himself again. They ate in silence, Jaeger gobbling ravenously.

"More?" Zephyr asked. She noticed that Jaeger's consumption of food was marked more by fear than pleasure, but she put part of this down to his recovery from near starvation.

He nodded tentatively as if unsure that such a request could be made. "This is so good!" he mumbled through his food. Zephyr asked the server for more food for Jaeger. She left him in silence for a few more minutes, then asked, "And is that what happened to you?"

"Yes," he said. "I was moved on to new opportunities."

"But what does that mean?"

"It's what happens to anyone who is old, or redundant, or when the Chief decides to restructure. I didn't really know what it meant until it happened to me."

"But you're not old," she interjected, "so were you redundant or were you restructured?"

"Neither," said Jaeger, staring out over the water. "I told the Citizens they could be free."

Zephyr couldn't conceal her puzzlement. "That they could be free?"

Jaeger nodded.

"Free of what?" she pressed.

Jaeger gulped, and leaned forward as if sharing a confidence. "The Brotherhood."

Zephyr looked puzzled again. "Are you the 'Brotherhood'?"

"No!" he said emphatically. "No. I'm a Citizen. Almost everyone at Mainbranch is like me—Citizens. Except for millions of the Brotherhood. We were all taken. We all work for the Brotherhood, but we're not the Brotherhood. Sometimes we have to fight for the Brotherhood." His tone was contemptuous.

Sensing his anxiety, Zephyr said firmly, "There is no Brotherhood here."

Jaeger looked at her, wanting to believe her, but he was still watchful. She nodded, affirming by gesture—*Believe me.*

He broke with her gaze and looked out over Loch Speare, sighing. Another silence extended between them, until Zephyr asked, "Did you tell the Brotherhood they were free and that's why they sent you away?"

"Ha!" Jaeger barked. "No. No. I told *Citizens* they could be free." He grinned. For the first time his voice was clear and definite. His eyes sparkled with real mirth.

"And how did you get that idea?"

"I dreamed it," he said.

CHAPTER 14

SPRING, 276TH YEAR OF THE EUTERRAN AGE (E.A.)

All are reminded that in matters of decision we do not seek
a dictate from a ruler, nor majority rule, nor consensus,
and least of all, agreement negotiated by compromise.
What we seek is unity and clarity in right Practice
and that which is opening. Patience is essential.

— THE BOOK OF MEMORY

"WE GATHER SEEKING UNITY in clearness in the matter of Jaeger, foundling, this twenty-fourth day of April, the two-hundred seventy-sixth year of the Euterran Age," Lars Beckett announced. He was sitting in a circle with Zephyr Fey, Flynn Menpaa of the East Watch, Otis Bede, Lydia Ross, a woman of Bede's Dan, and Ocean Claybourne. Both Claybourne and Ross were Lightminders. There followed a short silence, then Beckett called, "Otis Bede." All turned to Otis, except for Claybourne, whose expression was one of rapt inward attention.

"I came upon the foundling Jaeger during Tarshin about seventy kilometres east of the Massif. He appeared near death, dehydrated, starving, injured, unconscious. In memory of unity, I brought him back for care and recovery with the help of some from the East Watch." He nodded to Flynn who acknowledged his gesture. Otis continued. "On the second day after I found him, Jaeger told me his name, that he came from a place called Mainbranch, that he had been captive there for most of his life, and that he had been 'bounced,' which I gather means exiled. Because of his physical state, he spoke seldom and incoherently. But since recovering, these bits of his history have stayed consistent. The day after finding him, I started back for the Massif but he was unconscious for most of the journey into restoration territories and inside the Thornway. I saw him again two days ago and he seemed much improved, thanks to Zephyr Fey's efforts. I'm not sure what to make of him—whether he's a danger to us or not. We've all passed quarantine without incident, including him. Maybe he's teachable, but only in the first practices which can still be attained in later life. Maybe not at all."

"Could you tell where he might have come from, apart from what he said for himself?" asked Beckett.

"No," Otis replied. "We've surveyed east from here for several hundred kilometres and as you know, we've found many ruins but no surviving groups of people. Not being permacultured, that whole land is empty of anything but bush food and I doubt that Jaeger knew much about how to find or prepare it. All the pre-Ruination highways are choked with kudzu, so he couldn't have come that way. There are lots of ruins, some dangerous, some not—but there has been no sign that way of any group of any size for at least fifty years, though we have, as you know, encountered foundlings from the south and west. So it's like he dropped from the sky, or didn't come from the east. Whatever else he is, he's not bush-smart and I think he speaks truly when he says he doesn't know where he came from or how he got to be where he was."

Beckett paused before he spoke. "Zephyr Fey?"

Zephyr sighed, pondering what to say. "He recovers, but he's been mistreated. He's probably delusional."

"Every foundling is delusional," Flynn said, interrupting their clearness practice. "Excuse me," he apologized. The group settled back into waiting.

"He recovers," Zephyr resumed, "but my heart's not clear in this matter even though I think he means us no harm. I hope he's teachable. I hope he had no other errand in coming here. And yet I find it hard to imagine that anyone would mistreat him so, simply to camouflage a spy. The people he calls the 'Brotherhood' sound deluded and dangerous. Otis found him near death. So maybe his story is as he tells it. But he speaks strangely sometimes. I'm open to waiting. If he keeps eating, he should also take up Active Practice; it's our custom and he's able. Maybe Lars or Lydia can take him for short errands. If he's teachable, we will teach him. If he wishes to stay with us, we'll accept him as we've all been accepted. If he wishes not, our only course is to take him back more or less where we found him. But there I think that he would surely die. For now he stays on Forest Drift."

All let Zephyr Fey's words sink down into their collective silence. After a time, she spoke again. "And one more thing. Jaeger told me there were one or two thousand people whom I take to be forced labourers. They call themselves 'Citizens' but their captors call them 'skrala'—an odd term. But Jaeger insists there are many millions of the Brotherhood. If that is true, we should be mindful of it."

"I find that unlikely," Otis interjected. "It would take a lot of land and energy to provide for so many. Not even Euterra could martial so many resources, not even if we mined every landfill we know of. I believe that the Brotherhood may have told the skrala that there were millions of them as a way of intimidating them. But since the Ruination we've found only remnant bands of people here and there, and none nearly as populous as Euterra. It's hard for me to imagine that there could be millions of the Brotherhood this close to the east of us and we wouldn't know about them. If they pose a threat to us, I don't think it will be because of their numbers."

"Perhaps not," Flynn interjected. "But then again, as our history teaches us with tears, it doesn't take many to cause regret. What do we really know about him? Zephyr Fey must know that two weeks isn't long to be in quarantine. Some plagues take longer to manifest. Remember that we lost a third of all Euterra in the plague of 17, and just because we wanted to show compassion to a foundling such as this. I think he's dangerous in proportion to what we don't know about him. The Brotherhood sound like parasites, or the descendants of parasites. Do we really want to welcome them here?"

"Jaeger says he isn't part of the Brotherhood, whatever they are," Zephyr said. "They sound like over-lords of some sort. When I asked him if he too was a member of the Brotherhood, he looked terrified by the idea."

Lydia Ross spoke up. "When you told me that name—Brotherhood," she said, nodding at Zephyr, "I spent some time in the Hall of Memory, trying to find some reference to it. It sounds like they might be a patriarchal throwback to pre-Ruination times. The term 'Brotherhood' was sometimes adopted by gangs or organized criminals. Or it may be that they are another foundling group merely trying to make their way—although that interpretation is hardly consistent with how the foundling was treated."

"I did some further research," Lydia continued, "about various 'brotherhoods' from that period, very few of whose stories were reassuring to me. Nearly all of them turned out to be violent, ideological, and, by our light, completely delusional. In those days there were groups similar to our Guild of Tears whose role was to protect the people in time of difficulty. But in at least one report, at the height of the Ruination, they turned against the people they were supposed to protect and decided instead to protect each other and their families. But there the historical trail goes cold and we're only left to imagine what might have happened to them."

"Do we really want to go out of our way to risk meeting such people, or giving them shelter here?" Flynn pressed.

Zephyr bristled. "But I said Jaeger *isn't* one of the Brotherhood. And even if he was, what are you saying we should do with him?"

Flynn shrugged. "Take him back where Otis found him. Give him a compass and a pack of food and let him go. We've done enough—fetched him back from death—now let him set his own course."

Presently Beckett said, "Zephyr Fey has spent the most time with the foundling and therefore I think this friend's words are weighty. But even though he may intend us no harm, he could still do us harm in ways we haven't foreseen. I agree that we can include him even as we keep watch and wait for clearness. Otis Bede and Lydia Ross have offered Mizar Dan. Their Dan has already sought clearness and reached unity in the matter. We could move him off Forest Drift after Sam Faron's wending."

Until that moment, Ocean Claybourne had sat motionless in the circle, her body alert with the discipline of attention, eyes closed, hands cupped in her lap. Now her eyes opened softly as she regarded each person in turn. The silence among them deepened. Claybourne said, "My sense is that we have no clearness in this matter, at least for the time being. Thank you to Otis Bede and Lydia Ross for taking the foundling into Mizar Dan. But I'll suggest that we send another survey into the area even as we take more time to know this foundling. We'll meet again for clearness in this place in seven days time. I'll bring your greetings to the Siderium."

There followed another space of silence, before Beckett said softly and with finality, "Friends rise."

As the group rose from their circle, Bede and Claybourne briefly caught each other's gaze. He was absorbing the meaning of what she'd said. Claybourne's ebony face showed both determination and a kind of soft sadness for she knew who would go on this errand and guessed the danger waiting there. There would be perils enough on the road itself, and where the road ended in trackless wilderness, which was changing by the year, shifting through protean moods that no one could know with confidence from one year to the next—to say nothing of what the Brotherhood itself might be. Otis was first to release her gaze, sensing that might also release her from concern. But it didn't. She was a Lightminder, after all.

CHAPTER 15

SPRING, 276TH YEAR OF THE EUTERRAN AGE (E.A.)

And this delusion is like a chain
One link enclosing the next—
First arising as the ancient energy of desire
Then desire seeks attachment to objects
And objects please the self and strengthen it
And self would possess them against all others
And find a life in them lest it perish.
And so arises property
Whose claims set all against all;
Then all manner of violence
Both within and without
And slavery, and oppression, and war.
That is why it is said:
Skillful Practice eschews cumber.

— THE BOOK OF PRACTICE

In what moment of delusion did humans get the
idea that it's possible to own anything?

— APHORISMS OF HYRAM BOWEN

BECKETT EXTENDED HIS HAND to Jaeger, smiling. "I'm Lars Beckett," he said. "We've met before, but you weren't awake for it." Lars, Lydia Ross, Otis and Jaeger were all sitting in Jaeger's room on Forest Drift. Jaeger tried a smile, nodding his acknowledgement.

"This is Otis Bede, who I'm sure you remember. And this is Lydia Ross, one of Otis's Dan," said Lars. Lydia was perhaps thirty-five, slender, with an elven lightness of bearing and a glance that was both soft and penetrating. She wore a seamless, hooded, logan green robe that fell from shoulder to foot with a braided cord girdle around her waist. "It's Mizar Dan that has offered to settle you in Euterra. Lydia and Otis will help you find your way around and explain how we live here."

Jaeger placed his palms together in the Euterran greeting he had seen when he was with Zephyr. The others acknowledged his attempt with polite nods, though it mildly annoyed them that he used a gesture the meaning of which he probably had no inkling.

Lars said, "I'll leave you in the care of these two good people for now." With that he stood up, turned and disappeared into the passageway, closing the door behind him.

Jaeger sighed uneasily, waiting for something to happen. He was too much of a novice in the Euterran way of life to notice that nearly every meeting of people in this place began with a short silence. They embraced the moment with full attention like birds settling down on a fragile clutch of eggs. But it made Jaeger feel vaguely uneasy and after only a minute or so, one of his knees twitched impatiently.

Lydia was first to part the silence. "Welcome here," she said, shifting her gaze more directly to him. Jaeger nodded. "We don't know much about how you lived in Mainbranch," she continued, "but in finding your place here with us, you need to belong to a Dan. Otis and I belong to Mizar Dan. Mizar Dan has agreed to embrace you if you want to join us."

Jaeger looked puzzled. "What's a Dan?"

"Dans are groups of people who live together and care for each other," Otis replied. "Dans include both people who are related and others who are not. The webbing among us is our friendship. That's the main thing. Anyone can leave a Dan at any time, but to join another Dan requires unity among that Dan's people to embrace the newcomer. Children born in a Dan are children *of* that Dan, not the children of their birth parents. All Dan members share the care and upbringing of all our children. Most of the time it's the birth parents who care for the children they birth, but this doesn't relieve the Dan of its role. Dans care for their children if their natural parents die, or if one of them decides to leave the Dan. Our Dans take care of us when we're sick, educate us, and look after us when we're elders or for some reason are unable to look after ourselves." There was a pause as Jaeger took in these strange ideas.

"Is anyone not in a Dan?" Jaeger asked.

"Never for very long," Lydia replied. "To be without a Dan is to be without a livelihood, without a home. We're not forcing you to join Mizar Dan, and sometime later you may decide to join another Dan that will have you. There are several thousand Dans in Euterra alone, to say nothing of the

Permie villages and Guilds. You should eventually find one to your liking. But for now, Mizar Dan has agreed to receive you. The only alternative is for us to return you to where we found you and from there let you go where you wish."

Jaeger shuddered, but said nothing.

"There are a few more things," said Otis. "Long ago, before the Ruination, people had what they called 'private property.' These were things, sometimes great quantities of things, that they kept for their own use to the exclusion of all others. The idea of private property seeped into almost every part of life and probably prepared the Ruination itself. Property even came to include land, other sentient beings, and things essential to the continuance of life like water, soil, and forests."

"As early Euterrans deepened our understanding of right Practice, the idea of property made less and less sense to us," Otis continued. "It seemed to us to be a very destructive delusion. We bring nothing into existence ourselves, so how could we ever imagine we *own* anything? Dans hold all material things in a commons of their members. The same custom extends to Euterra as a whole. If we want to use some tools or a workshop, we go to the Hall of Elements and find them there for everyone's use. If we want to use an art studio, we go to the Hall of Practice and use it there. And so on... When we belong to a Dan, all the goods of the Dan are ours, and also none of them are ours. We find it skillful not to use or keep anything to the exclusion of others, but others don't keep anything so as to exclude our use of them either. Of course, everyone has use of some personal items like clothing or sentimental mementos, but all other needs are provisioned by the Dan in common with others. If you need anything, just ask the Cellarer. In Mizar Dan, that would be Oma Jessie. Over the generations we've found this to be a skillful way of life. We decided to trade the delusion of private property for a life that is free now of most forms of violence and coercion. It was always violence of one sort or another that stood behind private property. Since none of us owns anything, we have fewer reasons to fight with each other."

"I think I understand this," Jaeger interjected. "I'm a Citizen. Citizens in Mainbranch have no property either."

Lydia glanced at Otis, and back to Jaeger. "That may be true," she said. "But in Euterra this is a free choice. In Mainbranch, it sounds like it isn't. We're telling you these things now because Mizar Dan is planning an Embracing for you. You'll be asked to agree to some things if you wish to embrace the Dan and allow the Dan to embrace you. We want you to understand what this is about before it happens."

"There's a bit more," Otis added. "In Euterra, Practice is very important to how we live. We think of Practice as having two parts. They are Active Practice, and Stillness Practice. Belonging to a Dan involves both kinds of Practice.

The Active Practice we do for about twenty hours a week, more or less. It's through Active Practice that we deepen in various ways, and also how we get our living. Dans can provide for their people only if the people take up Active Practice. Exactly how we do this is something you'll learn as you live with us. At the beginning and end of every day we also engage in Stillness Practice. Of course, we'll help you learn that as well. Are these things acceptable to you?"

Jaeger teetered between confusion and desperation. "I don't know what to say," he said. "This is still a strange place to me. Euterran ways are hard to understand. But I don't want to go back to the forest."

Lydia found Jaeger's eyes searching hers, almost pleading. "Jaeger, no one will take you back to the forest unless you want to go. But living in Euterra means belonging to a Dan. That's how we all live here. And whenever someone joins a Dan, it's at first a time of mutual discernment. Later on the Dan will meet again to test its unity about you living with us, and you will also be asked to decide for yourself if you want to continue with us. But that may be a year or more from now. There's no hurry with any of this."

Jaeger nodded, still tentative, but looking more reassured than before.

"There's one more thing," Lydia continued. "We'll take you now for the Embracing, but your room in the Dan may not be ready for a few days. The one there at this time is Wending—approaching the end of his incarnation. So you'll be staying here on Forest Drift until then. You can start Practice right away, of course, and you can join us for feasts and for the Wending if you like." Lydia smiled. Jaeger looked back at her, still perplexed, but nodded his agreement.

"Very well then," said Otis. "Shall we go?"

CHAPTER 16

SPRING, 276TH YEAR OF THE EUTERRAN AGE (E.A.)

Of those who come in peace, there are no strangers or
guests among us. All are included as one family, one
Dan, without distinction, special privilege, or title,
according to the uniqueness of each person, but ever
mindful that we are all children of the same world.

— THE BOOK OF MEMORY

"THIS WAY," said Otis Bede. The trio left Jaeger's room on Forest Drift and made their way to the lift which they boarded without delay. Jaeger looked around somewhat nervously.

"What is this?" he asked.

"This is Dawngate Lift," said Lydia. "It's a kind of elevator. This part of it carries people. Another part carries freight. It takes us from one drift to another. Do you have lifts in Mainbranch?" Jaeger looked surprised. Reading his concern, Lydia said, "Zephyr Fey told me about your city—Mainbranch."

Jaeger nodded tentatively. "City?"

"Ah!" said Lydia. "There I go, making an assumption. It's a city, no?"

Memories rushed into Jaeger's mind: the hulking cube of the HQ, the principal building in Mainbranch, but only for the Brotherhood. Only for the Brotherhood. And spreading around it, the Developments—the Shacks and Dives of the skrala. Beyond that, rubble and metal and glass—and plastic everywhere, when it wasn't burning. No-go zones. Bucket shops sometimes. A perpetual choking haze. "What's a city?" Jaeger asked.

Lydia glanced tentatively at Otis. "It's a place where many people live together to make a community. Many people. Many Dans together. Like Euterra."

What's a community? Jaeger wondered. "Mainbranch has the HQ," he said, "and the Developments. Many people live there. Everyone has equal opportunity to achieve their full potential, they tell us, but I'm not sure it's a community."

The trio fell silent as Lydia pressed the controls and the lift slid upwards through a featureless shaft with rock walls. A rosy light surrounded them as it filtered along the pink granite higher up. Suddenly they emerged into bright light as their lift ascended through another drift on its passage upward. Jaeger gasped as he got his first glimpse of a lengthy passage running far out of sight to his left, many times longer than Forest Drift, and a double colonnade of gothic arches carved into the glowing stone, crossed by rays of brilliant sunshine. Crowds of brightly garbed people bustled in the passageway and a plaza hollowed from the rock to his right. A fiddler busked near the lift entrance, accompanied by someone beating a bodhran drum. No sooner had Jaeger taken in this sight than their lift continued its vertical climb through the sheer rock.

Jaeger leaned back against the wall of the lift cage as if pushed by an unseen hand. Lydia touched his arm to steady him. "Are you alright?" He gazed back, nodding but speechless.

The lift emerged through the floor of another drift, which appeared equally as long and populous as the previous one, but with light streaming in from side passages and from overhead lighting. No sooner had this passage registered in Jaeger's awareness than they were pushed farther up into the twilight of the lift shaft. They passed two more levels before surfacing on yet another drift, which was the lowest level of a multi-levelled interior space that Jaeger could see soaring five stories overhead. Walkways ringed its entire perimeter bordered with balustrades and its columns reached upward in delicately carved arches reminiscent of gothic cathedrals but deftly shaped to resemble tree limbs. Tier after tier of drifts were visible around its perimeter and the plaza at its centre was as crowded as all the other passageways. The lift carried them past one drift after another until at last it went gliding up its transit shaft again.

By this time Jaeger was gripping the webbing of the lift frame. He looked pale.

"A little nervous with heights?" Lydia asked.

Jaeger looked back at her, agape: "So many people! So..."

The lift passed through another dozen drifts before it emerged again into another vast gallery, also lined with colonnaded walkways. But this gallery opened to the sky above, light drenching its interior revealing level after level of terraced gardens. And in the far wall of the gallery, perhaps half a kilometre away, Jaeger could see the multi-storey facade of a sizeable complex of buildings.

"The Siderium," said Lydia, sensing his question.

"I've heard this name before," Jaeger said. "What is Siderium?"

"It's the heart of Euterra," Lydia said, "and its brain as well. I'll take you there. Soon."

The Dawngate Lift stopped on Ariel Drift. All stepped off the lift, which immediately continued its upward movement.

"This," said Otis as he removed a wheeled device from a storage rack, "is a spinner. Ever ridden one?"

Jaeger looked at the device with interest and apprehension. "A bicycle?"

Otis nodded. "Yes, that's one old name."

"I've read about them," Jaeger said. "But bicycles were deep-sixed by the Brotherhood. No bicycles in Mainbranch."

"Too bad," said Otis. "They're fun. Want to try?" He pulled down another spinner from the rack.

"Is it alright to use it?"

"Of course. Why wouldn't it be?"

"What if the owner wants it and it's gone?"

"All the spinners here are used by everyone on the drift," said Otis. "You simply take one down, go where you like, rack it up again, until someone else who needs it takes it wherever they want to go. But all these spinners stay on this drift."

Jaeger accepted this explanation without further comment and tried to straddle the device. He pushed off and wobbled comically for some time, making tight circles near the lift station, but before long was peddling in a straight line.

"Well done!" said Otis. "It's quite a walk to our Dan if we don't use these. So I'm glad you're a quick learner." Jaeger nodded again, almost smiling. Presently, the trio set off cycling down the passageway.

After for some minutes, they approached the southwest end of the Massif where the morning light was softened as it shown through the colonnade arches into the drift. "Here we are," Otis announced as he dismounted from the spinner and left it leaning against the drift wall. Jaeger and Lydia followed suit.

They passed through an arch that led into a short side-drift ending with a large glass window to the southwest. Two wide doors made of sturdy and beautifully oiled white pine stood in each of the side walls of the passageway. Otis pushed open the one on the right. "This is Mizar Dan," he said, and stood aside for Lydia and Jaeger.

They came into a spacious room hollowed from the pink granite with beautifully finished walls. The farthest wall was made of sliding glass panels identical to the ones that lined Jaeger's room on Forest Drift. As in his other quarters, these windows separated the interior of the room from a sunspace which was fronted by another wall of glass. Beyond this was a narrow balcony crowded with potted herbs and flowers with a view of Loch Speare and the blue dome of sky above it. Remembering the many drifts they had passed on their ascent, Jaeger pictured the Massif as being honey-combed with such dwellings.

But the balconies had been fashioned at such an angle that they would barely be visible from the ground looking up. From a distance, he imagined that one might see them, but it would be difficult to distinguish them from the normal striations in the rocky face of the Massif.

Sitting in the sun-drenched space were perhaps thirty-five people on cushions spread in concentric arcs around the floor and in niches that were hollowed out of the walls. The central figure in the room was that of an aged woman who alone sat in a chair. Many in the room smiled at Jaeger, Lydia and Otis as the three of them entered. A dozen of them were children. It appeared that they had all been waiting for this moment. A girl, about ten, broke formation and came racing across the room, leaping into Otis's arms and clamping him around the neck. "Spark monkey!" he laughed, hugging her, then wrestling her playfully to prise her loose and set her back on her feet. Still clinging with one arm around his waist, she inspected the new arrival with unabashed curiosity.

"Everyone," Lydia announced, "this is Jaeger." All present clasped their palms together and bowed their heads slightly in greeting, with two of the children giggling excitedly. Otis motioned for Spark to return to her cushion, but she pulled him along by the hand to sit next to her.

Jaeger's attention was drawn to the old woman, a tiny figure by any measure, her face deeply wrinkled, but her posture erect and supple looking for her age. She wore a plain, cream-coloured robe with a cowl lined with scarlet material, but no other ornament. Her hair was entirely white, cut very close to her head giving her an androgynous appearance. Her pale blue eyes looked unflinchingly into Jaeger's. Before her gaze, he felt stirred, transfixed, exposed as if stripped naked, but still regarded with palpable affection and respect.

Beside her was a brass bowl polished within to a lustrous shine, partly filled with water, and covered outside with embossed figures and symbols Jaeger couldn't identify. Beside the bowl lay a small, leather-sheathed mallet. Across her lap lay a broad band of some woven textile that had hanging from it many as yet unworked threads wound on bobbins that had the appearance of oversized beads. Morning light was waxing into the commons room flushing warmth over the pink granite walls. Lydia inclined her head for Jaeger to follow, and they walked together toward the elder. Lydia motioned for Jaeger to sit on the cushion at the end of the central aisle.

"This is Oma Jessie," Lydia said. "She is Elder in Mizar Dan. Oma, this is Jaeger." With that, she stepped back, and settled herself on another of the floor cushions.

Oma Jessie gazed silently at Jaeger for what seemed a very long time, her body utterly motionless. She began to smile, her eyes crinkling mischievously, her expression seeming both to invite him into some private jest, while also searching him with the most inscrutable intensity. The entire room and all gathered there, including the children, were caught in the same amber moment—waiting to breathe again.

Suddenly a tiny giggle escaped her which went trickling into the room. The suspension so palpable before, suddenly eased, and though no one else laughed, all breathed more freely.

Continuing to regard Jaeger closely, Oma Jessie cocked her head slightly to one side and asked, "Do you know what the Embracing is?"

Despite his previous conversation with Lydia and Otis, Jaeger felt at a loss in the moment. "Yes," he stammered. "I mean no… I mean, I don't know."

Oma Jessie's smile broadened slightly. "That's a good answer," she said. "No one *really* knows what the Embracing is."

For the first time since he sat down, Oma Jessie released her gaze on Jaeger, her eyes dropping to the woven band she held in her lap. "Do you know what this is?" she asked.

Jaeger shook his head.

"This sash," Oma Jessie said, "is the history of Mizar Dan. It's woven up from the threads of all our lives. Some Dan Sashes in Euterra are centuries old. Every thread is someone's story—someone's life. The sash is made of the threads of the people's lives who are with us now, or who have been with us in the past." She looked again intently at Jaeger. "Do you wish to have your life woven into this sash—to cast your lot with Mizar Dan?"

Even though Lydia and Otis told him that his stay in Mizar Dan might be temporary, Jaeger sensed a gravity in every word the elder spoke. She was kind, but what she said was to be taken seriously. Jaeger weighed her question for what seemed to him an appropriate length of time and said, "Yes."

Oma Jessie nodded. "Well and good," she said. She picked up the mallet that lay beside the brass bowl, and firmly struck its lip. The sudden sound opened out like a flower blooming from her hand, reverberating, spreading its one note bouquet farther and farther into some utterly mysterious inward distance. It was like the world could open into itself revealing hidden rooms and galleries.

Oma Jessie let the bowl sing until it faded to silence. Then she spoke:

"Mizar Dan, affirm this in unity—
That when Jaeger hungers, we will give him to eat;
That when Jaeger thirsts, we will give him to drink;
That when Jaeger is naked, we will clothe him;
That if Jaeger is sick, we will care for him;
That we will shelter him and keep him in our good counsel;
That we will share Practice with him and share our wisdom with him;

That should he suffer loneliness, we will befriend him;

That Jaeger's children shall be Mizar Dan's children to raise, guide and protect together with Jaeger;

That Mizar Dan will in all ways needful to it, encourage Jaeger in right Practice of attention, compassion, generosity and gratitude, and help him uproot whatever is unmindful, loveless, selfish or ungrateful in himself;

That Jaeger will be one of us until the Dan may ask him to depart, his free choice to leave our Dan, or his death.

Your word of unity?"

All present, with a single voice said, "We will strive so to do!" Jaeger felt a jolt as this affirmation split open the silence that came before. Oma Jessie turned her gaze back to Jaeger, her eyes twinkling. She struck the bowl once again, and again it reverberated until it finally came to silence. She continued:

"Will you, Jaeger, affirm this unity—

That when we hunger, you will give us to eat;

That when we thirst, you will give us to drink;

That when we are naked, you will clothe us;

That when we are sick, you will care for us;

That you will shelter us and keep us in your good counsel;

That you will share Practice with us, and share your wisdom with us;

That should any here suffer loneliness, you will befriend them;

That our children shall be your children to raise, guide, and protect together with us;

That you will, in all ways needful to Mizar Dan, encourage us in diligent right Practice of attention, compassion, generosity and gratitude, and help uproot from us whatever is unmindful, loveless, selfish or ungrateful;

That you will be loyal to this Dan until the Dan may ask you to depart, or of your own free choice you leave us, or unto death.

Your word of unity with us?"

Jaeger paused for only a moment. "I will," he said, "with all your help."

Oma Jessie nodded. "Then on behalf of Mizar Dan, I embrace you Jaeger. Please understand that what I've said is not an oath, not a creed, but a spirit we aspire to. We lay nothing on you as a burden but rather offer the hand of friendship in community." She revealed a skein of yarns from beneath the sash she was holding and held it up. "Would you like to pick the colour of your thread?" she asked.

Jaeger sensed that his choice of colour was important, weighty, the significance of which he would only grasp later. Weighty was a word much used here. Its true meaning, he sensed, would be another learning for later. After looking at the skein with some care, he pointed out a vibrant green thread. The elder nodded and smiled more broadly. "An excellent choice," she said. She pulled the end of the thread from the skein and began plaiting it into the sash, making the smallest beginning, then laying Jaeger's thread into the mass of others.

Having started the thread into the weaving Oma Jessie laid it aside, reached for the mallet and struck the bowl once again. When the ringing faded to silence, those gathered erupted in applause, jumped up from their cushions and surrounded Jaeger hugging him and slapping his back. At first it startled him, all the touching and attention. But after several moments of this he began to revel in the welcome.

Lydia started introductions. "This is Alex Bowen, Carrie Seth, Ty Lightfoot, Kat Argo," she said, reeling off name after name until Jaeger's head was spinning. She ended with the girl clinging to Otis. "And this is Spark Ross, my daughter with Otis."

In the jumble of new faces and names Jaeger was overwhelmed but tried not to show it. Since being taken into his quarantine on Forest Drift, he'd had no contact with other Euterrans besides Zephyr and Lars. But with Lydia's introductions over, most of the adults started to disperse to their various pursuits and things settled down a bit.

"This is Mizar, our commons room," Lydia said, indicating the room they were in. "This is where we take our meals and be Dan together. First sitting is at sunrise; first feasting about an hour later. The hours are struck on chimes from the Siderium, so you'll know when to rise." Jaeger began to register more features of the space now that it was emptier. Sitting niches had been hollowed from the walls in various places which were covered with cushions and folded blankets. The room itself was substantial—perhaps ten by twenty metres—one wall of which was a glassed-in sunspace with a view of Loch Speare in the distance. In another room that could be reached from the commons room was an extensive kitchen and an enormous pine table that took up that end of the room. There were also other tables and a few chairs about. Tapestries, textile artworks, paintings and sculptures adorned the walls or occupied small niches as in his room on Forest Drift.

"First sitting?" Jaeger asked.

Lydia smiled. "That is our first Stillness practice of the day. Almost all of us Practice. Spark will take you to the Siderium to start learning Stillness practice tomorrow. For now, let's get you settled." Lydia motioned Jaeger to follow her.

"If there is anything you need, ask Oma Jessie," Lydia said. "In addition to being Dan Elder, she's also our Cellarer. She has helpers, of course, but being a Cellarer means Oma Jessie procures and distributes whatever we need including our food and other personal provisions. I don't know how you lived in Mainbranch, but here in Euterra we practice a very simple life. Oma Jessie is here to distribute the things we really need, but not everything we might imagine wanting. As you probably already guessed, she can be—firm. Being both an Elder and a Cellarer, she constantly reminds us that sufficient of anything is always enough and that we can live in peace with each other and with the Earth only by living simply. So if you ask her for something, don't be surprised if she questions you about whether you *really* need what you're asking for." Lydia chuckled. "It can be gruelling! But at the end of it, we're usually more mindful than before of the difference between needs and passing cravings."

They left the commons room into a passageway that ran for some distance parallel to the balcony and sun space. There were a number of doors along one side, and above each door a glass transom allowed light to filter in from the rooms on the other side. Some were stained glass, giving the passageway a jewel-like quality. Jaeger couldn't take his eyes off the stained glass. It was something entirely new in his experience.

"This is so—beautiful," Jaeger sighed.

"It pleases me to hear that," replied Lydia. "Ariel Drift is one of the oldest in Euterra, so we've had time to beautify this space—and so far, without cumber. We think beauty is essential to tranquility, wouldn't you agree?"

Jaeger mused a moment. "I know that word—'tranquility.' But I don't know if I've ever had the feeling."

"We'll see," Lydia said. "You haven't started Practice yet. Maybe once you do, you'll find some tranquility there."

— • —

They made their way through the hallway, passing one door after another, until Lydia stopped at one of them. "This will be your room when Sam Faron makes his Wending," she said. "Right Practice in this moment will be to keep silence." With that, she pushed open the door only wide enough for the two of them to slip inside, then she pulled it closed behind her.

The room was spacious and warm, being of the same pink granite found nearly everywhere Jaeger had seen so far. Like the commons room, this room had a double glass wall for its western side creating a sunspace between the room and the balcony beyond. It sheltered fewer plants than were outside the commons room, but more of them were flowers and herbals. The walls were relatively unadorned but the floor was covered with mats of softly woven kudzu and hemp. A block of stone had been relieved from one wall leaving a broad shelf upon which was a sleeping pad. Under the bed some spaces had been hollowed out to accommodate wicker baskets that just fit the voids for storing clothing and other articles. There was a wardrobe standing against one wall and also a chair, a small, simply made table, and on the table, a few articles. A pair of spectacles. Several articles of clothing neatly folded and piled. An earthenware bowl, a cup.

On the sleeping bench lay a wizened man curled under a thick blanket of lamb's wool. One of his hands rested on his chest, and twined in his fingers was a string of worn, wooden beads. Jaeger had expected this man Faron to be alone in his room, but instead the floor was crowded with people. Most were children from the age of four or so to early adolescence. Some of them leaned together or held each other, or leaned against a wall. But they were all seated around Faron in concentric arcs with him at their focus. There was some rustle of movement as people shifted position or whispered quietly to each other, but this did nothing to disturb the silence that otherwise filled the room. On the sleeping bench above Faron's head a young woman sat cross-legged with a book open on her lap. Beside her were a water-filled brass bowl and a small mallet like the one that Oma Jessie used in the commons room. She wore a light blue robe and her posture was utterly attentive. She made no sound, no word as she simply regarded Faron and waited.

From Jaeger's experience, death was often painful, solitary and ugly. People in Mainbranch seemed to die of everything—disease, work mishaps (*lots* of work mishaps), and sometimes 'performance reviews.' Those who didn't die in these ways often just disappeared once they attained a certain age. They moved on to other opportunities. No one ever knew exactly of what these other opportunities consisted, or where they might be, and such an aura of menace surrounded them as to deter anyone from asking. Jaeger could not remember any instance of anyone simply dying from old age—or peacefully.

Lydia leaned closer to Jaeger. "Do you want to stay for a while?"

Jaeger glanced from the old man to Lydia. He felt anxious, but also reassured by her presence and so many others in the room. "Yes," he whispered. So they found a place on the floor, and, like the others, watched in silence.

Some time later, the door pushed open and Oma Jessie shuffled into the room. A leather satchel hung at her side. A rustling sound lifted from the group like a breeze on a warm afternoon, and settled again. She glanced around the room, as if getting her bearings, and then smiled. Her eyes fell on the sleeping platform and the motionless figure there. Perhaps she sighed, or perhaps it was simply an intake of breath that carried her over some invisible rise in the ether. She shuffled to the side of the bed and regarded Faron in silence. She reached for his hand, holding it like some creature new born.

"I've loved you long, Sam Faron," she whispered to him.

Though he had all along appeared to be asleep, he roused now, squeezing her hand. "And I you," he replied, barely audible.

"Nice blanket you have," Oma Jessie said. The corners of Faron's mouth moved toward a smile, but then he dropped into a deeper stillness. His breathing changed, sounding more effortful, as if he had at that moment taken up a task that required him to push forward against some invisible obstacle. Oma Jessie squeezed his hand again, and moved to the side to take a seat on a chair that had been there all along, waiting for her, though Jaeger hadn't noticed it when they arrived.

The old woman settled herself and let the satchel she carried settle beside her. She opened the satchel and withdrew the weaving Jaeger had seen at his Embracing into Mizar Dan. Her fingers, deft and graceful, searched through the skein of woven threads picking out one that was rusty red. She attended closely to the red thread, drawing it forward into the others.

Presently, Lydia leaned toward Jaeger. "That's Anais Reine," she whispered, nodding toward the woman sitting by Faron's head. "She's a Lightminder. When she senses Opening, she will chant *The Lai of Wending*. It is loveliness…"

In the next moment something changed; Jaeger couldn't have described exactly what. Somehow the form of the old man grew subtly translucent as if it was fading or being translated from its present form into something different. His body also seemed to shrink, folding back into itself, making him appear smaller. These changes were so subtle that Jaeger wavered between believing his senses and assigning the experience instead to some trick or distortion of his perception. But he was not alone.

Anais Reine leaned slightly forward, gazing at Faron intently, and then she picked up the mallet beside her and gently tapped the brass bowl with it. A ringing sound momentarily filled the room and faded. She cocked her head to one side, listening closely, and poured more water into the bowl, tapping it again. As she did so, Sam Faron's body seemed to relax and settle toward an even deeper stillness. Reine sounded the bowl again, this time striking it firmly. The tone resonated through the whole room. The sound seemed to be drawing the space in upon itself rather than expanding out from the bowl. Reine dropped her gaze to the book open in her lap and, taking the note she struck as her starting pitch, began chanting *The Lai of Wending*.

Reine's chant had a quality of movement in it—a tonal exit from the mood prior to its onset, which had been that of suspension and waiting and silence—and was now actively spinning itself forward toward some mysterious metamorphosis. Her voice was a clear, solid alto—a surprise wrapped in the hours of stillness that went before. The words she chanted were clear and firm and resonant without being loud. Jaeger sensed no tone of regret, nor of grief, nor even of solemnity, but rather a clarity and focus and hope that was palpable. Listening to her, Jaeger felt that something momentous was about to happen, a bird was about to fly, a blossom about to burst open and everyone would see it.

As the *Lai* was chanted, it began by addressing Sam Faron by name, recalling his dearness to all assembled, then it spiralled outward in a great saga of departure and return, of manifestation and disappearance, of arising and subsiding—all of it a capsule of Euterran metaphysical belief, but wrapped in the tenderness of a very personal love. The very quality of Reine's voice carried this overtone, the preciousness of each individual life and of Sam's life, but swept up and contained in a much greater, ever-evolving mystery that carried them all along toward its still hidden destination. As he listened, Jaeger recognized this as yet another example of the importance his hosts placed on memory, and on reminding themselves over and over again of the things they shouldn't forget, even as they lay dying.

Even though Sam Faron had ceased long ago to make any sort of movement, Anais Reine kept chanting. If anything, the intensity of what she sang grew stronger without becoming louder. She seemed somehow capable of *deepening* the penetration of her voice into everyone's heart without the performance in any way feeling invasive.

And then the chant was over. Everyone in the room was suspended in the final fading of that single voice toward silence. Unbidden, everyone waited. For what, Jaeger wondered?

A small sigh went up from Oma Jessie and then there was a tiny metallic 'snip.' She held a small pair of scissors in her right hand that had just parted Sam Faron's thread. She carefully tucked the end of it into the weaving making it invisible among all the other threads. "There," she said.

With that, people started to shift about in the room. The younger children were led out while others passed by Faron's body, touching his hand or his cheek as they passed. Reine remained in motionless concentration, eyes half open, while the others slowly cleared the room.

———•◆•———

Lydia and Jaeger found their way into the hallway with the others. They said nothing to each other for some moments until they returned to the common room. Jaeger wandered toward the sunspace wall, feeling attracted to its light, even as the sun outside was setting. Its rays came through the glass warming his face. He was full of emotions he couldn't name. Lydia came to stand next to him.

"Sam will be remembered," she said.

Jaeger looked at her, searching her eyes for a moment, and then back through the window. "Why?" he asked.

She sighed, waiting for words. "His life expressed a lot of things that are important to us—gentleness, friendliness, humility, great simplicity. Did you see those things on the table in the room back there? Those were *all* his personal possessions—not just at the end—but for most of his life. Even the best of us usually accumulate more cumber than that. But not Sam. Not Sam. He loved us, not things. He left no marks, no traces except our memories of him. His life was—*clear*. He always used to say that too much cumber would keep him from dancing!" Lydia smiled. "He was a good dancer," she said with finality.

"And Oma Jessie?" Jaeger pressed.

Lydia glanced at him, then back to the sunset. "You felt that, did you?"

Jaeger shrugged. "I felt...something. I don't know what."

"Poor Oma," Lydia said, her voice softening. "She has a duty as Dan Elder to cut the cord at every wending if possible. But this one must have been harder for her. She and Sam spent most of their lives together. Before the Ruination, people gave themselves in marriage. Marriage could be a very spiritual thing, but more often than not they were legal agreements to share property and live together. Mostly these arrangements didn't work out very well. When we founded Euterra, we decided that marriage was something we could do without. Too often it was a source of suffering for everyone, especially children. So our Dans provision us for life and provide a kind of extended family for all our children. Adults are never expected to make lifelong commitments to each other. The essence of life is change and we think our custom fits better with how changeable we can be."

"Nevertheless," Lydia continued, "many of us pair off with others for life, and we raise our children together, but always within the larger nest of the Dan. Sam Faron and Oma Jessie were one particularly charming example. We still prize a special faithfulness to one person. We still admire and honour love that lasts a lifetime. Now we recognize that kind of love as a serendipity. We no longer judge or marginalize people who for many different reasons may not have found such a gift manifesting in their own lives."

Jaeger was not sure what to make of Lydia's words. For the Citizens, among whom he had grown up and beside whom he had laboured, all of these were alien ideas, alien experiences. So much of their lives was controlled and managed by the Brotherhood that there was scarcely time or energy for anything but survival. All days were alike, all were filled with the pursuit of a bitter subsistence or the service demanded to maintain the Brotherhood in their relative affluence. While there were certainly people in Mainbranch that Jaeger cared about, and missed since his banishment, his *Retirement Party*, as had been the case for people of his ilk for millennia, love made them vulnerable to control, to manipulation, and to oppression in ways that few would risk.

Jaeger surfaced from his jumbled thoughts. "How did all of you come to this? I mean, how did this place come to be, and all of you?"

"Ah, well," Lydia said. "For that maybe you should consult one of our teaching elders—we call them *Telders*—like Hyram Bowen. He can often be found at Fogg's Inn on Procyon Drift. He also lectures at the Siderium, but he's far more entertaining after two or three meads. Full of tales, that one. But there will be time for that soon."

She turned away from the window, silently communicating to Jaeger that he should follow. She headed toward the door of the common room, speaking over her shoulder. "Perhaps that's enough for today," she said. "If you wish, I can take you to the lift station that will bring you down to Forest Drift at Dawngate. From there you can find your way to your room where feasting will be brought to you as usual. I'll come by early in the morning and bring you back here. First sitting is at dawn, first feasting about seven, there…" She pointed back at the window.

Jaeger noticed for the first time subtle arcing lines etched into the outer window wall. He looked at her, puzzled. "It's a timepiece," she said, "and also a calendar. When the sun is over here," she indicated the highest point on the arc, "it's Zenith—time for feasting. And when it's down here," she pointed to another part of the arc, "it's November; up here, June; down here, morning on the 6th of December." His expression of puzzlement turned to amazement. "Did you have no timepieces in Mainbranch?" Lydia asked.

"Only the horn."

"Ah—'the horn'?"

"And the siren," Jaeger added. "When it's time to fight."

Lydia glanced at him as she reached the door. His expression was deadpan. "Well," she said, "we have no horns of that sort. All our horns are musical ones. And no sirens either. I'll stop by when it's time for feasting. Explore, mingle, meet people. But for now, please stay on Forest Drift until we can prepare your room. Tomorrow Spark will take you to the Siderium so you can start learning Practice. After that, we'll get you an errand posting." She smiled, and added, "'No errands, no eats.'"

They left the commons room, secured a pair of spinners and set off back down the drift to the lift station. There they took their leave of each other, Jaeger descending again to the more familiar surroundings of Forest Drift and his quarantine.

CHAPTER 17

SPRING, 276TH YEAR OF THE EUTERRAN AGE (E.A.)

*Be vigilant for Opening. It can manifest in presence and
in absence; in vision and in blindness; in what is new and
in what is old. Especially it can manifest in dreams.*

— THE BOOK OF PRACTICE

CITIZEN FITZ STOOD five stories up atop Parking Block gazing over its balustrade at the green cloud of forest rising from the earth far to the west. Spring now well advanced, it looked like smudges of finger paint in the space between earth and sky. It was impossible to distinguish the forest from the trees.

Beside him stood Citizen Dexter, a weaselly sort of man with a week's growth of stubble on his face, unruly hair greying at the temples, and eyes that darted evasively even when he might be relaxing during a moment un-programmed by his Brotherhood overseers.

Parking Block was a building from Great Recession times that Citizens had converted to living quarters by walling in the voids between floors and subdividing the interior into family-sized accommodations. Windows were small both to limit access by potential attackers and for want of glass. Its name came from a time lost in confusion and forgetfulness and no one could now say who 'Parking' had been. There was consensus, however, that he must have been a powerful and wealthy man to have had so many buildings bearing his name. Parking signs had been found fairly often in Mainbranch and in many other towns the Brotherhood had recycled. So Parking must have owned many buildings indeed.

Fitz was a tall, rangy man with large hands, leathery skin, and the mannerisms of a person seasoned by hard physical work, work which had done nothing to dim his intense blue eyes. He gave the impression of an intelligence too narrowly confined by the vagaries of history and his local predicament. So perhaps it was some combination of his native intelligence and the broader hope that defied confinement that drew his eyes toward the west, and fixed them there.

"He's not coming back you know," Dexter pronounced fatalistically as he looked off in the same direction as Fitz.

"Who?" asked Fitz.

Dexter snorted. "You know who."

Fitz remained silent.

"No one comes back. Not after they 'move on to new opportunities.'"

Fitz shrugged.

Dexter persisted, an edge of anxiety in his voice. "What do you suppose that even means?" It wasn't clear that he really wanted an answer. What is death? What is madness? What are 'new opportunities'?

"I suppose," said Fitz, "that it's a good sounding name for a bad thing."

"A bad thing…" Dexter echoed. "Yeah. A bad thing probably happened to Jaeger."

"Probably," Fitz conceded.

Dexter became edgy again. "So why the hell are you standing up here, looking over there, like he's going to come walking back out of the woods or something?"

Fitz shrugged again. "Why can't you simply enjoy the nice day?" His voice was vacant, as distant as the tree line.

"He's not coming back," Dexter repeated. His tone was defiant, as if sheer force of conviction could assert the certainty of something about which he couldn't be certain.

"Maybe he doesn't have to," Fitz said enigmatically.

"What the hell?"

Fitz glanced at Dexter, registering his companion's discomfort with possibility, with potential, with anything abstract. Dexter was firmly grounded in life's substance, not its movement. Movement agitated him.

Returning his gaze to the line of forest, Fitz said, "I would like to see Jaeger again. But if I don't, he did leave us his dream."

Dexter looked incredulous. "His dream? His *dream*?"

"Yes. Thinking about his dream makes me feel good. I don't know why. I'm not even sure what the feeling is, exactly. But I like it. I don't want to stop dreaming it."

"Fucking dropping dollars!" Dexter spat. "You can look at the bush all you want on your own time, but we have no time here for dreams! We are *skrala*, my friend, and don't forget it. And the Brotherhood rules. So don't forget that either. We can all grumble and complain and nurse the memory of our grievances, but nobody is coming up with a better plan. Our only chance of anything better is to do what we're told, hope to hell we find the Motherlode, and other than that, take a chance if we see one."

"The Motherlode is pap!" Fitz dismissed.

Now Dexter was angry. "It's not!" he said. "It's not, I tell you. We'll find it someday—out there—" he swept his arm toward the bush, "—somewhere. We're right to be looking for it. The Brotherhood is right too. We'll find it. We have to. If not in this life, then the next. It's the only way out of this hole we're in."

"Maybe you're right," said Fitz in mock agreement. "The Motherlode would solve things for sure. But have you ever thought that maybe that's not our only choice. Maybe something else is possible?"

Dexter sighed. "Like what?"

Fitz still gazed westward. "I can't say." He continued to look at the forest and the trees.

CHAPTER 18

SUMMER, 2027 C.E.

*Right Practice in time of dire necessity is to avoid
cumber. Take only what is needed for a new life—
which is surprisingly little. Travel light. Go quickly.
One who waits for others never departs.*

— THE BOOK OF PRACTICE

BEAMER FARRIS, Laurel Fey and Jako Menpaa threaded their way slowly
through darkened streets littered with debris and derelict vehicles. They drove
without lights in a cube van they had painted black so as to draw as little
attention as possible to themselves as they maneuvered through the suburbs.
It had only been twenty-three days since the most recent and final collapse
of the electrical grid, but it seemed like years. A cascading series of outages
and overloads finally laid the entire system flat on its back, unable to recover.
Seeing this as a signal opportunity for their own designs, vandals commenced
destroying even more electrical equipment as they anticipated some final 'rev-
olution' that would set the world at rights. With the collapse of the grid went
cell networks, WiFi, satellite communication and a great many public services.
When the grid went dark, so did the Internet, the main backbone of which
was never designed to operate longer than a day or two on back-up power.
Yet even during those last desperate hours when emergency generators still
worked, there were cascading server failures all across the Internet as routine traffic jammed the servers that still operated. There was no human guile
involved—just one thing after another that few had anticipated and no one
could stop. Without the Internet, commerce was impossible. Without commerce, people soon became desperate for the necessities of life. Worst of all,
society as a whole lost its memory and with that, its mind. The Cloud, which
was so taken for granted, so routinely assumed to be available to answer any

question at any time, had simply evaporated like the virtual entity it was. To the billions who relied on it daily, its disappearance abandoned them to isolation, amnesia and confusion. It was a kind of mass social dementia. From this new position people then had to procure the necessities of life according to the harsher logic of a non-virtual world. This transition was eventful for everyone and lethal for most.

The fact that Beamer and company had an operating vehicle of any sort was itself enough to make them a target. Nearly all vehicles were at this point either out of fuel or vandalized beyond use. They paused at every reasonable opportunity to siphon gasoline from stranded vehicles and were successful often enough to keep going. But this tactic could not be sustained for long and of this they were acutely aware as they picked their way through the darkened streets. Any shard of glass or metal ripping through a tire wall might be enough to end their forward progress and any hope of escape from what had clearly become an impossible situation. Fortunately, they didn't have to transit the urban core itself, but could instead navigate its less travelled byways in search of their destination. Speed was impossible even where the streets were free of detritus. Decades of neglected street maintenance was the price of the hard budget decisions that came with climate change and economic contraction. Nowhere was their route a smooth one.

"You know what they say?" asked Jako, who was driving.

"What do they say?" Laurel took the bait.

"They say nothing focuses the mind as wonderfully as the prospect of being hanged in the morning."

"That's old," she said, but still laughed at how it fit their situation. "Samuel Johnson, isn't it?"

"I know it's old, but I couldn't resist," said Jako. "I suppose after this no one will remember stuff like that."

"That can't happen!" Laurel blurted. "We can't let that happen! We can't just forget everything."

"A great deal is being forgotten right now," Beamer said. The thought made him feel both despairing and liberated—despairing by the thought of losing so much that people had given their lives to discover and make, but liberated as if by the slate cleansing of a good house fire. Maybe the vandals weren't all nut cases merely acting out their rage. Maybe they were the unconscious instruments of the rubble-making phase of what would later become a renaissance. Beamer briefly entertained the image of a nursing tree, but it quickly faded to black.

"When we're done with this run," Laurel pressed on, "I think we should organize runs to libraries before all the books are burned for fuel. Tonight we have, what, five other teams out collecting plate glass, for godsake? *Plate glass!* Why don't we collect books and maps and stuff too? We can't forget Alexandria."

"Alexandria?" Jako asked, screwing up his face. "Who's she?"

"The ancient library at Alexandria in Egypt. It had thousands of scrolls—all the knowledge of the western world at the time. Then it was burned down by a mob of fanatics led by a nut case bishop. It probably set humanity back by a millennium. 'All of this has happened before and all of it could happen again.'"

"The Cylon Leoben in *Battlestar Galactica*," quipped Beamer.

"Be serious!"

Beamer smiled. "I am," he said. "It was *you* who quoted a Cylon."

"Say we'll salvage libraries. Say we'll set up our own library on the Massif. Say we're going to learn something from this ruination and not forget it all!"

"As you know very well, what I say doesn't matter any more or any less than what anyone else says. I'm not the dictator. But what I can say is that if you bring that idea into one of our meetings, I will say that you speak my mind—unless I feel led otherwise." He grinned at her. It was good to see Beamer smile—so like his name—and so rare since Tatum's death. Laurel and Beamer were friends, but not more than friends, except in so far as a collapse of civilization can bond people quickly.

Turning to Jako, Laurel asked, "And you?"

"What can I say?" he quipped. "Samuel Johnson, Alexandria and *Battlestar Galactica* all in one conversation? How could I disagree?"

Laurel nodded with finality. "Good. It's settled then."

"Well…" Beamer cautioned.

"I know, I know. It has to be in right practice. But I think this is an opening. It just *has* to be. We'll do this thing. We'll curate libraries."

"Said like the bookworm you are," Jako said.

"I'm an archivist," Laurel said, "and that's a lot different than a bookworm."

"So you're a worm of a different colour," Jako countered. Then he muttered, "Still a worm to me."

"Let's just get through this run first, shall we friends?" Beamer urged.

Beamer's reminder brought them back to the task at hand, and they crept along for another ten painful minutes. Every time they turned a corner they expected a barricade or a gunshot through the windshield, or one or another of the shocking surprises reminiscent of Hollywood disaster movies. But none of it happened. The streets were empty of people and they were able to thread their way along, only once having to get out of the van and clear debris that blocked their way. Then the van rolled quietly to a stop.

"I think this is it," said Jako.

They stopped in front of an ordinary looking bungalow on a tree lined street. Ordinary except that on this night it was utterly dark but for the wan light from a shrinking moon. All the houses were dark and silent. Many showed signs of having been burgled or vandalized. Jako backed the van as far into the driveway as he could, and turned off the engine.

"Okay," said Beamer consulting some notes. "Here we should have John and Clovis Hofsted and two children, Brody and Cate. We also will have some tools to load up if they're still here."

"Who are these people?"

"John is an elevator installer and maintenance man. Clovis is a nurse. Brody is eleven, I think, and Cate is nine."

"An elevator installer?"

"It's a long story. They had already been recruited for Badger Coulee before all this hit the fan, but they hadn't moved yet. This family was alright as of last night when we were last in touch with them. Hopefully nothing has happened in the meantime. But you should be prepared for anything."

Jako didn't ask for details. "Let's do it," he said flatly. They left the van, closing the doors quietly. Jako went to the rear of the vehicle to open the panel door while Beamer approached the rear of the house. He opened the storm door and rapped five times in quick succession, paused, then five times more. He waited. A faint light appeared inside as Jako joined Beamer on the patio outside the back door. The light disappeared as the inside door opened a crack.

"Beamer Farris?" came a whisper from inside the house.

"The one and only," Beamer whispered back. "We're your ride out of here, John."

The inside door opened, fully revealing a thirty-something man with several days growth of beard. He had on a head-mounted light such as those worn by plumbers, making him look vaguely like a cyborg. Beamer and Jako stepped inside the house and descended a flight of stairs into a finished lower level, then navigated through a short maze of boxes and mattresses apparently intended to keep light in the basement from being seen from above. But even then, the room they entered had its windows blacked out and only a tiny light shining toward the floor in one corner. The pungent odour of excrement emanated from a slop bucket in one corner of the room. Also, there were considerable numbers of empty food packages strewn about.

"Thank God!" said Clovis, her voice shaking. She held both of their children in a vice-like embrace which only relaxed when she saw her husband enter the room.

"Mrs. Hofsted," Beamer acknowledged. "This is Jako Menpaa who will be your driver tonight. We're here to take care of you." He looked at John. "The tools you want to take?"

"They're in the garage upstairs, unless someone has made off with them. But people these days don't seem to steal tools—I guess because that implies work." He gave a weak smile.

"I'll get that stuff in the van," said Jako turning toward the stairs. "Please get your family and belongings together. Time is not on our side. We have one more pick-up tonight."

"No argument there," said Hofsted, who with Clovis, quickly assembled duffles and other gear they had packed.

In another two minutes all were loaded in the van and Jako was again negotiating the remains of suburbia. The Hofsted family did their best to make themselves comfortable in what amounted to a large, windowless box lurching its way along, then slowly out of the city and into a more rural area where they could make better time. For short stretches, they even hazarded turning on their headlights, but doused them again as soon as a clear way forward presented itself.

"Next up is Cynthia Burgess and her partner Cat Wallace," said Beamer, again consulting his notes. "We're looking for Concession 6, Range 11, Lot number 17."

"Without a GPS," Jako mumbled.

"Without a GPS," Beamer confirmed. He unfolded a large sheet of paper in the truck cab. "These things were called maps," he said facetiously, "and they worked fine before GPS. Cynthia has a PhD in permaculture and Cat is a musician. They're homesteading out here somewhere."

"A fucking *musician?*"

"It takes all kinds to make a world."

"Huh," said Jako. "I guess we'll at least have music on the Titanic."

"We're not on the Titanic, remember?"

"Looks like it to me," said Laurel as she peered through the darkened windshield at the bush passing by.

Beamer muttered to Jako, "Shut up and drive. Concession 6, Range 11, Lot 17. You can't miss it."

"I can't miss it, eh?"

"Look," said Beamer. "That's all I've got…unless you want to try postal box 2214, group 6, rural route 7."

"Sometimes you're cruel, you know that?" said Laurel. "Just cruel."

In the same instant there came a sudden "thud!" on the hood of the van as if someone had thrown a rock at them.

"Lights on!" Beamer shouted. "That was a fucking bullet! Step on it! Go, go, go!"

Jako's knuckles turned white on the wheel as he lit up the headlights and floored the vehicle which lumbered only slightly faster down the road. "It would help to know where the hell we are!" he hollered over the roaring engine.

"How would it help? How would it help?" Laurel snapped.

"Just drive!" said Beamer. "Up to the next crossroad, then kill the lights."

As they approached the next intersection, Jako turned off the headlights again and brought the van to a stop. They could hear the faint crying of children coming from the back of the van. Beamer jumped down from the cab, taking a flashlight along.

"Where are you going?" asked Laurel, incredulous.

"Gotta pee," Beamer lied. He went to the back of the van and cracked open the loading door. He shined the flashlight on his own face and said, "Sorry for that. We just had a little run in with some bugs on the windshield. Nothing to worry about. We'll be out of here pretty quick." The whimpering in the van lowered and Beamer closed the door again. Then he went to the front of the van and played the flashlight on all four corners of the gravel intersection. Over the last few days he'd noticed that street signs were disappearing, probably being taken down by people who didn't want to be found anymore, or by others who might want to confuse interlopers searching for plunder. If so, he had to admit that it was working. After playing the light on three of the corners, the fourth at last displayed a sign: CSN Rd 6. The sign crossing it read: RNG Rd 11. *So far, so good*, he thought. He ran back to the van and jumped in.

"Looks like we've been driving on Concession Road 6 all along," he said, "and this cross road is Range Road 11. So we just need to find Lot 17. It's gotta be left or right on this range road. Laurel?"

"Laurel what?"

"You're the one with the intuition. Which way should we turn?"

"Who me?" she cried. "Why me? Because I'm a woman? Oh don't you start!"

"Left or right, Laurel?"

"Oh—turn left!"

Jako turned left and then flashed the headlights one more time to reveal the road ahead. At this place, it was relatively straight but he still felt anxious to put more distance between them and wherever the bullet had come from. "You know," he said, "we're going to have to turn the lights on for a while or we could drive right past this place. I don't think they'll have a porch light on for us." After driving for about a kilometre, he slowed the van down and began creeping along while everyone fixed their eyes on the shoulders of the road.

"Stop!" said Laurel. "There…" she pointed. About ten metres off the road, nearly obscured by vegetation, stood a solitary post with a number on it: 15. "Lot 15?" she said.

"Maybe," said Beamer. "If it's a lot marker, they will be about one and half kilometres apart. All ahead, dead slow."

Jako watched the odometer reel off the distance to where the next lot marker should be. Nothing. He stopped the van. "We have to go back. We must have missed it."

"No," said Laurel. "Keep going. Maybe it's just gone or something."

"It's gone for sure," said Jako.

"Just shut up and drive," said Laurel.

"Why does everyone keep saying that to me?"

Jako inched ahead for another few hundred metres, slowed down again and they resumed looking carefully for the lot marker. It appeared, again almost buried in roadside vegetation.

"This is progress," said Beamer. "Let's try for a turn-off of some kind."

What they saw first was the barest glint of metal in the right hand ditch just off the road. It was a drain culvert and probably under a graded driveway. Jako slowed to a crawl as they approached it, and turned in. Once on the side road, he turned on the headlights again to inspect the condition of the road before driving farther. "Looks passable," he said. He left their lights on as he drove forward. If the end of the road was an ambush, there was no way they could turn around anywhere at this stage. Black alder and hazelnut bushes crowded right up to the edge of the two-track, swishing along the sides of the van. They had been committed to keep driving forward from the moment they turned off the range road. After what seemed like a long time, the two-track widened abruptly into a sort of small parking lot with a lightless house just beyond. A sign stood near the driveway: "Burgess & Wallace"

"God I'm good," said Jako.

"*You're* good?" said Laurel, incredulous. "Who said 'turn left'? Whose intuition did we use? Hm? Hm?"

Beamer jumped down from the van as a light winked on inside the house. He went to the back of the van and opened the door. To the Hofsteds: "Stretch break, pee break, snack break. Then we're back in the saddle. Please don't stray off too far." He then turned and walked toward the house.

A woman appeared who was only slightly older than himself. "Doctor Burgess, I presume?" Beamer asked.

"And you're Beamer Farris, I hope. Give the password, or my husband will shoot you."

"Really?" said Beamer.

"Well," she said, "the threat of it keeps the rabble out. If only we really had a gun."

"Yes," Beamer replied, "we've already had one run-in tonight."

"Really?" Cynthia said with concern. "Anyone hurt?"

Beamer shrugged. "Maybe the window washer tank. But it was close enough to raise my hair. Given other circumstances I would love to linger here, but are you ready?"

"Got some boxes to load and our personal gear, then we can fly."

"Boxes?"

"Seeds, cuttings, bulbs and cultures, you know. That sort of thing."

"That sort of thing," Beamer echoed. "Okay. Load her up. Where's Cat?"

"On his way," said Cynthia. "He's saying good-bye to his instruments, except for his harp. He's bringing his harp. He says if he has to leave that, he would die. I believe him."

"One harp then," said Beamer, waving them on. "Sorry we don't have any window seats in this pig, but it's roomy and in the back you may have a measure of protection in case we run into any more bullets."

In a few minutes they were loaded and ready to go. Jako turned the van around and headed out the driveway to the range road.

They drove the rest of the night in a compromise between speed and vigilance. As false dawn began to touch the eastern sky, the van slowed and made a torturous hairpin turn to the right, plunging through a wall of hazelnut bushes. Thus commenced a slow ascent through a dense stand of white spruce broken only here and there by small patches of aspen. The van came to a stop in what resembled a very narrow campground parking lot shielded from the sky by a canopy of enormous white pines. Everyone tumbled out of the van. The children had slept for most of the ride and appeared in the best shape of anyone. Not far away were low shelters painted in camouflage colours, from which came the smell of food cooking.

"We'll rest here for the day," said Beamer. "At nightfall, we'll head off to the Massif. It will take all night to get there. Others will come to help with your gear. Sorry about the remoteness factor, but it only seems prudent these days."

"Are we hiding?" John asked.

"We either hide or we fight," Beamer replied. "I would prefer to hide as long as we can and fight only if we have too."

"Then will we be hiding forever?"

"I doubt that," Beamer said, sounding resigned. "The world we knew is gone. It will take a long, long time before anyone can afford the luxury of looking for us. And why would they if they don't know we're here? They say it takes a person about six weeks to starve to death. And they get too weak to act up long before then. So I would say in a month or so, only nasty people would be left coming up the driveway. But of course, I may be mistaken. Trouble could come looking for us long before we're ready for it."

CHAPTER 19

SPRING, 276TH YEAR OF THE EUTERRAN AGE (E.A.)

When acting on the Three Happy Memories, one is practicing. Bearing in mind the Nine Cautionary Memories, one is practicing. That is why it is said: Practice is sometimes departure from Practice.

— THE BOOK OF PRACTICE

OTIS BEDE SAT in a Siderium meeting room with a circle of a dozen Elders and Lightminders. His attention was fixed on the ebb and flow of his breath as the minutes passed and the circle deepened together. He imagined what might be asked of him, but immediately named the mental image as such and gently let it go—a distraction.

Presently Ocean Claybourne spoke. "Welcome here, friend Otis Bede," she said. He opened his eyes, nodded his acknowledgment, and waited for her to continue.

"As you may have guessed," she said, "we have a request for you. The found-ling Jaeger continues to puzzle us. As Zephyr Fey, Lydia Ross and Lars Beckett have all told us, he seems to have been abused during his stay with those he calls the 'Brotherhood.' He says he was taken as a child and held against his will. He calls himself 'skrala.' This term is unknown to us but it sounds—un-fortunate. Lydia says he's settled in Mizar Dan with you and will soon be assessed for his suitability to begin training in Stillness practice. He's an adult and apparently never received training of any sort as a child that would suit him for life here. So he may be unteachable and is almost certainly delusional. But Nota Dorne will explore the matter with him. And Lydia and Zephyr will continue to invite his story as he feels able to tell it."

Claybourne paused for a couple of moments and looked around the gath-ering. Then she took a long breath and continued. "But I have a concern about the Brotherhood which friends in this circle share. We've no knowledge of any sizeable group from the eastern regions we've surveyed so far. Much was lost during the Ruination and the Great Forgetting that may have been edifying in this matter, but there's nothing for it. It would be helpful to us to know more about the Brotherhood, how and where they live, and whether Jaeger's description of them is accurate. If they are a remnant group from pre-Ruination times, they may present a risk of which we should be aware. We want to be mindful of their presence and behaviour and to bring this knowledge into Practice. We need to discern in this matter how best to live in relationship with them so as to manifest light and protect life."

"So," Claybourne went on, "we're asking if you would be willing to do a survey—this one to find the Brotherhood group and observe as much as you can. This is entirely voluntary. It's not our desire that you place yourself in danger. We urge discretion. Travel alone. Forest coat. Return no foundlings, even if you come upon more of them. Take some pheros of such kind as you think might be useful, but only at greatest need. Find the Brotherhood, observe, and melt away. We know you already have experience as a surveyor, but this errand requires haste, not detailed observation of everything between."

Claybourne paused, her eyes searching Otis before she spoke again. "We're mindful that you have vowed Tarshin, that you've followed this Practice for the last four years, and that encountering the foundling interrupted one of your runs. How far had you progressed in fourth year Practice?"

Otis's eyes fell, hinting at his disappointment, perhaps even shame. "I was running the sixty-seventh circuit."

"Ah, I see," Claybourne sighed. "The fourth year of Tarshin prescribes eighty kilometre runs over one hundred consecutive days, along with the prescribed memorials, fasts and meditations, is that correct?" Otis nodded silently. Claybourne continued. "While the Siderium has the utmost respect for your decision to break the Tarshin Practice and attend to the foundling, your choice nevertheless compromised the integrity of the vow for this year. In fact, no one knows quite how interrupting the Practice at this point might affect you. As I'm sure you are aware, people have died attempting Tarshin Practice in the past, but no one has ever interrupted it for a reason like a foundling rescue. The Siderium therefore recommends that the vow remain broken for this year and that you repeat fourth year Practice next year, hopefully without loss of light. We hope you can find your way to unity with this advice because we want both to thank you for your generosity and compassion in helping the foundling, but also to maintain the integrity of the Tarshin vows. If you can find yourself in unity with the advice, then you would be free to pursue the survey we're asking you to do." Claybourne's voice became even gentler. "The co-dependent arising of these circumstances doesn't appear to us to be coincidental."

Claybourne's words faded back into the silence as the group continued to sit together for some minutes.

Otis's first response was disappointment. In their collective silence, he watched the feeling arise within him. Its first appearance was a compound of anger and sadness. But these he quickly traced back to his own attachment to expectations he had for himself and his attachment to the esteem that he would gain in the sight of others should he survive the Tarshin. This, in turn, he saw as arising from unresolved clinging to his own goals, his own expectations for himself, his desire to excel, and his hunger for recognition from others. But an even deeper part of him recognized these as psychic manifestations that had nothing to do with right Practice in the Tarshin Way. He watched these inner states arise from their source, and with insight watched as they gradually cooled and disappeared again.

Even as Otis's sense of loss welled up, at the same moment, he recognized right Practice in the Siderium's advice, and how much his disappointment was inflamed by attachment. In fact, he realized he knew it from the moment he decided to stop and attend to Jaeger. He would lose not only that day's run, but the sequence of the runs and the cumulative effect they would have had on his Practice if they had been done without interruption. Once broken, there was no way the Practice could be repaired mid-stream. It would be like trying to stop a dive halfway into the water. It needed to be restarted from the very beginning and there wouldn't be time in the current cycle of the year to do that. His choices would then be to spend the remainder of the year in Tarshin preparation broken by craft or permie shifts, or to undertake the survey, which was a much better use of his experience and training. The Siderium was right, even though he continued to feel disappointed.

"Alright," said Otis.

"Thank you Otis Bede," said Claybourne. "Have a care, friend."

------ • • • ------

Jaeger made his way into the commons room just in time to see everyone in the Mizar Dan assembled and sitting on cushions, except for Oma Jessie who sat in a chair. Everyone was utterly still, most with eyes closed, some gazing out over Loch Speare bathed in the first full light of morning. Seemingly from everywhere at once, a chime-like tone swelled in the room, ringing and ringing with a deep throated mellowness that caressed the ear. Jaeger noticed Oma Jessie with her hand poised over an ancient brass bowl, running her finger along its rim, then releasing the note by withdrawing her hand and placing it in her lap.

"Attention," said Oma Jessie. "Wake up!"

Jaeger sat down, though he didn't know what he should pay attention to. At first, he looked around nervously, but when he realized no one else was taking particular notice of him he relaxed a bit. Seconds lengthened to minutes and the minutes seemed to lengthen endlessly until he lost track of time. He slipped toward boredom and then reverie. He reacted with a start when the note from the singing bowl swelled again.

"Friends rise," announced Oma Jessie, as everyone in the Dan stood up and began to disperse in all different directions for their morning errands, some nodding and smiling at Jaeger as they passed by.

Moments later Jaeger saw Otis and Lydia embracing near the entrance to the common room. Spark was balled up on her cushion, hugging her knees together under her chin, choking back sobs. Lydia and Otis looked grave. Otis released Lydia and turned to Spark.

"Don't cry, chickadee," he soothed. "I'm coming right back."

Spark uncurled and sprang upwards clasping him around the neck. "But you just got home!" Spark whispered emphatically. "You said you'd take me to the North Ford and on the Snake. You said we'd pick berries and start learning the medicine plants there."

"I know, little bird," Otis replied, setting her on her own feet again. "But I must go walkabout again for a few days. The North Ford will still be there when I get back. Wake up, Spark," he said tenderly. "Pay attention, love."

The girl took a deep breath, her knees dropping into a cross-legged position. Slowly her hands slid from around his neck and down into her own lap. She inhaled again deeply, closing her eyes, doing her best to still her sobs. She stayed with this for perhaps ten seconds, then started sobbing again. Otis hugged her again and placed a long kiss on her forehead, then released her.

Lydia stood by stoically, nothing disturbing her poise, but it was obvious she was as upset as Spark. "It's not fair," she whispered.

"No, it's not what we want," Otis agreed, "but I'm called to survey and have been in those parts before. I'm the right person to go. The Tarshin is interrupted anyway and the survey is important."

"You mean dangerous," Lydia interpreted.

"You know I never do dangerous things." He smiled at her.

They regarded each other silently for several moments. He reached for her again, kissing her tenderly. Then he retrieved his backpack which stood on the floor nearby, a remarkably small bundle considering.

"Go with the Light," Lydia said, her voice wavering.

"Remember unity," Otis said softly, "and we'll be together no matter where I am." He pulled his pack over his shoulder and disappeared through the passageway.

Lydia turned and noticed Jaeger standing there, looking perplexed. "Is Otis going somewhere?" Jaeger asked.

"Yes," answered Lydia, wiping her cheeks. "Just for a short while we hope."

"Where?"

"I don't know," said Lydia. "Otis is a Surveyor. His work is exploring parts we've lost track of in the Great Forgetting. He makes maps—notes and things—when he gets back."

"How long will he be away?"

"I don't know. Sometimes only a few days, sometimes many weeks. I think this walkabout will be a longer one," she said, partly to herself. "Come, let's find you something to eat." Lydia turned to Spark who was once again hugging her knees and rocking to comfort herself. "Chickadee, please take Jaeger with you this morning to the Siderium, to start his Stillness practice, will you?"

Spark glanced up at Jaeger, doubtful. "Isn't he sort of big?" she asked, palming the tears off her cheeks.

Lydia suppressed a smile. "We're all the same size inside, little bird. Jaeger's never learned Practice, so he needs to begin at the beginning, just like you are. His size has nothing to do with it."

"Never learned Practice? Everyone knows Practice," Spark said smugly.

"Not where Jaeger comes from, love."

"Besides," Spark put in, "I'm not a beginner."

"Then you can help Nota Dorne teach him."

Spark brightened a little as she pondered this opportunity. She looked more closely at her charge. It gave her pleasure to think she might know something that an adult didn't. She decided they should be friends. "Oh, alright," Spark agreed.

"Just bring him back by Zenith. I want to take him for an errand detail later on. Or maybe Lars will do it. Anyway, back by Zenith."

CHAPTER 20

SPRING, 276TH YEAR OF THE EUTERRAN AGE (E.A.)

To lose one's mind and fall into a nightmare is the normal course of human affairs. To keep one's mind and stay awake is the more evolved path. This is simple but not easy.

— THE BOOK OF PRACTICE

"*I'M* TEN NOW, but I'll be eleven by next Solstice," Spark announced in a formal tone. "You can follow me," she said, leading Jaeger out of Mizar Dan by the hand. He followed docilely.

"We can take spinners," she continued, "but we can see more if we walk. It's not too far to Siderium from here. Lydia says you don't know anything, so maybe you'd like to see things."

"Lydia says I don't know anything?"

"Yes," Spark confirmed. "But none of us knows anything until someone teaches us, isn't that right? She also says you're delusional. But Practice will help with that. Without Practice we're all delusional, wouldn't you say?" she said cheerfully. Jaeger kept his peace.

As if she was addressing someone younger, Spark said, "These hallways are called drifts. Do you have drifts where you come from?"

"No," Jaeger answered.

"Oh," she said. "How strange. How do you get from place to place then?"

"Where I come from, we don't live in a mountain."

"Ah! Well, I guess you wouldn't need drifts then would you? They all have names, but I don't know them all because there are an awful lot of them. Some I haven't even seen yet. We live on Ariel Drift. That's the name of a star. Did you know that? All our drifts are named after stars, except for Forest Drift, I guess. We walk down here until we get to the Molly's Quay Lift Station, drop three drifts until we get to Laurel's Garden, and then we can go in to Siderium from there. Easy, right?"

"Easy," Jaeger agreed, "if you know your way around."

"I do," Spark said proudly. Many of the doors that opened onto the passageway led to other living quarters, other Dans, but on the opposite side of the passage were many alcoves and shops of various sizes. All were devoted to craft manufactures. In some, textiles were being woven into goods from clothing to floor mats to seating cushions and beds. In other shops, woodworking was underway. Jaeger saw shoemaking, too, and pottery. None of these shops appeared to be commercial outlets. As he followed Spark through the busy passageway,, his senses were pervaded with a continually changing bouquet of scents from wet clay to wood shavings to the musky smell of wool to incense to soaps and ointments.

Presently they came to a lift with words carved into the stone wall that read 'Molly's Quay.' They stepped on and it descended slowly past three more drifts when Spark touched a control and the lift came to a stop. They walked through a short passageway with bright light pouring into it from around a corner. They emerged into a sizeable courtyard arboretum laced with pathways planted with many types of flowers and trees. Bright sunlight shone down from an open roof above. It now being late in the spring, the garden wafted fragrances from every direction. Spark headed off along a path taking them left toward the centre of the garden which was occupied by some sort of sculpture. Pathways left the sculpture in many different directions, all radiating from this central object.

"All this," Spark said, and swept her arm around, "is Laurel's Garden. Her whole name is Laurel Fey. She lived long ago. She made us this." Spark pointed to the sculpture. "It's called 'Fey's Table,' but its whole name is—"Spark glanced up as if the sky would help her to remember the name, then said, "'Fey's Periodic Table of Well-being.'" She chuckled again. "But it doesn't look anything like a table, does it?"

In the middle of the garden was a circular plaza a dozen metres in diameter. At its centre was a composition of stained glass cubes of many colours arranged according to a complex geometry. At first the effect was overpowering and chaotic. But as Jaeger looked closely at the object, it was clear that specific relationships existed among its parts, not some random assembly. Different colours were arrayed in regular relationships to each other and to other parts of the structure, some of them circular, loops within loops. There were layers of colour like strata of rock, only they were crystalline, transparent. And at some points, there were bridging bits that connected layers, sometimes with many links and sometimes only one. Some sort of fluid, passed through channels within the composition carrying particles of something glittering and lightsome.

"What is *that*?" Jaeger whispered, a whisper, he thought, being the only appropriate tone in the presence of such a thing.

Spark grinned broadly. "It's the geometry of love!" she said matter-of-factly. "And it's Practice. At least sort of. See all those cells? Each one is some sort of practice. Today, you'll be starting with that blue one way down there." She pointed down into the structure, again pleased that she had already mastered something Jaeger was just starting. "Laurel Fey invented it back when the very first Euterrans came here. It wasn't very big then, but it was her idea anyway. Now lots of people work on it all the time. It's how we make Practice better and better. You'll like it," she said, nodding confidently.

"I will?"

"Of course," said Spark. "It's how you'll be happy! Do you have no Practice of a good life where you live?"

Jaeger was still transfixed by the sculpture and the currents of light moving through it. "Where I live?" he echoed vacantly. "Happiness? I'm not sure."

Spark shrugged. "We have to go because Nota Dorne will be waiting for us. You can come back here any time you want."

"Spark," he said, "what is that stuff sparkling and moving around in there?"

"Ha! That's power. Come this way," she said, grasping his hand again and leading him toward a broad stairway.

"And this," she said with another flourish of her hand, "is Siderium."

At some distance across the garden rose a multi-level facade terraced into the rock with many balustrades, stairways, ramps and windows. As they approached, Jaeger realized it was a single building hewn from the stone, much taller and larger even than the HQ in Mainbranch. It appeared to extend upwards all the way to the surface of the Massif, and possibly beyond.

"What is this place?"

"It's Siderium," Spark repeated. "It's where we learn Practice. It's our library. It has labs—but I don't know what they do there. It has our government. And the Lightminders are there."

"Lightminders?"

"Yes," said Spark. "I'll show you someday. But we have to hurry or we'll miss Practice." She bounded up a low flight of stairs tugging on Jaeger's hand until they emerged into a small alcove with two cushions on the flagstone floor. Warm sun bathed the space which looked out over the meticulously tended gardens and trees.

"We'll need another cushion," Spark muttered. Leaving Jaeger standing where he was, she disappeared around a corner, reappearing shortly with another cushion which she tossed down on the terrace.

From where he stood, Jaeger caught sight of movement in another alcove a short distance away. He saw a man of about forty, tall but not lanky, clothed only in a loin cloth, his body spare and tightly muscled. He appeared to be practicing very slow, continuous movement from one contorted position to another. He was never still, nor hurried in moving through whatever it was that he was doing. As the movements continued, Jaeger wondered at the strength and control that must be required in such performance. Presently the man came to a standstill in an erect standing posture with palms touching each other in front of his chest, in the gesture Jaeger recognized as the Euterran greeting. Then he reached to the side and retrieved a tunic the colour of sunrise that he pulled over his head—a garment that fell from shoulder to floor with a narrow girdle of braided kudzu. This man's clothing was decidedly plain, even by Euterran standards. Jaeger had noticed that while the Euterran way of life was extremely simple, they seemed to indulge in a fine aesthetic sensibility in clothing, especially in the use of colour. Spark looked up at Jaeger with a serious expression. "Beautiful, isn't it?" she observed, clearly referring to the man in the other alcove.

"What is he doing?" Jaeger queried.

"T'ai-yo," said Spark. "It's very old. A special kind of Practice. That's Nota Dorne, our Telder," she said. "He's very famous, a *weighty* Telder, they call him. But he's not fat. As you see. . Ha! Sometimes he's kind of stern—well, *very* stern actually, but he's always kind. He's hard to describe. He can see your heart. Curious, wouldn't you say?"

Jaeger pulled his gaze away from the man and looked back at the young girl with the perplexed expression that he often wore these days. "Yes," he said, "he sounds very curious. He can see hearts?"

"Mmm," Spark nodded, "but it doesn't hurt."

The man Jaeger had been watching strode in their direction, his movement more like gliding than walking, until he joined them in their own alcove. He carried a small bowl of water, hardly more than a teacup full. He sat down on a cushion and indicated with a gesture that Spark and Jaeger should do likewise. He set the bowl aside.

"Good morning, friend," he smiled at Jaeger as he offered the Euterran greeting gesture. While his expression was warm, it also conveyed gravity.

"Good morning," Jaeger said, returning the gesture.

"I'm Nota Dorne."

"Jaeger."

"Welcome here, Jaeger."

"Jaeger doesn't have a last name," Spark interjected, "but Otis Bede found him far from here and brought him back to Euterra. He's a foundling. It turned out he wasn't sick. Now he lives with us in Mizar Dan. Lydia says he's delusional and doesn't know anything. So I asked her if I could bring him with me to learn Practice." She smiled brightly at Dorne.

"Ah..." Dorne said, returning her smile with a slight incline of his head, "I see." Then turning to Jaeger: "Do you know Practice where you come from?" Dorne's gaze became calmly penetrating and was made more so by how he held his body. There was an unguarded attentiveness present in him. Jaeger sensed that this attentiveness suffused every muscle and joint of Dorne's body. His whole presence *was* the question he asked, and listening respectfully, but uncompromisingly, for an honest answer.

"No, I don't think so," Jaeger said, aware that he was waffling.

"Ah," Dorne smiled indulgently but without condescension, recognizing Jaeger's lie as what it was, but also accepting it without judgment. "If you knew Practice, then you would know that you know. As it is, you probably are delusional."

"I don't believe so," Jaeger protested.

"It's nothing to go on about," Dorne said soothingly. "We all go delusional unless we Practice continually. We all forget unless reminded. So shall we begin?" Jaeger felt like he was being drawn into a lake without ever having swum, but said nothing.

"Sit on the edge of the cushion, thus," Dorne said. "Keep your back straight but not rigid. Put your right hand in your left with upturned palms like this. Keep your head straight and level, eyes lightly closed or half open, whichever you like, but focusing here." He indicated a spot on the floor a metre in front of where Jaeger was sitting. "Practice is in the body as much as in the mind. Details matter. Posture feeds awakening. For today, let's just start with breathing. Pay attention only to your breath. When your attention wanders, as it certainly will, as soon as you notice it wandering, return it to your breath."

"That's it?" Jaeger asked.

"That's it—for today."

Dorne turned to Spark. He retrieved the bowl of water he had put aside and set it in the space between them. "This is for you today," he said. "Do it."

Spark squirmed excitedly on her cushion, and said: "Can we recite the Beginning Reminder first?" she asked.

Dorne smiled. "Don't you think Jaeger has enough to think about already?" Spark looked crestfallen. Dorne relented. "Where is the beginning?"

"There is no beginning," Spark replied, smiling and wiggling into a more comfortable position on her cushion.

"When do we begin?"

"Now we begin."

"How do we begin?"

"We pay attention. We breathe. We wake up."

"Who attends?" Dorne asked.

"No one attends."

"And who breathes?"

"No one breathes."

"That's right," Dorne said. "And who is waking up?"

"One who is already awake."

"So what *is* here?"

"Attending. Breathing. Awakening," Spark whispered.

"Just so," Dorne said.

"Attending, breathing, awakening have no beginning," Spark whispered, "and they have no end." She sighed and her body settled into the most subtle posture of stillness-holding-attention that Jaeger had ever seen. She looked feline, both perfectly still and yet as if ready to spring. Dorne did likewise. Their bodies sang with an energy impossible to name, almost impossible to see, but unmistakably felt.

Jaeger closed his eyes as both Spark and Dorne had, but within moments glanced again at the two of them with the same uneasiness he had felt earlier in the morning. *What on earth are they doing?* he wondered. Surely it couldn't be as simple as just paying attention to his breath. But after some minutes of wondering, and thinking, and imagining, and trying to associate this with *anything* familiar in his experience, Jaeger found his own eyes closing. At first, he was assaulted by a flood of images and thoughts and random emotions. But as time passed, he began to slip toward boredom, and in the boredom, the avalanche of thoughts and memories slowed and began to settle toward stillness. And in that dark interior space, he noticed breathing—only breathing—for the longest time. Until he heard something else. Something bubbling. He opened his eyes enough to see Spark and Dorne sitting face to face and between them on the stone floor, the small bowl of water. It was boiling.

CHAPTER 21

SPRING, 276TH YEAR OF THE EUTERRAN AGE (E.A.)

In Active Practice we perfect character, deepen in community
with other beings, and produce needful things. These should
not be thought of as separate, nor is their order arbitrary.

— THE BOOK OF PRACTICE

There is no such thing as a free lunch.

— APHORISMS OF HYRAM BOWEN

TWO DAYS AFTER his Embracing Ceremony, Jaeger took up occupancy in Sam Faron's former quarters in Mizar Dan. There continued to linger in the place the aura of the Wending witnessed there, but also the sheer density of the stone over which a human life could pass like a breeze and disappear. As he pondered this paradox, Jaeger found it oddly consoling—the thought that one could be sustained and transformed at the same time in the same place.

The morning feast was over and Jaeger sat through the first Stillness practice of the day with his Dan-mates as unsure of what to do as he was discomforted in so long a time of silence. Nevertheless, the silence seeped into him and stayed with him when he returned to his room. So when the tap on his door came, it sounded like a rock fall against the background of his inner quietude. Jaeger pulled the door ajar revealing Lars Beckett.

"Ah!" said Lars on seeing him. "Today we begin Active Practice. Are you ready?"

Jaeger shrugged. "I'm not sure what I should be ready for."

Lars flashed a quick smile. "Understandable," he agreed. "We'll fix that soon. Come as you are. If you need any special clothing or tools, they'll be provided. Please follow." He turned down the passageway and Jaeger went after him.

"Where're we going?"

"Down this way." Lars waved forward as they left the Mizar Dan passage-way and entered Ariel Drift. "It's not far. We won't need spinners." He set off hiking at a furious pace for a man his age and Jaeger kept up only by taking an occasional double hop. "Hyram Bowen once told me a very ancient saying: 'There's no such thing as a free lunch.'" Lars chuckled. "Active Practice is how we get our lunch."

"You mean *work*?" Jaeger asked.

Lars stopped. "What'd you say?"

"You mean you *work* to get your lunch?"

"Hmm," Lars said. "That's a very old word—work. I think I've seen it before in the archives in the Hall of Memory, but it's not a word we've ever used in Euterra. Where did you hear it?"

"It was my whole life in Mainbranch." Jaeger's tone was bitter.

Lars gaped. "Truly? That must've been horrible! But are we talking about the same thing? If I remember, work was involuntary labour done for someone else whose interests were not your own, often dangerous, and involved tasks you want to escape from as soon as possible. Then people were given money that they used to buy what they needed to live, and occasionally some comforts."

"That's pretty much it," Jaeger confirmed, "except without the comforts."

Lars shook his head and resumed walking. "Well, that's not what we do in Active Practice. Active Practice is how we get our living and we all do some every week. But we have a choice in what we do, and *how* we do it matters a great deal. We don't need money, so that's not involved. While we choose what we do, we may not always choose pleasant things—so discipline is part of it. Some say that the best Practice is to choose the things no one else wants to do, at least some of the time. But in Active Practice we try to perfect character and deepen our awareness of each other in ways that only practicing together can achieve—to make us better people. Active Practice also strengthens com-munity and helps us grow in compassion. We do both of these in the process of making the things we need to live. Active Practice is how we provision our livelihood. 'Work' as I understand it, was a means to an end, something most people preferred to escape if only they could get the end without the means. For us, Active Practice is the end. Getting our living from it is a side-benefit."

They turned down another short drift and came to the Centre Lift station. "Here we go," said Lars as he stepped on the lift platform and set the controls to descend. Jaeger followed, and they plunged downward until they arrived at Gemini Drift, forty-two levels deeper into the Massif. On the way down, the lift passed by another enormous gallery many stories deep. It housed several sizeable tangles of pipe, tanks, and machinery. The smell of warm lubricants suffused the air and pumps could be heard throbbing away in the depths.

Guessing Jaeger's question, Lars nodded, "It's called The Machine, although there are several of them down here. This device pumps our water, recycles our wastes, generates our electricity and produces the bio-gasses and distillates we need for manufactures and for running the wains. I can give you a tour some-day if you wish." The lift kept descending and the Machine passed from view.

After descending more than forty levels, the lift came to a halt and they both stepped off the platform, walked a few paces and then down another short drift that opened into a spacious gallery. It was crowded with people. There was a low din in the room as some mingled and chatted while others moved through the space, seemingly with purpose. The walls of the gallery were covered by large display boards with thousands of lines of printing, each of which included a small lighted number, lending the room a certain festive atmosphere.

"First we need to get you a pendant," said Lars. "Everyone gets a pendant. With it you can go to any of the General Stores and pick up whatever you need of material goods that aren't provided by your Dan. Of course Oma Jessie is the Dan Cellarer and she makes provision of basics like food and clothing and personal care items for the whole Dan. Many other things like tools, mu-sical instruments, art supplies, toys, and so on can be borrowed from one of the lending libraries. But there might be something else you want, though I can't imagine what, that you can get from the General Store, and when you do, you'll need to give them your pendant number. They help us keep track of the supplies we have on hand and when something runs low, to make more of it."

Lars pressed through the crowd with Jaeger in tow until they reached a clerk seated behind a counter. Lars leaned toward him and said a few words Jaeger couldn't hear over the steady rumble of the crowd, then returned with a small metal pendant with a number embossed on it, which he handed to Jaeger. "There you have it," he said. "You'll also need to show that to whoever is overseeing your Active Practice today. It helps us keep track of how many peo-ple are engaged in what errands, and also that everyone is doing their share."

Jaeger looked askance. "What if someone doesn't do their share?"

Lars grinned. "That doesn't happen very often without cause—but some-times it does. Generally such things are handled by Dan Elders. Dan-mates know what each other is doing and there is plenty of informal encouragement for everyone to do their part to support the Dan. It's simply natural that we do so—as well as an incentive to compassion. Every living thing makes its living somehow. We're no different. If someone doesn't heed their Dan Elder, then it might be referred to the Drift Council. It's very rare that anyone absolutely refuses Active Practice, but should that happen, Drift Councils can banish them from Euterra. People would probably then discover that it's much hard-er to provide for all of their own needs themselves than it is to participate in Active Practice. No one has ever been banished in my lifetime. But I admit, we do have a few who need extra encouragement now and then. It's just that in Euterra, because we're all members of Dans, it's harder for free riders to hide."

Accepting Lars's explanation at face value for the moment, Jaeger resumed inspecting the gallery. "What *is* all this?" he asked.

Lars looked around. "Many things are required to provision Euterra. We need food, clothing, tools and furnishings, energy and water, and much else besides. Some needs are attended to by the Guilds like the Permies or Carvers. Others need Active Practice from people with lengthy training who are licensed by the Siderium to do what they do. But many require no special training beyond what might be needed for that errand. So those sorts of errands are listed here on the boards. Anyone can come here, find an Active practice they want to do, enter their pendant number, and join the group doing that errand until enough people have joined. Then that station is closed for the day and you have to pick something else. There are thousands of errands listed here and usually you can find something you'd enjoy doing."

"But what are all the numbers?"

"Well," said Lars, "what this place really is, is a sort of auction house for Active Practice. We needed some way to match the errands that need doing with people wanting to do them. Obviously, some errands are more pleasant than others. Remember I told you that we do about twenty hours of Active Practice a week? We can do more if we wish, but twenty hours is the custom. The numbers beside the errand names on the boards are adjusted to reflect the popularity of that particular errand. So errands that a lot of people want to do are assigned a lower hour number, while less desirable errands have higher hour numbers. The less desirable the errand, the less of it you have to do to fulfill your twenty hours of Active Practice for the week because you get more than one hour of credit for each hour you practice. It's a way we have of letting people choose what they want to do, but also providing an incentive for less desirable errands to get done. People willing to take on those activities often wind up doing only ten or twelve hours of Active Practice with more time left for leisure, sports, Stillness Practice, the arts, love-making—whatever."

Jaeger continued to look around at the mass of people making their errand selections and assembling in groups to set about the day's activities. "I'm showing you this today," Lars went on, "so you could get your pendant and know where to get your Active Practice errands later on. But I thought today you might come with me to one of the Permie food forests. It's where I often do my own Active Practice. You might like it."

Jaeger looked apprehensive. "Does that mean going—out?"

Seeing his anxiety: "It'll be fine," Lars said. "I'll be with you and several hundred other people. Besides, I don't think this Brotherhood of yours knows we even exist."

Jaeger shuddered. "The Brotherhood knows everything," he said resignedly. "I doubt that," Lars said. Turning, he said, "Let's go this way."

They made their way out of the Auction Gallery and back to the Centre Lift which carried them and at least another twenty Euterrans down even farther into the Massif. They passed no more drifts on the way down except for one which was under construction. Rough tunnels had been hewn both east and west of the lift station. Stone carvers were busy doing finishing work close to the lift shaft. But they passed by it before Jaeger could see much of their work.

Presently the lift slowed and many people got off in another large gallery Jaeger had never seen before. He and Lars joined the crowd stepping off the platform. The gallery was crowded with people, spinners, wains and larger vehicles that were loading up and moving out of a spacious gate in the north wall of the Massif.

"This is North Gate," said Lars. "We can take some spinners and make it to the north food forest in half an hour." Moments later they recruited two spinners, mounted up and peddled out of the North Gate and into a dew-soaked spring morning. The air was chilly but the sun, now fully risen, promised warmth.

They peddled for a considerable distance along a road paved with blocks of the same stone as comprised the Massif. "Most of the stonework you see here including the road is made using material we remove as we build the city," said Lars. After about twenty minutes they passed through a small village of cottages made of fieldstone or scree from the city. "This kind of building takes more time but we think the results are handsome buildings strong enough to stand against the weather and they can last for half a millennium or more. Since they rarely need replacement, such buildings actually require less labour and materials than pre-Ruination architecture."

As they peddled through the village Jaeger also saw some buildings woven up from willow or alder, making dome-shaped structures of living vegetation. They were like giant baskets woven upside down and anchored to the earth by the roots of their parent material.

Noticing his interest, Lars said, "Those are called willow-wolds. We've learned how to weave trees and vines into useful structures—especially for buildings that don't have to last very long or that don't need to be completely weathertight. Almost everything else we make of stone, timber and tile."

Jaeger nodded without speaking, taking pleasure in what he saw. The willow-wolds possessed the same quality that suffused the whole landscape. He didn't know what to name it. The road they followed seemed to be passing through a forest, but—as Jaeger began to realize—it only *seemed* to be a forest. There were many trees, to be sure, and low bushes and mid-story vegetation of many species. But something about their arrangement didn't suggest a jumble of struggling competitors. The wood had a quality much different from the wild land he had crossed in the custody of the Brotherhood. *That was it!* Jaeger thought, suddenly seeing it—the quality that marked *everything* he was looking at here. They weren't passing through a forest at all: it was an *arrangement*, a landscape that had been consciously designed—to what end, he did not know. This was unlike anything he had ever seen in Mainbranch.

———•◆•———

Jaeger abruptly stopped peddling. When Lars noticed him falling behind, he slowed his own spinner, turned around and went back. Jaeger was straddling his spinner, sweat beading on his face as his body shivered. He was breathing hard and glancing around erratically.

"You alright?" asked Lars.

Jaeger sighed deeply, as if trying to catch his breath. "Yes," he said, "I think so…"

"Are we going too fast? We can slow down."

Jaeger shook his head. "That's not it. It's something about this place…this forest…" His voice trailed off.

"Ah," said Lars, nodding. "My apologies. We're in a permie forest. They can be very powerful places. But when you come into one for the first time, you mostly sense it emotionally before your thinking really catches up with what's happening—if ever," Lars chuckled lightly. "It takes long Practice to understand this place, but you can feel what it's doing right away. Take your time. There's a saying by a Samurai master from ancient Japan that matters of little concern should be treated seriously, but that matters of great concern should be treated lightly." Jaeger nodded without reply. When his breathing slowed, they remounted their spinners and pressed on.

Presently, they came to a place where the road widened to a sizeable plaza, crowded with abandoned spinners and wanes. There was an outbuilding just off the plaza, perhaps a tool shed, Jaeger guessed. Many pathways threaded away from the plaza in every direction into a forest that looked and felt wilder than that through which they had already come. People looked busy with tasks the purpose of which was not readily apparent to Jaeger, but there was a happy chatter in the air.

"Please follow," Lars said. He turned onto a path that led into the forest with Jaeger following. They walked for some distance over hill and dale, which should have been pleasant enough, except the trail summoned flashes of Jaeger's recent ordeal. Once he stopped, breathing hard, then resumed following Lars. Lars said nothing, guessing what might be happening, but left Jaeger to himself and the wholesome energies of the place they were walking through.

They came to the crest of a hill covered mostly in spruce and birch, but also with many snags and trees felled by the ever more intense and frequent storms that swept over the land. Beckett stopped, letting Jaeger catch up to him. When they met, Beckett extended his arm, pointing downslope on the yonder side of the hill crest.

Jaeger looked, but could see nothing but trees. Lars smiled, then stabbed at the air more emphatically. "Right there," he whispered. Jaeger continued to search where Lars pointed, then suddenly descried a figure sitting cross-legged on the hill side only a few metres away. The man's form appeared to abruptly jump out from its background of vegetation and dead fall. He looked to be sixty or seventy years old, long white hair pulled back to a single braid that reached from head to waist. His frame was lean, almost boney, but completely at ease sitting in the leaves. He wore the same type of general issue tunic and draw-string pants of Euterran design that Jaeger was given on his arrival.

The old man appeared to be gazing intently at the surrounding forest, and how the hillside they stood on sloped downward and around in both directions to form a large, bowl-shaped depression. At the lowest point in the depression there bloomed several hundred deep purple flowers pushing up from tight bundles of spear-shaped, deep green leaves as tall as a person's waist. Sunlight poured into the opening they made in the forest canopy igniting and intensifying their colour.

"*Iris germanica*," the sitting man said without turning toward them. "Magnificent, aren't they." He turned to acknowledge Jaeger and Lars. His expression was friendly, but also carried a certain aloofness, as if he intended not to allow this interruption to distract him from his task for long.

"This is Isaac Penn," Lars said. "Isaac, this is Jaeger…just Jaeger."

"Ah yes," said the sitting man, smiling. "Our new foundling. I'm honoured to meet you. And how are you finding our forest, and our—*peculiar* ways?" Jaeger saw again the same thing he noticed during his Embracing Ceremony with Oma Jessie—a sense that he was with someone who both participated in the conversation and also stood beside it, witnessing it.

"It's a lovely place," said Jaeger, taking care with his words, "and yet—strange."

Penn's eyes narrowed, twinkling. "Ha!" he barked. "I'll say!"

"Isaac is a Designer," Lars continued. "He's one of the Permie Guild. Their Active Practice provides our food and many other things. Designers are the elders of the Guild."

"You're *too* kind, Lars," Penn's tone was gently dismissive. "Lucky thing being an elder doesn't confer one iota of distinction. But we all play our parts. Mine is to sit here until I can hear the trees."

"And what do you design?" Jaeger tried.

"Worlds," said Penn.

Lars snorted. "You exaggerate!"

"It all depends how big you are," Penn said, his eyes still twinkling. "Let me put it this way: We try to rearrange the creatures of this world so as to meet our own needs as well as theirs, but we try to do it in conversation with who's already here. Sometimes it takes a long time to hear the conversation—is all."

"And this?" Lars asked, nodding toward the little dale.

"*This* is challenging," Penn said. "The tricky bits are in the curves. The depression is bowl-shaped, creating a whole series of micro-climates and different soil zones at different elevations and azimuths respecting the sun—to say nothing of saving the irises. We would usually add some minor terracing here to help retain moisture on the slopes and then guild any trees we add. But if we did that, you see, less water would reach the irises and since they are moisture loving plants, they would probably die out. I've been watching it for two years, but I think I'll have it in another year or so—if I don't compost myself first right where I'm sitting. Ha!"

Jaeger chuckled politely. Penn was as strange as the forest he sat in, but convivial enough.

"Very well," said Lars, all business. "I wanted Jaeger to meet you, but we should be off to find some sweatier task and let you return to your Practice."

"As you wish," Penn said. "But you're welcome to stay."

"Thank you," said Jaeger. "Maybe I'll join you for my next Active Practice."

"Maybe you will," Penn replied, returning his full attention to the task, which Jaeger suspected he had never really left.

Lars and Jaeger left Penn to his contemplation and returned in the direction they had come. Once they were out of earshot, Jaeger said, "He's a strange one…"

"You have no idea," Lars said. "But he's a brilliant Designer. He's right out here where the food forest meets wilderness. His work is very subtle, very sensitive—and also incredibly productive."

"Food forest?" Jaeger asked.

"Yes," said Lars. "Before the Ruination, food was produced on farms that grew just one or two crops. Their main goal was to make money. Naturally, this ruined the land. If the Ruination hadn't happened the way it did, it probably would have happened eventually from the collapse of agriculture. Anyway, when the first Euterrans arrived here, we decided to produce our food using permaculture instead of agriculture. We cultivate hundreds of different plants and animals in the same landscape instead of just one or two. It takes more people to grow food this way, but it takes a lot less machinery, and it's much more tolerant of the changing weather."

"And what makes Penn a Designer?"

"He studied permaculture from the Siderium, but other qualities are also required that we can't teach directly."

"Like what?"

"Well," said Lars, sounding amused, "did you notice how every flower in sight had turned toward him?"

"No," said Jaeger, credulous.

"That's why Penn is a Designer and you and I are not. Now, please follow." Lars turned again on the trail and they set off back toward the plaza, but before reaching it, they turned aside and headed up into a stand of large white spruce.

———•—•———

In another few minutes, they came upon a group of people scattered over a hillside that was covered with trees of various kinds, all clad in blossoms of white or pink. Fruit had been a rare delicacy in Mainbranch and Jaeger had never seen a fruiting tree. Certainly he knew chokecherry and dogwood, but Citizens' diets were mostly limited to grains and root vegetables as these were the easiest foods to produce.

"This is a fruit orchard," said Lars. "Some of the trees here still need guilding. So let's find the orchard trustee and get an assignment." He asked one of those working in the orchard where they could find the trustee and they were directed upslope to a woman who was handing out tools and sending teams of workers in various directions. She sent Lars and Jaeger off to a stand of young fruit trees barely three metres high and they set to their task.

Lars pointed out that the trees occupied a site that sloped gently southwards and they needed to remove sod from the upslope side and deposit it along the downslope side of each tree parallel to the crest of the hill above, creating a kind of level ring around the bowl of each tree about four metres in diameter. When repeated for many trees, the effect was to cornice the hillside making it more likely that the movement of water downslope would be slowed by the little terraces they were building, watering the trees in the process and generally retaining more water in the landscape.

After reshaping the tree bowls, Lars and Jaeger made small incisions in the sod around the trees sufficient to drop in a few seeds of a potherb or the bulbs of perennial flowers, garlic, onion, or chives. These plants, Lars explained, served to repel rabbits and pest insects that might attack the trees.

As they worked, Lars noticed that Jaeger had a tendency to throw himself into this activity as if driven by some unseen lash—a habit, he speculated that Jaeger must have acquired during his time in Mainbranch. He had constantly to urge Jaeger to slow down, pay attention to what he was doing, listen more attentively to his intuition about where to plant various seeds and bulbs, and in general enjoy their activity as Active Practice. However this instruction seemed to find little purchase in Jaeger's understanding. Lars thought it likely that his companion had little experience with many of the plants, and no experience at all of productive activity with conviviality at its centre rather than sheer output of labour. As the morning passed, Lars resigned himself to the possibility that Jaeger's re-education would likely take considerable time and he should be satisfied with whatever might be achieved one day at a time.

The pair stayed in the food forest for the remainder of the day, stopping only for a mid-day meal. Lars continued to point out features of the forest design. He spoke of how the many varieties of plants related to the landscape they'd been settled in, the movement of the sun, the variation introduced by regular seasonal changes punctuated by increasingly erratic severe weather events, the steps Euterrans were taking to try to accommodate these events in the food forest designs—all of which Jaeger noted with appreciative nods but little of which he could absorb in such spate.

By late afternoon the two had returned their tools to the tool shed at the plaza and had mounted their spinners to return to the Massif. On their way, however, they were suddenly halted by a loud, intermittent, whooping sound coming from behind them. Jaeger was mystified and more than a little anxious but Lars pulled his spinner off the road and motioned for Jaeger to do the same. Jaeger could see other spinners behind them also making way for whatever the cacophonous thing was that was overtaking them. Presently a vehicle appeared which was clearly powered in some other way than human peddling. It moved at speed and sounded an alarm as it approached that cleared the road as it went. When it passed Jaeger and Lars, it emitted a low hum and appeared to be carrying a half dozen people, two of whom looked unconscious, lying on stretchers inside the vehicle's cab. Jaeger caught a glimpse of one of the passengers whose body looked burned along most of its left side. The other figure on a stretcher was motionless, but was also burned. The strange vehicle hurtled on down the lane at a truly manic speed compared to the spinners and wanes that were gradually resuming their journeys.

Jaeger looked at Lars, startled and confused. "What was *that*?" he asked.

Lars looked grave. "I'm not sure," he said. "The carriage is a blitzer. We don't have many powered vehicles in Euterra, but the ones we do have are used mostly for emergencies and heavy transport. Something's up..." his voice trailed off uncertainly.

Jaeger looked doubtful. "That's not what I mean. What happened to *them*?" he said, clearly referring to the victims in the vehicle.

Lars continued to look down the lane in the direction of the disappearing blitzer, his expression concealing as much as it revealed. "I don't know," he said again, trying to sound convincing. Jaeger waited in silence, curious and anxious, sensing that Lars knew more than nothing. "It's a long story," Lars said, hoping that would dismiss the subject. Jaeger continued to wait.

Lars shrugged. "Long ago, before the Ruination," he said, "people used many dangerous things. When the Ruination happened, all kinds of them were lost or forgotten, including where were dumps of dangerous chemicals, how to dispose of them, what to do with them. In the Ruination, people were so occupied with day-to-day survival, they didn't think about such things. They had always been out-of-sight out-of-mind for most people anyway. But soon following the Ruination, the waste dumps and chemical sites started leaking, breaking down, and sometimes blowing up."

"I know that," Jaeger interjected, finally linking something in Lars's story to his own experience. "In Mainbranch, I was Citizen on work detail. We mined old landfills—for anything we could use. Sometimes they blew up."

Lars nodded. "Just so. The landfills made methane and sometimes now when we dig into them, the methane explodes. You have to be very careful."

"Is that what happened to them?" Jaeger asked, looking at the blitzer disappearing into the distance.

Lars shook his head gravely. "I don't think so," he said. "The people in the blitzer are Trefoils. After the Ruination, we created many different guilds—groups of Euterrans with specific errands. Most produce things like food or furniture or they carve out new drifts or serve as Helders. But some guilds were established to dispose of poisonous leftovers from the Ruination—or if we can't figure out how to dispose of them, then to contain them and prevent them doing harm. We've learned a lot about how to do that over the last three centuries, but there are some things that still present a danger we don't know how to fix. We can only contain them."

"The Trefoil Guild appeared only about ten years after the Ruination," Lars continued. "Their call to Active Practice is to watch over a nuclear reactor about one hundred and twenty kilometres from here. We managed to shut the reactor down long ago but now it's falling apart and it's upwind of Euterra. It's a problem. Sometimes accidents happen. The people in the blitzer were wearing Trefoil tunics, so…"

Jaeger looked pale, and baffled. "What's a nuclear reactor?"

Lars looked back at him, almost despairing. "Like I said," he deflected, "it's a long story. Today it's probably enough to say that a nuclear reactor was an ancient device for making electricity which used a very dangerous fuel. They no longer work for making energy, but the fuel they used continues to be a problem. Let's get going."

Both men peddled along for some time without speaking. They went more slowly than on their outward bound trip, partly because it was the end of a day of physical work, but also because they both were attending more to the sensations and beauty the late afternoon offered.

Eventually, Lars spoke. "You know," he said reflectively as he peddled, "many years ago, when I was much younger, I was part of a survey detail to a site about a thousand kilometres west of here. We were doing the usual—looking for plate glass especially, but anything at all in the town site that might be useful or could be made useful by recycling and re-fabricating. We were surveying part of what had been a small village. It was peculiar because most of the buildings were small, probably living quarters for people back then, but all were fallen down long ago and mostly covered over with windblown soil and decayed vegetation. So the whole area was a field of low sod mounds laced through with trees that found places to take root, and lots of bushy undergrowth. But every now and again, something stuck out of the sod that reminded me of what lay beneath—a bit of plastic pipe, a stainless steel oven rack, a window pane jutting upward like a broken tooth."

"I'd already decided that there wouldn't be much of use in such a place," Lars continued, "and I was on my way back to the rest of our survey team when my foot tripped against this bit of stone, pink granite like that of the Massif, sticking up from the sod, as if it wanted to be found. The rock had been sliced and polished, though the polished side was already becoming some-what dulled with age. I pulled it loose from the sod and saw that it was a grave marker for someone named Tatum Barnes. Sometimes people had these things made ahead of time, especially if they thought their death might be soon, then only the final date needed to be added."

Lars stopped peddling and stood in the middle of the lane. Jaeger followed suit. "You know," he said, his voice choking with emotion, "I've kept that stone, all these years. I don't even know who Tatum Barnes was. I don't know why I keep the stone. Each generation is born and thinks the world it finds is the very first world, unmarked by any malady or loss. But everything that is rests upon the bones of what went before, and sometimes a very great many of them. Sometimes we think that we're more highly evolved than pre-Ruination people. I hope so. But most of them were just trying to make their way, trying to get by on the light they had. Tatum Barnes was probably one of them. I'm glad the Ruination cleared away the old way of life." Lars's teeth clenched for a moment, and then his expression softened. "But I'm sorry for her." He stood straddling his spinner in the laneway, his body tight and shaking. Jaeger grasped his shoulder gently. Lars looked at him, acknowledged the gesture and then mounted his spinner again. "Let's go," he said. Jaeger nodded without saying anything and presently, they were again peddling toward the Massif.

As they made their way Lars appeared more weighed down than Jaeger had yet seen him. Jaeger wondered if this shift in mood was because of the story Lars had just told, or because of the blitzer carrying more casualties from Euterra's war with the past, or perhaps because of something entirely hidden about which Lars had not yet spoken to him. Whatever the cause, Jaeger sensed that their conversation was at an end. He realized, however, that Euterra faced more perils than being discovered by the Brotherhood. The serenity that most Euterrans displayed was purchased at a price that they paid every day.

CHAPTER 22

SUMMER, THE 276TH YEAR OF THE EUTERRAN AGE (E.A.)

One good question is better than a thousand answers.

— THE APHORISMS OF HYRAM BOWEN

JAEGER STEPPED OFF the Molly's Quay Lift into Procyon Drift, which had been mucked out as a double-wide thoroughfare with a double high ceiling. It was lined with crafter's shops, cafes, and personal services. Since his cycling trip with Beckett, Jaeger had explored more of Ariel Drift, and Spark had brought him to the Siderium, but he was now starting to range farther afield on his own. Procyon drift was at first overwhelming, crowded as it was with people, spinner traffic and bustling activity of every sort. He turned right and followed the course of the drift with his eyes as it curved away to the left in the far distance. He started walking in that direction, passing a luthier's shop, a small theatre, a clothes maker, a cobbler's shop and several cafes. The whole space was filled with different kinds of music that changed every time he turned a corner or walked fifty metres. At last he spied a sign for Fogg's Inn.

Fogg's Inn was where Jaeger was told he could find Hyram Bowen, one of Euterra's most esteemed Telders—a teaching elder. As to what Bowen might look like, Jaeger was told he would be unmistakable. He could apparently be found either lecturing at the Siderium or holding forth at Fogg's Inn. The latter sounded to Jaeger like it could be the more congenial place for first acquaintance.

Fogg's Inn was a dimly lit honeycomb of small alcoves carved into the walls of a somewhat more spacious central room, one wall of which included a bar. There were many heavy wooden tables, intricately carved in grotesques of both natural and mythical inspiration. Most tables were occupied, servers moving among them with trays of food, lager, ale, and mead. The hum of conversation filled the air along with the sweet muskiness of the ale. Several patrons paused in their conversations to register Jaeger's arrival, size him up as a first time visitor, and then returned to their talk. Jaeger felt distinctly uncomfortable as he had no experience of such a place, but resolved to make a circuit of the room looking for the unmistakable before making good his escape.

After passing several alcoves, Jaeger saw a plump, aged man with wavy white hair that fell to his shoulders, though the very top of his head was bald. He was dressed like most other Euterrans in a colourful but otherwise unremarkable simplicity. The only thing Jaeger could see which might distinguish him was the Telder's insignia, a triple strand of braided kudzu fibre with a pendant of blue stained glass, an item of apparel worn by all formal teachers in Euterra. He was holding forth animatedly with a much younger male companion. Jaeger slid into an empty booth near them and decided to listen for a while before introducing himself.

"Don't you ever think," pressed the younger man, "that maybe we here in Euterra went a bit too far in reaction to the Ruination? Individuals used to matter back then. People were judged and rewarded on their merits, their own accomplishments. They weren't lumped together like we are in the Dans. A man could set out on his own and make something of himself without being dragged down by the halt and the witless."

"We're all at risk of becoming halt and witless sooner or later, a truth that is generally lost on those who are still young and healthy," Bowen replied. "But I can agree that such a story has a certain appeal. It's just that one big problem with it is that it's *not true*. We *aren't* individuals! We can tell ourselves stories based on all manner of false but amusing assumptions: 'Suppose we were all just isolated individuals, then, imagine the adventures we could have!' But to my mind it's right up there with, 'Suppose there were dragons, or unicorns, or we had magic potions, then imagine the adventures we could have.' While such stories might be entertaining, no one should think on that account that a real culture can last very long if it's based on a false story. Before the Ruination, a few individuals enjoyed great power and affluence. But the vast majority of people didn't. The question is not whether some one individual should be free to excel and enjoy the fruits of her own accomplishments: The question is whether one part of a body can truly thrive while the rest of it is diseased and rotting."

The younger man shook his head doubtfully. "But back then people had democracy. They could rule themselves. They could vote for their leaders and have a say in public affairs. Here we just consult endlessly and take orders from the Lightminders."

Bowen looked shocked. "How can you say that?" he said. "The Lightminders rule no one and you know that. They witness and they testify. That's it. We can take their advice or not. And as to democracy," Bowen said, bristling in feigned umbrage, "it was an adversarial way of governing from the very beginning and by the end left most societies frozen solid in competing demands. Voting just created paranoid winners and alienated losers—hardly better than tyranny. It's just that in democracies, the mob elects its tyrants while in full-on tyrannies they don't. You have more opportunity in the Euterran Dan Councils, Drift Councils and the General Assembly to participate in governance than you ever would have had by voting once every five years. I would much rather live in a society where everyone is looking for unity and believes it's possible, than in a viper's nest of competing interests that aim to win all at their neighbours' expense."

Clearly the younger man was unconvinced, but when he spotted Jaeger listening intently to their conversation, he relented and slid out of his seat opposite Bowen.

"This is the person you're looking for," the younger man said to Jaeger.

Bowen glanced at Jaeger and gesture toward the empty seat. "Well, sit down you fool! That's why you've come here isn't it?" To his earlier companion he said, "To be continued!" The younger man nodded and stepped aside to make room for Jaeger.

"I've had enough today," he said to Bowen, and added, jerking his head in Jaeger's direction, "Take it easy on him the first time." He walked off toward the exit from Fogg's Inn, waving casually as he left.

"Can't hold his mead!" Bowen shouted after him, and chuckled.

"Are you Hyram Bowen?" Jaeger asked.

Bowen looked amused. "Who else could I be in this incarnation—being what I am?"

"My name's Jaeger."

"Of course it is. You're the foundling chap, right?"

"Right."

"And Nota Dorne or somebody put you up to coming down here because you have questions."

Jaeger nodded, feeling awkward. "It was Lydia Ross, actually," he said. Now that he had Bowen's attention, he was at a loss for questions. The man was not unfriendly, but he was somewhat intimidating.

Bowen said, as if to himself, "Why don't they ever send me someone with answers?" He smiled impishly. "And you don't know what to say because where you come from they don't have history, right? That Fey woman—what's-her-name?—told me you came from—where is it you came from?"

"Mainbranch."

"Right, Mainbranch. That's it. If I tell you about Euterra, you have to tell me about Mainbranch. Deal?"

"What's a 'deal'?" Jaeger asked.

Bowen leaned back, inspecting Jaeger more closely. "You *are* bushed, aren't you son," he said. "A 'deal' is an agreement."

Jaeger hesitated, then nodded. "Deal."

"Publican!" Bowen roared. "Two mead to seal the contract!"

A portly man at least as old as Bowen approached their booth with two glasses brimming with a golden liquid. "There're no publicans here, Telder Bowen," he said with mock formality. "Say that again and I'll drag you to the Siderium for spreading false doctrines and corrupting our youth."

"And then you'll make me drink hemlock, right?"

"Someone has to teach you manners."

"I'm beyond teachable," Bowen growled.

"*Now* you speak my mind!" The innkeeper set down their drinks, turned and waddled off into the dimmer reaches of the inn.

Bowen turned back to Jaeger. "We drink this slowly," he counselled, his eyes just a little rheumy. "Not everything was lost in the Great Forgetting, at least not the art of fermentation. But still, we practice mindfulness which more than compensates for affluence, thank the Central Harmony. True pleasure cannot be found in over-consumption." He tipped back his mug carefully and took a measured slurp from its surface. He swallowed only after holding the mead in his mouth for a moment, followed by smacking his lips. Then his gaze fell on Jaeger with focused intensity. "So?" he said.

Jaeger was startled by Bowen's sudden attention and scrambled to pose a question. He decided to ask something that had bothered him since his arrival in Euterra. "So, what was the Ruination?"

"Good question," said Bowen. "Big question. But the wrong question. The right question is: '*Why* the Ruination?'"

"Oh," said Jaeger, hoping to avoid further blunders: "So, *why* the Ruination then?"

Bowen looked at him momentarily as if he was prey. "The Great Forgetting." Then he burst out laughing, more playful than mocking. Jaeger flushed nevertheless. "So it's really true," said Bowen. "You really have no history in, in…"

"Mainbranch," Jaeger offered.

"Mainbranch—just so. Well, where to start then?" Being a Telder, Bowen might have summoned a professorial voice, but there had never been professors in Euterra, much to his chagrin. He knew of them from history and coveted their prerogatives, but in actual experience, he knew them not at all. So instead, the mead having had some tranquillizing effect, he adopted a less formal tone.

"I don't think anybody knows what caused the Ruination," Bowen said, "because it wasn't just one thing. Maybe one thing caused it, or maybe one thing triggered it, but then everything just toppled in on itself and everyone got swept along. *Something* happened about two hundred seventy years ago, more or less, as far as we can tell. I say 'more or less' because it didn't happen on a single day. It was more drawn out than that, for maybe a decade or more.

I say 'as far as we can tell' because part of the Ruination included the loss of our memory of it. The Great Forgetting was one result of the Ruination—although some say that people started forgetting long before the Ruination—which might mean that the Great Forgetting caused the Ruination, rather than the other way around."

Jaeger looked puzzled.

"Confusing, isn't it?" Bowen sympathized. He took another long draught of his mead, savouring the subtle after-taste of honey. "Well, let's put it this way: We know that about two hundred and seventy years ago, more or less, there were a lot more people around than we think there are today—although we don't even know for sure how many of us are left. Before the Ruination, some people lived very affluent lives. They believed in the most bizarre cocktail of myths, delusions, willful ignorance, and institutionalized violence that history has probably ever seen. They had no concept of Practice, of transference, of connection, or of sufficiency. Their idea of a good life was to consume as much as possible. Their technology changed the whole world. They even tried to make material consumption satisfy non-material needs, which really pushed them over the edge. They wolfed through resources and polluted like there was no tomorrow—which very nearly turned out to be true, except for the Opening…"

"The Opening?" Jaeger looked blank.

"Even more confusing, eh?"

Jaeger nodded.

"Well, those were confusing times." Bowen sighed, and went on. "The material economy of the day was making such an impact on the land and the oceans that some people feared that nature would collapse and take down the economy too. But that didn't happen."

"What did happen?"

"The economy collapsed first. It simply blew itself apart under the strain of what it demanded from people, and from nature, and the sheer psychopathy of the people in charge. We still debate the details of how this happened even now—at least us historians. The Ruination is an event that we remember today with both sorrow and gratitude. We call it the Opening. We mark the beginning of the Euterran Age from that time. Of course the economic collapse was horrible. Many people suffered and many died in all the chaos that followed. But ironically, when the economy stalled, the environment was saved, the collapse of which would have been even worse. It would have meant our extinction. But instead a window of opportunity opened through which some part of humanity could escape the extinction event that was certainly in the cards if we just carried on with business as usual. It opened the way for the Emergence."

"Business as usual?" Jaeger asked.

"Yes, business. While everyone contributed to the Ruination, it was mostly caused by corporations—organizations created to make money, which was called 'business.'"

Jaeger pondered this, then nodded. "Like the Brotherhood," he said.

Bowen's attention was suddenly riveted: "*What did you say?*"

CHAPTER 23

SUMMER 2027 C.E.

Nature tinkers up whatever may be possible from what it has at hand. It looks within itself for what it needs. In the process it becomes more, and changes what it is becoming. It changes while staying the same. Thus in turn more is provided with which to tinker. This is never-ending.

— THE BOOK OF ELEMENTS

JAKO EMERGED from the Dawngate Lift, a cage barely two metres in diameter, but an immense improvement in comfort and convenience compared to scaling Starsis Massif while packing in everything they needed on their backs. Behind him the lift was jammed full of cartons of books, the gleanings from a university library that had been the goal of their most recent expedition. It had taken them nearly a year to bore from the top of the Massif to the bottom, creating the first lift shaft. It connected to their first ground level gate which they christened 'Dawngate' because it was on the eastern edge of the Massif—and because Laurel thought it sounded poetic—though it resembled a cave mouth more than a gate.

"How'd it go?" she asked.

"Routine," said Jako as he started lugging the cartons out of the lift cage. "Which is fine with me. But I thought apocalypse would be, you know, more exciting—more like Mad Max. We didn't see anybody. It's kind of creepy really. Apart from that horrendous stink in the city for the first month or two, we haven't run into much that doesn't resemble a ghost town, like people just got up and left."

"Maybe they did."

"Doubtful," said Jako. "We haven't gone poking around in many houses or apartments yet, but I imagine a lot of people are still there. Some got sick.

Some maybe got killed by foragers. A lot probably just died without their medication, or from the heat, or bad water, or something. How many ways are there to die? I'm sort of glad we're not running into anyone now because if we did, they'd be survivors and they'd probably be pretty mean."

"Like us?" Laurel quipped.

Jako puffed out his chest. "Yeah," he said. "Like us. Or like me anyway. You're not mean."

"Don't cross me," she said. "Besides, I don't think you have to be mean to survive. You have to be mean to hurt other people, but not to survive."

"Unless hurting other people is *how* you survive."

"But that can't be true. It's too Hollywood."

"You just don't want it to be true." Jako sounded resigned.

"No," Laurel insisted. "Think it through. If you survive by killing other people, then you wind up killing off all the cooperative, peaceable people. In the long run then, the only people left would be those who go around killing other people. They'd probably wind up shooting first and talking later. We'd become more and more dangerous to each other. Not a very good survival plan."

"Which history shows," said Jako.

"But that's only true in a limited sense for a few cases and a few especially vicious people. Vicious people can only survive if there are more non-vicious people around who they can exploit and who comply with what they demand. We can't survive alone. We certainly can't flourish alone."

"Well," Jako conceded, "maybe. But I was in the Black Watch, the Royal Highland Regiment—and know this: If you have a carrot and someone else has an AK-47, pretty soon he'll have your carrot *and* his AK-47 too."

"But you can't grow carrots with an AK-47," Laurel retorted.

"Right. Brilliant." He decided to change the subject. "So how are we doing for space?"

Laurel surveyed the growing stack of cartons. "Well, once we get this stuff processed and put away, we have room for maybe ten thousand more. Then we'll either have to let the rest go, or else start working on another drift."

"But we need other stuff too," said Jako. "I'm amazed everyone has agreed to invest so much work in the library. We still need wire rope, and more glass, and tools, and more of everything."

Laurel was unfazed. "We need more of what we need, not more of *everything*. We need what we need to make a good life, not to jam ourselves full of every imaginable thing we can remember from the way we used to live. Most of it was crap anyway. We're going to be just fine. You'll see."

"I wish I had your confidence," Jako said.

"It's not confidence we need," she said. "We need a vision. Just picture it, Jako. Right here, carved into this rock—a massive library with all our books in it, and learning places, and public lecture halls and performance spaces, and maybe laboratories where we do science again, and maybe temples or something, all built in, right here, in this great big rock. And there is sun everywhere and flowers and trees worked in somehow, and people everywhere who are mentally and emotionally and artistically alive—not paid scholars and professional performers, but everyone—everyone doing something. It would be a place of light, of enlightenment, maybe…" Laurel looked as if she had just stumbled upon the answer to everything. "That's what we could call it: the Siderium!" she burst out. "Sidereal is stuff to do with stars, isn't it?"

"You know," Jako said, ignoring her outburst, "they're not making any more of that stuff called diesel that makes the trucks go. When our little hoard is gone, it's gone. And even if we had as much fuel as we want, we would still need parts for the vehicles, and the last time I looked, they weren't making them anymore either."

"Which is why we have to evolve somehow," said Laurel. "We need to keep our eyes peeled for whatever way is opening. We'll have to make a life without the stuff we can no longer have, like we did before we had it. Remember?"

"No." said Jako flatly.

"Where's Ai Changming?" Laurel said, mostly to herself. "I want to talk with him about a library."

----●◆●----

The day was fine and everyone had gathered outside. Beamer was sitting on the rock outside his grotto, which had been enlarged to a much more habitable space.

"Friends," he said. "I don't see the lights coming back on—anywhere. So I guess you might call this a turning point in history—if history had points instead of moments." A chuckle rippled through the group among those who caught his dry wit. "I think this may be it for the foreseeable future," he continued. "We may be it. We may be the human story from now on, or at least until we find some other people, hopefully friendly ones. But the world feels bigger now, doesn't it." Many heads nodded.

"So here's the deal," he said. "We have to be careful from this time on and think things through. We only have a few thousand litres of fuel left, so our salvage runs have to be really carefully planned, both in what we're going after, and how we go after it. We don't have fuel for random search missions or explorations or side-trips to the spa. Every drop counts."

A man waved from the middle of the group and spoke up. "I agree," he said. "We have to be careful with fuel and everything else. But it's not necessarily accurate to say we're running out of fuel."

Beamer smiled. "You have a secret stash we don't know about? An oil well, or a refinery perhaps?"

"Well, yes. Sort of. I mean, we could make more." Heads turned abruptly.

"Make more?"

"Yeah," said the man. "We just need to build a pyrolyzer."

Beamer raised an eyebrow. "A what?"

"A pyrolyzer. It's a gizmo that breaks down organic matter—*any* organic matter—to produce biochar, which is a great fertilizer, natural gas, and a distillate pretty much the same as diesel. Certainly our vehicles could burn the stuff. Once you get it started, it's self-powering."

"And you could build something like that?" Beamer pressed.

The man nodded. "I could build you one that would fit in a wheelbarrow, but a larger one would be desirable, and even better if we had more than one."

Beamer looked around the assembly. "Friends," he said, "if we're in unity on this, I dub this man Pyrolyzer Meister."

The man waved his hand again. "Alright," he said. "Then I have to make two or three runs to the city to get what I need."

"Try to make it two," said Beamer.

"Okay," the man replied. "But then I'll need the big truck—and a dozen people to help me." A score of hands shot up across the assembly.

"Brilliant," said Beamer, smiling. "Okay then. We build a pyrolyzer—a bunch of pyrolyzers."

Gradually the group recognized itself as a community and their sense of community was embedded in the Starsis Massif where they had chosen to settle. It seemed natural therefore that they would rechristen the Massif to reflect their dreams for it and the collective project they were seeding there. Several names were suggested, but eventually the group settled on 'Euterra'--a fusion of 'eu-' meaning happy, well, healthy, and '-terra' meaning Earth. Who proposed this name was lost in the confusion of those times, but forever after the edifice they built on the Starsis Massif would be called *Euterra* and its inhabitants 'Euterrans.'

From the outset, Euterrans faced a multitude of seemingly impossible challenges, but not without serendipity now and then. While the Snake River was at first an obstacle to their access to the Massif from the east, they later realized it delivered nearly limitless fresh water to their doorstep plus it acted like a moat on their northern and eastern flanks. Several settlers turned out to possess engineering skills which proved to be invaluable. In addition to enabling Ai Changming to realize his architectural vision for their settlement, they also found a way during their second year in the Massif to tunnel a spillway and tailrace to the Snake and install a small turbine generator. The power from this, while used at night mostly for lighting, could be seconded during the day to operate compressors and pneumatic drills that greatly speeded the construction of Euterra's first drifts.

In the early years of the Ruination, the settlers of Euterra were sorely pressed for food and very tempted to cultivate the top of the Massif. But wishing to remain more or less hidden during this time of crisis, and concerned about the legacy they might leave to future generations of beauty and unspoiled wilderness, they restrained themselves from harvesting the forest on the mountain. Again, luckily, some among them were knowledgeable of wild foods and how to catch fish from the river and the loch. When their numbers were still relatively small, browsing food from wild sources provided some basis for their living. Added to this were collection parties to nearby towns which were sometimes successful but usually dangerous and unproductive. When one looked closely at the mounds of things that jammed houses and stores, hardly any of it was useful in actually making a living. Nevertheless, enough food was secured over the first few years to allow the permaculturalists to start designing food forests. And so it was that with each year their production increased and life gradually became more tolerable, and eventually abundant.

The way of life that was emerging in the mountain was scrupulously frugal and conserving of everything. Rebuilding the consumer society of the past appeared increasingly ludicrous if not impossible. All organics that couldn't be composted were pyrolyzed for gas, biochar and distillate. Crop residues and dead fall from tree pruning were shredded and added to methane digesters that produced yet more gas and high value compost. A craft culture was reborn that either recalled or redeveloped all manner of hand tool manufactures using natural materials and salvage from pre-Ruination landfills. And any materials that were brought to the Massif were scrupulously recycled again and again.

Of all the materials the early Euterrans collected from pre-Ruination cities, the most prized was plate glass, with synthetic rubber being a close second. Requiring large, specialized machinery and enormous quantities of materials and energy, making glass in large sheets was well beyond the abilities of early Euterrans. But glass was essential to building cells and common room spaces for the Dans that could be heated passively from the sun. The Massif itself provided an enormous heat sink that moderated fluctuations in temperature both over the course of a day and seasonally. But a truly comfortable space that was completely solar heated and cooled required a double wall of plate glass. Fortunately, a great deal of this material was available in pre-Ruination architecture and many collection trips were organized to secure it.

So by degrees, Euterrans made a life where they found themselves coming to know their place and its possibilities in changing times with more and more intimacy. Nothing was easy, but it did become easier with each year, and each generation.

CHAPTER 24

SUMMER, THE 276TH YEAR OF THE EUTERRAN AGE (E.A.)

When undertaking a hazardous errand nothing is gained
by hesitation. It is best simply to charge right in, like a wild
animal. More often than not you will be successful. There
is regret only in not having died on your own terms.

— THE BOOK OF PRACTICE

OTIS BEDE SECURED a spinner and quit Euterra by the Dawngate, passed over the Dawngate Bridge and headed east. He was a powerful cyclist and the East Road was well paved for nearly a full day's ride to the east. All of this land had been permacultured for years. Side roads struck off to both the south and north leading to small settlements of Permies and Guilds in the countryside. The East Road meandered in its course passing around ancient peat bogs, small lakes, rock outcrops and other features of less certain origin or consequence. Otis knew that the land eastward also contained old landfill sites belching methane that could explode without warning, mine sumps full of toxic tailings and water, and even the remains of pre-Ruination towns that offered opportunities as well as many risks. But most of these were beyond the Thornway, a hedge designed by the Permies encircling Euterran lands and made of various species of thorn bushes and shrubs with an understory of toxic ivies and gooseberry brakes. The Thornway was a full kilometre thick and ran for hundreds of kilometres both to the north and south. It had been planted over two centuries before, when Euterrans felt more of a sense of threat from pre-Ruination remnant groups. Its effect was to passively funnel travellers of any species toward the East Watch where notice could be taken of their arrival.

Despite the fact that Otis had departed Euterra at first light and pedalled hard all day, it was early evening before he reached the Thornway. The road was overarched by vegetation and its pavement narrowed to a single lane going into the Thornway. When he at last reached the East Limit, the pavement ended at a path of hard-packed earth that plunged onward into a dense forest of spruce, fir and pine, but was also in many places festooned with kudzu vines. Nothing but wilderness lay beyond the East "Limit" as far as anyone knew, but psychological boundaries persisted and filled some ancient need. Practically the only people passing beyond the East Limit or the Thornway were surveyors or Tarshin-ru.

There was a small clearing where the Thornway ended with a shelter covering a dozen spinners carefully racked up out of the elements. Otis stowed his spinner, then noticed beside the path a slender cord leading up into a tree with a paper tag attached to its end. It read: "Safe travel friend Otis Bede." He untied the line which had been used to tree a cache of food, his last supper before leaving Euterran territory. He smiled at the generosity of his benefactors, those who stood the East Watch, but who neither he, nor anyone, would ever see unless at greatest need. Their part was to see, not to be seen. He knew they were watching him, and that even now news that he was passing the East Limit was on its way back to the Siderium.

Otis settled down to eat his supper, and as deeper shadows filled the forest beyond, he found himself a rude sleeping place to pass the night.

He awakened with the dawn chorus of the birds which commenced shortly before sunrise. A mist had risen overnight in the forest, leaving it dew-soaked and dripping. He made a scant breakfast from the remainders of his evening meal, and rummaged in his packsack for the forest coat he would use during travel. The garment looked terrible, consisting of shreds of cloth and dreadlocks of kudzu, hemp and alpaca fibre dyed the colour of the forest understory. Wearing a forest coat, a motionless person was effectively invisible, and even someone moving about would be hard to distinguish from the woodland background. Even in water he would appear to be a floating mat of vegetation.

On his last journey, he had travelled eastward for over three weeks. But that had been a survey assignment which required that he measure distances, memorize features and species assemblages, memorize the locations and assess the risks associated with ruins, toxic sites or other artifacts from the Ruination, and of course, note the location, size and level of development of other human groups in the region, all of which he had to do without making his presence known. Such surveys required that he pick his way along, committing to memory every detail of the landscapes he passed through. Of particularly interesting plants or animals, he might take samples or seeds. But his main task was to rebuild knowledge of the regional geography which had again become unknown territory following the Ruination, the Great Forgetting and several generations with more urgent priorities than knowledge of geography.

This time, however, he could make faster headway. His training as a surveyor had for its foundation his natural curiosity and practiced attention to detail, habits he must now consciously suppress as they would only slow him down, at least until he reached the place where he found Jaeger.

Otis set off down the path hoping to make good time as far as possible before it was necessary to plunge into the bush going cross-country. The path itself remained arm's width for only a few kilometres past the East Watch, narrowing down to little more than a boar track beyond that. From there on, the highways offered by the woodland were those created by animals, and they had their own agendas which didn't necessarily include heading steadily east. He had to take advantage of the animal trails when they suited his purpose, and then break way on his own when they didn't, cutting back-sight blazes all the way. All of this was laborious.

He knew from records of past surveys and old maps of the region that another day's march east there was a very large marshland as the contour of the land lost elevation in that direction following the watershed of Loch Speare. This he planned to bypass by navigating more to the north since the marsh in that direction was bordered by a wooded upland. The upland offered easier going than marsh grass and bulrushes, which would require him to break trail. During his second day, he made fair time until the land started its descent toward the wetland where he turned slightly north, keeping to higher ground. Nevertheless, he had to cross little valleys between the hills that were wetter than the upland terrain. At one point he changed course even more as he stepped in quicksand near the bottom of one hill, a feature that would have swallowed him whole had he tried to keep going that way. But before becoming too mired in it, he slogged his way out, lucky to keep his boots.

Otis kept a weather eye peeled for sheltered places to sleep. This entailed finding spots with dense overhead protection, not mere cover from the wind. Climate warming was now well past two degrees Celsius and with it came a much strengthened water cycle. Rains could be torrential—lasting days at a time. Especially in summer, when storms could bring hailstones as big as a man's fist with bruising and sometimes lethal results. Permies were constantly on the lookout for more weather tolerant trees and crop cultivars. As many surveys were launched these days in search of those precious food resources as from any mere geographical curiosity. But his immediate challenge of finding sleeping places was also complicated by the fact that other creatures sought them too. Finding a congenial place to bed down might also include evicting an existing occupant, or fending off later arrivals who thought they might lay a claim. Seasoning this competition was the fact that in these parts, humans were not at the top of the food chain.

He pressed on through this country for another two days before reaching the eastern extent of the marshland, garlanded by purple loosestrife. Farther to the east the land rose into the rock-strewn, hilly terrain of the ancient boreal forest it had once been. Given his rate of travel, Otis guessed he was still less than three hundred kilometres east of Euterra. Near dusk on his fifth day abroad, he reflected that the journey had been in every way routine, when downslope from where he planned to sleep for the night came the sound of screaming.

CHAPTER 25

SUMMER, THE 276TH YEAR OF THE EUTERRAN AGE (E.A.)

*One of the greatest advances in education and research
achieved by the first Euterrans was the abolition of schools.
Instead of basing education on institutions, Euterrans
based it on relationships between mentors and mentees.
The task of credentialing people to perform specific social
or economic functions was delegated to other bodies.*

— THE BOOK OF MEMORY

JAEGER AND LYDIA busied themselves with cleaning up the cooking utensils from the morning meal in Mizar Dan. Everyone in the Dan had an earthenware bowl, small plate, mug, and an eating utensil that combined the features of a spoon and a fork. Everyone washed their own utensils, with the exception of the cooking pots, which was a job that circulated weekly among the members of the Dan old enough and able enough to perform the task. Even Oma Jessie did her shift.

"So, how did you find Practice?" Lydia asked.

Jaeger smiled. "Spark's a very enthusiastic guide."

"Yes," said Lydia, raising an eyebrow. "She usually lights a fire around here. Growing up fast..."

"Does everyone in Euterra do Practice?" Jaeger asked.

"Most people do," Lydia replied. "We all learn Practice from an early age— as soon as children can sit still for five minutes or so, they begin Practice. Every day in Euterra starts and ends with Practice, as you've seen."

"Why do you do it?"

"Well, to appreciate that, you need to pursue it for more than a few days. We learned from our history that before the Ruination, Practice wasn't done by everyone. In fact, it was only something a few people did. Our Telders think it was one cause of the Ruination. People in those days had no centre. They didn't know who they were, why they were here, what they were supposed to do in this life. They had no insight into desire or other mental states. Lacking respect for their centre, to say nothing of the Central Harmony, they were directionless and lost—like arrows without feathers. They possessed great power but little wisdom and so they destroyed themselves. It must have been horrid!" She shuddered. "They nearly destroyed any chance for their children as well. Beamer Farris could see the Ruination coming and he brought the first Euterrans to this place. He knew some Practice. He urged everyone who came here to Practice. It was one of the first things we did together. It was why we built Siderium. All people need help remembering what's important. Practice helps us do that. Without it, we would probably eventually go insane, like the people before the Ruination."

"So Practice is the first law of Euterra, and all of you are followers of this Beamer Farris?" Jaeger asked.

"Not at all," Lydia said, chuckling. "We're friends of Beamer Farris, not his followers. And we have no laws in Euterra—at least not with the meaning that word had long ago. Practice can't be legislated. But Practice is sweet. Most of us discover that sweetness immediately. One taste and very few people choose to leave it aside again. It'd be like giving up honey to chew on ashes and sand instead. No one is forced to Practice. But anyone who's learned Practice understands that stopping Practice would be like throwing yourself off the Massif. Why would you do it? Nevertheless, a few people are lazy and some think they can live without Practice—at least until they discover they can't."

"When Spark took me to meet Nota Dorne, we passed through a garden she called Laurel's Garden," said Jaeger. "In it was an object she called 'Fey's Table.' She said it *was* Practice—sort of. What did she mean?"

Lydia pondered for a moment. "Hmm," she said. "Spark is precocious, and it's hard to know sometimes what she means when she says things like that. Practice is everything to us. It's the foundation for our way of life. If you were to make a physical model representing Practice, it would be Fey's Table. Maybe that's what she meant."

"But what does that mean?" Jaeger's voice belied his struggle to understand.

Lydia took a deep breath. "Well, Laurel Fey wanted to make a physical object that would help people understand a different way of life from that of the pre-Ruination world. She wanted this object to both reveal and help us remember whatever we knew about what makes for a good life—not just material riches, which was the main obsession of pre-Ruination societies. Not only that, but she wanted her Table to be continually transformed by future generations of Euterrans as we discovered and proved more and more about what made for a good life. The model you saw in the garden is our current best understanding of how to be happy and well both in relation to each other and to the Earth. But when we discover something new, we add a block to the model. Or maybe we find an easier or more direct way to achieve the same result if we take out a piece, combine pieces, substitute others or change some aspect of the structure. Fey's Table has eleven times more elements in it than when she first built it, all discovered and added by later contributors. Everything about it is important—how cells are grouped, their relations to each other, the interactions among them, the order in which a person engages in the practices the cells represent. It's a work of genius, actually."

Jaeger made no immediate response, pondering what Lydia said. Then he said, "One other thing. There's a fluid or something running around inside the model. Spark said it was power. What does that mean?"

Lydia cocked her head slightly. "Well that's a bit harder to explain. From early days we noticed that certain practices strengthened other practices or made them easier—like they were linked somehow in these self-reinforcing loops. Then about a century after Laurel Fey, another Telder and researcher named Barqua San Martino suggested that the Table be thought of in terms of energy relationships as well as personal or social practices—or in other words, that as a result of linking practices in certain ways, it was as if an energy of well-being was amplified in a person's life. It didn't necessarily mean that the energy became stronger, exactly, but that it stabilized and steadied. San Martino also thought that it might be possible to channel this energy to specific tasks, or to amplify it in collaboration with others—though this has not yet been proven."

"Like boiling water," Jaeger said.

"What did you say?"

Jaeger shook his head. He felt that he might be probing something off limits to foundlings. "Nothing, really." Changing the subject, he asked, "And the Siderium is your school?"

"Interesting that you use that word," Lydia said. "'School.' That's a very old word."

"That's what Lars said when I talked about work," said Jaeger.

"Ah, yes, indeed. That too is a word we seldom use anymore. The Siderium is one place we learn things, yes. But our Telders say that before the Ruination, most children were kept locked up in places they called 'schools.' In some schools they were subject to every sort of regimentation while in others there was absolute chaos. We have nothing similar in Euterra."

"So how are children educated?"

"We use the Skills and Knowledge Exchange—the SKE. We have many mentors and tutors who help others learn what they want to know about various subjects. Anyone of any age can go to Siderium and get the SKElist for whatever they want to learn, if one is required. The Siderium sets the SKElist for all knowledge areas that require licensing. Everyone, regardless of age, is free to learn whatever they like, from whomever will tutor them, at whatever pace is congenial and at whatever time they find agreeable, until they've mastered the SKElist. Of course not all learning is individual—some things are best learned in groups. And not all subjects have SKElists, so learners and mentors can do what they wish. There are many such subjects. But when someone's Active Practice affects the welfare of other beings, such as being a Helder or a Permie, we expect people to master certain skills and knowledge before undertaking that Practice. For these activities, there are SKElists. For other things like art history or poetry, there are no SKElists."

Lydia paused, then asked, "Do you have schools in Mainbranch?"

Jaeger's gaze became distant again as he searched for words. "Yes," he said tentatively. "I suppose you would call them that. We have boot camps. Citizen's children in Mainbranch stay in boot camps, at least the children that are allowed. They can't be running loose everywhere. They learn only what they need for their jobs. Anything more is inefficient."

"But who makes up your SKElists?"

"We don't have SKElists. The Brotherhood decides everything. The Brotherhood picks the children for the jobs the Brotherhood wants done."

Lydia sensed again the strangeness of this man, this foundling. He seemed detached, distant, beyond merely being a newcomer to Euterran culture. She wondered if this was an effect of his near death experience in the bush, or a longstanding trait.

"So what sorts of Active Practice do people do in Mainbranch?"

"Only Citizens work," Jaeger replied. "The Brotherhood 'manages.' Citizens' work and work. Citizens grow food, recycle, go raiding, keep accounts—accounts are very important—the Brotherhood wants good accounts. Who manages Euterra?"

Given Jaeger's past experience, Lydia wondered what sense he would make of any answer she could offer to his question, but perhaps he would understand later on. How does one make sense of a foreign language when immersed in it for the first time? One just does, somehow.

"How Euterra is managed is rather like how we manage the Dans. Everyone is in charge and no one is in charge. We have the Dan Councils which are meetings of all the members of one Dan. The Dan Councils send someone to represent their Dan on Drift Councils that are made up of all the Dans on the same drift. Some are bigger and others smaller, but all their voices are equal in Council. The Drift Councils send representatives to the Euterran General Assembly. At every level, we meet for clearness on whatever must be decided or done and we don't act until we have both clearness and unity. Sometimes this can take a long time, but everyone is included in some way."

"And the Lightminders?" Jaeger interjected, remembering the conversation he overheard in Fogg's Inn.

"Until you've deepened in Practice," Lydia said, "that might be harder to understand. The Lightminders sit *within* the General Assembly, not *above* it. Some Assembly members might be Lightminders themselves, but most are not. The Lightminders' special charge is to discern way opening on any question before the Assembly but also to introduce matters to the Assembly that may arise from their Practice. All Euterrans are encouraged to Practice and members of the Assembly are no exception. We want to bring the fruits of Practice into all our decisions and be guided in those decisions by the light that Practice provides. But Lightminders perform this errand with special discipline. Another way to think of it is to imagine the Lightminders are an *organ* in a larger body. You might even think of them as eyes of a special sort—eyes that see inwardly. Without them, we would be running into things we ought to avoid, or we might fail to act or refrain from acting, depending on the circumstances."

"So the Assembly makes your laws?" Jaeger asked.

"Ha!" Lydia smiled. "There's another of those old words again. Where did you hear it?"

Jaeger shrugged. "In Mainbranch. The Brotherhood makes many, many laws in Mainbranch."

"I see," said Lydia. "Well, I suppose if we needed laws in Euterra, it would be the Assembly that would make them. But soon after the Ruination, when we ended private property, we also discovered we didn't really need very many laws. Almost all laws were about property rights. No property, no need for laws."

"But what if someone steals something?"

"Why would they do that?" Lydia asked. "Anything can be got by asking your Cellarer for it, getting it from a library, or going to a General Store. Why would anyone steal something they can have just by asking? It's pretty much the same with what used to be called the laws of copyright, of patents, of wills and estates, of trespass, of vandalism, of all forms of burglary and robbery, almost all family law, certainly corporate law and that of contracts, and so on. They're all about property. We *do* have laws against personal violence, but conflict over property in one form or another used to be the main cause of such violence, so we see such acts only very rarely—and Practice is a huge help as well. We also have strong customs—I'm not sure you would call them 'laws'— around licensing various sorts of Active Practice that require SKElists."

Jaeger was sunk in thought for several moments, revealing little, if anything, about how much of what Lydia described made sense to him. Then he looked up suddenly, riveting his gaze on her. "Lydia!" he said, his voice dropping to a panicky whisper. "The Brotherhood is dangerous," he said, pleadingly, clearly needing her to understand something he could barely articulate.

"Dangerous to whom?" she asked.

"To Euterra," Jaeger said. "To everyone."

"Dangerous how?"

"If the Brotherhood finds out about Euterra, they'll come here. They'll come and…" his voice trailed off as if the effort to express himself through his anxiety was simply too great.

"Is the Brotherhood looking for us?" she asked.

Jaeger's eyes continued to dart around anxiously. "The Brotherhood is always looking," he said. "But I don't think they know about Euterra—yet."

Lydia reached for his hand and held it firmly. "Jaeger," she said, waiting until she had eye contact. "You're safe here. Euterra is very great. No one will harm you here." She could feel the tension in Jaeger's body slowly draining away as he let himself accept her reassurance.

At length he said, "You're very kind to me. I don't want danger to come here."

"Of course not," said Lydia, "and we won't let that happen, will we?" Jaeger gazed back, dubious, but willing to accept her resolve for the moment.

For her part, Lydia's only thought was for Otis.

CHAPTER 26

SUMMER, THE 276TH YEAR OF THE EUTERRAN AGE (E.A.)

A near universal delusion of the pre-Ruination era was that "reality" was an objectively existing set of conditions and relationships independent from the human perception of them. It was only discovered much later that reality is a function of social relationships which are in turn a function of consciousness. Change the focal length of consciousness which is constitutive of social relationships and reality itself is changed.

— THE BOOK OF PRACTICE

AGAINST ALL ODDS, one of the buildings that had been conserved in Mainbranch was a sports stadium. If the HQ was the brain of Mainbranch, then Metro Stadium was its heart. As was often the case in Mainbranch, the origins of the names of places or structures had been lost. No one knew who, or what, a "Metro" was. It had always been called that and it survived for want of a better name. Even in times of direst need, the Brotherhood somehow kept the stadium operating. Citizens and the Brotherhood alike came in their numbers to whatever might be offered—sporting events, public executions, and most especially, Promotions. Attendance at Promotions was particularly good. They were, after all, required for all Citizens and everyone except the ill or the aged infirm who had not already been sent away to new opportunities. Despite the modest size of the HQ, and despite the few hundred Brotherhood who attended any one Promotion, it was widely believed among Citizens that the Brotherhood vastly outnumbered them. Somewhere there were millions of them, or so it was believed. Citizens were given to appreciate the fact that some of the Brotherhood tore themselves away from their vital work on behalf of Mainbranch to attend Promotions with Citizens in the spirit of teamwork.

So it was that on this day Citizen Fitz found himself caught up in the flow of people, mostly other Citizens, who were filling the stadium. The Brotherhood, for their part, had exclusive sections in the stadium and segregated passageways to reach them. For this Promotion, as usual, a sizeable stage had been set up at the centre of the stadium with a podium and sound system in place. It was rumoured that the Chief might even be in attendance. Fitz let himself be carried along as the stream of bodies passed through a portal into the stadium proper, then along an aisle to a row of seats which filled until the movement of people stopped and everyone sat down. The Brotherhood cadets, distinguishable by their insignia, badges and uniforms, jostled through the crowds passing out armloads of small pennants affixed to short sticks specially made to be of no use as weapons. Most Citizens accepted these trinkets without notice or comment. It was expected that they should have them and expected that they should wave them at the appointed times. While there was a certain energy present in the sheer mass of people, it contained no quality of anticipation or levity.

Presently, the sound of drumming came from the stage as a number of people made their way onto it. Leading them was an elaborately garbed figure that everyone recognized as the Chief, but almost no one knew by name. Behind him several members of the Commission found their seats, while behind them, there appeared a considerable entourage of almost a hundred others, some of them Brotherhood and some Citizens. As the drums pounded on, a dozen minimally-clad young women ran out to the stage apron to perform an attention-grabbing gymnastic display. This performance provided a distraction from the cuing and shuffling that was happening on stage as people found their assigned seats in the pecking order. When things finally settled down, the cheerleaders romped off stage as they had come on, and an imposing-looking figure stepped up to the mic. Even from this distance, Fitz could see it was the Expediter, Axel Caine.

At first Caine stood mute in front of the mic, clearly waiting for the gravity of his glaring countenance to quiet the crowd, which it did in due course.

"Chief!" Caine growled into the mic, then sweeping his arm vaguely rearward, boomed, "trusted Commissioners, esteemed Brotherhood, Citizens, visitors and friends!" Fitz wondered briefly who might be a visitor or a friend? But before he could weigh this possibility, Caine continued: "Welcome to our two-hundred and fifty-seventh Promotion. It is my special privilege and pleasure today to introduce His Excellency, Trustee and Protector, Benefactor and Leader of Mainbranch—the Chief!" The Chief stepped forward from his seat at the centre of the front row on stage and extended his hand to Caine as he approached the podium. They shook hands and Caine surrendered the podium with a shallow bow. Anemic applause issued from the crowd.

The Chief waved perfunctorily at the mass that filled the stadium, then spread his arms wide to grip both sides of the podium. His ropey arms left no doubt that he was the person in charge and graced the crowd by generously sharing his precious time.

"Esteemed Commissioners," he started, "Brotherhood and Citizens. Welcome! It's my pleasure to officiate today the many sacred duties that lie before us." He actually did sound like he was enjoying himself, which Fitz found puzzling, perhaps even incredible. "We have quite an agenda here," the Chief continued, looking down at some document on the podium, "so without further delay…"

First he called up about twenty of the Brotherhood cadet graduates who formed a cue to his right and filed past one by one as the Chief called their names. They were already garbed in the grey Brotherhood uniform, but in this ceremony they received cranberry-coloured berets which completed the uniform and made it official. Then they were pinned with a badge which made them official Protectors and Order-keepers of Mainbranch. It was seldom clear exactly what it was that they protected Mainbranch from, since it had been years since they had last recycled another settlement and generations since anyone might mount a credible attack on Mainbranch itself. Nevertheless, Fitz supposed they were essential to the collective security as rumours were constantly circulating about threats gathering at their borders, or even within Mainbranch itself. It was particularly the threat from within that the Brotherhood repeated with such regularity, especially among the Citizens.

Following the cadets' investiture, the Chief called to the stage individuals and small groups who were being recognized in some way for signal contributions to Mainbranch. Nearly all of these people were Citizens, not the Brotherhood. It was said that the Brotherhood held their own special ceremonies in private on other occasions. But Promotions were occasions when rank and file Citizens were in the limelight.

There was an extraction team awarded for their work in recycling more material from the landfill mining face than any other extraction team that year. For this they were all given breeding licences to pick any woman they wished from Citizen ranks and to whom they would have exclusive access until a child was produced. In previous years, this had been a particularly coveted prize during Promotions and it continued to be so, judging from the hoots and applause from the crowd.

Next, the Chief handed out posthumous Orders of Loyalty and Obedience to the widows of eleven extraction team workers who had been asphyxiated in a methane pocket, also in a landfill, when their Foreman ordered them into a pocket in the mine face that everyone deemed hazardous. In the best Citizen tradition, the extraction team had soldiered forward, ignoring personal risk for the greater prosperity of Mainbranch.

Of course members of the business sector, most of them Brotherhood or Citizen collaborators with the Brotherhood, received Creative Destruction Awards. With these awards the Chief took the opportunity to harp on and on about the importance of innovation, rational utility optimization, and the deft, invisible hand of the market, nearly all of which flew straight over the heads of all but a few of those assembled, though everyone could sense from the Chief's tone how very important it all was.

Between each of these presentations the cheerleaders would bolt on stage and lead the crowd in chants and cheers that everyone had learned from childhood. What started as lacklustre applause and half-hearted recitative chanting gradually built to stronger, if decidedly tribal, crowd responses. The mere presence of several thousand of one's compatriots seemed to amplify this enthusiasm, regardless of what was actually happening.

When the last awards had been conferred, most of them honorary rather than material, the Chief turned to the crowd with his arms raised high. He smiled broadly, though his eyes held no mirth. In another few minutes the crowd quieted again and the cheerleaders straggled off stage.

"Commissioners, Brotherhood and Citizens," he said. "We live in times of pride and of peril. Is this not true? Imagine with me now—" he invited, and when Fitz heard these words he felt a little thrill. It came from the mere invitation that they should imagine something together—to enter into a relationship of such intimacy with so powerful a man. Many others must have felt the same way because a hush came over the crowd like a prayer meeting.

"Imagine with me now," the Chief repeated, his tone more reflective, "our pride and our peril. You are people of wisdom; hard-working people endowed with common sense and good intentions. But just imagine my fellow Citizens"—*What boldness! What humility!* Fitz thought, *that the Chief, a leader even of the Brotherhood, should number himself among mere Citizens!* "Just imagine the possibility," the Chief went on, "that we may be the only people left on Earth." He paused again for effect. "Or maybe not. Maybe we have company out there someplace, aliens who are maybe sitting on *our* Motherlode. Both thoughts are disturbing, aren't they? Is this not true?" Several heads began to nod, first among the Brotherhood on stage, then in the crowd more generally.

"Peril and pride, my fellow Citizens, my brothers and sisters. But of what can we be justifiably proud? And how are these perilous times?"

The Chief shook his head in mild amazement, as if his next comments should be obvious to all. "I'm proud of all of *you!*" the Chief bellowed, setting the PA system squealing. "I'm proud of you. Our life here is not easy, god knows. But you labour on, day and night, because you believe, with me, that better times are coming." There was a rustle of expectation in the crowd. Was the Chief going to announce that the Motherlode had been found at last? "Better times are coming," he repeated. "They have to because we have our best Brains searching for the Motherlode and we know, we just *know*, that someday we'll find it." The crowd deflated slightly. "And then it'll be like the Great Recession never happened. Everything will get back to normal. We'll all be millionaires again just like the folks before the Recession. We'll have big houses and, and all *that*." Apparently the Chief couldn't be specific. "They could even fly when they wanted," he said, extending his arms, winglike, in the air. A gasp shuddered through the crowd. "Yes, my fellow Citizens, they flew, whenever they liked, almost like birds. Our Brains have told me that. And we too will fly, and have fine clothes, and eat meat at every meal. And this is coming, my fellow Citizens. I can feel it as sure as the rain. And it makes me so proud of you that you too believe. You too keep this faith, this dream alive, the only dream we need, the only dream we can have." A few in the audience shifted uncomfortably in their seats as they sensed this oblique reference to the doings with Jaeger. But the matter had become unmentionable in public and especially within earshot of any of the Brotherhood.

"So I'm proud of these things and you should be too. We're making it in tough times. We have new business ideas every week. Every week brave Citizens go on recon missions looking for the Motherlode and we know that someday, somehow, we'll find it. We'll find it because we *believe* we can. And what we believe we can do *will* happen, my fellow Citizens. We fully expect that our economy will start growing again real soon and when it does, there'll be bonuses for everybody—Citizens and Brotherhood alike." A sound rumbled through the crowd that mingled applause and cheers, but it soon died. This was a speech they had heard many times before in several variations. Today, Fitz thought, the Chief was especially animated, conveying a quality of expectation that wasn't always a feature of his speeches.

"But what about our peril?" the Chief said, his tone suddenly turning dark. "What could possibly menace such a great people—such a great city? Could it be aliens? Could menace come from them? Well, let me tell you my fellow Citizens, we've found many aliens in the past and we've recycled all of them!" He slammed his fist on the podium sending a thunderous rumble through the PA system. When the rumbling stopped, his voice became steely and subdued: "And if we find any more of them, we'll recycle them too, especially if they're sitting on *our* Motherlode!" Applause erupted from the stands and the Chief waved them off in humble dismissal.

"No, my good people. I don't think aliens could be our problem. As I said before, maybe we're alone, and maybe we're not. But I think we're alone. We may discover new landfills and recycling opportunities—probably will—but I don't think we'll find other people. Aliens get scarcer every year. If we do find some, I feel pretty sure there won't be many. So basically we're it, and this is as good as it gets. So where could peril come from then?" He let the question hang ominously until finally adding "From us," in a revelatory tone. Once again people shifted uneasily in their seats, a few looking at each other.

"Yes, from us," the Chief repeated. "We've met all our challenges and over-come them all. The result is this great city we share. What has made all this possible is our common belief and our single dream—our dream of a future of peace and prosperity. It's the only dream we need. It's the dream rooted in our human nature. It's natural to want more, to strive more, to overcome opposi-tion and resistance, to meet all challengers with courage and determination. These are enviable qualities in a people. Nothing from outside us can prevail against them. And believe me fellow Citizens, we have the power to crack the skulls of anybody who opposes us."

"So the peril, you see, can only come from within, from among us. If we stop believing in our dream, if we believe instead in strange dreams from peo-ple who really aren't of the same mind as we are, then our peril appears. If we keep it together, we have a bright future. But if we listen to alien dreams, they'll become far more dangerous to our peace, our prosperity, and our secu-rity than any real aliens could be."

The Chief paused to let his message sink in, then continued. "Of course, we all have a part to play in this. If you see anything or hear anything that sounds off the map, let us know—let my office know, through the Brotherhood in your Developments. We'll get to the bottom of it right quick and you can rest secure that Mainbranch and protecting our way of life here will be our top job."

"And let me say again how very proud I am of all of you, and how proud I am to be your Chief! That's it." The cheerleaders tumbled back on stage and started prompting the crowd for applause which rose as a slow tide, never cresting at great height, but applause nonetheless. The Chief hurried off stage and was escorted quickly into one of the passageways leading out of the stadium.

The crowd was now standing up as the drums burst to life on stage. People were making their ways toward the exits when Fitz caught sight of Dexter several rows down. Dexter looked at Fitz, then raised his eyebrows in a "how-about-that" expression. Fitz nodded without adding further nuance, but sud-denly he felt under surveillance, more than usual.

CHAPTER 27

SUMMER, THE 276TH YEAR OF THE EUTERRAN AGE (E.A.)

One of the profoundest insights at the foundation of
Euterran culture is that Nature is barking mad.

— THE APHORISMS OF TELDER BOWEN

"IT SOUNDS LIKE MAINBRANCH," Jaeger said, as he tried to absorb Bowen's description of the Ruination.

"What?" asked Bowen. "What part?"

"All the parts. People at each other's throats, scavenging for stuff, killing people, fear, the Brotherhood—crazy stuff."

"That's how you lived in Mainbranch?"

Jaeger nodded: "I couldn't see it while I was living there," he said. "But I can see it now, since coming to Euterra. I didn't know there was any other way to live than being a skrala, than working for the Brotherhood. But now I know differently. My dream was real."

"Your dream?" Bowen asked.

"I had a dream—before my Retirement Party took me to new opportunities. I dreamed the arena where we play sports and all the Citizens were there and the Chief too."

"The Chief?"

"Yes," Jaeger said. "The Chief is top dog, alpha male, big shot, for the Brotherhood. Everybody does what the Chief says. He takes care of us, manages—things. He grows our economy. We must always grow or else we'll die." Jaeger seemed distracted, falling back into memories that tightened his body, masked his face. He looked up at Bowen, and gave a little start as if coming back to the present. "In my dream," he resumed, "the Chief was hollering at all the Citizens and we were smiling and nodding. Then one, and then another, stopped nodding." Jaeger's voice quivered, his eyes welling up. "One after another, we stopped nodding, stopped smiling at the Chief. We just *stopped*." Jaeger's expression pleaded with Bowen to grasp the significance of this image.

"And what did that mean to you?" Bowen asked. "That all the Citizens stopped nodding and smiling?"

"The Chief turned to smoke," Jaeger said, slapping his palm on the table top, testifying to a miracle.

"Turned to smoke?"

"Yes, smoke. Citizens can be free, if we just stop nodding and smiling." Jaeger sounded like he had just discovered some new law of nature, or a divine revelation, the significance of which was lost on Bowen.

"Well yes," Bowen said, trying to sound like he understood. "I guess that would happen, wouldn't it."

Jaeger looked lost in thought. Bowen raised two more fingers to the inn-keeper who reached for more glasses for another round of mead.

Surfacing again from his memories, Jaeger asked, "How did all this happen?"

"All this?"

"Yes—all this that happened to us, to people. How did this happen?"

"It happened," said Bowen matter-of-factly, "because we behaved naturally."

"Naturally?"

"Yes."

"You mean we nearly went extinct just by doing what comes naturally?"

"More or less," said Bowen. "Think about it. All species survive by feeding and breeding. Those that feed and breed most tend to leave more offspring. If there ever was a species with no taste for feeding and breeding, probably it would have left fewer offspring and would soon have disappeared. So, for a long time, nature has been selecting for creatures that feed and breed to the limits of the food and space available. Humans appeared from this same process. So like every other species on Earth, we *naturally* want to feed and breed to the limit of what is possible. And for three billion years that worked pretty well. So well, in fact, that a lot of us came to believe that feeding and breeding was the whole point of life."

"And that's what caused the Ruination and the Great Forgetting?"

"Well, no," said Bowen, "not exactly."

Jaeger looked puzzled again.

"Along came humans," Bowen continued, "from the same evolutionary process as other species. But we had some really amazing equipment—big brains, opposable thumbs, upright walking, and culture, for example. We could do things never before seen on Earth. We could invent languages and tools and humour. We could tell ourselves stories about how amazing we were. We could even tell ourselves stories about things that didn't exist. And because we see no other species doing these things to the *degree* we could do them, we started thinking of ourselves as special, as somehow set apart. On our bad days, we thought we got kicked out of paradise because of bad choices we made. On our good days, we thought our technology exempted us from the laws of nature and we could do as we pleased. But we remained just as much a part of nature as any other species. We're animals who have to feed on other plants and animals to live. In Euterra we call this the First Cautionary Memory and we build a set of practices around it so we don't forget it—*ever*. But most important for the Ruination is that in addition to our big new brains and opposable thumbs, we kept all the old desires to feed and breed to the limit of the available resources. That is to say, we are *naturally* inclined to feed and breed ourselves to extinction."

Bowen paused, looked down into his empty glass and shook his head. Then he resumed his story. "What caused the Ruination, and opened a window for something else, were not the instincts to feed and breed, but the *combination* of those instincts and the new traits that appeared in humans for language, toolmaking, and so on. Every other species on Earth thrives to profusion if possible, but no past species has ever brought the whole planet to ruin in the process. For that you need technology, and consumer culture, and political hierarchies and an amazing bunch of truly deluded ideas packaged in really appealing stories. What caused the Ruination was human beings, behaving naturally, but to an extreme degree never before seen in nature. Consumer culture was based on the ancient habits best suited to life in the jungle, but monstrously amplified by technology and a mistaken story about what makes for a good life, until they threatened our extinction."

Jaeger pondered this, and began to shake his head.

"You doubt this?" Bowen asked.

"Are you saying that humans caused their own extinction?"

"No," Bowen said quickly. "*Nature* caused it. Humans are just part of nature, doing what nature does."

"But that's absurd!"

"Why's it absurd?"

"Because it would mean nature is suicidal—crazy," Jaeger sputtered.

Bowen shrugged. "Well, let's not pretend that nature has a personality or intentions or anything of the sort. But why do you think it's impossible that nature might contain something self-destructive? Humans are part of nature, you've already agreed. We evolved from it; we subsist only within it. People occasionally go crazy and sometimes kill themselves. So clearly, nature can be crazy, can it not? And if it can commit suicide in the case of individuals, why not collectively as well? History showed us doing a more and more thorough job of it as the technology of killing advanced."

Jaeger continued to shake his head. "I just can't accept the idea that nature is self-destructive."

"As you wish," conceded Bowen. "For centuries many people believed that nature was benign and wise—going all the way back to the Stoics. But looking back, it does seem that the way life evolved on Earth includes a self-destructive wrinkle. It became visible only when human beings appeared with our special talent for amplifying that wrinkle. This isn't because we sinned, or because we are somehow above nature, but exactly because we carry on the age-old tradition of how life works on this planet, but to an extreme degree."

"So if nature itself is crazy, you're saying there's no way people could avoid the Ruination?" Jaeger asked.

"The only way to avoid the Ruination would be to evolve *beyond* it—which we did in the Emergence—but not enough of us, nor in time, to avoid the Ruination."

Jaeger's face dropped. "But how could that be possible if nature is crazy?"

"Ha!" barked Bowen. "Good thing for us she has her lucid moments."

The innkeeper arrived at their table with the second round of mead—not counting Bowen's previous rounds. As Jaeger mulled over all that he'd heard, it continued to confound him. "First you said that the Ruination was caused by human beings behaving naturally, and that nature is crazy. Then you said nature has lucid moments. Is nature crazy or not?"

"Let's put it this way," Bowen said. "Solutions to life's problems that are common sense in one situation can become self-destructive in a different situation. That's what happened to us. When there were only a few thousand pre-humans living pretty much like other primates, following our natural instincts assured our survival just like that of other species. So the instincts for consumption, even over-consumption, were selected in us, like in other species, because early in the game it increased our chances of survival. But as I said, when these new abilities developed in us, and our numbers increased to many billions, and we spread all over the planet, then instincts that had served us well in the past became self-destructive in our new situation. And I assign the cause of that to nature, not to human beings, at least in the sense that we had any say at all in how this whole story was being written."

Jaeger still looked doubtful, so Bowen pressed on: "We humans not only felt pushed around by our ancestral instincts to feed and breed, another whole layer of trouble arose from our big brains. Not only did we feed and breed, we thought that because these activities gave us temporary pleasure, they could provide us with pleasure that could be increased without limit. And not only that, but the more we consumed the more contented and secure we'd be. And not only that, but we thought that following these instincts would assure our survival. The big brains that made so many wonderful things possible also made us vulnerable to profound delusions."

Bowen paused for a draught of mead, wiped his mouth, and continued. "We evolved within certain environmental conditions including climate conditions.

Our huge population depended on a stable climate for food and water. But we were so successful at feeding and breeding that we changed the environment. Few people even thought that was possible until it was too late. This new order of things presented different selection requirements for survival, most of them *cultural* as it turned out. The acme of consumer culture was reached when it was so successful at reshaping the world that it couldn't continue."

"So how could any escape be possible in such a situation?" asked Jaeger.

"Indeed," Bowen nodded. "That's a good question, isn't it? Honestly, I don't know. But here's my guess."

"Early versions of Euterran philosophy appeared thousands of years before the Ruination. They were a long-standing possibility for us in the evolution of our culture. But for a variety of reasons, they stayed at the margins of history as long as centre stage was monopolized by the aggressive, the grasping, and the violent. It wasn't until these natural tendencies in human character had played themselves out to an extreme degree in consumer culture, nearly to the point of extinguishing our species, that 'way opened,' as our Lightminders say, for a new culture. This event we call 'the Emergence.' Given the dramatically different circumstances following the Ruination, the Euterran way of life offered many more survival advantages than the old way did. In a sense, you might say that our way of life was always a possibility but it didn't find its day in the sun until the Ruination. It's too bad it had to emerge from a near-extinction event rather than a more gradual process of developing consciousness. The Ruination nearly destroyed us all. But it didn't. We leave off an old way of living not because we suddenly become enlightened, but because the old way is simply no longer possible. And sometimes that's how things go."

"So you're saying," Jaeger said, attempting to make sense of it, "that Euterra is just as much an expression of nature as the way of life that produced the Ruination?"

"How could it be otherwise?" Bowen replied. "I admit, I was being facetious when I said nature was crazy but she has her lucid moments. I don't see how Euterra could appear unless it was potential within us as much as pre-Ruination consumer culture was. Just as most people who lived before the Ruination were behaving 'naturally' by living more or less unconsciously, narcissistically, consumptively, and violently, we, following the Emergence, use Practice to set our older instincts and impulses in a different context. For us, our evolutionary past is something we're trying to grow out of, not something we just accept, or indulge, or exploit in others, or let run rampant in ourselves. Before the Ruination, people accepted living without insight as normal and therefore saw no alternative for themselves. They saw everything else on the planet as mere resources for satisfying ever more numerous and delusional needs. They didn't see life as trying to evolve beyond its beginnings, to somehow heal the wrinkle in itself that made it self-destructive, and which offered a role for humans to play in that process. Before the Ruination, people were choiceless slaves, and lived like slaves—to one degree or another regimented, driven, oppressed, resigned, fearful—because they believed it was the only way people *could* live—because of 'human nature.' Our mutation, if you want to call it that, was the capacity to cultivate insight through Practice. The key thing is that what mutated in us was not our bodies, but our culture. Culture is the only tool we have to compensate for what nature would otherwise incline us to do—which would be to end ourselves. Here in Euterra we now know that without Practice we would suffer the same fate as most other species, and at our own hand to boot. So nature both laid the trap and offered an exit. Almost everyone fell in. Only a few found the exit and we are their descendants."

CHAPTER 28

AUTUMN, 2029 C.E.

In everyone's death, as in everyone's life, character is revealed.

— THE BOOK OF MEMORY

THE CUBE VAN lumbered up through the black alder thicket to the clearing that Beamer and his friends had made some distance from the road. It had been months since they had received any more refugees to Euterra, but the clearing was still used as a marshalling area for items being collected from what remained of the pre-Ruination cities. A half dozen people staffed the location to receive and refuel the vans, load the goods they retrieved on small pedal-powered cargo vehicles, and make their way toward Dawngate. With these vehicles they could reach their destination in four or five hours. On foot, the trip would take more than a day.

As the cube van rolled to a stop, two people hastily piled out, Beamer being one of them. Jako, who was driving, gunned the engine to get the van under the camouflage tent in the clearing.

"Cid, brush the road!" Beamer called urgently to one of those who stood watch at the parking area. "And somebody bring me the walkie."

Cid Argus ran down the bush road to where it met the crumbling highway. He hastily pulled a tangle of black alder branches and other brush across the turn-off, and made his way back up toward the clearing. Depending on the direction their visitors were coming from, concealing the turn-off might be enough to render them invisible. If they came from the other direction, the subterfuge would be less convincing.

Another of the watch came running to Beamer with a walkie-talkie—a pair of which had been retrieved on one of their expeditions, together with some rechargeable batteries. Two years later, they still managed to keep them charged using a solar powered charger.

Beamer grabbed the walkie. "I sure hope they're not having tea," he said, pressing the call button. After an agonizing ten second wait, the device crackled to life.

"Starsis Massif," came a voice. "How may I direct your call?"

"Cut the crap," Beamer barked. "We're at the clearing. I think we were followed back. Big truck load of goons, maybe twenty of them. We're heading back. If we're not there in two hours, close the Dawngate and raise the lift cage all the way up. Over."

There was just the hiss of white noise for what again seemed an agonizingly long time, then: "Okay. Two hours; then close the gate and lift the cage. Over."

"Maybe load the guns too," said Beamer.

Another silence. Beamer could only imagine the panicky conversation that was happening on the Massif at this moment. The walkie-talkie hissed to life: "Load the guns. Copy that."

"Out," said Beamer with finality. No reply came from the mountain. "Everybody over here!" he hollered. All those at the site assembled around him. "Everybody, forget the gleanings. Get bikes and head for the Massif as fast as you can go. I'll follow when I can."

"I'm staying with you," said Jako.

"The hell you are," said Beamer.

"The hell I'm not."

"Look, maybe if these guys just find me here by myself they'll think I'm some screwball good-ol'-boy trying to make it on my own. Then they can make off with the trucks and stuff and that'll be that."

"I don't like this at all," Jako said.

"Neither do I. But these guys are probably armed and there's maybe two dozen of them. Do you want the six of us to take them on? Really? Besides, I'm a way better talker than you are."

Jako looked around reluctantly. Then Beamer said to all of them, "Get your asses in gear. I'll be right along. Go, go, go!" The group moved away, and each one grabbed a bicycle. Jako pulled the camouflage tent flap over the rear of the cube van in a futile effort to conceal it from view while others pulled branches and other debris over the trail that led to the Massif. In a moment they were gone, leaving Beamer alone. He busied himself by pulling more branches over the trail leading to the Massif, but once this task was complete, he waited, listening intently.

In minutes Beamer heard the growling diesel engine of a truck making its way slowly along the highway. It was coming from the same direction that he and Jako had taken back from the city, which meant that they might have a chance of being undetected because of the angle at which their bush road met the main road. So silent was the bush that Beamer thought he could hear even individual bits of gravel popping from under the tires of the pursuing vehicle as it rolled steadily forward.

Then came a shout. "Hey!" The truck squeaked to a stop, its engine idling from a single point that seemed awfully close. They had been found. There were some doors slamming, indistinct voices, then the truck engine roared again as it made its turn onto the bush road and laboured up the incline toward the clearing where Beamer waited.

In the moments that remained, Beamer weighed various possibilities. It may be that the visitors would simply shoot him as soon as they saw him, no questions asked. They would then explore the clearing, hot wire the trucks and take them and their contents back to wherever they came from. But certainly they would search for other potential spoils and would find the bike lane leading back to the Massif. They might explore this for some distance, give up, or make plans to return later and find out where it went—in which case they could appear unannounced on Euterra's doorstep at any time.

Maybe, though, they would not be too thorough or too smart. Maybe after finding the vans under the tent, they would consider it a good day and go home without searching more. Maybe they would not be inclined to gratuitous murder and would simply leave Beamer alone and go away. Or maybe Beamer would be made a slave, although another mouth to feed would make prospects of long-term slavery unlikely, in which case they would kill him then. And maybe those weren't really guns he saw when he and Jako had crossed paths with this bunch, but were instead tennis rackets or croquet mallets and they were all just out for a drive in the country, looking for a picnic spot.

In the end, at the very last moment available to him, Beamer grabbed the only remaining bicycle and wiggled it around the brush barrier and onto the trail. He waited there as the truck rumbled into view and its engine died. It was a five tonne chassis, possibly an old grain truck, with a tarpaulin cover. There were two men in the cab, both burly and stolid looking. They slid out when the vehicle stopped. Presently more men emptied from the rear box—eleven in all. Fewer than Beamer had feared but more than he'd wished. At first they formed a defensive perimeter around their own vehicle and scanned the bush, as if they knew what they were doing. Several, but not all, had shotguns and there was one rifle among them. Two others carried machetes. Soon, however, what at first appeared to be some modicum of discipline quickly evaporated and they became a randomly moving mob. They scurried out in all directions from the truck like a pack of looters, each one wanting to be the first to find plunder. They immediately saw the tent and with many a whoop and holler, invaded it like sixteen-year-olds after a beer at the football game. They spent some minutes exploring the contents of the tent and the vans it sheltered, then a few started to straggle out of the tent and resume their survey of the clearing for other opportunities. Two walked directly toward Beamer, though they hadn't seen him yet. As soon as he moved, they certainly would. He decided this was what he wanted.

Making no pretence of hiding, Beamer mounted the bike and started pumping hard away from the clearing. Something that sounded like hail went rattling through the vegetation ahead of him, followed by a dull "pop" from the direction of the men behind. This, he decided, was buckshot. Clearly they had no intention of negotiating a peaceful coexistence. He peddled faster to get himself out of shotgun range, and hoped he would be out of sight before someone brought up a rifle. The lane was too narrow for their truck, so if they were coming in pursuit, they would have to follow on foot.

Some time later Beamer stopped and dismounted, certain that his pursuers, if they had followed him, were still far behind. He turned on the walkie again and pressed the call button.

"Beamer?" came the reply, immediately this time.

"Yeah," he said. "I'm on my way back. Are all the birds home to roost?'

There was a hiss of static, then: "All but Jako and Cid. Over."

"What the hell?"

"Don't know where they are. Everybody else was ahead of them. Over."

"Okay," said Beamer. "Call me when they arrive. In another hour, pull up the cage and don't drop it again for anybody. Understand? Over."

"Who's behind you, over?"

"Thirteen of them. That's all. Thirteen. Over."

"Have a care, friend. Over."

"Yeah. See you soon." He left the walkie on monitor, mounted his bike again and resumed peddling.

In a bit more than two hours, Beamer made the Dawngate Bridge. It was a narrow wooden structure that spanned the Snake River immediately east of the Dawngate itself, thus eliminating the need to scale the Massif much farther to the north, a more laborious route. He crossed the bridge and cycled directly into the Dawngate entrance, an opening in the rock that looked like a cave. But if it was merely a cave, Beamer knew, why would there be a bridge leading to it? The lift cage had already been raised leaving a gaping shaft going upwards together with the wire ropes and counter weights for the lift itself. Beamer set his bike aside and then went outside again. He cast his eyes up the side of the Starsis Massif which appeared to be little more than a featureless wall of granite. There was nothing to do but wait. He sat down near the gate entrance and leaned his back against the rock.

For a long time, there was nothing but the distant sibilance of the Snake River cataract below the bridge, and the occasional whoosh of onshore breezes from Loch Speare moving up into the forest. Then came the hissing sound of large wings cutting the air as an enormous raven swept around the rock face and landed with a double hop directly in front of Beamer.

"You again," he said with affection.

"Ache-uck!"

"Yeah, I wake up sometimes—" Beamer said with a weary smile, "but I keep falling asleep again, you know?"

The bird cocked its head and fixed its bottomless black eye on him. It came another hop closer, then turned abruptly as if it sensed something in the distance. It took flight, creaking loudly. There was a space of near silence, then a cacophony of raven calls starting up in the far distance and steadily coming closer. Beamer got to his feet, gazing at the green wall of forest beyond the bridge. There emerged the group of men led by those Beamer had seen first getting out of the truck. They walked like a mob, swaggering, confident in their numbers. Thirteen, Beamer counted. There were thirteen of them. He hoped it was *their* lucky number.

Beamer walked out a few paces from where the bridge met the rock face on his side of the cataract. The group of men stopped on the other side of the bridge, some of them raising their guns.

"Friend," Beamer greeted, smiling broadly. "I don't think you'll be needing guns here."

The man who appeared to be the leader turned to one of his companions and said something inaudible. Then he turned back to Beamer and shouted, "I'm not your fucking friend!" He appeared to be stalling for time to look over the cliff side, search the shadows inside the gate for potential ambush, search the rocks below the bridge for who might lurk there. "Do we have a grievance so soon?" Beamer asked, trying to sound amiable. "We've barely met."

"Whatchya got in the cave?"

"That's where I keep my bike."

"Bullshit!" The man spat out the words. "I think we'll have a look for ourselves."

Beamer raised a hand. "Friends," he repeated. "There's nothing here to interest you. You got my hoard back in the clearing. Please, go in peace."

"Or what?" the man said as he began to stride forward.

"Or you'll be sorry," said Beamer evenly.

The man paused, looking at him. A brief moment of doubt crossed his face, but then he sneered and continued forward. "And who the hell is gonna make me sorry?" he said.

"You'll be sorry," Beamer said, "because what goes around comes around, and sometimes sooner than you think."

"What a bunch of hippie crap!" the man growled, and fast as a snake he raised his rifle and fired.

From a fissure in the granite wall, Jako looked down at the group of men moving forward onto the bridge. "As you wish," he whispered, nearly choking, and pulled the trigger. Through the scope he saw the top of the first man's head shatter like an egg. There immediately followed a fusillade of gunfire from a dozen directions on the Massif and from the forest wall. It didn't stop until all the men lay dead on the bridge or the road leading up to it.

Jako dropped his rifle and started scrambling down the cliff face like a mountain goat. He was in a desperate hurry to reach the shelf of rock outside Dawngate, but there was no quick way to do so. It took him minutes to reach the bridge level, by which time nothing was moving. A maddening silence hovered over the scene.

Overhead, ravens began to assemble, at first in ones and twos, then in small murders until they filled the trees in a single conspiracy of over a hundred birds. They muttered and gargled their eulogies together in subdued voices. Time to sound the alarm had already passed, they seemed to know. Now was the time simply to bear witness. They shook their wings and turned their heads askance as they waited.

Beamer lay on his back on the rock pavement, his eyes gazing quietly into the sky. He had a small hole in his chest from which issued little sputters of blood as he coughed and wheezed. Jako got to his side and lifted him off the pavement by the shoulders, but when Beamer moaned Jako held him still. "Okay?" Beamer wheezed.

"Everyone's okay," Jako said hoarsely, the words almost strangling him..

Beamer's eyes swept away from Jako's face toward a seemingly empty space near his feet. There. "Ah! Tatum!" he whispered. He gave a little smile. Then his body relaxed toward utter stillness.

CHAPTER 29

A ship at sea, making a course change of only one degree,
can make landfall in a completely different country.

— THE BOOK OF MEMORY

IF THE SEVERAL MUGS of mead that Hyram Bowen had imbibed were having an effect, it was not evident. As the evening wore on, Fogg's Inn saw its patrons disappearing, except for the most loyal regulars—of whom Bowen was a charter member. Jaeger, however, was feeling a bit more affected, this mead stuff being new to his experience. Nevertheless, he pressed on with his questions for Bowen.

"Tell me more about the Emergence. What was it?" Jaeger asked.

"Ah," said Bowen, "that's hard to say—exactly. For starters, we don't think of it as something that happened a long time ago and is now over. The Emergence is a process we've started to go through. No one knows how long it will take or where we will wind up, if and when it's ever over. It's like steering a boat and making a tiny course change which doesn't seem like much at the time, but it ends up taking you into an entirely different ocean that calls for more course changes of its own. All you can be sure of is that you made a little course change at some time and now you're a long way from where you started."

"So what was that little course change?"

"There were probably several of them. But what you most need to know about Euterra is that it's a *sensibility*—or a way of thinking and feeling, that takes physical form as a different way of living from pre-Ruination times." Bowen took a swig from his fresh glass of mead and continued. "Think of it this way: Before the Ruination people thought that a good life was a matter of arranging the outer conditions of their lives to try to satisfy their desires. They took desires for granted, as if they were unquestionable facts of life, as if they were nothing dangerous. If you asked them why they desired what they desired, or what, exactly, a desire *is*, and whether catering to desires is a good way to achieve well-being, they would probably have been offended. They identified so strongly with their desires and the things they had acquired in trying to satisfy their desires, that questioning any of that was like questioning their personhood—their legitimate right to exist, to 'have a life,' as they would have said back then. They thought of their lives as forms of property. So just about everyone was focusing on the material condition of their lives and they were pretty much unaware of their trans-material condition. They even saw the two as opposites." Bowen paused to chuckle. "If you think about it, this attitude is almost hilarious because if you approached these very same people with a proposal about investing money…"

"Money?" said Jaeger.

"Ah, yes, well that's another whole story," Bowen said, arching an eyebrow. "But just follow me here for a minute: If you had made a proposal about how to invest money to these same people, they would probably question you very closely about whether this proposal was what it appeared to be, they would interrogate you as to whether it was likely to provide a good return, whether the source of the proposal was trustworthy and what your track record was on delivering results. On and on. They would have asked all these questions about money, which is a mere idea with no physical power to change our lives in the least apart from our belief that it can—but their *desires* they accepted without question. Most strange! What would have happened, do you think, if they subjected their desires to the same interrogation as they did to investment opportunities? Is this desire what it appears to be? Will indulging this desire really deliver what it promises? Is this desire trustworthy and how often does pursuing it really achieve well-being? And so on and so forth."

"That's why Laurel Fey's work on her Periodic Table is so vitally important to the Euterran way of life," Bowen went on. "Instead of blindly following our desires assuming that all we need to do to be well is to find the right objects to satisfy our desires, Fey instead gave us a way of interrogating desires themselves to determine *scientifically* whether they actually bring us to a good life. And we discovered in the process that before the Ruination, we had been asking the wrong questions all along. The question is not how many things are enough things to satisfy my desires and attain a good life, but rather, how many desires are enough desires for a good life? And will pursuing them really achieve the well-being I think it will?"

Having hardly any personal experience of money to say nothing of investing, and being affected by the mead, Jaeger felt benumbed.

"Anyway," Bowen continued, waving his hand, "the tiny course changes that distinguish the Euterran outlook started with *stopping*: We stopped assuming that a good life could be found by re-arranging the outer conditions of our lives. We stopped trying to satisfy desires that could never be satisfied. And we stopped believing that a way of life that likely promised human extinction could ever provide for well-being. But neither did we go to the other extreme of withdrawing entirely into an inner world of fantasy and wish fulfillment. The Euterran outlook focuses attention on the *relationship* between the inner, subjective, and outer, objective conditions of our lives. So we're neither a society of mystics nor of materialists; we live on a third rock we don't even have a name for. But the way to find that third rock, and to more or less stay on it once you discover it, is what we call Practice."

"So we don't take desires for granted. Desires are natural but dangerous. They were selected by evolution and became innate to human nature because they offered some value in helping us feed and breed to the max. But the idea of directing all of one's attention to satisfying desires, especially material desires, is sheer lunacy. The promise that satisfying desire is the way to have a good life is a lie, plain and simple. We know it to be a lie because it fails the test of experience. No sooner do we lay hold of something we think will satisfy a desire than we find the object of desire changes, or desire itself moves off in some other direction only to catch fire again in some other part of our lives. Almost everyone went mad in this tragic tail-chase. Given this insight, even if we could return to a pre-Ruination way of life, I don't think many Euterrans would do so. Once having tasted honey, who wants to chew sand?"

Jaeger watched Bowen carefully, weighing his words. His life in Mainbranch hardly afforded the luxury of time or energy to ponder such questions. He felt like a stranger in a strange land.

Bowen sighed. "But the Emergence is what it is," he said, "because it's a collective happening, a cultural change, not just an insight experienced by a few spiritual prodigies as in ancient times. We're still not sure how this happened. But others have written about ideas or changes that slowly ripen in the depths of our human experience and when the time is right, they can surface in many places around the same time. Maybe that's what happened with the Emergence. In any case, a lot of people for whom this change in outlook was latent or already underway somehow found each other, and Badger Coulee, and Beamer Farris, at just the right time. Had this not happened when it did, the way it did, Euterra wouldn't be here today."

"So you try to live without desire?" Jaeger gaped. The idea of it sounded farfetched.

Bowen shook his head, smiling. "No, no. That's impossible. Like I said, desires are innate to human nature, part of what we are as a species. What's different about Euterran culture is that we don't believe anymore that pursuing desire will make for a good life. Desire is there, all the time. Practice teaches us how to notice it arising, like any other subjective thought or image—and how, if we practice detachment, it passes away like any other idea. Practice teaches us how chasing after fantasies can have serious consequences for the Earth and for other people if we pursue them without bringing a critical awareness to what we're doing. We don't just blindly let desire have its way with us."

"Another part of the Emergence," Bowen went on, "has to do with technology and how we use it to change the world. Before the Ruination, as I said, people took their desires for granted and used technology to reshape the material world which they thought would make them happy. Since there was no end to desire itself, and no limit on the number of things we might desire, technology was continually rearranging the material world. Many species rearrange the physical world to make it more congenial to their needs; so this was nothing new. But in the case of human beings, using technology to change the world was something we did to an extreme degree. We did it to such a degree, in fact, that we almost rendered the Earth uninhabitable for human beings. And while there were many voices even in pre-Ruination culture saying that well-being is something that comes from the inside out rather than the outside in, it was mostly lip service. In truth, very few people believed that a good life was something we fashion by changing *ourselves* rather than changing our material surroundings. The Emergence included a widespread shift in how we thought about well-being. We'd always known that very few material things are required for a good life, but in the Emergence we actually started living as if we believed it. And by living it, we demonstrated its truth. In the process, we also discovered that we needed a lot less technology for a good life than we thought."

Bowen sighed. "My greatest regret," he said, sounding weary, "is that we didn't take this direction long ago—before so much was lost, so much life, so much—history. But maybe the way it happened is the only way it could have happened. Who can say?"

"So, you mean the Great Forgetting?" Jaeger asked.

Bowen nodded before downing the last of his mead.

"What was it?" Jaeger asked with some impatience.

Bowen smiled wryly. "You're relentless, aren't you?" Jaeger shrugged, sensing that despite what he said, Bowen was still enjoying his rhetorical flight.

"One of the supreme ironies of the Great Forgetting is that in the process of it happening, we've also forgotten how it happened. Our historians have many theories, but to prove or disprove any of them requires information we've lost, or never had. So the debate is both endless and fruitless."

Jaeger leaned forward eagerly. "But what do *you* think?"

"Humph." Bowen shook his head. "What do *I* think? I think the Great Forgetting was the most recent and catastrophic example of a long process of forgetting that started with the invention of writing, and then of books in which writing was preserved, and eventually in devices like computers and the Internet which we lost in the Ruination."

Jaeger looked perplexed.

"The Internet was a way of linking computers together over large areas of the Earth. It made communication much easier and also offered a way of storing vast amounts of information," Bowen said. "Once we invented writing, we started committing our experiences to writing rather than to memory. As the need for memory declined, so did memory itself. When writing fully developed, the measure of what a person claimed to know was the number of books they'd read, not so much what they could actually remember. This process became more pervasive when printing made cheap books abundant and more people learned to read. This was in many respects a great advance over the monopoly on knowledge held by a literate elite. But the keeping of written records evolved pretty naturally to the invention of libraries where many such records could be stored and studied, which in turn prepared the way for catastrophes like the sack of the library in ancient Alexandria in Egypt, or the book burnings under various fanatics from Savonarola to Hitler to radical Islamists."

Jaeger's head throbbed from all of the historical references, all new to him, but he kept listening nonetheless.

"Anyway," Bowen continued, "by pre-Ruination times the better part of human knowledge was being stored in computers—not even written down any more. And even later in the story, information was stored in something they called 'the Cloud,' a network of computers connected by the Internet. None of these things survive today in anything like the form they took then. We simply don't have the materials, tools and energy needed to make such things anymore. But back then, because the Internet and the Cloud were supposedly designed to survive even a nuclear attack, people thought of them as secure, almost immortal—the perfect place to store everything, forever. Of course people continued to store knowledge in their memories as well. But the confidence they felt in the security offered by the Cloud turned out to be illusory. For one thing, the Cloud still required electricity to operate, and it was the security of the electrical grid that pre-Ruination people took most for granted. They also connected or controlled a great many other devices using the Internet—everything from their power dams and airports to their food supply and communication systems. With everything connected in this way, something in which pre-Ruination people took great pride, they were also vulnerable to what used to be called 'cascading failures.' That's sort of a fancy way of saying, 'one damn thing after another.'"

Bowen sighed. "No one today, least of all me, really knows how the cascade got started. But something happened that had widespread and pretty long-lasting effects on the electrical grid, and with it, collapsed the Internet.

Maybe it was something from the sun, or an act of war, or really bad weather that caused an overload, or just a minor technical fault that somehow got out of hand. At any rate, somewhere in the world, something happened that collapsed the grid, and we think because of the Internet, the collapse spread worldwide. As it happened, the grid was essential to powering the Internet, but the Internet had also become essential to operating the grid. I can't really explain the technology of how it all happened, but the effect was catastrophic. Within hours, there were emergencies everywhere and within days, the global economy virtually stopped. Elders, the handicapped, those dependent on special medicines or medical devices and services were all dead or disabled in a couple of weeks. Massive civil unrest, vandalism, terrorism and criminal opportunism emerged everywhere, making it harder to get things back in operation. Governments went into panic mode ostensibly to preserve public order, but with the hidden agenda of protecting the power of established elites. Things became unmanageable very, very quickly. That, of course, was the onset of the Ruination."

Jaeger felt his mind stretching, trying to imagine this by-gone world of so many people and so much complexity. But there was nothing in his experience to compare it to.

Bowen continued. "But the Great Forgetting part has to do with what was lost when the Internet and the Cloud collapsed. Without electricity, without sophisticated computers and other machines, whatever was stored on those devices for all practical purposes essentially disappeared. And supremely ironic was the fact that many of these devices were deliberately designed never to be repairable or to operate for very long. What people then possessed of knowledge was whatever remained in their heads—which turned out to be precious little. As social and economic conditions worsened, then we started losing people as well as machines. We do know with certainty that one effect of the Ruination was a worldwide population collapse, though we still don't know how deep the collapse went. We know that apart from Euterra, there are no major human settlements within a thousand kilometres of here in any direction, which doesn't bode well for the rest of the world either. With every death, especially of highly trained people, humanity lost a little bit of its collective knowledge about everything—including the knowledge of how to rebuild or repair the technology that made pre-Ruination civilization what it was."

"So," Bowen sighed, "you might say that if pre-Ruination society was the high point of human development, then three centuries ago we fell into a hole we still haven't got out of."

"Would *you* say that?" Jaeger asked.

"No." Bowen snorted. "I wouldn't. A great many precious things were forgotten in the Ruination—no doubt. But in my view, most of what was lost didn't matter a damn. And some things were lost that I hope stay lost. There is no doubt in my mind that the direction pre-Ruination civilization was headed would have ensured the extinction of human beings and many other beings as well. And I don't think there is any way we could say that the purpose of human life is to rebuild or surpass pre-Ruination culture. What the Ruination did was to shatter beyond repair the contradictions that made pre-Ruination society so toxic to a good life. We no longer have to be troubled to conserve or reform that particular pathway of human evolution. Most of what was forgotten doesn't matter because we're now evolving along a different pathway made possible by the Opening which was the Ruination. It's tragic that so many people suffered so much, but it happened as it happened, and almost certainly not by conscious human intent. We prepared all this for ourselves more or less unconsciously—a fault we hope to avoid in the future."

The two men sat there for some moments, still absorbed in the world their conversation had created---a world of imagination and memory. By degrees they again became aware of the clinking of mugs, muttered conversations, a burst of laughter, the sounds of Fogg's Inn.

CHAPTER 30

The purpose of human life is to bring the light of consciousness into the unconscious darkness from which we evolved. Of course, there may be more.

— THE BOOK OF MEMORY

LYDIA ROSS EMERGED with Jaeger from the headframe for Molly's Quay Lift atop the Starsis Massif. Considering that the Massif had been continuously inhabited by Euterrans for nearly three centuries, its upper reaches looked remarkably wild. Headframes for the other lifts had been fashioned from laid-up stone and salvaged steel, but Molly's Quay Lift rose into the centre of an outcrop that merely required hollowing out to serve its purpose. Flagstones had been laid around the lift entrance to make a small terrace with a few built-in sitting benches. Otherwise, the landscape around it looked entirely natural with the exception of a paved walking path about a metre wide that led away into the forest.

"Please follow," said Lydia as she stepped onto the path. They walked silently for some time through groves of towering fir and spruce trees that offered a densely shaded corridor. Here and there moss bearded the branches with grey rags of life. Ahead of them on the path, dragonflies clattered in their ancient improbable dance.

As they followed the way into the forest, Jaeger noticed a number of small plaques no larger than his palm stuck into the ground at the base of the trees. The plaques looked like bronze, time having weathered them to a warm patina. On closer inspection, the plaques displayed names: Loca Hendricks; Ismael Zedek; John Lucas; Ferin Mosley; and on and on. Virtually all of the trees appeared to be tagged like this.

"What is this?" Jaeger asked, pointing to a plaque.

Lydia paused in her stride. "The names of the trees," she said. Jaeger puzzled over this, yet another mystery of Euterran culture to grapple with. "Well," Lydia continued, "they are actually the names of people buried under the trees. We bury our dead very soon after we die, washed and shrouded, but otherwise just as we passed. It's also our custom to plant a tree over our graves, so that our physical elements can be drawn up into the trees to sustain new life. Today though, most burials occur off the Massif in the surrounding countryside. Most people want to be buried on Permie sites where they can become something edible and sweet." She smiled. "All the trees on top of the Massif are the transformed bodies of the first Euterrans. So you might say that this entire forest is the standing presence of our ancestors, still alive among us, but in a different form."

"So you think people somehow survive after death?" Jaeger asked.

Lydia raised an eyebrow. "That's an ongoing discussion," she said. "Practice is the centre of our lives and Practice is always based on facts that we can verify over and over again. We never ask our children or ourselves to take anything on faith. We know for a fact that the physical elements making up the human body pass endlessly through the living and non-living cycles of nature. In *that* sense we are all physically immortal."

Jaeger shook his head, doubtful.

"But I think your question is about something more," Lydia went on. "Some Euterrans believe that something of a person migrates through death to a new life, reappearing again and again. The Tarshin practice of deep remembering sometimes provides intriguing clues that some of us have lived before, perhaps many times. Others say these are false memories arising as pure psychic constructions that have no corresponding reality beyond the person's own experience. While we continue to be very interested in the question and it sparks lively discussion and even some research, little evidence has been found to decide the question one way or the other. So I would have to say that most Euterrans are agnostic on the question, open to new discoveries, loyal to their own views, and mostly respectful of those who differ. The fact that Practice is very important to us is of relatively little help in such matters because the whole of life isn't compassed by Practice. We know there is much that falls outside of Practice, outside of our individual or even our collective awareness—outside even of what the Lightminders can perceive. So we must remain open on the question. Do you think you've been here before?"

Jaeger stopped in mid-stride to gaze into the misty green passageway through the trees on which they walked. "I've never really thought about it," he said. "But maybe. Yes, maybe. Yes, I think so."

"How do you know?" Lydia asked.

Jaeger shrugged. "I don't know how I know. I just do."

"Then for you, it is a truth of your experience, but the rest of us will have to wait for evidence we can all see and understand."

She stepped off the paved walkway and onto another path worn bare on the Pre-Cambrian rock. It led off a short distance to the east, then opened in a small glade dotted with paper birch and aspen, species that added horizontal flourishes to the feathery vertical forms of the spruce and fir trees. The path was a depression worn into the rock by the passage of many feet over a long time. The open space in the forest rose slightly from the south to the north, and on its north side was a grotto with a partially walled-in entrance. Granite rose up in an arc from west to east as if someone had spooned molten rock into a smooth pile but left a gigantic bubble at its centre. In this space had been laid shards, evidently from the surrounding outcrops, to fill the space except for generous window openings and a doorway on its south face. The stone work was festooned here and there with Virginia creeper, making it look even more like it was either emerging from, or dissolving back into, the Massif itself.

From somewhere, everywhere, there came a soft droning sound unlike anything Jaeger had ever heard. He stopped in mid-step, not sure if, or what, he was hearing. But it was there, like strings being gently brushed, now in ascending pitch, then trailing off in a lower range, and dropping again into stillness. After some moments, he noticed that these sounds were arising in response to the breeze that had been wafting through the open space in the forest that they had entered.

"Those are wind harps," Lydia said, guessing the question in his mind. "They're a little higher up on the outcrop where they can catch the air. We invented them shortly after arriving here. It seemed to be in right Practice for us to make some for this place. They make music from the wind. It's always different." She turned and walked a few more paces, leading Jaeger on to the entrance of the grotto.

"This," said Lydia in a hushed tone, "is First Haven—where Beamer Farris lived." They headed toward the entrance. All along the way, Jaeger saw bouquets of flowers, some very simple, others elaborate; some fresh as if cut the same day, others withered and dry, flaking into the scant soil and bunch moss, clearly never touched after having once been laid down. "We come here sometimes, just to remember," said Lydia. She moved more slowly and deliberately as they approached the door of the strange structure. It had no lock or knob but only a latch to hold it against the wind. She lifted the latch and they stepped inside.

They entered a modest but spacious room. Light streaming in the windows from the south was gathered in an echo of warmth by the substantial mass of rock that made up the west, north and east walls as well as its arched ceiling. The room showed little evidence of tooling, much less the elaborate and delicate attention to detail and finish that Jaeger had seen everywhere else in Euterra. It was sparsely furnished with a table, two chairs, a sleeping platform like his own in Mizar Dan, some food cupboards and space for preparing meals, a small wardrobe, a shelf for books. The space felt like it had been vacated for a very long time, yet it radiated a welcoming quality.

"Beamer Farris?" Jaeger asked.

"Yes," she said. "Beamer Farris brought the first Euterrans here—although we didn't call ourselves that at the time—just before the Ruination. He saved us. He knew what was coming and what we had to do. He lived here until he died in the first year of the Euterran Age. Now we mark time from the year of his death. This is exactly as he left it on the day he died. We've kept everything the same. Some think he levitated to the top of the Massif because we can't imagine anyone climbing it, but others think he climbed it one day simply because it was there. They also say he could talk to ravens and understood them when they spoke to each other. There's even a story that a raven fed him while he sat on this mountain doing first Practice. To this day, we still teach ravens human speech sounds so they remind us to 'wake up.'" Lydia smiled, as if amused by the thought.

"So what happened to him?"

"He was killed protecting Euterra." Her voice caught slightly on the words. "The only change we made in here was to hollow out that niche for him there."

Jaeger noticed for the first time an indentation carved in the back wall of the dwelling in which stood a graceful earthenware jar. It was unadorned in any way except for the exceeding skill of its craftsmanship.

"Every Euterran child hears the stories about Beamer Farris. We remember the price he paid to keep us safe here and to keep us free. Most Euterran adults visit at least once a year—usually just to sit a while—but many mark the day of his death with a special visit and remembrance. I thought you should see this place. Please follow now."

———— • ♦ • ————

In silence, they returned the way they had come, along the path to the paved walkway that would take them back to the Molly's Quay Lift. The lift dropped a dozen levels to slide to a halt at the Laurel's Garden Lift Station, and from there they walked through Laurel's Garden to Siderium Plaza. Jaeger had already traversed this expanse of gardens and walkways in the custody of Spark on the way to his introduction to Practice. A question lingered from that first visit.

"So, who was Laurel?" Jaeger asked.

"Ah. This garden is named after her—Laurel Fey. She was one of Beamer Farris's original companions, a lover of books. She is largely responsible for Siderium. She helped salvage many books from the Ruination, and other sources of information like maps and all manner of scientific instruments. When the rest of us were worried what we would have to eat, she was insisting that we build a library, and set up a research laboratory, first for permaculture research, then eventually every other imaginable thing. She established our first museum and our first collection of pre-Ruination art. She urged us all to cultivate daily Practice and she was one of the first contributors to *The Book of Memory*. She also had a hand in assembling the other classics—*The Book of Elements*, *The Book of Practice* and *The Book of Transitions*. All Euterran knowledge is structured in some way by these classics, and by her Periodic Table. Of course all have many volumes, many authors, and many parts which are not 'books' exactly, so Laurel Fey didn't build the whole edifice by herself. But she saw the Opening. She's a woman after my own heart. My own Active Practice is as an archivist."

"Laurel Fey, you said?" Jaeger interjected. "Is she any relation to Zephyr Fey?"

"Hmm." Lydia paused, looking thoughtful. "Great, great, great, great, great, great, great, great, great, grand-daughter I would guess—or thereabouts. In Euterra surnames pass to descendants of the same sex. So Laurel Fey's name passed through all her female descendants of whom Zephyr Fey is one. So yes, they are related."

Jaeger and Lydia started up a series of stairways and ramps that carried them higher and higher into the Siderium building. Presently, they arrived at a great gothic archway that was the entrance to a very long hall ribbed with beautiful columns and branching capitals. It resembled a canopy of trees. The passageway plunged back into the mountain a considerable distance and Jaeger noticed that it was one of the few places in Euterra where he saw artificial light. Three levels of balustrades and window walls lined both sides of the passageway and behind these were vast rooms thronged with people busy with all sorts of tasks unrecognizable to Jaeger.

Lydia swept her arm in an arc. "Siderium is a circular building, like a very big layer cake. At its centre is the Rotunda where I'm taking you. That's where the Lightminders practice. The rest of the circle is divided into quadrants—one quadrant devoted to Memory, one to the Elements, one to Practice and one to Transitions. This," she said, sweeping her arm to indicate the right side of the passageway, "is the Hall of Memory. And this," she said, and motioned toward the left wall, "is the Hall of Practice. The Halls of Elements and Transitions are on the other side of the Massif, opposite the Rotunda. All have many levels and all are gathered around the Light." She stopped and smiled at Jaeger. "And that's how we see things."

Jaeger didn't know what to say or what to ask. He walked silently beside Lydia as they went down the passageway to whatever lay ahead.

The colonnade they traversed intersected another passageway that crossed their path, curving away from them to left and right. Their passage terminated in another ring-shaped passageway that formed the circumference of a large circular room straight ahead. They came to a tall, magnificently carved wooden door. Lydia grasped its handle and paused. "Silence is right Practice here," she whispered, then pushed the door gently inward.

They stepped into a large circular room the ceiling of which arched overhead in the half-sphere of a perfect dome. At the centre of the dome was an oculus through which sunlight poured into the space. It was fashioned with mirrors and lenses that brought light precisely to the centre of the Rotunda regardless of the angle of the sun. The centre of the room was empty of any adornment or furnishing, but the floor had been laid up of quartz slabs studded with threads of wire gold. This gave the floor a milky, cloud-like quality suspending tangled threads of light. The floor of the room descended in circular tiers from its outer circumference to its centre, rings within rings, each consisting of a sitting bench hewn from stone. Most were topped with cushions of various colours. Jaeger guessed the space could hold several thousand people, but at the moment only a hundred or so were present, sitting in the first few circuits of benches close to the circle of light captured by the oculus. And at its very centre were perhaps twenty small children. They were occupied in some sort of play, with three or four adolescents moving among them, whispering instruction, handing them toys, gently moving them from one play group to another. Their company was hushed, and yet wide awake in its activity. And the circle of elders who completely surrounded them sat utterly still, utterly silent, holding them there in some ineffable spiritual embrace. Jaeger sensed that some deep and unnamable work was underway.

Lydia stepped sideways into the outermost ring of benches, moving in far enough to leave room for Jaeger to join her. Both sat down and Jaeger could see Lydia's eyes partly closing as she centred herself in Practice. He tried to do the same, but realized he was at first distracted by the thought that they would be sitting for only a moment, as if to 'pay their respects' to the place they were in. But as time passed, the thought dissolved into the enveloping silence of the Rotunda.

But was it silent? Jaeger's breath caught in his throat, suspended there, waiting, listening. Listening for what? Then he heard—*something. Something* was here. It was like an overtone resolving itself in a cavernous vault, a third, a fifth, a seventh—somewhere above whatever was dominant in him. It distilled light into sound and if sound could shimmer, this sound shimmered, higher and higher... But was it high at all? Suddenly he could feel a chorus of tones so low they seemed to shake the rock he sat on. It throbbed like some mighty engine deep in the Earth, and so pervasive that Jaeger's eyes, which had drooped closed, now popped open. He gasped suddenly.

Lydia felt Jaeger jerk and opened her eyes. His expression mingled surprise and delight and confusion all at once. She suppressed a smile as she inclined her head, indicating they should leave.

"*What was that?*" Jaeger gasped as the door of the Rotunda closed behind them. He leaned back against the wall, and slid slowly down until he sat on the floor, hoping he wouldn't sink into it and disappear. The stone was cool and solid and reassuring. "What was that?" he repeated, mostly to himself.

Lydia stood by, saying nothing, giving Jaeger time to recover his composure without embarrassing him by fussing over his shock. Then she said, "Whatever it was, it was for you. Now follow please."

In a few moments they went back through the outer hall again, where they sat down in one of the courtyards above Laurel's Garden. Lydia regarded Jaeger closely, then said, "Jaeger, Siderium is a very special place. I probably shouldn't have brought you here so soon, but I thought you could manage it. I'm sorry if you were frightened."

Jaeger smiled weakly. "I wasn't frightened, just—surprised," he said, trying to appear game. "I felt something similar in the Permie food forest when I was there with Lars," he said. "Who were the other people there?"

"They're Lightminders. As I said a few days ago, nearly everyone in Euterra does Practice. But some are drawn to give their lives to it. This may last a few weeks, or many years, or a lifetime. Their sole tasks are to practice mindfulness of the Light and watch for Opening."

"I don't understand."

"It would be unusual if you did," said Lydia. "Let me just say this for now: In the past, especially before the Ruination, people spent a lot of time looking backward. They killed each other over things that were written in three-thousand-year-old books. They defended creeds to the death, argued over tiny differences in belief, pledged allegiance to things they didn't even understand. And they let these arguments and creeds and books define them. They stopped being people in exchange for becoming embodiments of historical grievances. This trade meant that they didn't have to be responsible moral agents. They could simply appeal to the authority of their traditions when they made choices and didn't have to look for Opening."

"Lightminders practice by paying close attention to what is emerging, what is being born, what is manifesting at this moment—the Light appearing—the way forward. While we know our history holds important lessons that help us discern way forward—that's the whole reason we have the *Book of Memory* after all!—we see our history as something we're emerging from, not something we have to defend or that we're bound to repeat. Lightminders discern way forward for the community. We're not the guardians of a tradition or a deposit of faith. We look for cracks in the walls of the past, walls which would otherwise end our Emergence, our evolution. Our whole way of life is based on the idea that what's most precious about people is what we are becoming, not what we've been."

"So the Lightminders are your rulers?" he asked.

"No," said Lydia. "We're sense organs."

Jaeger and Lydia lapsed into silence for a few moments, then Jaeger said, "We?"

She regarded him evenly. "I'm a Lightminder," she said.

Jaeger pondered this. "And the children?" he asked.

"Before they're capable of formal Practice, we surround our children with silence, steep them in it. Not all the time, but regularly, and in small groups. Experience has taught us that the profoundest truths are best absorbed through experience rather than just described in words." She stopped and glanced up at someone approaching.

Zephyr Fey caught sight of Jaeger and Lydia. She was descending the stairway from the Hall of Practice which also housed Helder's Hall, a centre of healing practice. She smiled as she approached them, clasping her hands in the customary honourific. "Friends!" she greeted, trying not to look too gleeful when her eyes fell on Jaeger. She had to maintain some semblance of professional decorum. "Studying the difference between periwinkle and aster, I presume?"

"Zephyr!" Lydia said, smiling. "We've just been wandering the Siderium. What news?"

"Ha!" Zephyr said brightly. "Maybe this is Opening. When I saw you I thought we should introduce Jaeger to Soiree Dansante. There is one tonight, on Procyon Drift Plaza." She fixed her eyes on Jaeger. "Want to come?"

Jaeger felt his face grow warm—an unfamiliar feeling. "A Soiree-what?"

"Soiree Dansante," Zephyr said. It's a sort of party, with music, with food, with dancing. You should try it. You'd like it."

"By all means," Lydia said, chiming in. "I'll bring him. You can fetch him back to the Dan afterwards, if he can walk."

Zephyr grinned. "He'll walk. Or else I'll carry him."

"I can walk," said Jaeger, his whole body feeling too warm. "Why wouldn't I be able to walk?"

"We'll see," said Lydia.

CHAPTER 31

The story of our lives is written in our bones.

— THE BOOK OF MEMORY

IMMEDIATELY OTIS realized the scream was not human. But it contained that pained quality that registers with all other mammals as kindred suffering. He edged downslope and peered through a hazelnut break to see what might be afoot. There, a dozen metres away, a large and more recent version of a rock python was holding a boar by the end of its snout, cunningly avoiding its razor sharp tusks as it looped first one, then two, then three coils of its massive body around its prey. The scream would be the last sound from the boar, except for the cracking of its ribs and spine as the snake silenced its meal. It was easily six or seven metres long, and the encounter reminded him, if he needed reminding, to stay more to upland areas if possible. While it would be unlikely that such an animal would consume a full-grown man, it might well try.

He angled northeast again, away from the edge of the marshland and toward higher ground. There he found a stand of very large white pine trees where he made his evening meal, after which he decided to climb a pine and sleep above ground, draped around a branch and shrouded in his forest coat. While treeing himself was not certain protection against pythons, and ran risks of its own, there was a primordial comfort in doing so nonetheless.

With no mishap by morning, Otis carried on. He walked for another two days without incident of any kind, but he was conscious of passing through a landscape that was busy consuming what humanity had been. After almost three centuries, much of what people had made of their lives before the Ruination was gone, having been digested by the juices of corrosive weather and the tendency of a multitude of other species to treat human artifacts as food or raw materials for their own purposes. But here and there persisted remnants of that time long before when super highways laced the continent from end to end and plastic was everywhere. Here would rise from the forest floor the ruins of a massive column of concrete—perhaps an upright for a highway interchange—rotting to dust, the grey aggregate pierced with rusting iron bars. The rest of the road was patchy, pitted concrete mostly obscured by vegetation. A mound of moss here or a tangle of kudzu vines there might conceal the plastic remains of a car, but its metal parts would long ago have oxidized or survived as frosty lumps of aluminum or bits of glass. With every step he might pass a discarded plastic toothbrush, or the fantastic grotesque of some child's sipping cup, faded and dull looking, but tenaciously enduring the passage of years. Among the most durable of artifacts was anything made of stainless steel. For collecting expeditions, this material was especially prized as it could be melted down again and refashioned into any number of highly useful tools. Such litter was familiar to him from the several surveys he had made in his lifetime. But they never failed to evoke a combination of melancholy and relief: melancholy that so much had been lost, and relief that so much that had been lost meant so little in the first place. That people were willing to risk the future of the species for such detritus never ceased to appall him.

The next day he came upon a much larger heap of cumber, this mound stretching for several kilometres. Clearly the remains of a small pre-Ruination city. Passing around it would take him far out of his way, but passing through it would be a tedious process of threading through a labyrinth of things which were large, high, sharp or poisonous. Parts of it might also be occupied by animals who found its surroundings congenial to hunting, sheltering or littering their young. But he entered it nevertheless. His journey involved staying as much as possible to the borders of open areas where his forest coat offered some measure of camouflage, carefully testing steps when the support beneath or the footing was uncertain, and avoiding anything that might result in a laceration. Since he was alone and beyond medical aid, even a minor injury could result in sepsis that could be fatal. A twisted ankle could immobilize him for days. Long ago he'd learned that survival and heroics were incompatible.

It took Otis all day to cross the city. He made good time even though he was sorely tempted to conduct a side-trip into what appeared to be a mostly intact library or research centre of some sort. Many of the building's windows were intact, and the interior appeared to have minimal water damage, considering how long it must have been vacated. Shelving was visible from outside, some of it clearly holding books—perhaps dust now, but perhaps not, if the conditions were just right. There was also a wide array of glassware that might have been used in a laboratory, and was probably still usable if salvaged. He had to convince himself to carry on past this building, whatever it had once been. The purpose of his trip was not for salvage, despite the riches that may lie therein. Many other buildings close by were settling gently into the landscape as the process of decay lowered them there. The effect of this was to gently loosen large sheets of glass from decaying window frames, a material for which there was a continuous need in Euterra. Surveyors knew of this city, but he wondered if they knew of this particular site. He made a mental note and then pressed on.

On reaching the eastern edge of the city, he came upon a scene that made him stop. There was something different about the area just ahead. It looked like the rubble had been disturbed or reorganized. There is a peculiar property of naturally occurring ruins that brings to them a sort of physical perfection, sometimes even beauty, a formal harmony fashioned by the silent working of natural forces and the stability visible in things that have followed the law of gravity to find their own final resting places. But introduce a human hand and all of this is disturbed in a way that is unmistakable. Instead of 'ruin,' the place says 'recently occupied.'

Otis stopped, found a cranny in some fallen concrete and tangled aluminum where he could hunker down and sit. With his forest coat, he knew he was unrecognizable as a human, looking more like an ancient pile of leaves and twigs that had blown into a fissure where it was quietly decomposing. Beyond he could see decaying logs of wood and sheets of birch bark, which must have been much younger than the ruined concrete they were propped against. There were plastic pails about and bits of metal that had been sharpened and hafted. Near these objects, he could see what looked like a small pile of sticks but which he recognized were bones. They looked tangled up in something artificially coloured, perhaps a bit of polyester surviving from pre-Ruination times. Looking more carefully, he could discern several such bone piles—in fact, many. And they were scattered about the scene as if all the people had died at once and not from disease or starvation or some cause where the many who were well had cared for the few who ailed. Rather, it looked like all had scattered and dropped at once, like a gust of leaves.

Presently, he rose again and walked into the clutter of remains. The chaos of it exhaled a miasma of terror and disturbance. Whoever these people had been, they must have died at least a year before as their decomposition was complete. But the positions in which they lay, and the clutter of the site, made it clear that their end had not been a peaceful one. He sat down again opposite one of the corpses and looked carefully. Both the radius and ulna bones of the right arm had been shattered suggesting the arm had been broken at the time of death. Some hair was still visible on the tanned and desiccated scalp, but a large, deep gash could still be seen there just at the base of skull, separating it from the atlas vertebrae at the top of the spine. The bones of this person, who he decided had been a woman, told of a violent death and a difficult life.

Looking around the group, he guessed that they had lived at a subsistence level, perhaps even hunting and gathering. There were other remains among which were clearly those of boars, and many other smaller animals. But there was still something missing. He surveyed the gruesome scene for many minutes, asking himself over and over, what was *not* there? In the end, he gave up and decided to resume his trek.

He had daylight enough to make his way for another two hours, plunging back into the bush which seemed to go on forever. The peace he felt tramping along a more open forest floor than he had so far traversed contrasted with the low hum of anxiety he had felt while crossing the city. Out here he could see. Out here he could hear things and know their direction. Out here he knew what else was in the bush with him. As he walked, he kept an eye peeled in quest of early berries, and his vigilance was rewarded soon enough, giving him some sweetness to add to his supper. Farther now from any wetland that might be a haven for pythons, Otis decided to make a small fire and sleep on the ground. After a meagre meal, he settled down for the night. Then, on the border of sleep, it occurred to him, what was missing in that grim scene at the eastern edge of the city: *There were no children there.*

CHAPTER 32

Most of what we call education is reminding
ourselves of things we shouldn't forget. We are
a distractible species—often to our grief.

— THE APHORISMS OF TELDER BOWEN

"YOU SHOULD UNDERSTAND," said Nota Dorne, "that if you cast your lot with us, you'll need to know these things. Otherwise, nothing about life in Euterra will make sense."

Jaeger swept his gaze around another of the Siderium courtyards awash in mid-day light variegated with leafy shadows. He had become one of Dorne's mentees, though he sometimes sensed that Dorne doubted his capacity to learn what he had to teach. "Do I have a choice?" said Jaeger, resigned.

"You always have a choice. You're not a prisoner here. But if you choose to leave, we'd take you back where we found you. We'd give you some training and gear but we wouldn't risk trying to find Mainbranch to return you there until we know more about it. Or you could just walk out Dawngate on your own and go where you wish, though I wouldn't recommend it."

Jaeger shuddered. "Not back to Mainbranch!"

Dorne regarded him silently, then said, "I understand this is difficult for you—not something you chose for yourself. But if you give it a chance, you may find this practice congenial. Learning what you need to know isn't even possible unless you're at least a bit open to it. It's challenging enough at your age. Most Euterrans learn Practice as children, when their consciousness is most open. For adults it's more—challenging. But who knows? You might be teachable after all."

Jaeger nodded. "Alright. I don't mean to be ungrateful. It's just that things here are very strange compared to where I lived before."

"Which is another reason to apply yourself to Practice," said Dorne, "if only to reduce the strangeness. And sometime, I'd like to hear more about Mainbranch."

"Well, maybe you would, and maybe you wouldn't." Jaeger paused, then asked, "Where do we start?"

"We'll start at the beginning as we did with Stillness Practice. Take that seat and attend to me as if you could hear what I have to say only once, as if to memorize every word, as if your life depended on it—because it does."

"You mean people die who don't remember what you say to them?"

Dorne gazed at Jaeger intently. Humour was not his forte. He wondered if Jaeger was serious or facetious. He decided to take him seriously. One erred more often by taking things lightly than by taking them seriously. "History teaches us that if you don't remember what you're about to learn here, the absence of that memory will kill you, and sometimes others as well."

"I was only joking."

"I'm not."

Dorne dropped his gaze and folded his hands in his lap, took a deep breath and then exhaled it slowly and at length. With the next in-breath, he seemed visibly to draw together within himself everything he wanted to say on this occasion as a single, conscious intention.

"The first and most basic thing you need to know about us is that we prize life above everything else. Euterra exists to foster life and protect it. Everything we do aims to nurture life and yet more life. Everything we do is measured against this value. This sets our way of life apart from most cultures of history, especially pre-Ruination culture. They were takers. We are trustees."

"In a deeper sense," Dorne went on, "I mean that Euterrans generally believe that the purpose of human life is to nurture and protect all life. We know why we're here and what we're supposed to do here. We also know this is a community undertaking, not just an individual pastime. Most people living in past societies, especially leading up to the Ruination, had little or no sense either of their individual or their collective purpose. Their lives were inwardly hollow and lonely because they had no shared purpose beyond pursuing their individual pleasure. They thought mere freedom, which they guarded vigilantly, mattered more than what they did with their freedom. Freedom meant having choices, not making them. They were mistaken."

"And you've solved that problem?" Jaeger asked.

"Perhaps," said Dorne. "It would be impossible to say that we've settled the question for good. But we've found an answer that brings meaning and value into our lives right now. Later I'll tell you about the Lightminders and how they continually watch for Opening—whatever is emerging for us that will be the next step toward whatever we are becoming. The ultimate mystery is hidden from us but sometimes we get glimpses of our next step. The

Lightminders watch always for what might be the next step in our evolution, the next step into that mystery. It's our shared desire always to be moving toward it rather than somewhere else, or off in all directions at once as pre-Ruination people did."

"And how do you do that?"

"Ah! That is the Practice." Dorne smiled. "Practice is a very large subject. We can make a start if I tell you *about* Practice today, but you'll need months, probably years to actually learn it, much less master it. Most of us think of ourselves as students of Practice who never achieve mastery. Any who think they're masters clearly don't yet know what is Practice—and there are a few of them around."

"So what was it I learned the day I met you, when I was with Spark?"

"You learned sitting practice with attention to breathing," Dorne said. "It's the most basic skill necessary to learning anything else. That's why we teach it first to children, although Spark is far beyond that. It's a disciplined way of paying attention. If you don't first learn to pay attention, it's pretty much impossible to learn anything else, wouldn't you agree?"

Jaeger nodded. "So what else is Practice?"

"Practice is the collection of knowledge and skills that hold our way of life together, give it form, and preserve what we understand about the good life, the universe and everything. It's through Practice that we come to a sense of who we are, what our purpose is, how to fulfill that purpose, how to watch for way opening, and much more besides."

"Sounds—daunting," Jaeger said.

"Well, perhaps. But the alternative is chaos, or trial and error—mostly error. We believe that in principle, Practice can be discovered eventually by anyone with enough time and persistence because Practice is true and we can't avoid or deny the truth forever. It's just that we have so much in common, and so much has already been discovered by others, only a pathologically individualistic person would forego such help in favour of trial and error, or a stubborn but ignorant independence. But we're all free to go that way if we wish. In pre-Ruination times, it was the mainstream, though a stream without a channel."

"Euterran Practice revolves around the study of the Four Classics," continued Dorne. "These are *The Book of Elements*, *The Book of Memory*, *The Book of Practice* and *The Book of Transitions*. We call them 'books' but they aren't just books. Each book includes many volumes of things that are written down—that make up, in fact, whole sections of our libraries—but also includes practices, artworks, exercises, and artifacts all related in some way to the theme of each book. So we might say that each book is a compendium of knowledge of a certain type which is essential to our way of life. What the classics have in common is that each relates in a specific way to our prime concern, which is nurturing and protecting life. Of course not everything we do or make re-lates directly to this goal—some things neither promote nor threaten life, and therefore we may indulge them. But if there is one principle in Euterra that comes as close as anything to the old meaning of a 'law' it's the injunction to avoid activities or knowledge the object of which is to destroy life. We admit of very few exceptions to this."

"But you do admit of some," Jaeger said, probing, curious. It was more a tentative statement than a question, arising from a world more familiar to him.

Dorne broke eye contact, as if trying to conceal his expression of distaste. "Discussion of such exceptions does not further." His words sounded final, if not downright dismissive.

The two men paused in their conversation as if they had stumbled into a topic that was obscene, embarrassing. Jaeger wasn't quite sure what to make of it because he had had no similar experience during his stay in Euterra. He had no sense that the topic was forbidden, but just in very bad taste. Dorne, the consummately gracious mentor, dissolved the awkwardness by resuming his overview of the Four Classics.

"*The Book of Elements*," he said, "is about the material world. It includes everything we know about, and everything we know how to do with the nine-ty-eight naturally occurring chemical elements and the twenty synthetic ones as well—the elements constituting physical reality. We also recognize other 'elements' which don't fit the chemical definition of an element, but which are necessary for the persistence and flourishing of life. These include things like clean air without which complex life cannot exist, clean water, living soils which can support more life, and the genetic diversity of life itself."

"We also include some non-material elements," Dorne went on. "These are elements that we see manifesting through the material universe such as love without which symbiosis between humans and other beings is impossible; con-sciousness which is humanity's greatest endowment and without which fully human life isn't possible; and the material aspect of the Central Harmony. The Central Harmony is the source of everything else and is what manifests in way opening discerned by the Lightminders. But we think it must have manifested somehow from the very beginning in other beings as well. We can't penetrate exactly how this happened because their sentience is very different from ours and therefore difficult to grasp. We sense, however, the fact of a common ori-gin, a common love, which opens way for different beings in different ways but is the common ground that holds us all together in Unity."

Jaeger was thoroughly puzzled and was sure that it showed. Dorne looked indulgently amused. "It's still an area of active research. Let's say for now that Euterrans recognize the working of the Central Harmony in all the other physical elements. This means that even though we use the elements to make things we need, we still recognize in them this quality of mystery—even sacredness—which is entirely independent of their usefulness to us. Their value inheres in them simply because they exist, not because they may be useful to us. So you might say the universe is lending itself to us for our use, but always in the service of life and never in the cause of gratifying our ego-delusions, appetites for luxury, or to exercise power over others."

"That all sounds interesting," Jaeger said, though his interest was waning, "but what actual difference does it make in how you live?"

"It makes all the difference. Pre-Ruination cultures thought of the elements as insentient 'resources,' basically dead matter. They recognized nothing in them other than their physical properties. Like fish unaware of the water they swim in, they couldn't even see themselves as spiritual beings evolving along with the physical elements. But since we are made of physical elements and we are evolving in our sentience, this implies that there must have been something sentient present in the elements themselves from the very beginning. Otherwise, how could sentience arise from them?"

"In any case," Dorne continued, "if ever pre-Ruination people paused in their consumption of luxuries long enough to reflect on their own behaviour, they often bemoaned their materialism. But, in fact, they were not materialistic. Had they really loved the material world as much as they thought, they wouldn't have made shoddy, tasteless things destined only for landfills. They would have treated everything as if it was a sacred object."

"And Euterrans do this?"

"It's an ideal we try to attain, yes. The next time you go for Active Practice with the Permies, for example, notice the Permie Elders who are simply sitting still and looking at the landscape. They will do that sometimes for several years, registering its every feature, every mood, every shifting season. They will not lift a finger to change that landscape in any way until they're sure they understand it and what is possible for it without violating its essence, its own unique way opening. We've learned that only by working with that essential integrity—the Central Harmony appearing as a landscape—can we live in right relationship to it, that it can feed us without harm to itself, that we can be symbionts rather than parasites."

"Or watch any of the Euterran crafters," Dorne went on, "and how long they will observe, examine, feel or listen to the materials they work with. Nothing can be worthily made, whether a bit of furniture, clothing, a sculpture or a tool, without respecting the elements they are made of. And respect comes down to true knowledge, affectionate regard, and awareness of the indwelling sacredness of everything. That's why, from the very beginning of Euterra, Beamer Ferris urged everyone to build Euterra as an artwork, not just a shelter. Disregarding these insights leaves a dead world cluttered with trash."

Jaeger sighed.

"You're tired then?" Dorne asked.

Jaeger smiled weakly. "I feel like I've been trying to sip from a waterfall."

"Rest for a while as you need," said Dorne, "but know that this is Practice."

———— • • • ————

Later, Jaeger and Nota Dorne left the Siderium garden and went to the top of the Starsis Massif. They sat on a small expanse of granite bedrock fringed with spruce trees circling them on the north and east but with an open view of Loch Speare to the south and west. The day was brilliantly sunny and warm. The intensity of the light brought a surreal clarity to the texture of the rock and seemed to cause it to emit a slight metallic scent. Here and there rubbery lichens digested the stone with unimaginable patience. While they sat there, Jaeger's attention was captured by a row of subtle grooves in the surface of the rock.

"Sand worms," said Dorne without turning from his contemplation of the grey pool of the Loch below.

"What?" Jaeger said, jolted from his dreamtime. "Sand worms," Dorne repeated. "This rock is more than half a billion years old—pre-Cambrian they used to call it. Those grooves were left by very large worms burrowing into the sediment of an ancient ocean bottom at a time when they were among the most advanced forms of life on Earth. Provides perspective, doesn't it."

"Perspective?"

"Yes. I especially like these worm fossils. They help me remember things I should never forget—like knowing my place."

Jaeger sat without speaking, his fingers drawn to the grooved pattern in the surface of the rock, trying to imagine the unimaginably long time since that soft-bodied thing as long as a man had waited, burrowed down in the ooze, only its feeding parts exposed until some hapless creature came swimming by, then... He snatched his hand back from the fossil.

Dorne noticed the abrupt gesture but held his peace. "That's why we study *The Book of Memory*. Human beings need constantly to be reminded of things that are important but not necessarily urgent. We're very prone to distraction. We get sidetracked by things that are urgent but not important, and we forget what is important but not urgent. Even when we make great discoveries, we tend to forget them or let them be obscured by less important but more insistent distractions. So a good deal of Practice aims to help us remember things we shouldn't forget. One Great Forgetting was enough!"

"But isn't a book of memories simply what Telder Bowen calls 'history'?"

Dorne nodded. "It's certainly that. *The Book of Memory* includes everything Euterrans know from history before the Ruination and our own history here in the Massif since then. But it's about a lot more than merely events from the past. You could also call it a book of reminders—things we need to remember not only about what happened in the past, but also things of which we should be mindful every moment. It's fine to cultivate attention through sitting practice, but it's just as important what we pay attention to while doing so. We can do better than look at the back of our eyelids. *The Book of Memory* offers things worth paying attention to—worth remembering. It's a collection of things people need to remember in order to live rightly as symbionts with nature, and with each other. They're the non-negotiable facts of life."

"And to know your place," Jaeger said, feeling finally as if some things were falling into place.

"Yes—to know your place," Dorne repeated. "You may also hear people sometimes mention the Happy Memories and the Cautionary Memories. These are a special part of *The Book of Memory* that form the basis for some of our meditative practices and ethics. The Happy Memories are discoveries about life that are encouraging to keep in mind. Each one has a whole literature of its own, but in a nutshell, the First Happy Memory is that of Immortality. Euterrans believe that we are all immortal, evolving through many incarnations becoming more and more radiant along the way. So far, we can see no end to this."

"The Second Happy Memory is that of Relationship or Connection. None of us is an individual. We all arise co-dependently with other beings and with each other. Anything done to any of them is done to ourselves. This has been the case since the original entanglement of the material and spiritual elements in the beginning. So we are never alone and never free of responsibility for each other. It was in such remembrance that Otis Bede brought you to Euterra.

"The Third Happy Memory is that of Mindfulness. We humans can direct our attention and with practice we can stabilize it to the end that we develop greater freedom and self-understanding. By freedom I mean freedom from all sorts of mental and physical factors that would otherwise imprison us in negative emotions and destructive habits. In other words, we can cooperate in our own perfection while remembering that we are always on our way beyond where we are."

"The Cautionary Memories are exactly what the name implies," Dorne continued. "Forgetting them will cause suffering."

Here Dorne paused and appeared as though he was gathering together only the most essential kernels of two and half centuries of Euterran philosophy. When he resumed speaking, his voice took on a recitative quality, taking care that nothing was omitted, nothing overlooked. Jaeger listened intently, himself feeling drawn into the aura of Dorne's concentrated attention.

"We need to be careful to remember that we are heterotrophs," Dorne said. "We feed on other beings to sustain ourselves and must participate in those relationships as loving symbionts. And we also need to remember that human judgment is fallible—we can be mistaken and we should always be mindful of this by practicing humility, modesty and inclusiveness of others. We live amidst multiple time scales—meaning that many things are happening both faster and slower than we can directly perceive, which can be another source of mistaken judgment."

"We're prone to narcissism—forgetting that the ego is merely a useful social construct, not the measure or the reality of who we really are. We are prone to thinking that we are exceptional in various ways—thinking ourselves wiser than other beings or not subject to the usual laws of nature. And we're inclined to psychological projection when we attribute to others traits or motives which are actually our own. We're drawn to delusional egoism because consciousness itself requires that we abstract information from reality in order to make mental representations of it, and in the process to some degree we can lose touch with reality, to our grief."

"We can also fall victim to hyperactivity, with an innate bias toward action even in situations when non-action is clearly the wiser choice. As well, we tend to act impulsively—a habit we try to compensate through Stillness Practice.

"Finally," Dorne said, "we must be vigilant for the delusion of possession, that we can somehow permanently possess anything at all when in fact we are continually borrowing and using things we did not make nor do we understand. If we fail to keep these Cautionary Memories in mind, it's certain that we will behave insanely in some way or other. Every Euterran child learns the Happy and Cautionary Memories from the time they can first speak, and contemplation of them together with their various discourses and commentaries is a constant focus of Practice throughout life. In no way do we suppose the lists are complete and it's not enough to simply memorize a list. The aim of Practice is to help us conjure the insight we need so that we can perceive these truths as a personal experience. No one is asked to accept them 'on faith.'"

Dorne stopped, and Jaeger took some moments to ponder all of it. It was a lot to ponder. Then he asked, "And you teach *all* this to your children?" Dorne looked at him quizzically. "In a manner of speaking," he said. "It's not that we sit them down and tell them these things. That would hardly be helpful. What we teach them is Practice, and then we surround them with support for their Practice, nourishment for their Practice, different ways to Practice, posing questions and making suggestions until, with respect to each memory, they experience the truth of that particular teaching. We don't evolve by being told things. We evolve by having new experiences. So the process is more like gardening than it is telling people things. And when the fruit is ripe it falls by itself."

"So that's what you call *The Book of Practice*?" Jaeger asked.

Dorne gave half a nod. "Partly," he said. "*The Book of Practice* has many parts. If it's a verb, it's in *The Book of Practice*. One part of it contains all the practical procedures for doing everything needed to sustain us and foster more life here—everything from the steps of various dances, to how to make applesauce, to how to smelt iron ore—everything except the formularies and recipes contained in *The Book of Elements*."

"But in what we've been discussing today, other parts of *The Book of Practice* are involved," Dorne continued. "The earliest Euterrans recognized that consciousness is a powerful thing—maybe the *most* powerful thing. We also believe that people don't have consciousness; consciousness *has us*. While we cannot generate it on our own, we can nevertheless direct it according to our intentions. This may seem trivial, or obvious, but it's neither."

"As we develop in childhood, we don't become more conscious per se, but we can become more self-reflective in our mode of consciousness and with practice, more capable of directing and focusing conscious intentions. We've discovered that it's very important to both our personal and collective well-being that consciousness be directed in a disciplined way and with life-fostering intention. Lacking this, consciousness will find its own focus, often randomly, and too often forming fixations that are useless, unwholesome or that are corrosive to well-being. It matters what we offer a growing consciousness to feed on. And it matters that this process of growth not occur randomly. All of this is important because we're not just copying some dogmas from one generation to the next; Practice has consequences for the physical structure of the brain and how it works later in life. So Practice isn't just about adopting certain postures, doing certain exercises, or even thinking particular thoughts. It's about shaping the architecture of the organ of consciousness in ourselves."

"But aren't you manipulating children when you do this?" Jaeger asked.

"Of course we are," Dorne replied. "We continually study the effects of Practice on ourselves and how they either work in favour of, or contrary to, our life together. We adjust Practice as we discover new things that help make our lives happier and more symbiotic with nature. That we deliberately introduce our children to these practices and strongly encourage them to persist in Practice is something for which we make no apology. History shows that for over ten millennia, most people thought it was 'natural' and 'free' to let consciousness develop randomly. The results of this approach you can discover to your grief elsewhere in *The Book of Memory*. We think our way is better."

Jaeger shook his head doubtfully, though nothing in his personal history prepared him to debate what Dorne said. "You doubt this?" Dorne queried.

Jaeger shrugged. "I'm hardly in a position to argue," he said. "But something about what you say doesn't sit right with me."

"Maybe it's because you think we force Practice on our children and each other," Dorne speculated. "But that would be a misunderstanding. Very young children absorb whatever is around them—and in that sense, when we bring Practice to them, you might say they have no choice. But as the capacity for choice grows in them, what we invite them to do is more and more voluntary. The reason is that Practice cannot be done under force of coercion. It simply doesn't work that way. Practice is too complex, too demanding, and too interior to force on anyone else. What *does* happen, however, is that those who are practicing are becoming visibly happier all the time while those who don't practice generally are not. If you see others eating something delicious which they also offer to share with you, is it not a rational exercise of freedom to want some yourself?"

The two men fell into silence for some minutes. While they sat there on the Massif, a scoop of white pelicans came gliding along the Massif from the east, veering noiselessly past the wall of rock below them, then turning south, tracing their descending gyre over the grey surface of the Loch. Their formation was perfect, their turns in perfect synchrony as they made their way downward to their afternoon meal. "We don't have consciousness." Dorne's voice floated into Jaeger's reverie. "Consciousness has us." Jaeger suddenly felt himself locked to the movement of the pelicans, gliding round and round in their perfect mastery of the air.

Jaeger shook his head, rousing himself from his trance. "And you said something about a *Book of Transitions?*" His voice felt disembodied, as if it belonged to someone else. His attention was still captivated by the birds.

"Yes," said Dorne. "There is a fourth book, *The Book of Transitions*. You might say it's the most subtle and challenging of them all."

"How so?"

"*The Book of Transitions* is about some of the things we find most mysterious. If you just take an ordinary, commonsensical perspective on the world and life and everything, it all appears quite seamless and consistent. But if you investigate a bit more, reality has some wrinkles."

"Wrinkles?"

"Well," Dorne said, "everything I say from now on is metaphors. Yes, wrinkles. For example, we notice a discontinuity between the part of the world that is apparently non-living and the part that is living. If I put some dishes of carbon and sulphur and phosphorous and some bottles of oxygen, nitrogen and hydrogen on the table and then try to mix them up in different ratios,

I get pretty much nothing. Even if I mix them in the exact same ratios that they are found in living things, I still get nothing. But when they're combined *just so* in nature, they become alive. That 'just so' is a transition boundary between two radically different realms of existence and different kinds of beings. This is quite mysterious."

Jaeger was lost again. "When you start looking for these transition boundaries," Dorne went on, "you find them everywhere: for example, the transition from unconscious to conscious awareness; the transition from individuals to communities; the transition between mindful and mindless states of awareness, and several others. They are these little wrinkles that make it impossible to apply what you know about one side of the wrinkle boundary to the other side of it. *The Book of Transitions* is about our efforts to understand these things."

"Why would you care?" Jaeger felt a bit fatigued.

"We *do* care." Dorne's tone was firm but not defensive. "We feel drawn to them without knowing why."

"Like way opening," Jaeger said.

Dorne glanced at him in surprise. Was it an idle guess, he wondered, or was Jaeger beginning to understand something? "Yes," said Dorne, "like way opening. We have observed that when the Lightminders discern way opening, they are more often than not standing at a transition boundary of one sort or another."

"But what practical difference does this make to ordinary people?" Jaeger said, impatient from wrestling with so many new ideas.

"A great deal," said Dorne, "if you're the least bit curious about where you came from or where you're going. The very fact that you're sitting here in the form you have is the result of non-living matter organizing itself in such a way as to enable it to cross a transition boundary that makes you a living person rather than a pile of chemicals. We believe that human beings carry consciousness awakening in Nature. We are Nature looking back at itself for the first time—remembering itself—appreciating itself—aware of itself—and in that awareness capable of consciously choosing to care for itself. And awareness of these wrinkles is part of it. How is that possible?"

"In Mainbranch," Jaeger said, not bothering to hide his irritation, "we're too busy trying to stay alive to ask about how we got alive in the first place."

As if not hearing Jaeger's dismissal, Dorne went on. "And what will it mean, what will it be like at the end of your life, when you cross the transition boundary between your life and your death? Lydia tells me you were present at Sam Faron's Wending. You must have seen it, sensed it..."

Jaeger grew more sombre. "I saw...something," he replied, his voice trailing off.

"And there was more you didn't see that was present there—what you perhaps heard in *The Lai of Wending*, in those gathered, in Faron's body as he made his transit. Yes, you saw something, and it should be remembered."

CHAPTER 33

*There is no 'economic problem.' The material requirements
for a good life are modest and easily provided. Live
simply so as not to multiply violence and cumber. Better
to devote oneself to music, dancing, and deepening
Practice than to go off crosswise multiplying trouble
and adding cumber to cumber without limit.*

— THE BOOK OF MEMORY

LYDIA AND JAEGER stepped off the lift at Procyon Drift and headed toward the plaza which was already crowded with people and shimmering with several thousand tiny multicoloured lights. It was extremely rare to discover any more LEDs left from pre-Ruination times that might still work, but many had been gathered during, and just following, the Ruination. Treated with care and operated only rarely, they lasted practically forever. Now they were used only for special occasions like Soirees, and in special applications like surgeries or for lighting the inner reaches of Siderium libraries and laboratories. Euterrans generated some electricity from micro-hydro stations on the Snake River, pyrolysis and biogas generators, and some small wind turbines. But making electricity was easy compared to the devices that used it. No one knew how, or had the tools or special materials, to fabricate solid state devices like LEDs anymore. With the disappearance of fossil fuels and the immense power they gave people, and which was mostly taken for granted when it was cheap and abundant, manufactures that were common in the Industrial Age were challenging or impossible to produce in the Euterran Age. But Soirees Dansantes were social priorities in Euterra, and for them, stage lighting was set up as well as twinkling holiday lights kept from the salvages of past generations.

The Procyon Drift agora had been converted to a giant dance floor with a stage at one end and a buffet-style spread of all sorts of edibles and no shortage of beverages to help them go down. Many chairs and tables had been scattered around the edge of the room for elders and those who might later grow weary. Flocks of children were stampeding from one end of the plaza to the other, playing out the last of the day's energy before they would collapse, no matter how loud the music. As Lydia and Jaeger threaded their way through the crowd, Jaeger spotted Hyram Bowen gripping a mug of mead and holding forth in lively conversation. Lydia kept moving along, though, intent on finding Zephyr. Presently they spotted her coming through the crowd.

"At last!" she called, bringing Jaeger and Zephyr face to face. "You know I don't do well in crowds," Lydia said, smiling. "So I'm off to find some punch. Be well!" And she was swallowed in the crowd again.

"Punch?" asked Jaeger, feeling both terror and fascination in the midst of this scene.

Zephyr laughed, her eyes twinkling. In another time her usual persona might have been called 'professional,' or by some, even stoic. But on this night she'd given herself permission to drift in the light and crowd sounds and music with untethered pleasure. "It's a combination of fruit juices. Lydia is a Lightminder. They never ingest anything that might cloud them up or make them silly. Pretty tight if you ask me, but she takes her vows very seriously. She'll have a good time anyway—in her own way. Not to worry..."

"Punch sounds good to me," said Jaeger, wanting to be agreeable.

"Not on your life!" Zephyr laughed. "I'm your Helder and I prescribe mead, or maybe ale. We'll see how you handle your first dose and then take it from there. You need flexible ankles for what comes next and believe me, mead helps."

Jaeger was puzzled, as was often the case, but less often of late. He followed Zephyr to the bar and they started on some mead. Meanwhile, some musicians had taken the stage and opened an entirely new chapter in Jaeger's experience. It was also the first time he had heard amplified music of any sort. At first, this was terrifying. But as the mead suffused his brain with its golden aura, the music was tolerable, then pleasant, then positively exhilarating.

For a while Zephyr simply watched Jaeger take in the scene, the large number of people, and what for him must have been unimaginably exotic sounds and aromas and vibrations.

The band had many different drums, simple wind instruments, fiddles and a bass, and several guitars and a harp. Their first number started out with stately slowness, almost dignified in its cadence, but people laughed excitedly as they flooded on to the dance floor. Without any direction or prompting, they started forming circles of twenty or so people, alternating by sex. The circles began turning with individual dancers introducing what appeared at first to be a simple series of repetitive steps. Zephyr set down her mead and grabbed Jaeger's hand.

"Come now!" she shrieked in excitement. "You *must* learn *this*!"

Jaeger stumbled along behind her and found himself beside her on the edge of one of the turning wheels of dancers.

"Follow me," she called. "This way…step, step, turn half way, turn back, step back the other way, step, turn, turn, that's it. Now women only!" she said, just in time to save him following her toward the centre of the circle. But immediately she came twirling back to join him at the rim. "Now men!" she called and gave Jaeger a push. All the men in the circle moved toward the centre with simple steps on the way in, but performing a sort of prancing backward step that left Zephyr gasping with laughter as Jaeger tripped his way back to the edge of the circle. Then sideways they went, half turning, turning half back, and on.

At first to his dismay, then to his delight, Jaeger heard the music speed up a little with each passing bridge, and with each round, the dance became more intricate and more frenzied. Gradually the dancers with less skill or stamina moved themselves to the edge of the circle while the more skilled moved closer toward the centre. Jaeger edged back but kept up with clapping as everyone began cheering on the ones left in the centre. The dance was an odd combination of cooperation in the circle pattern, enfolding competition around who could keep up with the ever-faster tempo of the music, add the next layer of complexity to the steps, and just endure. Presently only two women and two men were left in the circle, one of whom was Zephyr. Her body *was* the music as she screamed with laughter trying to keep up with each tempo shift. The fiddlers sawed away like madmen, grinning through their sweat as she kept dancing and turning, her now bare feet pounding out the rhythms coming from the drums. In another moment the remaining dancers stepped away from her, leaving her there spinning in the middle of the circle. Then with shocking suddenness, the music stopped, Zephyr froze in place, and the last chord of sound echoed in the gallery above them. She stood on one foot, her other foot raised in front of her, and the only sound in the room was that of breathing. Then just as suddenly, she set down her raised foot and the room erupted in clapping and shouting. She smiled broadly and came spinning toward Jaeger as the band struck up another tune and people flooded back onto the floor.

Jaeger grinned at her. "That was wonderful!" he said. "*How* did you do that?"

"Practice," she smiled. "Where did I leave my mead?"

CHAPTER 34

*When on dangerous ground, one should exercise care
not to be made captive by one's own curiosity.*

— THE BOOK OF MEMORY

THE PRESENCE OF other people was announced first by a sudden interlude in the forest's conversation with itself. Only with the greatest care and awareness can someone move through a forest unnoticed. As it was, however, certain voices in the trees had suddenly fallen silent while others were raising an alarm. Otis Bede could hear the corvids, ravens and jays, scolding far off, as well as a manically chirping red squirrel. But crickets, tree frogs, many other birds, and the buzzing of some insects fell utterly silent. By contrast, the sound of human voices rising over the leaves shushing in the gently lifting air clattered in the distance. He stopped, instinctively stepping off the boar trail and crouching down, sinking into his forest coat camouflage. To all appearances he became a mound of moss. Moss whose sole purpose was listening.

The voices were unselfconsciously boisterous, confident in their assumed solitude. Otis listened for a long time. They neither approached nor receded, and they didn't move from one place to another. There was a good deal of shouting, but no laughter. All the voices sounded male. They were still too far away to clearly distinguish words but Otis decided from their tone and number that the speakers were wholly preoccupied with their own activities and might therefore be approachable.

Noise carried very far in the bush and what sounded just over the next hill turned out to be over a kilometre away. Otis had to cover this distance off trail. It took him the better part of the morning to close the distance. The corvids didn't quite know what to make of him in his forest coat, so they remained silent or went back to incessantly scolding the others who presented the more recognizable threat.

As he approached, he noticed the telltale signs of the outskirts of another urban centre—the edge of a road sign thrusting up from the ground which had somehow survived the centuries, the ground unnaturally contoured suggesting something buried beneath, a shard of plastic unearthed by some animal and discarded yet again as inedible, unusable, or both. He picked his way along staying as much as possible under cover and moving from one stationary pose to another. To a casual onlooker, it may have looked like a collage of texture and colour was shifting mysteriously between glances.

Though he could clearly hear their voices, Otis was still a hundred metres away from the work gang when he first spotted a human figure. He continued to crouch motionless in the dappled shade and sunlight of the forest edge. The space separating him and the other men was more open terrain, mostly meadow grasses, vetch, fire weed, and here and there, low raspberry brambles or alder brakes. He could make out that the men were working with hand tools, excavating the face of a landfill deposit. He counted at least thirty of them, digging, then examining whatever they may have turned up, then continuing to dig. Occasionally, one of them would pull something from the cliff of debris, extracting a piece of aluminum here, a usable glass bottle there; but a great deal of it was a slimy mass of long decomposed organic materials, paper, box board, wood, pretty much anything except metals, glass and plastic. Anything salvageable was tossed into one or another of several piles.

These people, Otis guessed, were the 'Citizens' Jaeger had described. While most of them worked, a few others were clearly supervising. It sounded to Otis like those men were shouting directions and sometimes urging faster work. The labourers appeared to comply, but only as long as their supervisors looked on. The overseers were marginally better clothed and cleaner. They also carried objects about a metre long that Otis had never seen before. They appeared to be made of metal and slung by straps over the backs of the foremen.

It was late afternoon when they started loading two wheeled barrows with what they'd collected, and then headed off down a lane which was better travelled but less sheltered than any wooded track Otis would walk down. So he waited until the entire parade was out of sight, then followed them by the racket they made.

They tramped along for another six or seven kilometres when he began to detect more sounds and odours of human habitation—wood smoke, perhaps cooking onions, bread, garbage, excrement and urine, freshly cut vegetation. The light was waning from its afternoon glare to the lengthening rays of evening. He decided he would wait close to the forest edge until dark, and only then risk a closer survey.

By nightfall the settlement had become nearly silent. Otis crept closer, looking for signs of a night watch. But nowhere near the road could he detect one. This might mean that the Brotherhood, if in fact these *were* members of the Brotherhood, felt totally secure, or totally dominant, or else totally alone in their region and therefore complacent. Or perhaps they were careless, or perhaps Otis hadn't gotten close enough yet to what the Brotherhood thought was worth guarding. He pressed on into what had obviously been a city in pre-Ruination times. Most of the larger buildings were in ruins or falling into ruins. But some of those small enough to be repaired with human scale tools and labour had been maintained to weather tightness and were apparently occupied. Here and there he could see dim glimmers of light from dozens of windows even though the streets were dark as a cavern.

As he explored, Otis began to construct a mental map of this sprawling mess of hovels and shacks. Anything still standing had been built of masonry or concrete poured before the Ruination. In several locations, ancient parking structures had been closed in to make massive tenements with solid walls broken only with tiny windows here and there. As he passed these structures, he tried to guess how many people lived in them, surmising that several thousand might occupy these tenements. But their mere existence, or even their occupancy in the past, was no certain guide to how many people they sheltered now.

Turning a corner, Otis was stopped suddenly by an incongruous sight. Rearing up from the slums that surrounded it was a massive, cubical building. It wasn't large by pre-Ruination standards, perhaps only twenty stories tall and a hundred metres square. But its aluminum and glass facade had been maintained, and many of its windows were lighted, though dimly. Otis could clearly see guards on station at its entrance though they appeared not to be very vigilant. By comparison to the surrounding warrens, this building loomed upwards, imposing and intimidating. This must be the HQ as Jaeger called it.

Otis decided he had accomplished all he could for one night and resolved to get out of the settlement again, find some cover, make himself a meal and settle down to sleep for the day, to resume his survey the next night. As he turned to leave, however, he felt the point of something cold and sharp at the base of his skull.

"Don't move," came a tense whisper. "Don't make a sound. Don't turn around." A vice-like hand came down on his shoulder and turned him roughly to the right. "This way," the same voice said. "Walk. Slowly."

CHAPTER 35

*History is a mental construct bound in the body. To
liberate yourself from your history, unbind your body.*

— THE BOOK OF PRACTICE

ATOP THE STARSIS MASSIF and toward its southwest corner was a broad
expanse of rock that was both smooth and level. Euterrans called it the Tarshin
Reach as it was often used as a practice space by Tarshin-ru. A late summer
sun found Jaeger and Nota Dorne on the rock together, wearing only the
generous pants of Euterran custom, Dorne being endlessly patient and Jaeger
feeling awkward, as he often did.

"Lift your hands together this way," Dorne said, "then settle down bending
your knees part way, like this." His arms lifted and then settled down again
like a bulrush nodding in a breeze.

Jaeger lifted his arms and then let them drop, forgetting entirely to bend
his knees.

Dorne returned to an erect posture, gazing for a moment at his unpromising mentee. His expression blended gentle concern with uncompromising
self-discipline. "Again," he said, "but this time, pay attention to your arms and
knees—the same way we pay attention to the breath."

Dorne demonstrated the movement again. Jaeger reprised his first performance. "Stand here," Dorne pointed. "Give your whole attention to your arm. Be
in your arm. Feel every millimetre of your arm, the pulse of your blood, the weight
of the limb. Wake up—and relax." Dorne lightly grasped Jaeger's wrist and then
slowly lifted his arm for him. "Every degree of movement here," he said as he
moved Jaeger's arm, "is a new moment of consciousness. If we don't pay attention,
they slip by and disappear. Every moment of consciousness is a moment of life we
are either present for, or not. Do you want your life draining away into the dark?"

Jaeger did his best to concentrate, but with the effort he grew more tense, and frustrated. He dropped his arm. "I just don't see the point of this!" he blurted.

Dorne returned to his statuesque poise. "There is no *point*," he said calmly. "This isn't something we do in order to accomplish something else. If there is any point at all, it's to be present. That's all. The test is over before the lesson begins."

"I don't understand what you're saying," Jaeger said, more puzzled now than frustrated.

"As I see," said Dorne, without a tone of judgment. "This is normal for anyone learning Practice, especially as an adult. You won't be able to understand what I'm saying until you start doing what I'm doing. Again." Dorne stepped back from Jaeger and they again started the strange dance of T'ai-yo—Dorne moving and Jaeger trying to shadow his movements. They repeated the same movement phrase over and over, without conversation, for what seemed to Jaeger like hours. The rock was very hard beneath his bare feet and the sun more than a little warm on the top of his head.

Dorne completed the movement phrase and then said, "Sit now."

Jaeger sat down on the rock with gratitude. It wasn't until they stopped the exercise that it registered with him how strenuous it had been. Dorne sat down as well, facing him. "The Second Happy Memory," Dorne said, "is that everything inter-exists. There is a great deal to remember about this, but for today, know that whatever you've experienced in the past has left its trace in you—in your body, as well as your thoughts and feelings. Thoughts and feelings are states of the body, just as states of the body are thoughts. We can be more present if we release that history. I don't mean by 'release' to forget, but rather to relax clinging. This is the whole function of T'ai-yo—to loosen your clinging." Dorne looked at Jaeger closely. He still didn't understand. But he was aware that he wasn't struggling with not understanding any more. That was progress.

"Sit as I taught you," Dorne said. Jaeger adjusted his posture, slouching less, his body becoming slightly more attentive. "Close your eyes. Lean your head forward. Relax your neck completely."

Jaeger did this, at first mistaking the gesture for something simple. But as he let the weight of his head settle forward, it was as if first the muscles of his lower neck, then upper back, then deeper and deeper into his back began gently to stretch and release. What appeared to his mind's eye was a wave of light passing up his spine and flooding into his skull. At first he gave up a little chuckle, as if being tickled; but that slight vibrancy of his diaphragm began to grow as if being amplified from within, a swell on the ocean's surface that gained height as it neared the shore until it overflowed—and he began to sob.

"Just so," said Dorne, who sat by.

CHAPTER 36

*Each pursues the path he knows, even though the
path that is known may be fruitless. But unknown
paths may also be fruitless. One must set out.*

— THE BOOK OF PRACTICE

OTIS BEDE FELT himself being steered down a street in Mainbranch
which was even darker than those he had been passing through all night.
The hand on his shoulder was very firm, turning him first this way, then
that, and all the while, the sharp pointed thing pricked the back of his neck
menacingly. They made their way a hundred metres or more, then turned
off the street into a narrow alley, went another dozen metres, turned again,
then down a flight of metal stairs. The hand pulled Otis to a stop only long
enough for another pair of hands to pull a cloth bag over his head and then
tie his hands together. No words were exchanged, but the hand on his shoulder clamped tight again, turning him left. Still in a hoarse whisper, the voice
said, "Walk." Otis walked.

They continued walking short distances, turning, walking more, then going
down more stairs, then walking more, turning more. From the beginning, Otis
had used his training as a surveyor to memorize the turns, count the paces,
count the stairs, but it was soon evident that they were walking in circles, or
sometimes figure eights, even though the stairs took them steadily downward.
Wherever he was being taken, it was along a labyrinthine pathway, one that
would be challenging even for Otis to retrace. No one spoke, but he could
still hear from their footsteps and the gritty surfaces they walked over, echoes
from walls and ceilings, some of which were close by, and others far away.
From this he guessed they were sometimes walking down tunnels or passageways and at other times emerging into larger rooms, some of them cavernous.

But there were no other sounds than those made by the walkers themselves. Occasionally he could smell damp. Twice their feet swished through shallow puddles, but not for long. After nearly an hour of traipsing about, Otis knew with certainty that he was five stories underground but he had no idea anymore where he was in relation to cardinal directions or the city above.

Presently they came to a halt. Someone pressed firmly behind his knees which crumpled his legs beneath him, but he collapsed onto a chair instead of the floor. His guide and someone else quickly looped ropes over his chest and belly, tying him to the chair, and then applied more loops to his ankles and wrists. After the knots were tested, the vice grip on his shoulder eased, although the sharp pointed thing remained, the thing that threatened to separate his skull from his spine.

The bag shrouding his head was pulled roughly aside. Otis blinked into a darkness scarcely less dark than the bag. It was impossible to guess the size of the room as its walls disappeared into the dark in every direction. Near him was a small table and on it a single oil lamp which smelled like biofuel. It created a tiny orb of light within which he and his two visible captors were suspended. There could have been a hundred more people standing there just beyond the reach of that dim glow and they would hardly have been visible. The small light amidst so much darkness seemed to erase space itself—an effect that his captors probably hoped would be unsettling to him but which, because of his Tarshin Practice, he found both familiar and comforting.

"Who are you?" asked one of the two captors.

"Otis Bede. And you?"

"I'll ask the questions." His voice was firm.

"Otis Bede," he repeated.

"What kind of name is that?"

"It's my name," Otis replied. "It's the only name I have."

"No one has two names except for the Brotherhood. And you're not of the Brotherhood. So which name is your real name?"

"Call me Otis, then. Friends use first names."

"You assume a lot," the man said. "Where did you come from?"

"West of here."

"There *is* nothing west of here."

"A long way west from here," Otis said, while trying not to add anything important. His interrogator ignored his answer. The man started fingering Otis's outer forest coat, examining it closely.

"You dress strangely, Otis Bede." There was a touch of sarcasm as he used both of Otis's names, but since he wasn't being asked a question, he made no reply. "Why do you dress this way?"

"I was hunting. It helps to wear concealment."

"Humph," the man grunted. "You're lying." He moved around Otis, passing behind him, out of sight, standing in the dark for some moments. Was it a whisper Otis barely heard, or some shushing of the air in this airless, silent place? Presently his questioner returned.

"You say you come from the west where we know no one lives. You say you have two names when no Citizen has two names. You wear camo, though very strange camo. You say you're hunting but you have no weapons. And we see you passing from house to house all night long and you hope to be our friend?"

"Nothing I told you is a lie."

"If what you said is true, Otis Bede, it's not all the truth," he said flatly.

Otis tried his own question: "Where is this place?"

"You are in your grave, Otis Bede, if you don't start speaking the truth." The sharp pointed thing pressed harder against his neck.

Had his captors been more menacing, he might have been afraid. As it was, he guessed they *could* become menacing if he continued to hedge his answers. The more pressing question in his mind was why they hadn't killed him immediately, right where they found him? Why take him captive? Why the interrogation? Since he would probably wind up dead anyway, he decided little could be lost by trying to seize the initiative.

"I came from a place called Euterra," he said.

"We have no knowledge of such a place."

"That may be so," said Otis, "but there is such a place. It's very far from here. I *am* hunting—for a place called Mainbranch. Is this Mainbranch?"

His captors made no reply.

"I'm wearing forest coat and travelling by night because I hoped to avoid this very thing."

"This very thing?" his questioner echoed.

"Falling into the hands of people like you who tie me up, blindfold me, take me down in a cavern someplace, and keep a knife to my neck, telling me this is my grave."

Silence.

"You said 'Citizen,'" Otis said, pressing on. "Are you a Citizen?"

The interrogator's voice became more strained. "What we are or aren't is none of your concern. I ask the questions."

Otis took the plunge. "Do you know Jaeger?"

———⋆———

A murmuration swelled in the darkness and just as quickly subsided. But it was enough; enough for Otis to know that there were definitely more people in the room than his interrogators and himself—many more.

A hand slammed into his chest roughly pulling together his tunic and yanking him forward against his restraints. "*What did you say?*" The other man said hoarsely. His face was only millimetres away from Otis's, his eyes glowing coals in the lamplight.

"Forty-six days ago, I found a man near death in the bush far travel from here. I brought him back to Euterra. He said his name was Jaeger. He said he was a Citizen from Mainbranch. We have no knowledge of Mainbranch or of people called Citizens. So I was sent here to survey for them."

The interrogator's grip on his throat tightened. "And Jaeger lives?"

Otis looked into the face of the man who was nearly strangling him. The man's eyes were wide and welling. "He lives," Otis managed to choke out.

The interrogator's grip loosened as he turned away staring into the dark and at the same moment the dark itself erupted with excited cheering and laughter. The man waved his hand into the dark, and the uproar died as suddenly as it had exploded. Another kind of energy crackled in the air now, even in the silence. He turned back to Otis. "And what is your interest in Citizens?"

"To know who you are. To be friends."

"Ha!" The interrogator said. "Friends with Citizens! Citizens have no friends except other Citizens. Again you tell half-truths."

"So what do you think is the whole truth?"

The interrogator's gaze was icy, unblinking. "You want to know if we're dangerous," he said. Otis made no response. The interrogator gave a derisive snort. "It's the Brotherhood you need to worry about—and maybe Jaeger."

"Why Jaeger?" For the first time, Otis felt panic raising his gorge. Unbidden, the image of Lydia burst in his mind—and that of Spark.

The interrogator finally released his grip on Otis. "Jaeger had a dream," he said through clenched teeth. "And now all Citizens have the same dream."

CHAPTER 37

*One of the most regrettable and often repeated lessons of
history is that more civilized societies can be extinguished
by the less civilized but better armed. This represents a
process of cultural selection which logically should leave
in existence only the most barbaric societies. That Light
continues to reappear in history at all is therefore a miracle.*

— THE BOOK OF MEMORY

THE VIEW FROM Jaeger's room was the southwest sky above Loch Speare,
now studded with brilliant stars. The moon had not yet risen. With little use
made of artificial light in Euterra, the dome of the sky was the deepest jet,
alive with stellar twinkling. He and Zephyr Fey had taken a meal together in
his cell and now sat on the balcony space outside his room surveying the early
summer evening.

"How are you doing?" she asked. "Here, I mean—with us."

He sighed. "Sometimes I feel like I've always been here, in Euterra; right at
home. But sometimes I feel like I'll never get it, never completely fit."

"Well it's only been a couple of months," she reassured him. "I think you
have real potential as a dancer." He could almost see her smiling in the dark.
"Are there things about Mainbranch that you miss?"

Jaeger snorted. "If you knew the place, you wouldn't ask that."

"But there must be *some* things."

Jaeger paused briefly, then said, "Of course. People mostly. Living in
Mainbranch as a Citizen is horrible. But I guess that people living in horrible
places somehow make the best of it, especially if they think it's all they can
have. It's strange, but in Mainbranch, when the Brotherhood had nothing to

fear from me, I was never trusted. Here in Euterra, I've always felt trusted, even though you have something to fear because of me."

"I can't believe that," Zephyr said.

"You must believe that," Jaeger said. "For your own safety and that of Euterra—you must believe that. All you know of Mainbranch or of the Brotherhood is what you know of me, but I'm neither of the Brotherhood nor really a normal Citizen. Telder Bowen told me about the Ruination and how people lived just before it. It's very much like that in Mainbranch and with the Brotherhood. It's like the Ruination never happened for them. The Brotherhood doesn't teach us any history. They don't think it adds value. So we don't know much about the past. But I bet if we did, if we told the story of the Ruination, the Brotherhood would just say it was another 'business cycle.' They believe a lot in business cycles, and invisible hands, especially when things go wrong. But you have to believe, Zephyr, that if they knew I was still alive, here in Euterra, they would certainly try to find me, and then they would find you and everything you've made here."

"And then?"

"And then," Jaeger shuddered, "they would feed on this place."

"But how could they? Euterra is very great!"

"Euterra *is* very great," he agreed. "But Euterra is gentle and the Brotherhood is not."

A silence lengthened between them that Zephyr immediately feared might become a lacuna in their relationship. So she spoke, trying to fill it. "How can you say that among the Brotherhood it's as if the Ruination never happened?"

"Because it's true for them," said Jaeger. "It's even true for most Citizens. They live in ruins they don't even understand, and still they think all is well. They say that the HQ has two whole floors they call 'the mall.' It's a place where people trade things and display things we've made for the Brotherhood, or things we dug out of landfills. But they think that someday they'll have more and more of these things, a bigger HQ with room for more of the Brotherhood, and more Citizens to work for them. They think they'll find a way, or else take what they need from someone else, if ever they can find that 'someone else.' But I think there may be no one else left in the world. That's why Euterra is in danger."

"And what do Citizens want?"

Jaeger sighed wearily. "Citizens want their own mall."

"You're joking!"

"Only a bit," said Jaeger gravely. "Citizens probably want freedom more than a mall of their own. But if they somehow got their freedom, I think very soon they would want a mall. Telder Bowen said, before the Ruination, that's what was most important to people. They spent all their time in malls shopping for things. The mightiest cities on Earth were ringed by malls. Zephyr—isn't that what people do when they're free to do what they like? Build malls?"

"I'm not sure what malls are," she said, "but they sound sort of like the Agora we have on Procyon Drift. People need things to live, Jaeger."

"Of course," he said, nodding. "But do we need to live for things? Everything people in Euterra need is given by the Cellarers, or else from the General Stores. The crafters' stalls on Procyon Drift don't sound anything like the malls that Telder Bowen told me about. And especially they don't sound like they came from the same spirit. The crafters here are mostly artists who just want to share what they do and enrich this place with their work. But before the Ruination almost everything was—what did Telder Bowen call it?— *cutthroat*. How can people who want to cut each other's throats ever be what you call a 'community'?"

Zephyr sighed, exhausted by the topic. "It doesn't really matter anyway," she said. "The way of material affluence is closed to us now. The Ruination assured that. Even if the Brotherhood found Euterra and 'fed on us,' as you put it, being takers and not makers, in a generation or so there would be nothing left. They would just do what they did in the Ruination—prolong their own extinction without knowing why they had lived. Survival without meaning. I would rather be wending to my next incarnation."

Jaeger squeezed her hand in the dark. "Don't go wending," he said in a hushed voice.

He could feel her shrug in the dark. "Euterrans are free. We can't go back to living in malls without deluding ourselves. We know that. We have to find way opening to some other way of being human."

Another silence lengthened between them, but one in which Zephyr felt closer to Jaeger rather than parted. Then she spoke. "Maybe the Brotherhood are teachable."

"Maybe," Jaeger said, sounding doubtful. "Or maybe Citizens are. I'm teachable, right Zephyr?"

She grasped his arm in the gathering darkness, and squeezed it. "You definitely are, my friend. You definitely are."

CHAPTER 38

To assume another to be one's friend may be a mistake. But to assume that another is one's enemy makes it so with certainty.

— THE BOOK OF MEMORY

OTIS BEDE HAD LEARNED that his interrogator was named Fitz. They regarded each other closely as Otis slurped down oat gruel and ate a half dozen boiled eggs. It being mid-summer, a few berries had been added to relieve the monotony of the gruel. He sensed that the berries were a precious luxury offered in a spirit of hospitality to a hungry stranger, for which he returned effusive thanks. But the eggs and gruel, plain though they were, were a welcome change from bush foods, and he could eat as much as he wanted, instead of as much as he found.

Fitz had brought Otis, unbound, up from the sub-basement where their first interrogation was held. They sat now in a sunlit room with two or three dozen other Citizens who watched him eat, and who listened closely to his conversation with Fitz.

"You're lucky we found you before the Brotherhood did," said Fitz. "Their methods of questioning are much more—complicated."

"I'll count myself lucky then," Otis said with a nod.

"The Brotherhood doesn't care much what happens here in the Developments as long as we all come to work the next day, or unless it's close to the HQ. Then they take notice. You were getting too close."

"Who are the Brotherhood?" Otis asked.

Fitz shook his head. "Citizens don't know. The Brotherhood just *is*. My whole life, all I know is the Brotherhood and Citizens. The Brotherhood gives orders and Citizens obey. Citizens work, the Brotherhood rules. They all live in the HQ—that big building you were getting too close to. Sometimes Citizens go into the HQ to work, but no Citizens live there. Well...No Citizens live there unless someone in the Brotherhood wants a Citizen woman or man. Then sometimes they go in, but they don't come out again."

"But where did they come from?" Otis asked. "How did the Brotherhood come to be here?"

Fitz looked back with the deepest expression of puzzlement, as if the question was a complete novelty. "The Brotherhood just is," he repeated. "The Brotherhood has always been here."

"And Citizens?"

"What about Citizens?"

"Where did you come from? Have you always been here, like the Brotherhood?"

Fitz's gaze seemed far off, as if parsing memories, an expression Otis had also seen in Jaeger whenever he was asked about his past—as if anything past was deeply mysterious or must be excavated from some Hadean depth. Fitz's effort to assemble an answer visibly strained him. "I...don't...know, exactly," he said. "Some Citizens are born here, in Mainbranch. But some of us can remember things—like from a time before we came to live here." He tossed his hands in the air. "But maybe that's just dreams."

"Like Jaeger's dream?" Otis asked.

Fitz's eyes snapped back to Otis, fiery, intense. "No," said Fitz with finality. "Not like Jaeger's dream."

Otis got the feeling he had desecrated sacred ground.

Fitz was silent for a moment, then spoke again. "When Citizens dream, each dreams his own dream. They're all different. Maybe they are memories we see in sleep. Maybe nothing at all. But all are different. When Jaeger dreamed and told Citizens his dream, then we all started having the same dream. And it didn't feel like a memory. It was more like a prophesy, or..."

"Or an invitation?" Otis proposed.

Fitz looked startled, then nodded slowly. "Yes. Maybe. Maybe an invitation."

"That's what we in Euterra call 'an opening,'" Otis said. "It's not a prophesy, exactly. A prophesy assumes that the future is fixed and some people can see it and others can't. But an 'opening' is a possibility, something which may or may not happen, depending on what we choose. More than one person can see an opening. Our Telders say that many people must see it or it's probably not a *real* opening."

"Maybe." Fitz looked again at Otis, his eyes almost pleading. "For as long as anyone knows, the Brotherhood has always ruled. They push Citizens to work more and more. If we find other people we kill them—except for young children. Children we return to Mainbranch where they become Citizens. The Brotherhood has better food, more food. They want more of everything. The

Brotherhood lives in the HQ. No Citizens go in there, above the first two floors, or they never come out. A few Citizens work in there, but very few. It's always been this way. We're the ninety-nine—but I don't know where that name came from. Long ago it meant something, I guess. To be a Citizen is to be ninety-nine—and to weep." His voice trailed off.

"Until Jaeger," said Otis.

Fitz looked up again. "Yes," he said, "until Jaeger."

"And what happened when Jaeger told his dream?"

A small smile lifted the corners of Fitz' mouth. "Citizens stopped weeping," he said.

Otis could tell that Fitz was seized with strong emotion, which he wanted to respect. So the two men sat across the table from each other and the silence between them lengthened. Eventually, Fitz broke the silence. "More porridge?" he asked.

"I'm well fed. Thank you," said Otis. He decided to broach the matter that had caused him to panic earlier. "You said that the Brotherhood, and Jaeger too, are a danger to Euterra. How is Jaeger a danger?"

Fitz raised his eyebrows, as if this should be obvious. "If the Brotherhood retires a Citizen," he said, "we never see them again. They go in the night. They just disappear. But when the Retirement Party took Jaeger to find new opportunities"—here, Fitz shuddered—"everyone saw it. It was like the Brotherhood *wanted* Citizens to see it."

"Because of his dream." Otis did not have to ask this, for he knew it to be true.

Fitz nodded. "No one ever returns when they go on to new opportunities. If the Brotherhood knew that Jaeger lives, they would look for him. That would be dangerous for your people—believe me—*very* dangerous."

"How many of the Brotherhood are there?'

"Millions," said Fitz.

"But I've seen the HQ," Otis said. "Millions of people couldn't live in a building that size. Are there other Mainbranches, other HQs?"

Fitz shook his head. "Only this one."

Otis tried to imagine possibilities. "Does it go underground?"

Fitz nodded. "Two levels," he said.

"That's still not room for millions of the Brotherhood."

"There are millions," Fitz insisted. So adamant was he that Otis gave up trying to question it. Whether or not it was true, Citizens clearly believed that the Brotherhood numbered in the millions.

Over the next several hours of conversation, Fitz unfolded for Otis an increasingly alarming tableau. Citizens were virtually slaves under the Brotherhood's control. "The Chief," a title meaning something like tyrant or dictator, together with a body they called "the Commission," controlled every aspect of life in Mainbranch. Not even the Chief's name was known to Citizens. Dissenters, malcontents, the aged, the disabled and the redundant (as decided by the Chief) were summarily "disappeared" at the hands of someone else they called "the Expediter" along with his "Retirement Party." Clearly, the Mainbranch economy was more parasitic than productive. It operated mostly by recycling materials from ancient landfills and periodic raiding if any hapless remnant group from the Ruination was discovered. Most of these, however, had been exterminated long ago. It also sounded like the Brotherhood continued some form of the very destructive practice of mono-crop agriculture except that they used horses instead of machinery. Otis speculated that in pre-Ruination times the Brotherhood may in fact have been a police force which during the Ruination event found itself to be the best armed and most organized gang in town. Hoping to preserve their own families through a time when social order was disintegrating everywhere, police headquarters became the command centre from which they and their descendants had been living for nearly three centuries. But all of this, Otis recognized, was idle speculation. He remembered as well that in pre-Ruination times, corporations were among the most durable, adaptable and psychopathic of human institutions. It could have been that some corporate entity simply hired the police as mercenaries to provide temporary protection which eventually became permanent. Otis's efforts to disentangle fact from legend or superstition or propaganda became increasingly arduous and finally he gave up. He would have to rely on his own observations.

"Would you let me continue my survey then?" Otis asked.

A murmur passed around the room and Fitz's expression grew firmer. "That's impossible," he said.

"I don't understand."

Fitz looked impatient. "We captured you—" he said, "easily. And so would the Brotherhood if we let you go. We don't doubt your courage or your strength, but it's clear that you don't hide very well, in cities at any rate, and you probably hide better than you fight. If the Brotherhood captured you, they would certainly torture you. Sooner or later you would tell them of Euterra, that Jaeger lives, and about those of us who captured you first without reporting it. We would all be retired very quickly and the Brotherhood would be on their way to your village with a Recycling Party. As I told you, children are not spared. Is this something you want? Do you think you can fight them?"

Otis was silent for a moment. "No," he finally said. "I don't. What would you suggest?"

"We know the HQ and the Brotherhood," said Fitz. "We know the Developments. Tonight we'll take you to the western perimeter and you can find your way out of Brotherhood territory. Somehow, you got here without being seen, so maybe you should return that way, or whatever way seems best to you. Don't come back here. Tell the people in your village not to come here either—*ever*. Be warned that the Brotherhood exists and that they are a danger to any who travel east. Tell Jaeger to stay in your village. If he returns here many will be retired because of him. *He* would be retired, this time for sure. As it is, if he stays in your village, just the knowledge that he's alive may be enough to keep our hope. For your part, forget we exist, Otis Bede. But don't forget we exist."

Otis found himself again being conducted through a labyrinth of tunnels, but this time without a blindfold. The Citizens had re-provisioned him and led him as far as possible toward the edge of Mainbranch. In his time with them, he gathered that there was a semblance of resistance to the Brotherhood's control. It lacked effective leadership, and some had hoped that Jaeger would provide it. Its adherents were also fractious and disorganized and thus unable to mount an effective opposition to the Brotherhood. There may even have been a minority of Citizens within a majority of others who, if not actively supporting the Brotherhood's rule, nevertheless tolerated it in the expectation that anything different could be worse. Or else they didn't imagine that anything different could exist. Perhaps most importantly, Otis surmised, they likely harboured a great diversity of grievances but no unifying vision for any new order that might replace the Brotherhood. Since their misery was not quite complete and the Brotherhood offered just enough incentives calibrated to quell any rumblings of discontent, a precarious equilibrium was maintained. The greatest threat to the Brotherhood's hegemony would be a dream of a charismatic individual—a dream others could share—that offered an alternative to the status quo.

As they went toward the edge of the settlement, Otis guessed there weren't more than a few thousand inhabitants in Mainbranch, only a few hundred of whom at most were the Brotherhood. But these were guesses. He hadn't completed a reliable survey and he wasn't likely to. His cover was gone and the risks were too great, both to himself and to his captors.

The maze they walked snaked through basements, access tunnels, ancient underground parking garages, and utility corridors. Eventually, it brought them to a crumbling steel stairway leading upwards toward a barely discernible rectangle of moonlight.

"The bush line to the west is about two hundred metres that way." Fitz motioned in the pale lamplight they used to navigate the tunnels.

"Thank you," said Otis.

"When you see him," said Fitz, "tell Jaeger that Citizens remember him. Tell him Fitz sends greetings. Ask him to keep us in his thoughts every day, but not to return here. He will want to if you remind him of us. He must not. Do you understand? *He must not.*"

"I understand."

"Make good speed then!"

Otis took leave of his escort and ascended the stairway alone. Reaching the top, he glanced back, but their faces had already been swallowed by shadow.

He remained close to the exit from the underground until his eyes adjusted to the light offered by a nearly full moon. He glanced around to get his bearings, noting the space he had to cross before he could enter the cover provided by the forest wall. He took care to cross this open space as quickly and silently as possible and made it to the bush without mishap. Once under cover, he debated what course to follow: Either return directly to Euterra, using Tarshin running at every opportunity, or take a more devious and longer route that might help him evade anyone following but at the cost of time? In the end, he decided to do both—taking every opportunity to make speed when conditions allowed, but dissembling his route when opening appeared to offer a way to do so.

He spent the rest of the night picking his way westward as fast as travel in darkness would allow. He knew he risked accident by travelling at night, but adrenaline fuelled him and experience offered counsel that a novice would lack. He thought he had escaped Mainbranch undetected. He was mistaken.

———— • ◆ • ————

Dexter had held the chisel behind Otis's neck. Dexter had steered him to the chair where he was bound and questioned. Dexter had been listening in the shadows to Otis and Fitz as they talked, but he had not been among those who escorted Otis to his escape. As Otis set out on his return to Euterra, Dexter had other business that took him away from the Citizens that night. Personal business. Business he hoped would be profitable—somehow—though he wasn't sure quite how. And after all, wasn't profit the key thing in life?

Dexter's enterprise took him first to the HQ, and then found him ushered into the presence of the Expediter, a man whose name no Citizen knew. But his role in Mainbranch was well known. The Expediter got things done. The Expediter had connections. He had access to the Chief. Knowing him could be profitable. Of course it could also be dangerous, but one ran at least as many risks as one sat.

"He's heading west," said Dexter. "He left two hours ago. You could still catch him."

The Expediter's gaze was unblinking, blank, like that of a snake. "Where's he going?"

"Back to a village he calls Euterra."

"There is nothing west of here," the Expediter said dismissively.

"He says there is."

"Boar shit."

"Well," Dexter said, not prepared to give up, "maybe he starts off going west and then turns somewhere."

"You don't know?"

"No," Dexter admitted. "He didn't say, exactly, where he came from or how far away it was, except 'west' and 'very far.'"

"Who else knows about this?"

"A few others."

"Who 'others'?" the Expediter growled.

"Look," said Dexter, "if I tell you my sources, you'll retire my sources, and that means no more news down the line, right?"

"Your sources!" the Expediter snorted, continuing to fix Dexter with a basilisk stare. He broke his fixation and shuffled randomly through some papers on his desk, as if turning his attention to other matters. "Get out," he said.

Two of the Expediter's assistants moved toward Dexter, who got up on his own initiative, but before turning to leave, said, "If there's a Recycling Party, I want to go."

"We'll see," replied the Expediter without looking up.

"I want first pick," said Dexter, a flash of greed in his eyes.

"We'll see. Get out."

CHAPTER 39

*In discerning present circumstances it is helpful to
consider the lessons of history. But be not their captive.*

— THE BOOK OF PRACTICE

LYDIA ROSS STOOD with Lars Beckett before a table strewn with documents she had been pouring over for days. In addition to being a Lightminder, Lydia was a curator in the Hall of Memory.

"We may know something more about the Brotherhood," she said.

"You've found something?" asked Lars.

"Maybe. The Brotherhood could be us."

Lars's face went pale. "*What?*"

"In a manner of speaking," Lydia qualified. "This goes way back—back to the second or third decade after the founding of Euterra. Chronicles from that time are spotty because we were so busy just surviving. As you know from our history, Euterra received foundlings in the early days following the Ruination. We did this partly from compassion and partly to assimilate them to us rather than have them go back to wherever they came from and spread news of us being here. Not all of our motives were admirable."

"In any case, around 17-18 E.A. there was an influx of foundlings that we didn't know were actually fleeing an epidemic. We had no places or practices for quarantine at the time. They made it here with the result that maybe as many as a third of us died as well. It was a very dark time, a traumatic time both for our people and for the very idea of this place. Following the plague, we came upon almost no foundlings any more. Today we think that the epidemic, on top of the Ruination, caused a world-wide population collapse."

"But what does any of that have to do with the Brotherhood?" Lars asked.

"There is a very brief account from a year or two following the epidemic of a split within Euterra itself. The epidemic was traumatic for us. Some were angered and disillusioned with how the situation was managed and felt we should revert to more traditional, pre-Ruination forms of governance. These were more grounded in power and coercion than in Practice and the guidance provided by the Lightminders—who themselves were only embryos of what they are today. Fortunately for us, those who wanted a different way of life left Euterra without violence and went their way—reportedly somewhere off east."

"And you think they became the Brotherhood?"

Lydia shrugged. "I don't know. Possibly. I'm just telling you what the archival evidence is for a human presence to the east of here. Maybe the Brotherhood was already there and the Euterran émigrés just joined them. Or maybe the émigrés became the Brotherhood. We'll only know for sure if we find the Brotherhood and it turns out that they kept some history. Remember that such a group would still include some people with personal memories of pre-Ruination society. If they did go that way, if they did try to resuscitate corporate forms of organization, they must have forgotten about us. It would be consistent. The old pre-Ruination corporations had no use for history, priding themselves on always being future-oriented. But it wasn't at all like Practice that is attentive to way opening. Instead, as far as we can tell, they chased after the future like a mirage. It was pure projection, pure delusion, but a very compelling delusion. In any case, following the plague and the departure of that group, we started building the Thornway and established the Watches in the east and elsewhere. Today, we scarcely remember why these things were established, which is fortunate but also perhaps perilous."

"Hmm," said Lars. "Is that all we've got then?"

Lydia shook her head, "A bit more. We have record here of a survey to the east, over seventy years ago, done by someone called Cy Timo. His reporting was excellent but inconclusive. He surveyed over a thousand kilometres east of Euterra—found signs of recent human presence—some of it violent. But his survey was interrupted by very bad weather—rain that lasted for weeks, with landslides, overland flooding, sink holes opening, everything. He lost two members of his party to bad weather. He had to turn back. But he reported finding unburied human remains—a remnant group I suppose—but people who appeared to have been killed rather than dying of some natural cause."

"And why would Timo think they'd been killed?" Lars asked.

"Well, the remains were mostly skeletal, but they were all adults. There were no remains of clothing among them, suggesting they had been stripped before they were killed. And all were arranged in a single row, as if they had been lined up deliberately. And Timo reported finding round holes in some skulls."

"Round holes?"

Lydia nodded. "Come with me," she said. He followed her out of the archive room to a small lift that descended several levels into the Hall of Memory, to its museum collections. There they stepped off the lift and walked down one of several lengthy passageways until they came to a storage room with many shelves and drawers. Lydia glanced at the drawer labels as they passed deeper into the collections, then stopped at a large drawer and pulled it open. From this she lifted out a long, heavy looking object wrapped in cloth which she unfurled to let drop back into the drawer.

Lars gazed at the object with curiosity. "What is it?"

"This," she said gravely, "was called a gun. It was a device that used a replaceable cartridge that went about here, I think." She opened the breech to reveal the firing chamber. "And it was ignited somehow, releasing a burst of gas that propelled a metal pellet down this tube and out this hole." She pointed to the muzzle. "These pellets could be cast a great distance with enough force to kill a person. They were extremely common during Ruination times and were widely used to influence other people before we learned how to communicate with each other and other species. We also have record of them being fetish objects—believed by their possessors to confer power and status."

Lars raised an eyebrow. "And you think this thing has something to do with Timo's survey?"

Lydia nodded. "The metal pellets that come from guns might have caused the holes in the skulls that Timo found."

"So you think the Brotherhood has these things?"

Lydia shrugged. "I hope not. If they do, they may not work anymore. Timo's survey was seventy years ago. Three generations is a long time. But it still would have been nearly two centuries since the Ruination if these things still worked. Maybe they would work now too. We have some cartridges here somewhere." She rummaged around in the drawer, then extracted a handful of cartridges. "I tried putting one in the gun, but nothing happened." She shrugged again.

"Do we have any more of these—these guns, I mean?" Lars asked.

"I haven't checked the whole collection. But there are eleven of them in this drawer and several hundred cartridges. They're not all alike, so I'm not sure what goes together with what."

"And you think some of them may still work?"

"I don't know. Maybe we could give one to someone in the Mechanic's Guild, or one of the research labs in the Hall of Elements and see if they can figure it out. They don't look too complicated really. Some records from the Ruination say even children used them back then. We should be able to figure it out. But what use would they be to us?"

"I can't see any use right now," said Lars, though he looked worried. "But it's helpful to know such things exist and that the Brotherhood may have them.

If these things all disappeared in the Ruination, then good riddance. But if they didn't, I'm afraid we've sent our friend Otis on a dangerous errand indeed. Best take one to the Hall of Elements first and see if they can make sense of it. Ask them if they can find a cusp in these things. Also, please check the collections to see if we have any more of them around."

Lydia's expression turned grave as she put the gun back into its wrapping cloths. "Of course," she said, and paused. "I've held Otis in the Light ever since he left," she said after several moments. "I sense no harm to him." But her voice lacked conviction.

Lars embraced her firmly. "Steady," he said. "Otis is very skilled in bushcraft. But if necessary, I promise you, we'll send another survey to look for him."

She sighed. "The eastern forest is very great. If Otis doesn't return soon, you'll never find him."

"If Otis doesn't return soon," said Beckett, "we'll empty all of Euterra to find him."

Lydia gave a wan smile that slowly morphed into a look of exasperation. "Foundlings!" she said.

———◦•◦———

It was later that night when a rap came to Lars Beckett's door. He opened it to reveal Nota Dorne standing outside. "Walk with me," said Dorne. Lars nodded silently, stepped out of his quarters and the two men left Beckett's Dan and strolled down the drift together.

"The thing Lydia Ross found was examined in the Hall of Elements," said Dorne.

"Lydia said it was called a gun," Lars said.

"The 'gun' then," Dorne said, "has no life-giving purpose so far as we can tell. It's not in right order."

"I gathered as much. Could you make it work?"

"No," said Dorne, "but we think we know *how* it works."

"Lydia tried, but she couldn't make it work either."

"Lydia was fortunate. There's a small lever on the gun that prevents it working unless it's in a certain position. Lydia must have had it turned off when she tried to make it work."

"So are these things dangerous?" Lars asked.

"Indeed so," Dorne confirmed, "if they can be made to work. But such a thing would not be in right order."

"Of course not," Lars said. He stopped walking and Dorne did likewise. He regarded the other man with gravity. "Did you find a cusp?"

Dorne nodded tentatively. "Possibly," he said. "As you know, cusps arose from the original entanglement of all things at the beginning. In theory, everything is linked to everything else at one level or another, meaning that cusps should be everywhere connecting everything. They would be the whole basis for co-dependent arising. But so far, Practice shows us patterns of layered relationships of unequal density. When they appear close enough together sometimes they display crossovers that allow for specific effects. Sometimes not. While everything in the universe is entangled, not everything is equally densely entangled, and not all relationships are equally determinative of outcomes. So, yes, we have found a cusp. But it may be—difficult."

CHAPTER 40

*Sometimes what appears to be peace is just a lull
during which evil is catching its breath.*

— THE BOOK OF MEMORY

AXEL CAINE REPORTED to the Commission and the Chief what he'd learned from Dexter. In the end, there hadn't been much debate. The rumour of an as yet unvisited settlement was enough to warrant a party of four and two tracking dogs. Some of the Commission were tempted to order a larger party as the prospect that this might at last be the Motherlode fired their acquisitive instincts. The Chief prevailed, however, and it was agreed that a smaller party would probably do. But by the time they had assembled, packed their provisions and equipment, Otis had a full day's lead. It then started to rain torrentially for several hours, followed by a gentler but nevertheless steady drenching. The Brotherhood party set out from where Dexter told them Otis had departed, and headed off in the same general direction, but with no assurance that they had actually picked up his trail. The dogs were listless because of the rain and indefinite in their tracking. Any sign of footfalls in the sand or muck of the many trails that led off generally westward were rapidly being blurred or erased by the rain. But the Brotherhood party pressed on trusting to luck that the dogs would catch scent of something, that Otis might dally, unaware that he was being followed, or some other fluke would work in their favour.

For his part, Otis had no intention of dallying. He pressed on, welcoming the rain even though it was cold and miserable. Despite his leave-taking from the Citizens, he thought of no reason why he would *not* be followed. Sooner or later, he thought, something would slip. Someone would say something, and the jig would be up. So he pressed on with a will, first taking up the path he arrived on to make as much progress westward as quickly as possible.

232 | MARK A. BURCH

He passed back along the large meadow space he had crossed before, but this time he skirted it along its southern edge. Beyond this he remembered a large expanse of granite outcrops to the north. This would take him somewhat off a direct westerly route, slow him down, but he thought, in the rain, walking on bare rock, he would leave less sign than other ways he might go.

Much to Otis's satisfaction, and much to his discomfort, the rain continued steadily for another two days and three nights. As luck would have it though, the rain was not violent, which was very often the case in this age, nor did it include hail, which could sometimes be as large as a man's fist. He travelled both day and night not seeing much point in stopping if stopping meant merely that he would be miserable in one place rather than being miserable while at least making better his escape. But by the morning of the fourth day he was exhausted and cold. He came upon a crevice in one of the outcrops which was overhung and dry inside. Here he made a small breakfast without a fire, did his best to hang his outer clothes to dry and changed his inner clothing to spares he carried in a waterproof for such a contingency. He then settled down in exhausted sleep.

When he awakened again the day was already far gone. He ate again, but hastily, without knowing why. Something caused him to tingle, as if he was being observed. Paranoia perhaps, but not a sensation he was entirely willing to ignore. He was gathering his gear when, still at some distance, he heard voices. Their tone was conversational, punctuated by shouted commands that he knew must be intended for dogs. Dogs were something he hadn't anticipated. He stayed concealed, noting instinctively how the leaves of trees lifted lazily westward. He would be downwind of the search party, at least until they passed by. Hopefully they were far enough south of him that the dogs wouldn't detect anything at all. He stayed crouched in his niche, waiting.

The Brotherhood party trudged slowly southwestward, gradually passing out of earshot. Otis stayed under cover until nightfall, giving the pursuing party several hours to move off ahead of him. Once he was in full darkness relieved only by a waning full moon, he decided to head north rather than west. If the Brotherhood party gave up and returned, there was still a chance they might cross his path and pick up a scent. So, despite the cost in time, he decided the best course was to go off crossways. Before striking off, however, he retrieved from his kit an ampoule of phero. While he had brought several pheros with him on the survey, happily there had been no need to use any. One of these was a pheromone released by mule deer when in distress. To a dog, it would be a powerful and confusing stimulant. The risk in using it was that it also attracted any cougars in the neighbourhood interested in an easy kill. Nevertheless, Otis dispersed the substance widely and quickly, then made his way northward into less familiar territory. If the Brotherhood kept going in the direction he saw them disappear, he thought grimly, they would be heading into the marshes—and the snakes.

He pressed on through the night and all the next day bearing north, then northwest as he began his turn back toward Euterran territory. Another day's march and he turned due west which he knew eventually would bring him squarely into the Thornway, but it was still a long trek away. Better weather eased his passage except for two occasions when it rained steadily for a day or more, stirring up epical clouds of mosquitoes and black flies. He blessed the memory of the Euterran entomologists who discovered and concentrated the repeller pheromones for these insects. He inoculated himself liberally with these pheros and pressed on.

On his fifteenth day after leaving Mainbranch, he came face to face with the looming wall of the Thornway. It was a towering, tangled barrier made of everything nature ever invented with thorns, toxins, irritants or allergens. A kilometre wide and a dozen metres high, it ran for several hundred kilometres encircling Euterra from Loch Speare on the southeast, wrapping around eastward, then running north and finally west to peter out in a maze of ponds, lakes, bogs and swamps which were practically impassible for reasons of their own. On the theory that good fences made good neighbours, the Thornway was designed as a passive defence of living beings planted and tended by generations of Euterran permaculturalists. Even if left untended, it would thrive and maintain itself without human attention for generations. Everyone agreed that it was an unfriendly looking thicket, but in times past it had provided a subtle form of control and direction that had saved Euterra more than once. To Otis it was his first sighting of the sweetness of home—though not without a certain grim irony.

Once he reached the Thornway, Otis turned directly around and started walking carefully back along the very same trail he had taken to reach it. A day's march eastward and he changed direction again, this time turning due south, but only after laying down another patch of the mule deer scent. He reasoned that, if the Brotherhood party hadn't simply got lost in the marshes on their first bearing, they might have turned around to return to Mainbranch. *If* on the return trip the dogs somehow caught his scent, and *if* the deer scent did not confuse them thoroughly, then there was a chance they might pick up his trail again going north. *If* they could track him on a trail at least four days old, over rock, after several days of rain, then they might have followed him all the way to the second patch of pheromone. At that point, he figured, there was a fifty-fifty chance that they would follow his trail to meet the Thornway, at which point it would appear that he had simply vanished in a dead end. *If* they turned around to re-trace their same route back, there was another fifty-fifty chance that they might detect his southward turn, or equally likely, just give up and go back the way they came. He reckoned that even though they had dogs, this was a sufficient number of 'ifs' to offer reasonable assurance of escape.

As it turned out, the Brotherhood had a less perfect knowledge of geography, and their dogs were less useful, than Otis could have guessed. After passing him unawares, the search party continued more or less due west to eventually meet the marshes. These they decided to try to cross rather than bypass, at least the first day. They blundered along until one of their dogs was seized by the nose and quickly embraced by a python which dragged the animal toward deeper water and soon disappeared beneath eerily silent ripples. This was a disconcerting development which induced the party to turn north, an equally unproductive direction, then back east in their growing desperation to get clear of the marshes. This they achieved with their one remaining dog, the whole party emerging sodden and exhausted having spent two days trying more to save themselves than to pursue Otis.

After resting for half a day, they set a course around the northern edge of the marshes, then made straight west from there, largely ignoring the search for Otis's actual trail in favour of going as far west as their provisions and the weather would allow. In due course this brought them face to face with the Thornway over a hundred kilometres north of the Euterran east limit. The Brotherhood's limited knowledge of regional geography included no record of the Thornway, much less of the east limit gateway. And even if it had, to an untrained eye, the Thornway could scarcely be distinguished from a natural feature of the landscape. In their present pursuit of Otis mixed with a vaguer desire just to locate his 'village,' the Thornway simply represented an obstacle to be got around somehow. For this purpose, turning south seemed just as likely to be effective as turning north, and on this arbitrary basis alone, they turned south, trying here and there along the way to penetrate the Thornway whenever an opportunity presented itself—which was never.

Long before the Brotherhood party had even reached the Thornway, Otis Bede made his way south and west coming at last to the East Limit Watch. He crossed into Euterran territory to be met immediately by a warm welcome from the watchers, a hearty meal and fast escort back to Dawngate.

Despite Otis's warnings that he might have been followed, it was several days before Caine and his companions probed and poked along the Thornway far enough south to discover the Euterran East Limit. The East Road which passed through the Thornway at this point looked for all intents like a gaping mouth lined with a multitude of tiny but razor sharp teeth. Nevertheless, the Brotherhood party pressed on through the shadows and between dense walls of sea buckthorn, thorn apple, and at ground level and mid-story, dense masses of gooseberry and poison ivy. As they passed farther into the Thornway, their forward movement slowed, becoming more tentative all the while. But presently they emerged and continued their slow movement west. In a few hundred metres they came upon the East Road—the outer reach of the flagstone paved roadway that disappeared into the distance, leading to Euterra.

"Stop!" said the Expediter holding up his hand and peering at the road. "What have we here?"

"A road?" said Ferguson, facetious with exhaustion.

"Indeed we have a road," the Expediter said, ignoring the other's impertinence. "But see," he went on, "it's not an old road, like the old highways. And it's not made like the old highways. To make a road like this takes a lot of people, and time, and organization. To have time to make roads people have to have extra food. To be organized, they have to have some kind of leader like the Chief. And *that* means they will have things we can use."

"So do we keep going and do some recycling?" asked Ferguson.

The Expediter shook his head thoughtfully. "Not now," he said. "Now we do something else."

CHAPTER 41

Among the paths offered by Practice are action and nonaction.
Action should never be confused merely with doing something,
and nonaction should never be confused with inaction.

— THE BOOK OF PRACTICE

OTIS BEDE SAT in the Siderium meeting circle looking tired and disheveled from his journey but decidedly relieved to be back. Without exception, the others in the circle regarded him with a combination of protectiveness and admiration. Present were Lars Beckett, Ocean Claybourne, Lydia Ross, Nota Dorne and Zephyr Fey.

Ocean Claybourne smiled in Otis's direction. "Friend Otis," she said, "while I understand the wisdom in it, there are times when I think our long standing custom of recognizing no titles or distinctions among us might be amended to include the occasional, extraordinary exception. This is one of those times. But I have no title to give you nor authority to confer it, so please accept our gratitude for your undertaking, such as we *can* give." Everyone in the circle inclined his or her head in agreement before they moved on. "What news, Otis?"

Otis sighed. "I found the Brotherhood," he said. "They are about eleven hundred kilometres east of here. I'm afraid I couldn't complete my survey as I was captured by the skrala, as the Brotherhood calls them, or 'Citizens,' as they refer to themselves. The Brotherhood is a ruling class of some sort. They live in a single building they call the HQ and are ruled by someone they call the Chief. I saw only six of the Brotherhood supervising a work crew of Citizens during my survey, but the Citizens themselves believe there are many unseen members of the Brotherhood. But judging from the size of the HQ, I wouldn't think that there could be more than a hundred or so of the Brotherhood. The Citizens are almost slaves. The Brotherhood's control over them is loose as long as the Citizens do as they're told. But if they age, sicken, or disobey, they disappear. No one knows what happens to them. They mostly live in fear of the Brotherhood—and in envy of them. Their whole people, the Brotherhood and Citizens alike, are parasitic on the land. They mine landfills for materials left from the Ruination, and they carry on rudimentary food production, but nothing like our Permies do. They're mining the soil just as they do the dumps."

At length, after Otis had finished offering an account of his journey, Lars asked, "Do you think the Brotherhood is a threat to Euterra?"

Otis nodded quietly. "Without a doubt," he said gravely, "if they knew we were here, they would come. I doubt they're teachable."

"And the Citizens?" asked Lydia.

"They know Euterra exists and that Jaeger's here."

"Friend Otis," said Nota Dorne, his formality barely concealing his rising concern, "how would they know that?"

Otis shrugged. "I told them," he said.

"*You told them?*" Dorne repeated, his tone cold and incredulous but restrained.

"Yes. They took me captive. I thought they would kill me, but I also sensed they were more curious than hostile and might be of help to us somehow. I didn't tell them where Euterra is, only that it exists. They were very excited by the news that Jaeger was alive and even more concerned that this be kept secret. They're very, very concerned to protect him because of a dream they say he had. A dream that involves them in some way. Many Citizens chafe under Brotherhood rule. Jaeger may carry their dream of freedom for them. Even if they can see no way to free themselves, Jaeger being alive keeps their dream alive, which keeps *them* alive. In fact, when they heard Jaeger was here, they were anxious to get me out of Mainbranch as quickly as possible. They feared that if the Brotherhood found out that Jaeger was still alive, both Jaeger and they would pay the price. So they provisioned me and led me out of Mainbranch again."

The group lapsed back into silence to absorb this new information and let it find its place in their awareness.

Presently, Lars unfurled the cloth covering of the gun he had brought to the meeting. "Did you see anything like this?" he asked Otis.

Otis glanced at it briefly, surprised by the sense of uneasiness it prompted in him. "Yes," he said. "Yes. It's like one of the things I saw the Brotherhood foremen carrying with the work crew at Mainbranch. What is it?"

"It's a weapon," said Beckett, "a dangerous weapon. Beamer Farris himself was felled by a weapon like this."

A stir passed through the stillness of the group. It broke their silence, but didn't disturb it.

"If the Brotherhood attacks Euterra with weapons such as this," Beckett continued, "many beings would suffer. It would be a cause for regret."

Zephyr had been pondering all this and spoke for the first time. "But if we have one of these, couldn't we use it to defend ourselves?"

Despite what Zephyr had said, and perhaps because of it, all eyes turned toward Ocean Claybourne. She sat silently, her eyes closed. Then she moved her hand gently to the side, as if brushing away some invisible presence. "To use weapons against weapons," she said slowly, as if explaining something to children, "would not be right Practice. It would multiply suffering. It would endarken us."

"So how can we ever protect Euterra?" Zephyr said, her voice strained. "We have the Guild of Tears, after all. What are they for if not for this?"

Claybourne closed her eyes again. Zephyr blushed with embarrassment at her own impropriety, but continued fuming silently. The others waited for opening.

Claybourne sighed heavily, then took another breath. "Euterra is not protected by us, dear Zephyr. You know that. And least of all is it protected by weapons opposing other weapons with violence. The Guild of Tears, while it still exists, has not been summoned for over a century. But that doesn't mean that we should resign ourselves to inaction should the Brotherhood arrive with ill intent, or that we take no hand in our own protection. We should remember that they may be teachable after all. From what Otis has said, it's clear that they suffer greatly, and the Citizens too. Right Practice would not add to their suffering."

"But I fear for us," Zephyr said, her voice quavering.

"And you fear for Jaeger." Claybourne's gaze was knowing and also accepting. "But fear too brings darkness, so wake up, Zephyr!" Zephyr took the gentle rebuke without offence and lapsed back into the silence.

Claybourne turned to Beckett. "Have you taken this thing to the Hall of Elements?"

"We have," he said.

"And?"

"They think they've found a cusp. But they need more time to test it."

Claybourne turned again to Otis. "And do you think you were followed from Mainbranch?"

"I was," he said. "What I believe to be a party searching for me passed me a few days out of Mainbranch. But they headed off southwest into the marshes. I made way always assuming they might be following, but didn't see them again after that. There have been no reports from the East Watch of anything unusual."

"Then we must continue in watchfulness," she said. "These visitors may appear at any moment, or perhaps never. Who can say?" She turned back to Beckett. "In the meantime, we should alert the watches all around. They may not necessarily arrive from the east. And please," she said with finality, "test the cusp."

CHAPTER 42

*To manifest something in the mind is easy. Even those
with no skill can do so without conscious intention.*

*To manifest something in action requires more skill to
transcend the mind–action boundary, but it can still
be done, though the result is usually imperfect.*

*To manifest something material is even more
difficult and requires transcending the mind–matter
boundary. Only the skillful can accomplish this.*

*To manifest something spiritual is supremely difficult
because it requires surpassing no boundaries at all. It
requires union. Few can do it. They are mostly children.*

— THE BOOK OF PRACTICE

IT WAS ANOTHER MONTH before the Brotherhood appeared in Euterran
territory, but when they did, their arrival was unmistakable. Summer had giv-
en way to early autumn and despite the continuing wild swings in the weather,
the deciduous trees continued their ancient custom and were dropping their
leaves on every breeze in great cascades of colour. The conifers serrated the
hills in olive drab, dusty silver, and shades of logan green except for the tam-
aracks, which stood out like yellow flames. But in the third century of the
Euterran Age, winter had warmed from the frigid iciness of pre-Ruination
times to a season of rain, fog and sometimes snow under leaden skies.

The Brotherhood party was a host that poured through the Thornway and
out along the East Road leading to Euterra. The East Watch noted their

passing and reported it without opposing it. To unfamiliar eyes, it was impossible to distinguish the Brotherhood from their Citizen underlings, but at least a thousand straggled through the Thornway in all. Despite how numerous they were, they all showed the wear of many days' travel through inhospitable country and a third of them at least were tasked simply with carrying baggage. In another part of the world, they might have employed pack animals to carry their cumber, but the remnants of boreal forest they traversed offered only rough footing and no grazing at all. A dozen metres to either side of the East Road lay forested hilly country strewn with ankle-twisting screes of rock parted from outcrops by the relentless action of millennia of ice and water. And all of this was hidden beneath patches of moss, lichen and algae that could be slippery as oil. So the Brotherhood party confined its movements mostly within the East Road itself, a narrow bottleneck they had nevertheless to pass if they hoped to reach Euterra.

As the road itself grew gradually broader with more intersecting byways leading off to Euterran villages, the Brotherhood party felt more encouraged that their path would lead them at last to a prize worth all their labour. They made no efforts to conceal their approach, confident in their numbers, and mindless of the damage they wrought as they made their way west. All around them were the fruits of generations of Permies who had, through one subtle intervention after another, gradually transformed a wilderness into a food forest that mostly tended itself. But the provisions it offered were unfamiliar to the Brotherhood travellers and may as well have been weeds. They tramped through a cornucopia gnawing instead on the meagre rations they knew.

———————

Jaeger and Lydia entered the Rotunda room of the Siderium with Spark in tow. As they approached, Jaeger saw a large number of people entering the Rotunda through all the portals that ringed its circumference. Once inside, they went down one of the stepped aisles about a third of the way to the centre space beneath the oculus as the rings closest to the centre were already full of people in meditation postures. First Spark, then Lydia, then Jaeger slid into one of the rings and took their seats on cushions. Despite the throngs of people coming in, an ambience of silence pervaded the space.

Jaeger leaned toward Lydia, whispering: "What is all this?"

"The Brotherhood is coming." She formed the words with such a flat tone that they jarred against the surge of agitation Jaeger felt when he heard them.

"*What?*" he blurted in a much louder whisper.

Lydia's eyes were drifting closed. Now would not be the time to look at Jaeger, to become infected with his panic, if that was what filled his heart. Her hand drifted to one side as if smoothing the hair of a child. "Peace, Jaeger," she whispered. "Wake up. *Listen.*" Appearing to ignore both Lydia and Jaeger, Spark settled herself into that disturbing calm of hers, a stillness so precocious for her age.

Lydia's hands settled in her lap, graceful against the background of her pale blue robe. Jaeger looked over the assembly and suddenly it registered with him that a great many of those in the central rings of seats were clothed similarly to Lydia. All, he guessed, were Lightminders, and there were now easily two or three thousand of them amassed in the Rotunda—plus many more differently garbed but equally attentive to the practice of their stillness.

Little by little, the rustling movement of people and clothing faded to silence. Here and there came an audible cough or clearing of a throat, but even this eventually subsided to only the sound of breathing and the return again to Jaeger of that sense of something deep, something utterly mysterious, beginning its obscure and silent work. He could witness this, he thought, but he wasn't yet part of it. He stood just outside of it, bearing witness as a bystander. What part had he to play in this? Who were these people, after all?

Then he noticed Lars Beckett, himself robed in blue, moving quietly toward the centre of the great circle. In the next moment, he saw with shock that Lars was carrying a hand gun and a rifle, devices with which Jaeger was sadly familiar—though, in Mainbranch, they could be used only by the Brotherhood. The assembly appeared to be regarding these objects with unwavering attention.

"There are many people now approaching Euterra along the East Road," Lars said slowly, his voice carrying like a ripple opening in the water. "Their intentions toward us are unknown, but we believe they have brought harm to others. They carry devices like these," he said, raising the guns for everyone to see, "and we believe they are capable of inflicting great suffering and death. They're called guns." Jaeger thought he could feel a slight rustle pass through the room, but if so, it immediately settled back to stillness. No breath stirred.

"Without these," Lars continued, turning while holding the guns aloft, "much less harm is likely." He laid down the guns and retrieved two cartridges from a pouch on his belt. "Without these cartridges," he said, "the guns won't work." He laid down the cartridges beside the guns and then retrieved two other objects from his pouch, so small they were hardly visible from just a few metres away. "Without these caps, the cartridges won't work. And within the caps, those in the Hall of Elements tell us, is a substance called tetrazene. Without tetrazene, the caps won't work."

Lars allowed this information to sink into the great collective silence that filled the room, a silence now awake, but unmoved. Then he said, "I'm going to Dawngate to extend welcome and good will when these people arrive. I'm going alone. Should more of us go, we might evoke fear in our visitors which wouldn't be in right Practice. I ask that you hold me in the Light until I return."

Many heads nodded silently in Lars's direction. "I ask your help in one other moment of Practice," he went on. "I ask humbly that Light be kindled and raise the temperature of tetrazene to ninety-one degrees Celsius—*precisely* ninety-one degrees Celsius." Lars then turned quietly, ascended through the rings of those now sunk in silent meditation and walked toward one of the portals. On his way, he passed Lydia and Spark, poised in their stillness. Lydia's eyes fluttered open as Lars approached, joining his for the briefest instant, then releasing him again. Only then did she notice that Jaeger was gone.

For her part, Spark was beyond reach. In her mind's eye, she simply rested within the purest bubble of stillness while all around her rushed the thundering vortex of everything else. She witnessed it there—the typhoon of arising and dissolving—without judgment, without attachment, without desire. And from the swirling wall of being and becoming, she saw emerge, according to her humble intention, something unimaginably tiny, branched like the spicules of a diatom, like a constellation, a tiny thing made of shining points of light. And the light in her beyond her comprehension mysteriously resonated with the light in the tiny thing, and in the depth of her mind Spark offered an intention: "If it please—warm!"

Lars walked toward Dawngate through passages that had become eerily quiet. Word of the visitors and the risk they posed to Euterra had spread throughout the city. Some had gone to the Siderium to join Practice there, but the Rotunda could hold only a fraction of their numbers. Many more continued Practice in their Dans as he passed through the empty drifts. All Euterra was breathing with an immense quiet.

He emerged from Dawngate, taking a few steps in the direction of the bridge, but stopped before a circular device of Celtic knotted design that had been hewn into the rock long ago. On this spot, Beamer Farris had fallen. For a moment, Lars's mind was flooded with a sense of the ironic circularity of history, the Beamer Tales of his childhood, the deeply mysterious way in which all life, all that is precious and clean, can pause sometimes before a nameless, gathering darkness. But these thoughts he let flow through him—a stream he witnessed without entering—a stream he knew never returned to the same place twice. All he could do now was be open. Anything more—or anything less—would be ruinous.

Presently, from along the East Road came a trickle and then a flood of people. At their head were a number of very large men festooned with antique firearms and bandoliers, followed by many more also armed with clubs, bars, machetes or anything serviceable as a weapon. The swagger of their approach became somewhat more subdued when they arrived at the bridge over the Snake River and they heard the cataract roaring far below. Some noticed how narrow was the bridge, and how confined they might be in this narrow space if under attack.

To the swarm at the edge of the bridge, this massive precipice put them in a tactically awkward position, but so long had it been since they encountered any resistance to their procurement of what belonged to others, they scarcely took account of it as a threat. Besides, facing them across the bridge was a single, unimpressive looking man who seemed to have no weapons at all. Incredulous, the horde stopped as the men standing point scanned the face of the Massif and the surrounding hills for who might be concealed there. But after a few moments, satisfied that they were unopposed, they started over the bridge, only to stop again a few metres from Beckett.

Lars raised a hand and said, "Welcome, all who come in peace."

One of the men at the front of the mob looked dumbstruck. Then a broad smile started to spread over his face, then a great barking laugh that nearly doubled him over. Others in the crowd picked up on the levity and started laughing as well. When eventually it subsided, the man's expression hardened like flint: "Do you know who I am?"

Lars regarded him evenly and with a calm that his counterpart found unnerving. "You're someone who is my friend."

"Your *friend?*" said the other, incredulous.

Lars stood still, holding the other man's eyes—a gesture the other found confusing. The Brotherhood leader conjured that this should be a challenge. But it couldn't possibly be so, coming from someone who looked like Lars did at that moment. He just stood there, hands together in front of his chest, face quiet, but eyes wide awake. Soon, however, the Brotherhood leader's puzzlement gave way to contempt, the only emotion he was capable of feeling toward anyone he perceived as weaker.

"I'm the fucking Expediter!" Axel Caine spat the words. "That's who I am." Then he levelled the gun he was carrying directly at Lars. In unison, everyone carrying a gun with a clear shot at him did likewise.

Now in this moment, something remarkable happened—because remarkable things occasionally do happen. The Expediter hesitated. His hesitation grew from a feeling entirely new for him. He hesitated because for some reason, for some unnamable reason, he simply didn't want to shoot this man. He perceived that he had a choice. And unknown to him, similar feelings were emerging in nearly everyone in the mob behind him. The only outward sign that Beckett could see of this was the slightest dropping of the gun barrels, as if unsure of their purpose. As this momentary hesitation stretched out into a pause, a lacuna in the chain of causation, the slightest turn in co-dependent arising, all present noticed something else. Beckett appeared to shine. This was the only word fitting to the vision—that he shined. And the shining waxed as they looked on. Light didn't appear around him, or upon him, but seemed instead to stream *through* him as if he were transparent, the thinnest of vessels, holding liquid light.

But all of this appeared only within the Expediter's moment of hesitation, in the narrowest space of openness in a consciousness which was otherwise habitually closed to such things—which was, in fact, hostile to them. The Expediter shook his head suddenly as if to dislodge something irritating. "Fuck me!" he growled, then pulled his trigger. There followed a dull click. Nothing more. Briefly shocked and briefly vulnerable, the Expediter pulled a lever ejecting the chambered round.

"Fire! Fucking fire!" he bellowed, followed by the pattering sound of trigger after trigger being pulled to no effect. Then there followed the clattering rain of misfired cartridges tumbling out of guns, round after round, until their magazines were empty or the would-be shooters gave up trying.

Not to be dissuaded, the Expediter pulled a formidable looking knife from his belt and roared to those behind him, "Come on!" The crowd then pushed forward, surging into the narrow passage of the bridge, but only half-heartedly, and only to stop with a gasp.

Jaeger came running out from the Dawngate and stopped beside Lars. He waved his arms wildly shouting, "Citizens! Citizens!"

Citizens and the Brotherhood alike halted like a wave that was stunned halfway to its crest and breaking there.

"Citizens!" Jaeger shouted again, his voice fierce now, and keening. "Don't smile!" he screamed. "Don't nod!"

The mass of people began slowly to turn upon itself like an enormous bank of clouds brewing a downpour. For a moment it manifested chaos, seeming to go nowhere in particular and everywhere at once. But then it found its strange attractor and began turning, like a flock of birds wheeling round a common centre. And in a moment a hundred vortices formed in the crowd, each turning around a human centre, and one by one, beginning with the Expediter, hands were laid on, bodies were lifted and hurled over the bridge railings and balustrades into the foaming river below.

In a moment, it was over, like some quaking wave in the Earth's crust that goes rolling away, monstrous and indifferent. Jaeger and Lars, standing together, looked out at the crowd of dazed Citizens milling about. Some wandered off roughly in the direction they came from. Some sat down where they were, exhausted-looking, as if just roused from a nightmare. The swell of energy that had lifted them all only moments before to run amok slowly settled back in glassy placidity.

Without speaking, Lars raised his arms and slowly gained their attention. All turned their faces toward him, again standing there as an unremarkable figure robed in blue. "Friends!" he called in a louder voice. "You've been long on the road in bad weather and bad company. Fall is upon us. Would you join Jaeger and me for some supper?"

CHAPTER 43

*As every winter is followed by spring, that which has always
been repeats its ancient dance, but sometimes with variations.*

— THE BOOK OF MEMORY

IT TURNED OUT TO BE the single largest foundling operation in Euterran history, but somehow eleven hundred and thirty-seven additional bellies were filled that night. Antares and Bellatrix drifts were converted to a reception centre and temporary accommodations for the Citizen guests. Euterrans' continuing concern about disease led them to impose a two-week quarantine on the new arrivals which confined them to the lowest two of Euterra's forty-six drift levels. But their trek from Mainbranch had been so arduous and under such brutal control, that being warm, dry, and well-fed without fear of other harm coming to them, quarantine seemed a small price for such benefits.

Of course from a Euterran perspective, lacking as the Citizens were in any experience with Practice or any of the other customs that defined Euterran culture in the new age, the Citizens were culturally delusional. But most would probably be teachable, at least to the degree possible of attainment given their ages. Mere social learning and imitation would achieve a great deal without formal training.

"How did you do it?" Jaeger asked Lydia one day.

"Do what?"

"Stop the Brotherhood."

"We didn't stop them, exactly," she said. "The Lab Guild in the Hall of Elements examined the guns in hope of finding a cusp somewhere. A 'cusp' is a point at which the minimum influence can achieve the maximum effect, even an influence like an intention. They found a cusp in the chemical bond between a pair of nitrogen atoms in tetrazene. Tetrazene is the explosive that makes the firing caps work in the rifle and handgun cartridges. Breaking this one chemical bond stops the whole works—all it takes is a little heat."

"And you command powers like this?" Jaeger asked, incredulous. "You can heat things just by thinking about them?"

"We command nothing," Lydia said. "We ask. And we don't 'think'—we *Practice*. Sometimes what we ask for is manifested, and sometimes it isn't. To desire a particular result too strongly is not right Practice. It may be that the Central Harmony is making its way differently than the way we would at first desire, and it will be from that direction that Opening appears, not the one we wanted or expected. So we ask based on our clearest sense of what is in alignment with the Central Harmony. To force matters simply isn't possible. Thinking otherwise is delusional."

"But how does it work?" Jaeger was still perplexed.

"We're not entirely sure," said Lydia. "As early as the twentieth century, it was observed that disciplined meditators were able to change the acidity and alkalinity of fluids, and the crystallization of freezing water, and even the behaviour of electric devices, simply by applying intention. What we call Practice includes various forms of meditation. We still have much to learn about *how* they work, but we know with certainty that they *do* work. Is it that much of a wonder then that a correctly framed intention might change one electron one quantum level to neutralize a chemical compound?"

"So all the Lightminders were involved in heating up that chemical—that tetrazene?"

"No. Only one. Lars asked everyone to Practice because we never know for whom Opening will appear. And it might not even have been a Lightminder that did it. Nearly all Euterrans keep Practice and it wasn't just Lightminders who were practicing that day."

"Only *one*?"

Lydia nodded matter-of-factly. "How many people do you think it takes to change history? In this case, though, we think it was Spark."

"*Spark?*" Jaeger gaped.

"In all likelihood, yes," Lydia said. "She's still pretty much a child and children have absolutely no doubt, no self-imposed limitations on what they think is possible. They're clear channels. Her ego doesn't obstruct her perception. She could have done it, I'm sure."

"But how could one child stop all those guns?"

Lydia smiled quietly. "Dear Jaeger," she said. "You've only been with us a few months. There's much you still have to learn—that we *all* have to learn.

Power isn't what you think it is. Power is only sometimes a physical a force. More often, power is intention applied at cusp. Spark knows that. Many children know it, or sense it intuitively. We just hope that with Practice, they won't forget it once they grow up."

———————

The autumn was aging into winter when the Citizens passed their period of quarantine and were welcomed to stay in Euterra until spring. Their tenancy was not without friction but most Euterrans appreciated the Citizens as victims of violence, all afflicted in various ways by their individual and collective history of living in constant dread of being 'disappeared' or sent on a 'retirement party.' Day by day, however, with some exceptions, most Citizens repeated Jaeger's experience of living in Euterra. Gradually their psychological centre shifted away from fear and toward manifesting that energy that holds every being in existence and draws it from life to life.

As the days of winter passed and the light began again to grow in the sky, much had changed. Jaeger emerged as a leader among the Citizens and began drawing plans for how they might return to Mainbranch. Neither all Citizens nor all the Brotherhood had come with the recycling party. Ties remained with family members and friends in Mainbranch, and hope was kindled that Mainbranch might turn a corner in its history, becoming a very different society in the future. There would be hold-outs among the Brotherhood who would not embrace this prospect—Jaeger felt sure. But he felt equally confident that some path would open making change possible. Dozens of Citizens who had few ties to Mainbranch elected to stay in Euterra and adopt its way of life. And some Euterrans decided to join the Citizens on their return to Mainbranch, to help them learn Practice, apply permaculture, and offer aid with healthcare, education and governance. Zephyr Fey in particular saw way opening to train a new generation of Helders among the Citizens and perhaps build a life that included Jaeger as well.

———————

Deep in an alcove at Fogg's Inn on Procyon Drift, Hyram Bowen peered over his flagon of mead at a young man who had just slid into the bench opposite.

"Are you Hyram Bowen?" he asked.

"Of course I am," Bowen growled. "Who else could I be in this incarnation, being what I am?"

"My name is Fitz," he said.

"Ah," said Bowen. "Of course it is. You're another of those Citizen chaps."

"Right," said Fitz. "If you have a few minutes, I have some questions—about the Ruination."

"Of course you do." Bowen chuckled and held up two fingers. "Innkeeper! Two more meads!"

END

COMING SOON

Euterra Genesis

by
Mark A. Burch

SET IN THE YEAR 2027, Euterra Genesis is the birth story of a way of life, an aesthetic sensibility and a spiritual intuition that survives the Ruination to carry its members into a very different future. As the storm clouds of the Ruination gather on the horizon, the seed of Euterran culture is quietly germinating in the former ghost town of Badger Coulee. Is Beamer Ferris just a young man alienated from the enticements of consumer culture, or is he a reluctant prophet in troubled times? Are his visions born of compulsion and anxiety or are they authentic "openings?" Can the love he shares with Tatum Barnes survive in the crucible of social chaos and environmental upheaval that is gathering around them? And what does any of this have to do with Fey's Periodic Table?

97107722R00159

Made in the USA
Columbia, SC
07 June 2018